ALSO BY SOPHIE LARK

Brutal Birthright

Brutal Prince

Stolen Heir

Savage Lover

Bloody Heart

Broken Vow

Heavy Crown

Sinners Duet

There Are No Saints

There Is No Devil

BROKEN VOW

SOPHIE LARK

Bloom books

Published by Bloom Books, an imprint of Sourcebooks
P.O. Box 4410, Naperville, Illinois 60567-4410
(630) 961-3900
sourcebooks.com

Originally self-published in 2022 by Sophie Lark.

Cataloging-in-Publication data is on file with the Library of Congress.

Printed and bound in Canada.
MBP 10 9 8 7 6 5 4 3 2

This one is for all my sexy, brilliant lawyer ladies,
especially Jeanne, Tia, Reb, and Logan.
I know you will catch all my mistakes
and I love you for it 🙂

XOXO

Sophie Lark

SOUNDTRACK

1. "Boss Bitch"—Doja Cat
2. "California Dreamin'"—The Mamas & The Papas
3. "Please Mr. Postman"—The Marvelettes
4. "Devil's Advocate"—The Neighbourhood
5. "My Truck"—BRELAND
6. "She's Country"—Jason Aldean
7. "Dirt on My Boots"—Jon Pardi
8. "Maniac"—Conan Gray
9. "Sunday Best"—Surfaces
10. "Say Something"—Justin Timberlake
11. "All of Me"—Brooklyn Duo
12. "First Day of My Life"—Bright Eyes
13. "Electric Love"—BØRNS

Music is a big part of my writing process. If you start a song when you see a 🎵 while reading, the song matches the scene like a movie score.

Spotify   Apple Music

THE GALLOS

CHAPTER 1
RIONA

I'M SITTING IN MY CORNER OFFICE WORKING ON LAND-PURCHASE documents for the South Shore development. People think that being a lawyer is all about arguing, but in fact you only spend a tiny percentage of your time in court or in settlement negotiations. The vast majority of my hours pass by right here in this room, writing, reading, or editing.

I don't mind being alone in here. It's my sanctuary. I have control over everything inside these doors. I have my desk set up just the way I like it, facing the two-sided view of the Marina City Towers, Michigan Avenue, and the Chicago River spread out below me.

Everything in my office is pewter, brass, cream, and blue—shades I find soothing.

I've got three watercolors by Shutian Xue on the walls and a sculpture by Jean Fourier in the corner. It's his piece called *Building Blocks*, which is supposed to represent the interior of an atom. To me, it looks more like a model of a solar system.

I watch most everyone else finish their work and leave for the night. A couple of my colleagues poke their heads through my door on the way out to give me a message—some work related and some just nonsense. My paralegal, Lucy, lets me know she'll finish the stack of lease agreements I gave her as soon as she gets back in the morning. And Josh Hale tells me I came in second in last week's pick-'em league, which means I won a whopping twenty dollars.

"I didn't think you even liked football," he says with a condescending smile.

"I don't," I say sweetly. "I just like winning your money."

Josh and I are not friends. In fact, we're direct rivals. The eldest of the firm partners is about to retire. When Victor Weiss leaves, either Josh or I will be the most likely choice to replace him. And we both know it.

Even if we weren't in competition for the partnership position, I'd still detest him. I've never liked the kind of person who pretends to be friendly while scavenging for information they can use to hurt you. I'd respect him more if he were an honest asshole instead of a fake-nice guy.

Everything about him annoys me, from his too-tight suits to his aggressive cologne. He reminds me of a TV-show host. In looks, maybe a Ryan Seacrest. In personality, more like a Tucker Carlson— always thinking he's twice as smart as he actually is.

Taking the opportunity to snoop, Josh scans my office, trying to read the headings on the documents spread out on my desk. He's relentless.

"Okay, bye," I say pointedly. Telling him to leave.

"Don't work too hard," he replies, shooting a little finger gun in my direction.

After he leaves, his cologne lingers twenty minutes longer. *Ugh.*

The last to depart is Uncle Oran. He's the managing partner of the firm and my father's half brother. He's always been my favorite relative. In fact, he's the reason I became a lawyer in the first place.

At family parties I'd corner him and demand to hear another story of odd and interesting legal cases, like the man who sued Pepsi for refusing to provide him with a twenty-three-million-dollar fighter jet in exchange for Pepsi Points or the time Procter & Gamble tried to argue in a court of law that their own Pringles were not, in fact, potato chips.

Uncle Oran is an excellent storyteller, well able to milk drama out of even the most convoluted cases. He'd explain precedent and statutes and how important even the tiniest of details could be…how even a comma in the wrong place could invalidate an entire contract.

I found Uncle Oran fascinating not only because he's funny and charming but because he's so similar and yet so different from my father.

They both dress well, in fitted suits, but Uncle Oran's look like something a Trinity professor would wear—always tweed or wool with wooden buttons and elbow patches—while my father's are pure American businessman. They're both tall with the same thick graying hair and long lean faces, but Uncle Oran has the coloring they call *black Irish*—dark eyes and an olive tone to his skin. My father's eyes are cornflower blue.

Oran's accent fascinated me the most. He'd lost some of it living in America for years. But you can still hear it gilding the edges of his words. And he loves a good Irish saying:

Forgetting a debt doesn't mean it's paid. Or *there's no such thing as bad publicity, except your own obituary.*

He's a version of my father who grew up in Ireland—an alternate reality, if we'd all been raised there instead of Chicago.

Tonight he knocks on my doorframe, saying, "You know we don't pay you by the hour, Riona. You can go home once in a while and still have plenty of money for those fancy shoes."

The shoes in question are a pair of oxblood Nomasei pumps, set neatly to the side under my desk. I take them off when I know I'll be sitting for a while so they don't get creases across the toes.

I smile up at Uncle Oran. "I knew you'd notice those."

"I notice everything. Like the fact that you've got all the South Shore land-purchase agreements in front of you. I told you Josh was going to handle those."

"I'd already started them." I shrug. "Figured I might as well finish."

Oran shakes his head. "You work too hard, Riona," he says seriously. "You're young. You should be out with friends and boyfriends. Once in a while, at least."

"I have a boyfriend."

"Yeah? Where is he?"

"About five miles that way." I nod my head toward the window. "At Mercy Hospital."

"The surgeon?" Oran sniffs. "He's still around?"

"Yes." I laugh. "What's wrong with Nick?"

"Well…" Oran sighs. "I wasn't going to say anything. But I saw he sent you roses the other day. *Red* roses."

"So?"

"Not very imaginative, is he?"

"Some people like the classics."

"Some people are intellectually lazy."

"What are the right flowers to send a woman?"

Oran grins. "I always send whiskey. You send a woman a bottle of Bunnahabhain 40 Year Single Malt…then she knows you're serious."

"Well, we're not," I tell him. "Not serious."

Oran strides into my office and scoops the stack of folders off my desk.

"Hey!" I protest.

"This is for your own good," he says. "Go home. Put on a nice dress. Go get your man from the hospital. Enjoy a night out. Josh will find these on his desk tomorrow morning, the lazy shite."

"Fine," I say, just to placate him.

I let Oran carry the folders away, and then I watch him head to the elevators, his leather satchel slung over his shoulder in place of a briefcase. But I have no intention of actually leaving. I've got a million other projects to work on, with or without the purchase agreements.

And this is my favorite time to do it—after everyone else has left and the lights have automatically dimmed across the floor, in total silence, the rest of the office dark, and only the city lights sparkling below me. No interruptions.

Well—almost none.

My cell phone buzzes on the desk next to me where it lies facedown. I flip it over, seeing Nick's name.

You still at it? Want to meet me for a drink at Rosie's?

I consider. Rosie's is only a couple of blocks away. I could easily stop for a drink on my way home.

But I'm tired. My shoulders are stiff. And I haven't had a chance to exercise yet today. I think about a glass of wine in the trendy, noisy bar compared to a glass of wine drunk in my own bathtub, listening to a podcast instead of a recap of Nick's day.

I know which one sounds more appealing to me.

Sorry, I text back. Going to be working late. Then I'll just head home.

Alright, Nick replies. Dinner tomorrow?

I hesitate.

Sure, I say. 6:30 tomorrow.

Nick and I have been dating for three months. He's intelligent, successful, handsome, competent in bed (I would guess all surgeons are—they understand the human body, and they're in full control of their hands).

I should want to go to dinner tomorrow. I should be excited about it.

But I'm just...indifferent.

It's nothing to do with Nick. It's a problem I seem to have again and again. I get to know someone, and I start picking away at all their flaws. I notice inconsistencies in their statements. Holes in the logic of their arguments. I wish I could turn off that part of my brain, but I can't.

My father would say that I expect too much from people. *No one's perfect, Riona. Least of all yourself.*

I know that.

I notice my own flaws more than anyone's—I can be cold and unwelcoming. Obsessive. Quick to get angry and slow to forgive.

Worst of all, I'm easily annoyed. Like when a man becomes repetitive.

It's only been a few months, and already Nick's told me three times about how he thinks the anesthesiologists in his department are conspiring against him after he refused to hire one of their friends.

"It's these South Africans," he complained last time we went to lunch. "You hire one, and then they want you to hire their cousin or their brother-in-law, and all of a sudden, the surgical unit is overrun with them."

Plus, he seems to think that now, at the three-month mark, he's owed a greater portion of my time. Instead of asking if I'm free Friday or Saturday night, he assumes it. He makes plans for us, and I have to tell him I'm busy with work or a family dinner.

"You know, you could invite me to dinner with your family," he said in a sulky tone.

"It's not a social dinner," I told him. "We're going over plans for phase two of the South Shore development."

Most dinners with my family are working dinners, one way or another. Our business and our personal ties are so deeply intertwined that I would hardly know my father, mother, or siblings outside of "work."

The fate of our business is the fate of our family. That's how it works in the Irish Mafia.

Nick has some idea about the Griffins' criminal ties—it would be impossible not to. We've been one of the largest Irish Mafia families in Chicago for two hundred years.

But he doesn't get it. Not really. He thinks of it like an interesting backstory, like people who say they're descended from Henry the VIII. He has no idea how current and ongoing organized crime is in Chicago.

It's always a dilemma in my dating life. Do I want a boyfriend who's ignorant of the dark underside of this city, who could never really understand my entrenchment in my family? Or do I want one of the "made men" who work for my father, cracking heads and burying bodies, with blood under his fingernails and a gun perpetually concealed on his person?

Neither, really.

And not just for those reasons.

I don't believe in love.

I'm not denying it exists—I've seen it happen for other people. I just don't believe it will ever happen for me.

My love for my family is like the roots of an oak tree: a part of the tree, necessary for life. It's always been there, and it always will be.

But romantic love...I've never experienced it. Maybe I'm just too selfish. I can't imagine loving somebody more than I love my own comfort and having my way.

The idea of being controlled by someone else, doing things for their convenience instead of mine…no thanks. I barely tolerate that for my family. Why would I want to center my life around a man?

I pack up my briefcase. Before I leave, I sneak into Josh's filthy cluttered office and steal back the purchase agreements off his desk. I started them, and I plan to finish them, regardless of what Uncle Oran says. He won't notice—I'll be done with them before Josh would even have looked at them. With my briefcase satisfyingly heavy, I head out of the office tower on East Wacker Drive. I walk home because my condo is only four blocks away from work.

I bought the condo just this summer. It's in a brand-new building with a gorgeous fitness center and swimming pool. There's a doorman and a fantastic view from my living room on the twenty-eighth floor.

It was past time. I'd been living in my parents' mansion on the Gold Coast. Their house is so huge that there was plenty of space for everyone—no real reason to leave. Plus, it was convenient to all be in the same house whenever we needed to go over business-related material.

But then Cal got married, and he and Aida found their own place. And then Nessa left, too, to be with Mikolaj. Then it was just me alone with my parents, with the distasteful sensation of having been left behind by my siblings.

I have no interest in getting married like they did, but I could certainly move out.

So that's what I did. I got the condo. And I love it. I love the quiet and the space, the feeling of being on my own for the first time in my life.

I wave to Ronald, the doorman, and take the elevator up to my apartment. I change out of my blazer, blouse, and slacks, putting on a one-piece swimsuit instead. Then I grab my waterproof headphones and head up to the pool on the roof of our building.

In the summer, they open the atrium overhead so you can swim under the stars. In the winter, it's enclosed from the elements, though you can still see the sky through the glass.

I love to lie on my back and swim back and forth, looking up.

I'm usually the only person in the pool when I come this late. Sure enough, tonight the space is dim and quiet, the only noise the water lapping against the rim of the pool.

It smells of chlorine and fabric softener from the fresh stacks of towels laid out on the lounge chairs. After turning on my swimming playlist, I set my phone on one of the chairs.

I'm about to jump in the pool when I realize I forgot to fix my hair. I usually braid it and put it under a swim cap so the chlorine doesn't dry it out. Red hair is fragile.

It's still in a chignon from work, twisted up with one of those two-pronged hairpins.

I don't really want to go all the way back down to my apartment. This will be fine, for one single time.

I put my hands over my head and dive into the water with one clean jump. Then I stroke back and forth across the pool, listening to "California Dreamin'" on my headphones.

♫ *"California Dreamin'"—The Mamas & Papas*

I'm wearing goggles, so I can look down into the bright blue water illuminated with pot lights from below. I see a dark shape down in the corner of the pool, and I wonder if somebody dropped something down there—a gym bag or maybe a canvas bag of towels.

Turning over, I lie on my back and look up at the glass ceiling. It reminds me of a Victorian greenhouse—the glass bisected by a lattice-work of metal. Beyond the glass I see the black sky and the shimmering pale disc of a nearly full moon.

As I'm looking up, something locks around my throat and drags me down under the water.

It pulls me down, down, all the way down to the bottom of the pool, heavy as an anchor.

The shock of something grabbing me from below made me let out a shriek, and now there's almost no air in my lungs. I kick and struggle against this thing that's caught hold of me. I claw at whatever's wrapped around my throat, feeling spongy "skin" with hard flesh beneath.

My lungs are screaming for air. They feel flat and deflated, the pressure of the pool pressing against my eardrums and my chest. I twist around just a little and see black flippers kicking by my feet and two arms in a wet suit wrapped tightly around me.

I hear the exhale of a respirator next to my right ear. It's a scuba diver—a man in a scuba suit is trying to drown me.

I try to kick and hit him, but he's got me pinned with both his arms constricting me like an anaconda. The water slows the force of any blow I aim at him.

Black sparks burst in front of my eyes. I'm running out of air. My lungs scream at me to take in a breath, but I know if I do, only chlorinated water will pour into my throat.

I reach behind me and grab what I hope is his respirator. I yank as hard as I can, pulling it out of his mouth. A stream of silvery bubbles pours up next to me. I hoped that would force him to let go, but he doesn't even try to replace it. He knows he's got more air in his lungs than I do. He can hold out while I drown.

My chest heaves as my body tries to take a breath without my consent.

In one last desperate motion, I yank the hairpin out of my bun. I twist around and stab it right where the man's neck meets his shoulder.

I see his furious dark eyes through his scuba mask. His grip relaxes for a split second as he flinches with shock and pain.

I pull my knees up to my chest and kick at his body as hard as I can. I shove myself away from him, rocketing upward to the surface.

My face breaks the surface, and I take a huge, desperate gasp of air. I've never tasted anything more delicious. It's almost painful how much air I drag into my lungs.

I swim for the edge of the pool, stroking with all my might, praying I won't feel his hand closing around my ankle as he drags me back down again. Then I grab the rim of the pool and shove myself out. Not stopping to grab my phone, not even sparing a glance behind me, I sprint across the slippery tiles to the exit.

There's two ways down from the roof—the elevator or the stairs. I take the latter, not wanting to risk a black-clad hand shoving itself between the elevator doors right as they're about to close. I run down two flights of stairs, and then I dash back out into the carpeted hallway, hammering on apartment doors until somebody opens up.

I shove my way into the stranger's apartment, slamming his door behind me and locking it.

"Hey, what the hell?" he cries.

He's a man of about sixty, overweight and bespectacled, still wearing office clothes but with a fluffy pair of slippers on his feet instead of shoes. He goggles at my swimsuit and the water I'm dripping on his carpet, too confused to form words.

When I look over at the living room couch, I see a woman of about the same age midway through eating a bowl of ice cream, with her spoon paused at the entrance of her mouth. On the television screen, a blond girl sobs over her chances of getting a rose or being sent home that night.

"What—what's happening?" the man stammers, no longer angry now that he's realized something is wrong. "Should I call the police?"

"No," I say automatically.

The Griffins don't call the police when we have a problem. In fact, we'll do anything we can to avoid contact with the cops.

I'm waiting, heart pounding, too scared to even look out the peephole in case the diver has followed me and he's waiting outside the door. Waiting for my eye to cross the lens so he can fire a bullet right through it.

I say, "If I can use your phone, I'll call my brother."

CHAPTER 2
RAYLAN

I LIE VERY STILL IN THE FALSE BOTTOM OF THE CART. I CAN FEEL IT bumping and jolting over the dirt road, then pausing outside the gates of the Boko Haram compound.

The insurgents have been holed up in here for a week after taking control of this patch of land close to Lake Chad. We've got intel that Yusuf Nur drove into the compound last night. He'll only be staying here for twelve hours before heading out again.

I hear Kambar arguing with the guards over the wagon full of rice he's brought. He's dickering with them over price, demanding they pay the full sixty-six thousand naira they offered and not a kobo less.

I'd like to strangle him for making such a fuss about it, but I know it would probably look more suspicious if he didn't haggle. Still, as the argument drags on and on, and he threatens to turn around and take his sacks of basmati back home, I have to stop myself from giving the boards overhead a thump to remind him that getting inside is more important than getting his money.

Finally, the guards agree to a price just a little lower than Kambar wants, and I feel the wagon lurch as we drive inside the compound.

I hate being cooped up in here. It's hotter than hell, and I feel vulnerable, even though Bomber and I are both armed to the teeth. Somebody could douse this cart in gasoline and set it ablaze before we could shoot our way out. If Kambar betrayed us.

We've been working with him on and off for two years, so I'd like to think I can trust the guy. But I also know he'll do a lot of things for the right price. He's done a lot of things for me when I scrounged up a good bribe.

Luckily, we pass into the compound without incident. Kambar drives the cart over to what I assume is the kitchen area, then starts unloading his rice.

"I hope that smell is the cow and not you," Bomber hisses at me.

For almost three hours now, we've been crammed in here together, like two lovers in one coffin. It's definitely a much more intimate experience than I ever hoped to have with Bomber.

He's not a bad guy—a little bit stupid, a little bit sexist, and pretty fuckin' awful at telling jokes. But he's a hard worker, and I can count on him to follow the plan.

We've been hired to kill Nur, the leader of this particular cell of Boko Haram. He's been running rampant over northeastern Nigeria, trying to block democratic elections and install his own theocratic state. With him at the head, of course.

He's taken hundreds of hostages, then murdered them when towns refused to open their gates to him or pay the outrageous ransoms he demanded.

Well, that ends tonight. Boko Haram is a hydra with a hundred heads, but I'm gonna hack off at least one of them.

I wish I had my normal crew with me. This job is dicey. I'd rather have Ghost by my side, or even Psycho. But the Black Knights are currently occupied in Ukraine. Bomber was the best option I had on short notice.

"I have to pee so bad," he mutters.

"I told you not to drink so much water."

"It's fuckin' hot, though…"

"*Shh*," I hiss at him.

I can hear at least one other person helping Kambar unload the cart. The last thing I need is for the insurgents to overhear Bomber whining.

I hear Kambar chatting with somebody a dozen yards away. Then a pause. Then the three swift knocks on the side of the cart that tell us the coast is clear.

I reach beneath me, flipping up the latch that holds our little compartment in place. The doors swing open, dumping Bomber and me out in the dirt underneath the cart. I see the bullock's hooves up by my head and two rickety wheels on either side of me. Bomber and I roll between the wheels, hiding ourselves behind a pyramid of oil drums.

Kambar doesn't even glance back at us. He climbs up in his cart again and flicks the reigns, whistling for the bullock to get going.

Bomber and I hide behind the oil drums for another two hours. Bomber digs a channel in the dust and releases his aching bladder, which I wish he wouldn't do two inches from my elbow, but there aren't any other options. I hear the cooks rattling around in the kitchen, making the dinner meal for the fifty or so soldiers inside the compound.

I smell the mouthwatering scents of sizzling lamb and bubbling tomato sauce.

"We could sneak in and grab a bite…" Bomber whispers.

"Don't even think about it."

At last, it's dark, and I'm pretty sure everyone is done eating. I see the glow of lantern light up in the window at the southwest corner of the compound. The room Nur is using.

"Let's go," I mutter to Bomber.

I don't want to wait until the night watch comes on. I want to act now, while everyone is full and drowsy, while the soldiers who watched the compound all day long in the hot sun are counting down the minutes until they can go have a cigarette and a drink, play cards, or go to bed early.

We've been watching the compound for days. I have a fairly good idea of where the guards are posted and what their patrol pattern looks like.

Bomber and I creep up the back staircase.

The compound reminds me of a medieval castle—all big rounded stones and windows cut into the walls without any glass. Instead of panes, colored cloth is hung to block dust from blowing inside.

There's no air-conditioning in places like this. They rely on brick or stone and airflow to keep the interiors relatively cool.

Bomber hangs back while I poke my head around the corner, checking for the guard. He's standing at one of the windows looking outward, his rifle set butt down on the stone floor next to him, the barrel resting against the wall.

Sloppy. These men have no training. They're ferocious enough against unarmed civilians, against women and children, but their sense of invincibility is unearned.

I creep up behind him and wrap my arm around his throat, covering his mouth with my hand and choking him out. I wait until he goes limp in my arms, and then I drop him gently to the floor.

I strip off the man's clothes. He's wearing desert camouflage with a green turban and face wrap. He's a much smaller man than I am, but luckily the top and pants are baggy, probably pulled at random out of a stack of uniforms.

I put his clothes on over my own, grateful for the turban because I can use it to hide my face. When I'm ready, Bomber covers me as I approach Nur's door.

Two guards bookend the door. These two know better than to set down their rifles or show any indication of boredom. If Nur caught them slacking, he'd shoot them himself or order one of his more creative and disgusting tortures.

The last time his insurgents took hostages outside Taraba, he ordered all their hands be cut off and hung by a string around their necks. Half the hostages died of infection or blood loss. Nur didn't seem to care.

Looking down at the floor to hide my face, I stride purposefully toward the guards.

"Message for Nur," I mumble in Kanuri.

The guard on the right holds out his hand for the message, thinking I've brought a note or a letter.

Instead, I cut his throat with my Ka-Bar knife.

He gasps soundlessly, bringing his hands up to his neck, more surprised than anything else.

The guard on the left opens his mouth to shout, swinging his rifle around at me.

I block the rifle with my arm, clamping my hand over his mouth. Then I stab him six times in the chest.

Both men drop at almost the same time. There's no muffling the sound of their bodies falling or the gurgling of the man on the right.

So I expect Nur to be waiting for me.

I haul up the man on the left and hold his body in front of me as I push my way through Nur's door.

Sure enough, Nur fires three bullets in my direction. Two hit the body of his hapless guard. The third splinters the wooden doorframe next to my ear.

Running straight at Nur, I throw the guard's body in his face. He stumbles backward, tripping over a footstool and landing hard on the luxurious Moroccan carpet spread across his stone floor.

I kick the gun out of his hand, then step aside so Bomber can shoot him. Bomber is right behind me, with a silencer screwed on to his SIG Sauer. He shoots Nur twice in the chest and once in the head.

Nur wasn't wearing a vest. Just a loose white linen top on which the bloodstains bloom like flowers. I can hear his last breath of air whistle out through a hole in his lung.

I'm always surprised how very human these warlords are. Nur is about six feet tall, soft shouldered, with a belly. He's bald on top, the patches of hair around his ears streaked with gray. The whites of his eyes are yellowed, and so are his teeth. I can smell his oniony sweat.

There's nothing special or majestic about this man. He's murdered thousands of people and terrorized many more. But right now he's dying in a dull way, without any last words. Without even putting up much of a fight.

Bomber and I wait until he's fully dead. I check for a pulse with my fingers, even though I can already see from his glassy eyes that he's gone.

Then Bomber and I latch on to the window ledge and rappel down the side of the building.

We're planning to go out through the drainage chute, where the kitchen staff dumps the dirty water and other refuse. It wasn't my first choice of exit, but Bomber and I have had all our shots, so hopefully we won't catch anything too nasty.

As we creep through the dark yard, the guards are beginning to swap shifts. In about ten minutes, they'll find Nur's body. They're sure to check in on their boss.

Bomber and I are passing through a narrow stone hallway to the kitchen when he hisses, "Long Shot, take a look."

I scowl back at him, annoyed that he's slowed down. There's no time to look at whatever caught his attention.

Still, I backtrack to the locked door. Peering through the tiny window, I see five small girls huddled on a bare floor. They're still wearing their school uniforms of plaid jumpers and white cotton socks and blouses. Their clothing is remarkably clean—they can't have been here long.

"Shit," I murmur.

"What do we do?" Bomber says.

"We better get them out."

Bomber is about to shoot the lock, but I stop him. I can feel something weighing down the pocket of the pants I stole from the guard upstairs. Fishing around, I find a set of keys.

I try each one in the lock, succeeding with the third. The door screeches open. The girls look up, terrified.

"Stay quiet, please!" I tell them in English.

I don't speak Hausa, Yoruba, Igbo, or any of the other Nigerian languages. I only memorized a few words of Kanuri for this job. So I'm just praying these girls learned English at school.

I can't tell if they understand or if they're just scared into silence. They stare at Bomber and me, wide-eyed and trembling.

I try the keys on the shackles around their ankles, but none seems to fit. Instead, I wriggle a rock out of the wall and lay their chain over top. Bomber smashes it with his rifle butt until the links part. I can't remove the metal manacles around their ankles, but we can slip the chain out at least.

Putting my finger to my lips to remind the girls to stay quiet, we hustle them down the hall to the kitchen. Bomber peeks his head in first. He sneaks up behind the cook and hits him over the head with a serving platter, knocking the man onto one of the rice sacks Kambar brought just that afternoon.

I drop the girls down the refuse chute, one at a time. It smells fucking horrible.

Bomber wrinkles his nose. "I don't wanna go in there."

I hear shouting on the upper floor of the building. I think someone just found Nur's body.

"Stay here and take your chances, then," I tell him.

Holding up my rifle to keep it out of the muck, I drop into the chute.

I slide down the foul dark passageway, hoping against hope that it doesn't narrow at any point. I can't imagine anything worse than being trapped like a cork in a bottle in this disgusting place. Luckily, I slide all the way through.

"Look out!" I call ahead to the girls, not wanting to plow into any of them.

Now their clothes are filthy, streaked with grease and rotten food. I grab the hand of the smallest one, saying to the others, "Go!"

Bomber grabs two more by the hands, and we run away across the barren ground, praying the dark and the sparse scrub will conceal us. It's good that the girls got so dirty—it helps mute the bright white of their socks and blouses.

I can hear the commotion back in the compound. The insurgents are running and shouting, searching the building for us, but lacking organization now that their boss is dead.

I'm trying to run as fast as I can, but the girls are slow. They're limping along, barefoot and stiff from however long they were trapped in that room. They probably haven't eaten.

"We've got to leave them," Bomber barks at me. "We have to be at the pickup point in forty-one minutes, or they're gonna leave without us!"

It's five miles away. There's no chance these girls are going to be able to run at that pace. Not in their current state.

"We're not leaving them," I growl.

The soldiers are in chaos, but soon they'll reorganize. They'll head out with their Jeeps and their spotlights, trying to find us.

Crouching, I motion for the biggest girl to climb on my back. I grab two more girls and set them on either hip.

"Are you insane?" Bomber says.

"Pick up those two, or I'll fucking shoot you myself!" I shout at him.

Bomber shakes his head at me, his beefy face red with anger. But he picks up the other two girls. Bomber is built like a linebacker. I know he can carry a few more pounds.

We start jogging across the rough ground, the girls clinging to us with their skinny arms and legs.

Even though they're small, I must be carrying over a hundred pounds. I don't know what the fuck kids weigh, but these three seem to be increasing in mass by the minute.

Sweat is pouring off my skin, making it hard for them to hold on to me. Bomber is puffing and blowing like a hippo, too tired to even complain.

We run until my lungs are burning and my legs are on fire.

"Two more miles," Bomber gasps.

Fuck.

Each jolt of my feet sends pain shooting up my back. My hands are numb, trying to cling on to these kids. I'm scared I'm going to collapse and not be able to get up again.

I try to pretend I'm back in basic training, when I had to run ten miles with a forty-pound pack on my back. When I wasn't accustomed to pushing my body and had no idea how far it could go.

I remember my first drill sergeant—Sergeant Price.

I picture him jogging beside me, screaming at me to not even think about slowing down. *IF YOU DROP ONE GODDAMN STEP, PRIVATE, I WILL KICK YOU IN THE BALLS SO HARD, YOU'LL SING LIKE MARIAH CAREY!*

Price knew how to motivate a guy.

At last, when I really think I can't take another step, I hear the drone of the chopper. It floods me with new life.

"Almost there!" I say to Bomber.

He nods dully, sweat flying off his face.

The last little bit of ground is uphill. I carry those girls up that ridge like I'm Samwise Gamgee carrying Frodo to the volcano. It is both the best and worst moment of my life.

I lift them into the chopper one by one, wondering exactly how the hell I'm going to figure out where they came from so I can get them home again.

"We don't have the weight capacity for extra bodies!" the pilot snaps at me.

"Then chuck something out," I tell him.

I'm not leaving these kids after I carried them all that way.

The pilot throws out the med kit and a couple of other boxes of supplies. Hopefully nothing too expensive—I'm probably gonna have to pay for all that.

Once Bomber and I are settled, the chopper lifts into the air. The five girls huddle together on the floor, clinging to each other, more frightened by flying than by the rest of the escape. Only one has the courage to peek out the open doorway to see the dark desert dropping away beneath us.

She looks up at me, big eyes shining in her little round face.

"Bird," she mouths at me in English. She links her thumbs together and flaps her fingers like wings.

"Yeah." I grunt. "You're a bird now."

As we fly over Lake Chad, my cell buzzes in my pocket.

I pull it out, surprised I'm getting service up here.

I'm even more surprised to see Dante's name on the screen. Last time he called me, I ended up shot in the side. It gave me one of my nastiest scars yet.

I pick up anyway, saying, "Deuce. You better not be calling me for another favor."

"Well…" Dante laughs.

Deuce never used to laugh much. I think he's doing it more now that he got his girl back.

Speaking of girls…

"Let me guess," I say. "You're calling me 'cause Riona wants my number. It's all right—I understand. The chemistry between us was palpable."

"Well, she didn't throw her drink in your face, so I guess by the standards of your usual interactions with women, it went pretty well…"

I snort. I only met Riona Griffin one time, but she made an impression on me. You don't see a girl that gorgeous very often. The fact she's arrogant and uptight and hates my guts just adds a little spice to the mix.

"So what are you really calling about?" I ask Dante.

"It is about Riona," he says. "But not how you're thinking…"

CHAPTER 3
RIONA

My brother, Callum, shows up at my building in less than ten minutes. He rescues me from the apartment belonging to the Greenwoods just in time. Mr. Greenwood is becoming increasingly insistent that we call the police. Mrs. Greenwood also seems impatient, either because she's missing the end of *The Bachelor* or because she's noticed her husband's eyes flitting over my bare legs several times. The striped bathroom towel the Greenwoods provided was made for their modest proportions and doesn't cover much more of me than my swimsuit does.

When they open the door to Cal, my brother strides into the apartment with Dante Gallo following along behind him. The Greenwoods retreat to their couch, not wanting to be anywhere near a man who can barely walk through their doorframe without turning sideways.

A wave of relief washes over me at the sight of my brother, who looks as cool and competent as always, and Dante, who could have ripped that fucking scuba diver in half with his bare hands if he had been in the pool with me.

I almost want to hug them both. Almost. But I'm not quite that far gone.

"Thanks for coming," I say instead.

Cal doesn't stand on ceremony. He puts his arm around me and squeezes me against his side. I think becoming a dad has made him soft. But also, it feels nice. Comforting.

"We already cleared your apartment," he says. "There's nobody there."

"Let's go back, then," I say, with a subtle glance toward the Greenwoods. No need for them to overhear any more than they already have.

"I don't know how a mugger got in the building with Ronald at the door!" Mrs. Greenwood frets.

I told the Greenwoods that someone accosted me at the pool, but I was vague on details. Mrs. Greenwood assumed it was a mugging when I told her I'd have to use her phone to call my brother.

"Thanks for letting me stay," I say to the couple.

"You go ahead and keep that." Mrs. Greenwood nods at the striped towel. I think she'd give me almost anything to get us out of her apartment.

We head back down the hallway to the elevators, my bare feet padding soundlessly on the carpet while Cal and Dante walk on either side of me like bookends.

"Do you know who the diver was?" Dante says in his deep gravelly voice. "Did you see his face?"

"No." I shake my head. "He had dark eyes. That's all I saw. Most of his face was covered by the scuba mask. He was strong…"

I shiver involuntarily, remembering how his arms locked around me and dragged me under the water.

"Are there cameras on the roof?" Cal asks me.

"I have no idea."

We take the elevator down from the thirty-second floor to the twenty-eighth. Even though Cal already went through my apartment using his spare key, Dante checks it again before we enter.

"I'm gonna shower real quick," I say to them. "Help yourself to a drink, if you want."

I turn the water on as hot as I can stand it and wash the chlorine smell out of my hair. As I turn my face into the spray, I feel another swoop of panic. I remember the awful heaving of my lungs, desperate for air. I shut the water off, drying off with my own properly sized towel, and change into yoga pants and a sweatshirt.

When I come back out to the living room, Cal and Dante are prowling around, checking the windows and balcony doors for any sign that someone might have broken in here earlier in the day.

"Does anything look out of place?" Cal asks me. "Is anything missing?"

"Not that I can see."

I would notice. My apartment is minimalist in the extreme, clean and well organized. My books are arranged alphabetically by author. There isn't a single dirty dish in the sink. I don't have plants or pets—I don't want anything living depending on me.

"Let's have a chat with Ronald, then," Dante growls.

Ronald is the main doorman. He and two others rotate shifts so there's someone in the lobby twenty-four seven, making sure nobody who isn't a resident or guest accesses the building.

Ronald is middle-aged, bald, paunchy, and friendly. He has a hint of a British accent that may be real or may be something he uses to endear himself to the tenants, who like the idea of a posh internationally imported doorman.

At first, he's hesitant to show us the camera feed for the swimming pool without clearing it through building management. However, my brother is very convincing with his light-blue eyes that cut right through you and his title as city alderman. Dante's imposing silent bulk is persuasive in an entirely different way.

Ronald takes us into a small back room with a single desk, chair, and computer monitor. "You can watch the video feeds on here."

"We need to see all the cameras on the roof," Dante says. "The ones that show the swimming pool."

"I'll see what I can do." Ronald sits down at the desk and clicks tentatively with the mouse. "We only got the security cameras this year, so I'm not entirely familiar with the system. I've only had to review the footage twice before, when Mrs. Peterson kept insisting someone was knocking on her door…"

"Were they?" Dante asks.

"No." Ronald chuckles. "It was her cockatoo, inside her apartment."

Ronald manages to pull up the swimming pool camera, winding back the recording to two hours earlier.

"Is that the only camera up there?" Callum asks.

"Yes. There's only one per floor," Ronald says.

The camera is mounted high in the corner so almost the entirety of the pool is in view. We can see the lounge chairs on both sides of the pool, the cabinet that holds all the extra towels, and the entryway where people enter and exit on their way to the elevators. However, the lower-left corner of the swimming pool is cut off.

We watch the grainy footage as a mother and her two young children paddle around, then a group of teenagers lies on the lounge chairs while an old man swims laps. After that, the pool empties, and for a long time, there's no one up there at all.

Finally, I see my own familiar figure come walking across the tiles. I watch myself turn on the music streaming to my waterproof headphones via my phone, then set the phone down on the nearest lounge chair atop a folded towel. Calm and oblivious of what's about to happen, I stride over to the pool and dive in.

My heart rate quickens as the seconds count down to what I know is about to happen. I feel the ridiculous urge to call out a warning to myself. I watch my tiny figure swim back and forth across the pool, knowing that any second, those steady laps are about to be interrupted.

What happens next looks strangely benign on the video screen. I simply drop below the water and disappear. The camera is too far away and the resolution is too weak to make out what's actually happening. You can see churning in the water and the dark shadow of a figure below, but it's impossible to tell that there are actually two people down there, locked in a deadly struggle.

I realize that if the diver had successfully held me down, all the camera would have captured is my body floating back up to the surface facedown. It would have looked like I cramped up and drowned. No one would have known I'd been murdered.

I watch myself struggle and fight below the water, just a dark blur in a haze of bubbles. Without realizing it, I'm holding my breath.

Cal tenses next to me, and I hear Dante give an angry grunt. I know they feel as helpless as I do, watching what already took place, powerless to do anything about it.

When my figure pops back to the surface again, I take a deep breath in the stifling space of the security room. I watch little Riona haul herself out of the pool and flee to the stairs.

Having failed to murder me, the diver abandons subterfuge. He pulls himself out of the pool as well, burdened by his oxygen tank and unable to use his right arm to its fullest extent because of the hairpin buried in his trapezius muscle. I can't see the hairpin on the video screen, but I can see the stiffness of that arm and the way the diver favors his left instead.

Ronald gives a little yelp at the sight of the diver. He hadn't realized until that moment what he was watching. "Who the bloody hell is that?"

We ignore his question, watching the diver strip off his flippers. He doesn't seem interested in chasing me. Instead, he picks up my cell phone off the lounge chair and carries it away with him.

Only once he's gone can I breathe freely again.

"Rewind the tape," Cal says. "I want to see when he got in the pool."

Ronald scrolls back and forth over the feed several times. We can't see the diver entering the swimming pool.

"Wait." Dante grunts, pointing with his thick finger at the screen. "What's that?"

He's pointing to a moment thirty minutes before I entered the pool. No figure is caught on camera. But I see ripples running outward across the water from the lower-left corner of the screen.

"He got in the pool right then," Dante says.

"He stayed off-screen." Callum frowns. "He knew how to avoid the camera."

"Is that the only way up to the roof?" Dante asks Ronald, pointing to the main entryway.

"No." Ronald shakes his head. "There's a maintenance elevator on the other side. You can't see it on camera. I told them we really should have two per floor, pointing in both directions—"

"Who has access to the maintenance elevator?" Cal interrupts.

"Just the doormen and the building superintendent," Ronald says. "But none of us would be putting on scuba suits and attacking residents!"

He puffs up indignantly, like Cal was suggesting Ronald himself might have been the one hiding in the pool.

"Give me that video," Cal says.

"What?" Ronald sputters. "I have to report this. I—"

"You're not telling anyone about this," Dante growls. "Give us a copy of the video, and then delete it."

"I can't do that! I could lose my job!"

"Ronald," I interject, using my most reasonable tone. "I was almost murdered in the pool because an unknown person gained access to your building. If anything's going to make you lose your job, it's the lawsuit I'll file against you, the property management company, and the owners of this building if you don't give me that video right now."

Ronald swallows hard. "Well…uh…when you put it that way…"

He sends a copy of the footage to Callum via email, then deletes an hour of video out of the database.

"Thank you," I say sweetly. "Now keep your mouth shut about this, and you'll see evidence of my continued gratitude in your Christmas bonus."

We leave Ronald alone in the security booth.

"You'd better come back to my place tonight," Cal says. "Or to Mom and Dad's."

I don't love either of those options. Cal has a brand-new baby. While I appreciate my one and only nephew on an intellectual level, I'd like to preserve our relationship by not being woken ten times in the night by his yelling.

My parents' house is barely more appealing. I just moved out on my own—I don't want to be back in my old room, especially not with my mother and father fussing over me in the wake of the failed drowning.

"I think I'll stay at a hotel," I tell him.

"Someone should keep an eye on you." Dante grunts.

I know that's his way of offering to do the job. But Dante has a kid now, too, and a fiancée—he and Simone are getting married in just a couple of weeks.

I shake my head. "I'm fine. I don't need a babysitter."

"Don't check in under your real name," Cal says.

"I know." I roll my eyes. "I'm not an idiot."

"This is serious." Cal fixes me with his cool-blue stare. "Whoever that fucker was, he's a professional. He planned this out ahead of time. He knew the building. The security system. He knew your schedule—when you get off work and when you swim laps at night. He went out of his way to make this look like an accident. That's top-tier hitman shit. Whoever hired him for the job isn't fucking around."

"I know," I say again, with less sarcasm. "Trust me, I'm taking this seriously."

I remember the water closing over my head and those iron arms dragging me down.

"We need someone to keep watch on you until we figure out who did this," Dante says.

I frown at him. "Who are you talking about exactly?"

"A professional."

I cross my arms over my chest. "You better not mean who I think you're talking about…"

"I called him on the drive over. He's flying back stateside tonight."

"DANTE!" I shout, thoroughly annoyed.

"He's good," Dante says. "Very, very good."

"I don't need a babysitter. Especially not *him*." I curl my lip in distaste. I met Raylan Boone once before, and I wasn't impressed. His cocky country-boy schtick is the last thing I need right now.

"Who is he?" Cal asks curiously.

"We were in Iraq together," Dante says. "He helped me save Simone."

"What's he done to offend you, sis?" Cal says, failing to hide his smirk.

"I don't want somebody following me around," I say coldly. "Especially not someone…*chatty*."

Cal and Dante don't even try not to laugh.

"Only *you* would prefer potential assassination to someone trying to 'chat' with you." Cal snorts.

"He's the best man I know," Dante tells me seriously. "He'll take care of you, Riona."

I know Dante means well, but I can't help scowling.

I don't want anybody taking care of me.

CHAPTER 4
RAYLAN

Dante drives me over to Riona's law firm on East Wacker. He warned me that the Irish princess wasn't exactly keen on having me as her bodyguard, but I was hoping we could get off on slightly better footing than last time.

"Nice to see you again," I say, holding out my hand to shake.

Riona looks me up and down like I'm a Bible salesman standing on her doorstep. Her green eyes look cool and frosty, like sea glass. "Is that what you're planning to wear?"

That surprises me because I actually showered and put on clean clothes before I caught a flight across the Atlantic. I'm wearing boots, jeans, and a button-up flannel, which seems to me to be about the most normal outfit a guy could wear.

"What's wrong with this?"

"Nothing." Riona sniffs. "If I need somebody to chop wood for me."

"Do you? 'Cause I'm pretty handy with an axe. Gimme three hours, and I'll buck, split, and stack a cord for you."

Riona shakes her head at me. "I hope to god I never find out what any of that means."

She turns around and marches away from me. I assume I'm supposed to follow, so I wave farewell to Dante and stroll along after her.

The law firm of Griffin, Briar, Weiss takes up several floors of the building. I've already been briefed by Dante that they handle all legal matters for the Griffin empire and some of the work for the Gallos as well, as the two families' interests have become entwined.

We've only gone about a dozen steps when we're intercepted by a tall trim man with iron-gray hair, a long lean face, and a tweed suit. The suit, combined with his tortoiseshell glasses, makes him look like he'd be more at home in a Dublin pub than in a Chicago law firm.

Sure enough, when he speaks, he has a hint of an Irish accent— just a flavor, enough to know he hasn't spent all his life in America.

"Riona!" he says, putting his arm around her shoulders. "Fergus told me what happened. You didn't have to come in today."

Riona colors. I can't tell if she's embarrassed by the mention of the attack or because she's being hugged in the workplace. Possibly both. "I'm fine, Uncle Oran."

"I assume you're Raylan." Oran releases Riona and holds out his hand for me to shake. He has dry slim fingers and a firm grip.

"Raylan Boone," I say. "Nice to meet you."

"I'm glad you're here to keep an eye on my niece," he says. "She's very valuable to us—to the firm and to the family."

"I'll do my best."

I can tell Riona hates this even more—being talked about in the third person and being entrusted to me like a package. She must care about her uncle because only that could keep her from firing off a sharp retort.

"Raylan can stay in my office," she says to Oran. "Out of the way."

"Oh, no need! Make yourself comfortable," Oran tells me. "We've got a pretty good espresso machine. Of course, I'm biased—I picked it out myself. Or there's a café on the ground floor."

He smiles, showing crowded teeth that definitely never had the benefit of American orthodontic care.

"Thanks," I say. "I'll drink any kinda coffee as long as it's brown."

Oran laughs. "A true soldier! I was the same way when I served in the IRA." He claps me on the shoulder in turn, then continues off down the hallway.

"Your uncle was in the IRA?" I ask Riona.

Riona shrugs. "That's what he says. But Uncle Oran never lets facts get in the way of a good story."

"He's your father's brother?"

"Half brother. Different mothers. Actually, there's a half sister in Cork who's even older. I guess my grandfather wasn't too careful on his visits home. Or too concerned with Grandma's feelings."

I don't think she particularly likes telling me this bit of messy family history, but Riona has a kind of brutal honesty. An interesting characteristic for a lawyer. I always thought of attorneys as silver-tongued devils who would try to convince you that black is white and wrong is right.

Riona is the opposite—she seems determined to state things exactly as they are and damn the consequences. Or other people's feelings.

"This is my office," she says, pointing to a room that looks more like an art gallery. "Don't touch anything. Don't talk to anyone. Just...be quiet so I can work, please."

Two bright spots of color burn on her pale cheeks. I think she's embarrassed for anyone else to see me.

I grin at her. "You can tell 'em I'm your cousin if you like."

"No thank you," Riona replies coolly. "I know how you treat your cousins where you come from."

I can't help giving a little snort. I've heard plenty of cousin-fucking jokes before, but the way Riona says it, with her particular edge of disdain, tickles me all the same.

She's a tough nut to crack.

And I've always liked a challenge.

Honestly, if she liked me right off the bat, I'd think she had terrible taste.

I settle down in a cushy armchair in the corner of her office, and I watch her work.

I'm not watching her all the time, of course—I'm also checking the ingress and egress points of the building, making a mental map of the office, looking over the rest of the staff, and watching their interactions: checking to see who's friendly with who, who's got a rivalry going on, and who looks particularly interested in Ms. Riona.

I notice one guy eyeing the pair of us every time he walks down the hall. He's got sandy-blond hair styled up in a quiff and a skintight blue suit with a bright yellow pocket square. Kinda dandy for my tastes, but he seems pretty proud of himself about the whole ensemble.

"Who's that?" I ask Riona.

She takes those pale green eyes off her work for just a moment so she can glance up and check out who I'm talking about.

"Oh," she says flatly. "That's Josh Hale. He's a sneaky little fucker who's vying for the same job as me. That's why he keeps trying to spy on us."

"How much does he want that job?"

"A lot," Riona says.

"Enough to want you out of the way?"

"Maybe. But I don't know if he'd have the balls to make that happen. He's not from a Mafia family. He's just your average cutthroat promotion chaser. The toughest thing about him is the fact he was on the fencing team at Notre Dame. Which he'll be sure to tell you within ten minutes of meeting you."

Once Josh is done staring at us, I see him head into a messy office at the end of the hall. He pops out again only a minute later, looking red-faced and irritated.

Meanwhile, a pretty girl in an orange dress has scooted her chair several feet to the left so she can peer through our window, too.

"What about her?" I ask.

"That's my paralegal, Lucy. I would guess she's looking in here because she thinks you're attractive. She's been single for a while."

Riona says the word *attractive* with a note of disbelief. Still, I can't help grinning over the idea that she basically admitted I'm cute.

"What're *you* working on?" I ask her.

"Purchase agreements for the South Shore development," she says curtly.

"Is that all you're doing?"

She sets down her pen, looking up at me with annoyance. "Why?"

"Well," I reply patiently, "somebody tried to kill you last night. I assume they had a reason. Seems like it might have something to do with one of your current projects…"

"It's possible," Riona says. "This is a two-billion-dollar development. That's enough money to kill somebody over. But it doesn't make much sense that they'd try to kill *me*. Drown me in the pool, and my family will just hire someone else to do the paperwork."

She says it calmly, without emotion. But I think I hear an edge of bitterness in her voice. Like she really thinks the Griffins would just carry on with their project, barely missing her at all.

"I don't think you get an office like this just by filling out paperwork," I say.

"I think you know as much about lawyers as I do about chopping wood." Riona sniffs.

"Fair enough." I smile at her.

Riona goes back to her work.

I sit back in my chair and think.

The Griffins have a hundred enemies. Rival Irish families. Rival Italian families. The *Bratva*. Polish Mafia…

Why try to kill Riona Griffin, though? And why try to make the drowning look accidental?

Most times when a Mafia boss orders a killing, he wants to send a message. If the intent was to threaten the Griffins or to avenge a past wrong, the hitman would have just shot Riona in the street. Or something much worse…

When you kill someone secretly, that's personal.

The hit was directed at Riona, and Riona alone.

Because of something she did. Or something she knows…

Riona works all day long without taking a break for lunch. My stomach is growling, but I don't want to give her the satisfaction of begging for food.

Around 6:00 p.m., she finally starts packing up the papers on her desk.

"Chow time?" I say.

Riona checks her watch. "I'm meeting Nick for dinner."

"Who's Nick?"

"My boyfriend," she says primly.

"Can't wait to meet him."

She frowns. "You're not coming."

"Sorry, darlin.' I'm your bodyguard. That means anywhere you go, I go, too."

She narrows her eyes at me. I can tell she's trying to decide whether this is worth arguing. On the one hand, I think Riona hates not getting her way. On the other, I'm fixing her with a look that makes it plain that I'm planning to stick to her like honey on a bear paw. She's not getting rid of me till this job is done.

"Fine," she snaps at last. "But I don't think Nick is going to like this."

"He might." I shrug. "I'm a pretty likable guy."

I grab my jacket and follow her over to the elevator.

"You got a car?" I ask her.

"No," she says. "I don't need one. I only live a few blocks from the office. And it's easy to get a cab or an Uber if I want to go anywhere else."

"Easy for someone to pretend to be a cab driver, too," I tell her, my eyebrow raised.

"Well, that's why you're here, isn't it? In case of murderous phony cab drivers."

I can tell she's already chafing under the inconvenience of having her plans and routines challenged. And this is only day one. We've barely gotten started.

Riona strides out to the curb, holding up her hand to hail the nearest cab. As it pulls up, I reach out to open her door for her.

"I can do it," she snaps. She pulls the handle herself and slides into the back seat. I follow her, sitting directly behind the driver.

"Where to?" he asks us.

"Amuse Bouche," Riona says.

"Great seafood at that place," the cabbie says cheerfully.

Riona ignores him, and me as well, looking out the window as we cross over the river.

"So tell me about Nick," I say.

"Why?"

"Because I need to know about everyone in your life. Everyone you've been interacting with."

"Nick doesn't have anything to do with…" She glances up at the cab driver, who's listening to a country song, drumming his fingers on the wheel. "Anything to do with what happened," she finishes.

"We don't know that. Because we don't know what happened or why."

"That's ridiculous. Nick's a surgeon. He's not—"

"What kind of surgeon?" I say.

Riona takes a slow breath, clearly annoyed with me. "He's a thoracic surgeon."

"And how long have you two been dating?"

"Three months."

"How did you meet?"

"Is this really—"

"Just answer the questions. It's easier than arguing."

Riona tosses her head, throwing her long flame-colored ponytail back over her shoulder. Her hair is the most vivid I've ever seen—not orange or strawberry blond. A true bright red. Her eyebrows and lashes are much darker, like the black points on a fox's ears and nose.

There's nothing delicate or girlish about Riona. She's a woman through and through. She has a long straight nose, wide mouth, strong cheekbones, and poker-straight posture. Tall, and not afraid to wear heels to make herself taller.

"Do you think I do anything because it's *easier?*" she says.

"Smart people don't do things the hard way."

"Know a few smart people, do you?" she says mockingly.

"Why you tryin' so hard to fight with me? We're not enemies."

"We're not friends either." She sniffs.

I just chuckle and shake my head at her, which annoys her more than if I'd gotten angry.

Riona may look like a fox, but she's got the temperament of a thoroughbred—haughty and high-strung. I don't think she's bad-tempered. She just doesn't trust easily.

I know how to handle thoroughbreds. I grew up on a horse ranch, after all.

Gently, I say, "Come on. Tell me where you met this Nick guy. Was it on Tinder? You can tell me if it was Tinder."

"No," Riona says, refusing to smile. "It wasn't Tinder."

"Where, then?"

"It was a friend's birthday party. I was opening a bottle of wine. The corkscrew slipped. I cut my finger. He helped bandage it."

"And he didn't send you a bill after, so you knew it was true love."

"No. He just asked to take me out for coffee the next day."

"Who was your mutual friend?"

"Her name's Amanda. We went to law school together."

"How does Nick know her?"

"He plays racquetball with her fiancé, Greg."

We're pulling up in front of the restaurant now. Riona says, "Satisfied? You're not going to interrogate him, too, I hope."

"Nah, of course not." I grin. "I'll be quiet as a mouse. You'll barely even know I'm there."

CHAPTER 5
RIONA

Nick is waiting by the host stand for me. He showered and changed after work, so he's wearing a pale blue button-up shirt that brings out the blond in his hair. I think he shaved for a second time because his face is perfectly smooth as he gives me a quick kiss hello. I can smell his aftershave and the industrial-strength antiseptic lingering on his hands and fingernails.

Nick could cosplay as a Ken doll without much trouble. He's tall, fit, and handsome, with a cleft in his chin. He has a softness to his features that makes him look boyish, even though he's almost forty.

He seems excited to see me, until he realizes the man who followed me through the door is also following us to our table.

"Raylan Boone," Raylan says, not waiting for me to introduce him. He grabs Nick's hand and shakes it. "Nice to meet you."

"Raylan is a security expert," I explain. "My family hired him. He's going to be shadowing me for the next few days."

"Or weeks," Raylan interjects.

"Okay…" Nick returns Raylan's handshake without quite the same level of enthusiasm. "Why, exactly?"

"There was an incident last night," I say. "Nothing serious. But we thought it would be better to take precautions."

Raylan's amused gaze flits over to me, noting that I haven't told

Nick what happened and clearly am not planning to tell him the details now either.

"What kind of incident?" Nick frowns.

"Nothing serious," I say breezily. "Let's order our drinks."

Nick and I sit across from each other at the small square table. Raylan sits on the side, like our chaperone.

"Serious enough that you need a full-time bodyguard…" Nick looks over at Raylan warily, like he's not sure how much to include him in the conversation. I'm sure he's wary for other reasons, too. Despite the fact that Raylan has the haircut of a hillbilly and hasn't shaved in weeks, he's still objectively handsome. His blue eyes look especially bright next to his black hair and thick dark eyebrows. His pointed incisors give him a wolfish look when he grins.

I could assure Nick that Raylan is also cocky, pushy, and completely not my type. But I'm not in the habit of assuring Nick of anything. It's not my job to soothe his insecurities.

Raylan isn't helping matters.

"Don't worry, Doc," he says. "I'll keep Riona safe. And anything you two lovebirds wanna talk about…just pretend I'm not here. Just like doctor-patient confidentiality, what the bodyguard hears, he keeps to himself."

He says it with that cheerful smirk on his face that makes you think he's teasing you, no matter what words are coming out of his mouth. Nick frowns. He hates being teased even more than I do.

The waiter comes to take our drink orders. I get a vodka soda, Nick a glass of wine.

"Just water, thanks," Raylan says.

"Still or sparkling?" the waiter asks.

"Whatever's free and cold."

"You can have a drink," I say to Raylan.

"Nah. I'm on the clock."

"There is no clock."

"On the job, then."

I don't know why it irritates me that he won't have a drink. I guess because I'd prefer to think of him as an unnecessary precaution, not an actual professional bodyguard.

Nick, seeing he's not going to get the information he wants out of me, switches to questioning Raylan directly. "So…how do you know the Griffins?"

"I don't," Raylan says. "Riona and I met through Dante Gallo."

That doesn't help. Nick isn't the biggest fan of Dante. They've met twice before—after which Dante said, *Yeah, he's nice. Bit high on himself.* And Nick said, *Do you usually stay friends with your clients after you get them acquitted of murder?*

"Do you, ah, work with Dante?" Nick asks with a note of nervousness.

"We were in the military together."

"Oh." Nick sounds relieved. "I considered enlisting, way back when. So I could get med school paid for."

"Hm," Raylan says blandly. "You don't say."

"I couldn't be a soldier, though. All that toilet scrubbing and 'drop and give me twenty' shit. Guess I don't like following orders," Nick says with a laugh.

I look over at Raylan, to see how he'll respond to that nice little piece of condescension.

Raylan just grins, his teeth white against his dark stubble and his tanned skin. "Guess you'd rather be the general in your operating room."

"Yeah, I guess so." Nick smiles back at him. He doesn't seem to notice the glint in Raylan's eyes, which isn't entirely friendly.

"'Course, if you fuck up at your job, the worst you're gonna do is kill some granny on your table," Raylan says casually. "You don't have to worry about watching all your colleagues, the anesthesiologists and nurses and other doctors, get captured and tortured and have their heads cut off. Or get blown to pieces right next to you. You don't have to worry about dying yourself."

"No…" Nick's smile fades. "But that doesn't mean—"

"I guess that's why in the military, we start small with scrubbing toilets," Raylan says. "Then we move up to making our beds. Then we proceed through drills and training and practice missions before we ever head out in the field. It's incremental progress. You get to know your brothers, and they get to know you. And nobody is promoted to a leadership position when they're too arrogant to follow instructions themselves. Because that's how it works when the whole team's life is on the line. Nobody's gonna serve under some shithead they don't even like, let alone respect."

Raylan is smiling pleasantly the whole time he's speaking. He keeps that same friendly Southern drawl. But I somehow become aware of his large strong hands folded on the tabletop. And the width of his shoulders under that flannel shirt.

Nick seems to become cognizant of the same thing—that Raylan is a trained soldier. Not to mention a good two or three inches taller than Nick.

He swallows hard. "Right," he mutters. "We should probably order. The kitchen can be slow here…"

"What should I get?" Raylan asks me, not bothering with the heavy leather menu and its array of choices spelled out in fancy scrolled print.

"Do you like steak?"

"Course I do. What's not to like?"

"Well, they're famous for their rib eye."

"I thought that cabbie said seafood was their specialty."

I shrug. "He also thought Columbus Drive was the best way to get over here."

"All right, you convinced me." Raylan grins. "Cabbie doesn't know his ass from his elbow."

Nick motions to the waiter.

"Go ahead," I say to the men. "I'm still looking."

"Rib eye, please," Raylan says. "Bloody, with a baked potato."

"I'll have the chicken and capers," Nick says virtuously. He hands his menu to the waiter and winks at me. "I plan to live past a hundred."

"I'll trade a decade or two for steak," Raylan says, totally unconcerned.

I can't help smiling a little. "I'll have the rib eye, too."

Nick looks betrayed.

I shrug. "I'm hungry."

When the waiter leaves us alone again, an awkward silence falls over the table. Nick tries a new conversational tactic, which I suspect is designed to exclude Raylan.

"I saw the Art Institute is showing an exhibit of El Greco," Nick says. "I got tickets for us."

That actually does excite me. "Thanks. I'd love to go."

Nick looks pleased with himself. Not content with that victory, he says, "I guess we'll need a ticket for your bodyguard, too. Are you a fan of painting, Raylan?"

"Not really." Raylan shrugs.

"You don't like Renaissance art?" Nick smirks.

Raylan takes a piece of bread from the basket in the middle of the table and spreads a generous layer of butter on it. "Well, El Greco isn't really Renaissance, is he?" he says, taking a large bite of his bread.

"What do you mean?" Nick frowns.

"Well…" Raylan chews and swallows. "The way he stretched out his people and made 'em all dramatic. Wouldn't you call that 'Mannerism'?"

Now I really can't help laughing, even though it turns the foolish look on Nick's face into a downright scowl.

Raylan shrugs. "We got books in Tennessee. Even a museum or two."

The steak comes to the table on sizzling five-hundred-degree platters, drenched in butter and parsley. The two-pound baked potatoes are piled with sour cream and hunks of bacon. The scent of grilled meat is heavenly.

Raylan and I attack our food like ravenous dogs. I haven't eaten a thing since coffee that morning. The rich, fatty rib eye is soft enough to cut with a fork. It melts on my tongue, intensely satisfying.

Nick cuts his chicken breast into small cubes, sour faced.

I can see Raylan wants to tease him about his order, but he refrains.

Feeling just a little bit bad for Nick, since my own meal is so damned delicious, I ask him about his surgery that afternoon.

Nick perks up, launching into a long and detailed description of the complicated thoracotomy that was brought to his hospital specifically for him because he's the only surgeon in the city with a 100-percent success rate on that particular procedure.

On that topic, the rest of the dinner passes by.

"Does anyone want dessert?" I ask the two men. "Or another drink?"

"I'm stuffed," Raylan says.

"Me, too," Nick says, less truthfully. He only ate half his chicken. I think he's had enough of this strange date.

"I'll get the check," I say.

Raylan says, "I already paid it."

"What? When?"

"I gave the waiter my card last time he came around."

"You're not supposed to buy my meals," I inform him. "If anything, you should be reimbursed for yours."

Raylan shrugs.

I know he was probably trying to avoid the awkwardness of Nick feeling obligated to pay for all three of us. But Nick seems more annoyed by this outcome, where Raylan has shown him up in foresight and chivalry.

"Let's get going," Nick says brusquely. "Are you coming back to my place, Riona?"

That's our usual routine, the one or two nights a week that we meet for a proper date. But I don't really see how that's going to work with Raylan tagging along after me everywhere I go. Is Raylan going to lurk in Nick's living room, while Nick and I head upstairs to the bedroom to knock boots?

"I'd better not," I say, with a glance toward the obvious impediment.

Nick gives a huff of frustration. "I'm leaving, then. I assume Raylan can help you call a cab."

With surprising consideration, Raylan hangs back so I can have a little privacy walking out with Nick.

"How long is this going to go on?" Nick demands.

"I don't know," I say honestly.

"Is there something you're not telling me? What's the reason for this? Because if he's some old boyfriend, or—"

"Don't be ridiculous," I snap. "I was attacked last night."

"You...what?" Nick's expression changes from annoyance to alarm. "Why didn't you tell me that?"

"I don't want anyone making a fuss. Especially not you. But that's why he's following me around for now."

"Are you all right?" Nick asks, more gently.

"I'm fine. You'll just have to be patient with a third wheel for a while."

Nick sighs. "All right."

He kisses me softly on the forehead. I really don't like when he does that, but I tolerate it because I know this wasn't the most pleasant evening for him.

I say, "I'll call you tomorrow."

"Please do."

I watch Nick jump in his Porsche and speed off in the direction of his house up in Streeterville.

I can feel Raylan standing behind me, close but not so close that he's towering over me.

"Back home, then?" he says.

"No." I shake my head. "Let's go meet up with my brother. I

want to know what he's found out about that diver. No offense, but I don't want to make this a permanent arrangement."

"Sure." Raylan smiles. "I get it. I spoil the romantic ambiance. I bet Nick is a real charmer when it's just the two of you."

There's no edge to his words. If I'd only just met him, I'd think he meant it sincerely enough.

But already, I'm getting to know Raylan enough that I catch the hint of a smirk tugging at the corner of his mouth.

He doesn't like Nick. And he doesn't give a damn if I know it.

CHAPTER 6
RAYLAN

RIONA AND I TAKE AN UBER OVER TO CALLUM'S APARTMENT, WITH a detour by the Gallo house. I don't like us hopping in and out of hired cars. I want to drive Riona myself, in a vehicle I know is safe.

So we borrow one from Dante.

It's the same Escalade he and I drove around in last time I was in town. I sink into the driver's seat, into the dent made by Dante's bulk. Riona seems similarly at home in the car, setting her water bottle in the cupholder automatically before she buckles her seat belt.

"Drive around in this car a lot, do you?" I ask.

"What's that supposed to mean?"

"You seem to know where everything is."

Riona gives an irritated sniff.

"What?"

"There's nothing romantic between Dante and me."

"I never said there was."

She rolls her eyes.

I'm driving us up Lake Shore Drive, the water spooling away beside us on our right. Riona looks out at the lake, which is flat and gray today, almost the exact same color as the cloudy sky.

I say, "I know he was carrying a torch for Simone all along."

"That's not why!" Riona snaps. "I mean, I knew he was in love with her. He said he wasn't, but it was obvious. It made me sad to see him hurting like that. There wasn't anything romantic between us either way—we were just friends. We still are."

"I believe you."

"I don't care if you believe me or not. That's the truth." Riona is quiet for a moment. Then she says softly, "He respected me. So often, men act like you have to prove yourself to them. When I showed up at the jail after they arrested him—you know about that?"

I nod. When the Griffins and the Gallos were fighting with the Polish Mafia, the Polish boss, Mikolaj Wilk, framed Dante for murder. Riona got the charges dropped.

"Dante trusted me to help him. Even though we barely knew each other. And our families had been enemies not long before." Riona links her fingers gently on her lap. She has lovely hands—pale and slim with clear polish over the shell-pink nails. "We're alike in a lot of ways. Disciplined. Hardworking. Unemotional. People respect that in a man. But with a woman, they say you're cold or harsh."

"People say that about Deuce, too."

"They don't hold it against him, though."

I think about that. How attributes are viewed in men versus women. How women are criticized for behaviors that might be seen as virtues in men. You see plenty of that in the military—guys getting complimented for their "leadership skills" and gals getting called *ball-busting bitches* when they give the same orders.

"You're right," I say after a moment. "And you're right that I shouldn't have assumed you and Dante couldn't just be friends."

Riona glances over at me, surprised that I actually agreed with her for once. She says, "People are always telling me what I should want or what I should feel."

"Is Nick one of those people?"

That was the wrong thing to say. I can almost see her barriers coming up again.

"You were lying when you said you don't like art," Riona accuses. "You were laying a trap for him so you could make him look stupid."

"For a smart guy, it was awfully easy to make him look dumb."

"You didn't like him as soon as he made that comment about the military."

"Everybody thinks they know what's it like to be in the army 'cause they watched *Saving Private Ryan*."

Riona nods slowly. "Right. And everyone's a lawyer because they watched *Suits*."

I laugh. "Well...that was a pretty good show."

Riona smiles just a little. "I watched it for the clothes. Donna knew how to dress. Joan from *Mad Men*, too. They don't always do the redheads right on TV, but with those two..."

I'm sorry that we're already pulling up in front of Callum's place. Right when Riona was actually starting to relax a little. It takes me a minute to be sure we've got the right place because the building looks like an old church, not an apartment complex. But Riona assures me this is the spot.

I never met Callum on my last visit—he was busy watching the birth of his son. I know all about him, though. He's married to Dante's little sister, Aida. He's the oldest Griffin child and heir to the empire.

I can tell straight off how much he cares about Riona. He brings us up to his cozy kitchen, which is small but warm, with exposed brick walls and butcher block counters. Plenty of the original church remains, including the long roof beams and several stained glass windows.

Despite how late it is, Callum's still dressed in slacks and a white button-up shirt, the sleeves rolled up. He keeps his voice low as he pours us all a drink, mindful of Aida and the baby asleep in the next room.

"How's Miles?" Riona whispers.

"Getting more stubborn by the day." Callum smiles.

He pours us each a glass of red wine.

"To family," he says simply.

This time, I take a sip. The wine seems especially good after the rib eye. It's funny eating and drinking like this. The two months before, I hardly had a single good meal. Now I'm in the lap of luxury. I'll have to be careful not to let it go to my head. Hunger gives you an edge.

I set down the wine. "What do we know about the diver?"

Callum opens his laptop and plays the security video for me.

Even though I can see that it upsets Riona, she watches the whole thing over again without taking her eyes off the screen.

"How did you get away from him under the water?" I ask.

She explains about the hairpin.

"That was lucky," I say. "And smart."

As the diver climbs out of the pool, I say, "He looks about six-two, two hundred pounds. Does that sound right, Riona?"

She nods. "He was strong. Young, probably—less than forty. Dark eyes." She pauses for a moment, remembering. "I think he was left-handed," she adds.

"Why do you say that?"

"When I was lying on my back, his arm came over my neck this way..." She mimes it crossing her throat from left to right. "I think that was his dominant arm."

"Good." I nod.

"Not much of a description," Riona says skeptically.

"It's better than nothing."

We watch the diver pick up her phone after he gets out of the pool.

"Have you tried tracking the phone?" I ask Callum.

"Yes. It turned on briefly in Greektown. Then it disappeared again."

"What kind of info is on that phone?"

"A lot of things," Riona says. "Personal and banking info. All my work emails...it's password protected, but you know that doesn't mean shit to somebody who knows what they're doing."

"Could the phone have been the target?"

Riona shrugs. "Seems like there are easier ways to steal it."

I turn to Callum again. "Do you know who brokers hits in Chicago? If this guy was hired locally, a broker could tell us who the diver was. And maybe who hired him."

"I know someone." Callum nods.

I want to go along with Callum for that. So I say to Riona, "Can I take you over to your parents' place tomorrow? Just for a couple of hours."

"Sure," she says, without much enthusiasm.

"Good. Now what about enemies? Who has a grudge against you at the moment?"

"Against Riona specifically—nobody," Callum says. "Against the Griffins—a whole fuck of a lot of people. Top of the list are the Russians. My father killed their last boss, Kolya Kristoff. The new one is an old-school gangster out of Moscow. His name is Alexei Yenin. He worked as an interrogator for the KGB, so as you can imagine, he's as vicious as they come."

I say, "Drowning isn't the Russians' usual style, but I could see a former KGB officer being a little subtler than most."

"Right." Callum nods. "Still, it's weird if they targeted Riona."

"Who else?"

"Maybe the Hartford family," Riona pipes up.

"Who's that?" Callum asks.

"A couple of months ago, Enzo Gallo asked me for help. Or, more accurately, one of the other Italian families needed help," Riona says, with an expression of distaste. "Bosco Bianchi was driving drunk and high with a couple of sixteen-year-old girls in his car. One of them went through the windshield. She was put in a medically induced coma. Bosco's toxicity test went missing, and I got his confession thrown out. The DA settled for eight months in medium security. The girl never recovered."

I can tell Riona feels bad about the girl. She's embarrassed that she facilitated Bosco's deal, but she doesn't shrink away from admitting it.

"Virginia Hartford was taken off life support last week," Riona says. "She's got a father and an older brother. If I were them, I might want revenge."

I write that down, same as I did the information about the Russians.

"Okay," I say. "We'll check that out, too. Anyone else?"

A longer pause, and then Riona says, "Maybe Luke Barker."

"Who's that?"

"He was a senior attorney at my firm. He got handsy with me at the company Christmas party, and Uncle Oran fired him."

"Where is he now?"

"I have no idea," Riona says coldly.

I mark his name down, too. "That's a good start. We'll run down those possibilities starting tomorrow."

It's getting close to midnight. I can see Callum trying not to yawn. He gives his sister a hug, telling her, "We'll figure it out, Ree. Don't worry."

"I'm not worried," she says. "I just want to know, one way or another."

"Say hi to Aida for me," I tell Callum.

"I'm sure I'll get the chance in an hour or two when Miles wakes us up." Cal groans.

Riona and I get back into the Escalade and head over to her apartment building.

"We can park in the underground parking," she says. "I have an assigned spot, even though I don't have a car."

I can see why Riona picked this condo—it's a lot like her corner office. High and lonely, with a stunning view. I can tell she likes things that are aesthetically stark and completely within her control.

It's only once we're alone in the apartment that Riona seems to realize I'll be sleeping here, within the bubble of her personal space.

"I'm fine on the sofa," I tell her.

"Right," Riona says, with an expression of discomfort. "I'll get you some clean sheets."

I unbutton my shirt and shuck it off, planning to wash up and brush my teeth at the sink like I usually do.

Riona comes back surprisingly fast, carrying a stack of fresh bedding. Her eyes flit across my bare torso, and I'm surprised to see her blush. I didn't take her for the modest type.

"Here." She shoves the bedding at me.

"What's wrong?" I say, not able to resist teasing her a little.

"Nothing's wrong," she says brusquely.

I'm pretty sure I got the honest Riona to tell a fib.

"Do you need toothpaste or anything?" she mutters.

"Nah. I brought my Dopp kit."

"All right. Good night, then."

"Good night, Riona."

She retreats into her bedroom, and I hear the muffled sounds of water running and light feet padding around as she readies herself for bed.

Because I'm a nosy fucker, I poke around her living room a bit.

It's alarmingly clean. Unlike Nick, Riona would do just fine in the military. Her books are lined up with soldierlike precision. I couldn't find a speck of dust with a hundred white gloves. Even her remote is set at a perfect ninety-degree angle on the television stand.

All that order makes me wonder. In my experience, when somebody clings that tightly to a sense of control, it's because something happened to them at some point in their lives that made them feel powerless.

I think of Riona describing Luke Barker and how he got "handsy" with her at the Christmas party. Her voice was as calm as ever. But I don't feel calm thinking about it. I feel a stab of something very like anger. I put Luke at the top of my list of people I plan to talk to.

I lay out a crisp clean sheet on the sofa to protect the cushions.

Then I lie down and slip into a light slumber. A soldier's sleep—the kind you wake from easily.

Riona's scream jolts me right off the couch.

Before my eyes are even open, I've jumped up and I'm running to her room.

I rip open her door and flip on the light.

She's tangled in her sheets, ripping and clawing at them where they're wrapped around her throat.

I pull her out of the bedding, wrapping her in my arms instead. She's only wearing a light silk camisole and shorts, and she's shivering, from cold or from fear.

"*Shh,*" I tell her. "It's all right. I'm here."

Embarrassed, she tries to pull away from me. But I keep my arms around her, pulling her against my chest. I feel her heart hammering away against my bare skin and her slim frame shaking.

"I thought I was drowning," she gasps.

Again, I feel that flood of anger that a man put his hands on this woman. Riona is desperate to seem strong and independent. But the truth is she's fragile in the way that all women are fragile—smaller than men and vulnerable to violence.

I have a sister. I'd fucking kill anyone who tried to touch her.

And I feel that same drive to protect Riona. To keep her safe. Not just because Dante asked me to. Because she needs it. She needs my help.

"I'm here," I tell her again. "No one's going to hurt you."

I feel her heart beating wildly against my forearm. It feels like a bird caught in a cage, struggling to get out. Riona's whole body is shaking.

But after a minute, she stops fighting and she sinks down against my chest, allowing me to hold her. Allowing me to warm her with my arms, so her shivering stops.

I don't think she'd ever allow this if she weren't exhausted and terrified. In fact, she'll probably be embarrassed in the morning.

But right now, she accepts my comfort.

I hold her like that for almost an hour, until her body goes heavy and warm with sleep.

CHAPTER 7
RIONA

I wake up alone in my bed with the sunshine streaming in through my window.

I slept in late, which is strange for me.

I can hear the clinking sound of somebody moving around in my kitchen. I realize it's Raylan, and I remember how I woke up screaming in the night.

My face burns, knowing what a fool I made of myself. Screaming like a little kid with a nightmare.

He had to come in and hold me, like I was five years old.

I hate that he saw me like that: weak and vulnerable.

On the other hand, the memory of the dream is still fresh in my mind. I was swimming but not in the clean, bright rooftop pool. It was night, and I was swimming in a huge dark lake. My hands looked ghostly white in the black water.

Something grabbed me from below and dragged me down. I could see the reflection of the moon on the surface, growing tiny like a pinprick of light as I sank down, down. The water was freezing cold and pitch-dark. The thing that had hold of me was monstrously large. It grabbed me with a dozen tentacles that squeezed all around my body—around my arms, legs, chest, and throat. It kept pulling me down no matter how hard I fought. And when I finally had to gasp for breath, cold water flooded my lungs.

I woke up tearing at the sheets that had wrapped tight around my body. I heard someone screaming, and it took me way too long to realize it was me. I touched my face and felt that it was actually wet and cold. I'd been crying in my sleep.

I hope to god Raylan didn't notice that, at least.

I'll admit, it did feel good when he held me. I was ashamed of myself. And embarrassed that he ran in there half naked, wearing just the boxer shorts he'd been sleeping in. But I couldn't deny how warm his arms were, and his bare chest pressed against my face. He was like a huge blanket fresh out of the dryer. His warmth seemed to seep into my body, calming me down.

But now I have to face him. And I'm self-conscious all over again.

Not wanting to hurry that particular meeting, I take a shower first and get dressed in a blouse, slacks, and a pair of loafers. Then there's nothing else to do but go out to the kitchen.

Raylan is messing around at the stove. He's got four different fry pans going—one on each burner—and he's wearing my apron over a fresh flannel shirt. His black hair looks damp and clean, like he already showered. I notice he didn't bother to shave, though. His thick black stubble makes him look rakish. Especially when he smiles, showing those sharp teeth.

I don't usually let men sleep over at my place. So I'm not used to somebody taking over my kitchen, using my fry pans and my spatulas, spattering grease on the stove top.

I don't even know where the hell he got all this food. I certainly didn't buy bacon and eggs and whatever he used to make French toast.

At least I can smell the rich scent of coffee. I pour myself a mug.

"Food's almost ready," Raylan says.

"I usually just have coffee."

"Coffee's a drink. It ain't breakfast."

Raylan dishes up two massive plates full of crispy bacon, scrambled eggs, thick-cut French toast slathered in butter and syrup, and some kind of hash made of peppers and potato.

He sets a plate down in front of me, taking the seat opposite for himself.

"There's no way I could eat all this," I tell him.

"That's brain food," he says, taking a huge bite of French toast.

"That's two thousand calories. Your whole day on one plate."

"Not *my* whole day. Takes a lot more than a plate of breakfast to feed this body, darlin'." He grabs a piece of bacon and takes a big bite out of that, too.

I shake my head at him. "You're gonna have a heart attack."

"When have you ever seen a cowboy die of a heart attack?"

"Is that what you are? A cowboy?"

"You bet. Raised on a ranch in Tennessee."

"What happened to it?"

"Oh, it's still there."

"Why'd you leave?"

"I got restless. Wanted to see what else was in the world. Besides…" Raylan grins. "I never said I was a *good* cowboy."

I have to admit the bacon on my plate does smell delicious. I pick up a slice and take a bite. It's crispy and chewy, as fragrant and satisfying as the rib eye steak the night before. If I keep spending time with Raylan, I'm going to become a carnivore.

"See?" Raylan says. "Not bad, huh?"

I try a bite of the hash, too. The potatoes are crisp on the outside, fluffy in the middle, well seasoned with salt and pepper, and sweet sautéed red pepper and onion.

"You're a good cook," I admit.

"You like to cook?"

"No. I hate it, actually."

"Why?"

"All that work just to make something that's gone five minutes later."

I don't tell him the other reason—I hate doing anything that's expected of me just because I'm a woman. Cooking, cleaning, childcare…I bristle against the idea that I should want to do those things. That I should let them consume me while men spend their hours on more "important" work.

My own mother was never a housewife. But she's always deferred to my father. He's the head of the family, and she's his right hand. I don't want to be anybody's hand.

That's why I'm never getting married. When Nessa married Mikolaj, I told her to take our grandmother's ring. It was supposed to go to me, as the eldest daughter. But I don't expect to ever use it.

I know nowadays people think they get married as equals. But when it comes down to it, someone's career and someone's goals have to come first. If one of you gets a job offer in New York and the other in LA, how do you pick where to go?

Selfishness is a recipe for divorce. I'm just going to skip all those middle steps and stay single all along. I like my own company. I like my own life.

Or at least I did before that diver came and fucked it all up.

"What?" Raylan says.

"What yourself?"

"You're frowning," he tells me.

"I was just… I'm sorry about waking you up," I say, not meeting his eyes.

"Hey." Raylan sets down his fork and puts his hand over mine. It's heavy and warm. It reminds me of how warm his arms were last night. His hand sends that same gentle calm through my body. "You don't have to be tough all the time, you know. It's okay if something like that affected you…"

I pull my hand back, pushing my chair away from the table and standing. "I'm fine," I tell him firmly. "Totally fine."

Raylan keeps eating his food, obviously determined to finish the whole plate.

Actually, I think he's eating every last bite just to annoy me. I'm standing there practically tapping my foot, wanting to get going.

"What's your rush?" he says.

"I have a lot of work to do today."

"It's Saturday."

"I'm in the middle of a huge project."

"Think that'll secure the partner position?" Raylan forks up his last bite of hash.

I flush. "Yes, actually."

"Isn't it kind of a given? Since your name's already on the door?"

"No, it isn't," I snap. "But that's exactly what people think. Which is why I have to work harder and stay later than anyone. Because otherwise, no matter how smart I am, no matter how much business I bring in, everyone assumes that I got where I am because my last name is Griffin."

"All right, all right." Raylan holds up his hands in surrender. "Lemme wash these dishes, and then I'll take you over to your parents' house."

He clears off the kitchen table, then stacks all the dishes in the sink and fills it with hot soapy water. Quickly and efficiently, he reverses what appeared to be an insurmountable mess in the kitchen. In less than ten minutes, every dish is washed, dried, and put back exactly where he found it, and the countertops and stove are restored to their former sparkling state. He even folded and rehung the dish towel.

"Does that meet with your satisfaction, Sergeant?" he asks, a gleam of amusement in his bright blue eyes.

Sometimes I get the uncomfortable feeling that Raylan can read every thought in my head.

"Yes," I say primly. "Back to normal."

I grab my briefcase, heavy with all the files I brought home for the weekend.

Right after I talked to Uncle Oran, I stole that stack of purchase agreements back off Josh's desk. Just as I suspected, he hadn't even touched them yet. He *is* a lazy shit. If he spent less time spying and schmoozing and more time working, he might actually have had a shot at the partner position.

I know Oran said to let Josh do it, but I already started on the purchase agreements, and we need them finished before we can move into phase two of the South Shore project. That's my family's number one priority right now, and the Gallos' too. We've sunk everything we have into it. I can't risk an idiot like Josh fucking it up.

CHAPTER 8
RAYLAN

I DRIVE RIONA BACK OVER TO THE GRIFFINS' MODERN MANSION ON the Gold Coast. It's a palace of glass and steel, a monument to how their family has grown and flourished in Chicago.

As we enter the huge bright kitchen, I remember that this is where Riona and I first met. I glance over at her to see if she's thinking the same thing. I catch her eye, making a little tinge of pink appear on her pale cheeks.

I don't know why I get such a kick from getting a rise out of her. I guess it's because she's so determined to keep that perfectly composed demeanor at all times. It's like she's setting up a challenge for me. And I've always been one to rise to a challenge.

Imogen Griffin is just finishing her breakfast. She's already dressed for the day in one of those classy business-style sheath dresses, her blond bob as smooth and sleek as glass.

Riona and her mother look a lot alike. Riona's a little taller, with red hair instead of blond. But looking at Imogen is like looking twenty or thirty years into Riona's future—proof of how gracefully she'll age. Like an iconic actress who only seems to become more regal with time.

I could have guessed that without ever seeing Imogen, though—Riona's too stubborn to ever let herself look less than her best.

Imogen comes over to Riona at once and kisses her on the cheek. "How are you, love?" She strokes her hand gently down Riona's hair.

I'm surprised to see that Riona allows this. In fact, she rests her cheek against her mother's for a moment. She obviously respects Imogen.

But she still won't admit that someone trying to murder her has affected her in the slightest.

"I'm fine, Mom."

"Imogen Griffin," Imogen says, holding out her slim hand to me.

"Raylan Boone."

"Thank you for coming to help us. Dante speaks very highly of you."

"I'm surprised." I grin. "He's usually so honest."

Imogen smiles, her blue eyes fixed on mine. "I've come to trust him. It never ceases to amaze me how even the bitterest of enemies can become friends. Or the reverse."

She checks the delicate gold watch on her wrist.

"I've got to go," she says. "I have a board meeting for the Chicago Library Association. Riona—Butcher and Meecham are here to keep an eye on things."

I assume that's her security team. I plan to give them a once-over before I leave, though I'm sure the Griffins are supremely careful who they hire for that type of position.

Riona is already spreading out her work on the small table of the breakfast nook. It's obvious she intends to dive right in.

I admire her work ethic. Makes it kinda tiring to watch her, though—she doesn't get much sleep.

Callum comes into the kitchen right as his mother is going out. He kisses her on the cheek, almost exactly the same way she kissed Riona. It's always funny to see the little habits in families— the gestures passed along like a silent code that only the members would recognize.

"How's Miles?" she asks him.

"I think he and Aida are soul mates. All they do is nap and cuddle and eat."

"You better be getting up with him in the night," Imogen says warningly. "Don't leave it all to Aida."

"Do you honestly think she'd allow that?" Callum laughs.

Imogen smiles. "No. Probably not."

Imogen waves goodbye to us all, and Callum pours himself a cup of coffee from the large carafe on the spotless white marble countertop.

"You want some?" he asks me.

"No, thanks. Just had a cup."

"How's the guarding going?" he says with a glance at Riona already bent over her work.

"Great."

"Really?" I can hear his mild disbelief.

"Of course." I grin. "What could possibly go wrong, following Riona around twenty-four seven, constantly right next to her, watching her every move, sticking right by her like I'm surgically attached? How could she not enjoy that?"

Riona doesn't dignify that with a response—she keeps her eyes on her papers. But I can feel the disdain radiating out of her all the same. Callum has to work hard not to laugh.

On a more serious note, I say, "How long have these guys Butcher and Meecham worked for you?"

"Six years for Butcher, eight for Meecham," Callum says. "We can trust them."

I nod. "Just checking every box."

"I appreciate that," Cal says. "You ready to see the broker?"

"Most definitely."

Cal gulps down his coffee and puts the mug in the sink. I can tell from the dark shadows under his eyes that he was telling his mother the truth—he's been getting up with a newborn. You can't hide that haggard-but-happy look of new parents.

"We'll be back in a couple of hours," Callum says to Riona.

"Don't hurry," she replies, still not looking up.

"I can drive," I tell Cal as we head back out to the wide curving driveway where I left the Escalade.

"Thanks," Callum says. "That's probably for the best. I felt like a zombie on the way over."

I get behind the wheel, and Cal climbs into the passenger seat, rubbing the inner corners of his eyes.

"I don't know what it is about interrupted sleep. Even if you get eight hours, it's not the same."

"Nope," I say. "Not even close."

I never sleep eight hours straight through anymore. Too many nights sleeping on sand or rock or dirt, always having to keep one ear open for interruptions—the kind of interruptions that can kill you. You never really recover that deep and peaceful slumber.

"So, who's this guy we're going to see?" I ask Cal.

"He's a connector. And a nasty piece of work. You armed?"

I nod. "Always."

"Good. Me, too. Hopefully it won't come to that, but I'm not sure he's going to want to cooperate."

Cal directs me as I drive us down to Riverdale. It's on the far south side of the city. The neighborhoods seem to get older, poorer, and more run-down the farther south we go. Instead of towering high-rises, I see squat concrete apartment buildings, boarded-up businesses, and vandalized bus stops.

Riverdale itself seems sparsely populated by contrast to the downtown core. Most of the area is taken up by rail yards, landfills, and industrial sites, including a massive wastewater treatment plant.

Callum tells me to drive up toward the Union Pacific railroad tracks.

"Right up there," he says, pointing to what looks like an abandoned warehouse. Every single window is shattered, and the metal sides are layered with what looks like twenty years' worth of graffiti—color and pattern so dense that it's hard to tell what any of it is supposed to represent.

"Is the car gonna be here when we get back?" I say skeptically.

"Who knows." Callum shrugs.

"They still have trains coming through here?"

"Yeah. A fuck ton of them. Probably five hundred a day. They get jammed up on the tracks and left overnight. Then guys who work at the rail yard tip off other guys about what's in the boxcars. And if it's something worth stealing—guns or TV sets or designer shoes—it goes missing that night. The railways are insured, so they'd rather save money on security versus trying to stop cargo from going missing."

"And your broker here—what's his name?"

"Zimmer," Cal says.

"I take it he facilitates the thefts and finds a home for the goods."

"Right, exactly. He's the middleman."

We get out of the car, walking across the broken pavement of the empty lot. It's hard to believe there's anybody inside the warehouse, but when Cal knocks three times on the metal door, it creaks open almost immediately.

A bouncer both tall and fat silently looks out at us. His head is so big and round that his piggy little eyes are just slits in the flesh of his face.

"Here to see Zimmer," Cal says calmly.

The bouncer pats us down with hands that are surprisingly small for his huge frame. Even that amount of physical exertion makes him breathe heavily.

"Leave your guns there." He grunts, pointing to a cardboard box set on top of a stool.

Callum drops his Glock into the box without complaint. I don't really like disarming in an unknown place, but if that's the price of entry, I guess we don't have much choice.

I drop my gun and follow Cal into the dim warehouse.

It's a strange kind of clubhouse in here. I see several dusty couches and armchairs and a whole lot of games: a pool table, air hockey, foosball, and three separate TVs with gaming systems. A dozen kids ranging from teens to early twenties are lounging around, killing each other in *Call of Duty*, and already drinking even though it's ten o'clock in the morning.

Callum beelines straight toward a guy who can't be more than twenty-two years old. He's wearing ripped skinny jeans, an oversize Fila sweatshirt, and a puffy pair of Yeezy boots. He's puffing from a vape, and he looks blazed out of his mind.

"Morning," Cal says politely.

Zimmer gives him a slow nod.

"Can we talk in private?" Cal says.

"You can say whatever you want to say," Zimmer tells him lazily.

"It's for my privacy," Cal replies coolly. "Not yours."

Zimmer regards him with narrowed bloodshot eyes. But after a minute, he hauls himself up from the oversize beanbag chair he was lounging upon and leads us to the back corner of the warehouse. Here we can all sit down on a sectional couch of uncertain age and color. Quite honestly, I'd rather not sit down, seeing as it's stained with mystery fluids. But those are the kinds of sacrifices you have to make when you're the guest of a gangster.

Zimmer sprawls out on his side of the couch. Cal and I sit at a ninety-degree angle.

"So?" Zimmer says, taking another long puff off his vape.

Without preamble, Cal says, "I want to know if you brokered a hit against my sister."

Zimmer lets out his breath in a plume of thick white smoke. It curls out of his nostrils and mouth simultaneously. His eyes peer through the smoke, dark and glittering, like a dragon.

"If I gave out that kind of information," he says, "what the fuck kind of broker would I be?"

"I understand that." Cal keeps his voice measured. "But here's the thing, Zimmer. We've never had any conflict. I stay up on the north end of the city. You run things how you like down here. We maintain a mutual level of respect. If you were to broker a hit against a member of my family, and I were to find out about it…I would consider that an act of aggression."

Zimmer takes another pull off his vape. His relaxed posture hasn't changed. But I can see a new alertness in his eyes and a tension in his muscles. His face is still, but there's a gleam of anger in his eyes. "I would consider it *aggressive*," he hisses, "if you came into my house and threatened me."

The silence stretches between Cal and Zimmer for several minutes. I'm not planning to say a goddamned word. Cal knows this guy; I don't—but I am watching everyone else in the room out of the corner of my eye. Keeping track of the big bouncer who's standing off on our right-hand side, close enough to be summoned at a moment's notice, and the rest of Zimmer's people, too, who might be fucking around on *Call of Duty* but are no doubt armed—every single one of them.

Finally, Cal says, "I have a piece of information in trade. I know a boxcar full of Rugers went missing from the Norfolk rail yard a couple of weeks ago. One hundred and fourteen guns spread out across the city, mostly here on the south side."

Zimmer's face remains impassive. I can tell this isn't news to him at all.

Cal goes on. "They picked up three of the men involved last night. Bryson, England, and Dawes. Two of them kept their mouths shut. But the third seems to think he can link you to the robbery. He's making a deal with the DA as we speak. I guess you fucked his girlfriend a couple of months back, and he's holding a grudge about it. He seems to think that, unlike your usual hands-off approach, with this particular shipment, you tested one of the guns. The same one used to rob the liquor store on Langley. Remember that? The one where the clerk got shot? Dawes says he knows where that particular Ruger is. He says it should still have your prints on it, along with the prints of the idiot who shot the clerk."

As Cal speaks, Zimmer sits perfectly still. But his face gets paler, until it looks as gray as the smoke seeping from his nostrils.

"I could tell you where they're holding Dawes," Cal says quietly, "so you can shut his mouth for him before he says too much. But I need to know who hired that hit on Riona."

Zimmer lets out the remaining smoke from his lungs. "All right," he hisses quietly. "All right."

He sits up straighter on the couch, leaning forward on his knees and speaking so low that I can barely hear him. "I didn't broker the hit myself. But I heard about it."

"Tell me what you know," Cal says.

This is the first time Cal's voice loses its casualness. There's an edge to his tone now, and I see the stiffness in his shoulders. He's angry, hearing it confirmed that someone dared hire a killer to attack his sister.

"I heard there was a hit happening, and nobody could know about it. It had to look like an accident."

Cal gives a small, almost-imperceptible nod. That's what we guessed.

"It was expensive. They hired this guy they call the Djinn."

"The Djinn?" Cal says, frowning like he doesn't believe Zimmer. "What the fuck is that?"

"That's his name," Zimmer says defensively. "I don't know his real name. Nobody does. You call him up—and he makes people disappear."

"Fine," Cal says, cutting to the point he cares about more than the identity of this hitman. "I don't give a shit. I want to know who hired him."

"I don't know!" Zimmer says. "I don't. When hits are hired, it's a double-blind system. The client doesn't know the hitman, and the hitman doesn't know the client. It's all anonymized. That way nobody can rat."

Cal scowls, obviously wishing he'd implemented a similar system between him and Dawes.

"So where's the snitch?" Zimmer demands.

"They're holding him in MCC," Cal says. "D Block."

Zimmer nods.

Cal gets up from the couch, our business with Zimmer obviously concluded.

The hefty bouncer follows us all the way to the door, where we retrieve our guns.

"Don't come back." He grunts as he cracks the door for us once more.

Cal turns and fixes him with a cold stare. "Don't give me a reason to."

Even the air of the run-down rail yard tastes fresh after the inside of that warehouse. We head back to the Escalade, which is mercifully untouched. No doubt anyone watching recognized Callum and knew better than to fuck with his ride.

It was bizarre watching the charming and well-bred politician melt away so I could see the Irish gangster underneath. It's easy to see the Griffins for what they are today—one of the wealthiest and most successful families in Chicago. You forget that their empire was built on blood and crime. That Fergus Griffin—and his father before him, and his grandfather before him—had no scruples about crushing anyone who got in their way. I suspect Callum is the same.

"You don't care if he kills Dawes?" I say to Cal.

"Why would I?" Callum fixes me with his icy-blue eyes. "He's a low-level criminal, not even loyal to his own boss. I don't give a fuck about him. I'd strangle him with my bare hands to keep Riona safe."

I nod. "Fair enough."

I let Cal do the talking in there because he knows these people and I don't. But I want to get to know this so-called Djinn. If I'm going to protect Riona, I need to know who he is and how he works.

For that reason, I call Dante and ask him to meet me at the Griffins' house.

He gets there around 1:00 p.m., carrying a large bag of Thai food. He spreads it out across the long marble countertop, saying to Riona, "Take a break and eat with us."

Riona sets down her pen, tempted by the scent of chicken satay and coconut rice. "I can take a break for a minute."

Cal, Riona, Dante, and I all dish up large plates of food. Cal and Riona use chopsticks, but Dante and I grab forks out of the silverware drawer. Fucking around with wooden sticks is the reason you don't see a lot of overweight Thai people, I bet.

While we eat, Cal recaps our meeting with Zimmer.

Dante doesn't look pleased at all when he hears the name *Djinn*. I ask, "You know him?"

"I don't know *him*," Dante says. "But I know he's fucking expensive. The best you can get around here. A professional."

I glance over at Riona to see how she's taking this.

She's picking at her pad Thai, obviously not thrilled to know that the person hired to kill her is a little too good at his job.

"Hey," I say to her. "We'll find him."

"I'd rather find the person who hired him," Riona says.

"I went and met with the Russians this morning," Dante tells us. "Yenin denied having anything to do with it. But he looked pretty fucking pleased about it all the same. And I doubt he'd tell us if it *were* him."

"We need to find out more about the Djinn," I say. "And check the other two people Riona mentioned having a possible grudge."

"I'll look up the Hartford family," Dante says.

"And I'll find the guy Uncle Oran fired," Cal says.

Riona pushes her plate away, having hardly touched her food. "I'm going back to work. Sounds like you all have it covered."

CHAPTER 9
RIONA

THE WEEK THAT FOLLOWS IS EXTREMELY STRANGE.

I'm not used to having another person with me constantly. Raylan stays by my side morning and night, no matter what I'm doing. I think he'd stand outside my shower if I let him.

I appreciate that he's taking the job seriously, but I like my alone time. I'm cognizant of him constantly watching me, even when I'm trying to work or read or exercise.

I guess it could be worse. His company isn't entirely unpleasant. He insists on cooking for both of us. "'Cause otherwise I'd starve," he says, apparently feeling that the volume and frequency of my meals leaves something to be desired. And he is a good cook. He makes pasta carbonara with fresh basil, bacon, and peas and a citrus-marinated chicken that he serves over risotto.

As I suspected during our dinner with Nick, Raylan is pretty damn smart under that country-boy schtick. While I'm working, he's often reading. He goes through half the books on my shelf, reading *The Bell Jar*, *Life After Life*, *Barkskins*, and *The Devil in the White City* all in one week.

"What do you mostly read?" I ask, curious about his taste.

"I like any book that puts you inside somebody's head," he says. "Like this *Devil in the White City* one. Have you read it?"

I nod.

"This H. H. Holmes guy. He's pretty fucked up. But it makes me curious anyway, trying to see why he did all the things he did."

Raylan is observant. His laid-back attitude doesn't fool me—it's obvious he sees a lot more than he lets on and files it all away.

I say, "You like watching people."

"Yeah." He nods. "I do."

"Why?"

"People are interesting."

"I find most people pretty boring."

"Am I boring?" He grins.

"No," I admit. "You're not."

Raylan isn't boring. He's intelligent and he's a paradox. From the way he talks about his family and the ranch where he grew up, I know he had a happy childhood. Yet he felt compelled to join the army and wander all over the globe. On the surface, he appears folksy and friendly. But he's a trained soldier who wouldn't hesitate to kill.

He has a competitive side, too. He likes to joke around, but I see his aggression surface under the right circumstances. Like when he joins me for my evening workouts.

I haven't gone back to the rooftop pool. Even though I know the diver isn't likely to come back when Raylan's right there with me, I can't stand the thought of slipping into the water again.

Instead, I go to the gym on the floor right below. It's got ellipticals and treadmills, squat racks and free weights.

Raylan joins me working out so, as he puts it, "I don't turn into a lazy ass just sittin' around watching you work."

The treadmills all face the bay of floor-to-ceiling windows so you can look down over the city as you run. Raylan takes the treadmill next to mine and sets it to a steady jog, keeping pace with me easily.

I like running. Dante and I used to go for runs together in the nicer spring and summer weather. It's getting too cold for it now.

I can go for a long time. Running suits people with slim builds. It's easier for me to go on and on versus someone like Dante or Raylan with more muscle. That's a lot of weight for them to carry.

I notice that Raylan sets his pace and incline to match mine exactly. He's probably doing it to annoy me. Or to prove something to me.

To test that theory, I turn my pace up from 6.5 to 7.2, and I increase the incline to 2 percent. Sure enough, he does the exact same thing, tossing me a wolfish grin.

"You can't outrun me," he says. "We're right beside each other."

"Oh, really?" I crank it up again, to 8.0 and 3 percent.

Raylan copies me. We're running at a decent clip now, both of us breathing harder and getting a little red in the face.

After five more minutes, I up the speed to 8.5. Raylan does the same.

"I can go forever like this," I tell him. That's not exactly true, but a little psychological warfare never hurt anybody.

"So can I." He winks at me.

I have to admit…the wink is kind of sexy.

I've been telling myself that Raylan is not that attractive and definitely not my type. I have no interest in a mercenary who wears flannel shirts and takes pleasure in teasing me like he's an annoying older brother. I like men who are dignified and respectful. Men I can take seriously.

Despite those absolute facts, I find my eyes drifting over to Raylan and the way his T-shirt is starting to cling to his broad chest as it soaks through with sweat.

I whip my head straight again and turn up the treadmill to 9.0.

Raylan matches me stride for stride. He's grinning at me, despite the fact he's breathing hard and a little drop of clear sweat is running down the side of his face.

"Really putting me through my paces, huh?" he says.

"You can stop anytime you want," I say, trying not to sound out of breath.

"No fuckin' way."

His growl sends a shiver down my spine.

To chase it away, I turn the treadmill up to 10.0.

We're really sprinting now. I've got long legs, but so does Raylan. I have stamina, but apparently he does, too. Neither of us is talking now. We're staring straight ahead, pumping our arms, both ridiculously determined not to give up.

I don't know why I started this competition or why we're both so intent on winning. I want to prove to Raylan that he can't beat me, and he apparently feels the need to do the same. We're running fiercely, doggedly, furiously.

I turn the treadmill up to 10.5.

"Are you training for the Olympics?" Raylan pants.

"You can give up any time."

He just laughs.

I have the strangest mixture of annoyance and admiration for him. I want to fucking beat him—I don't know why it's so important to me, but it is. And at the same time, a tiny secret part of me doesn't want him to quit. I know myself—I'm always looking for people to show weakness. To fail. And then I have disdain for them. A tiny piece of me wants Raylan to force me to respect him.

I can tell he's tired. He's red-faced, sweating, panting. So am I—maybe even more than Raylan. It's a battle of wills now. Our brains are driving our bodies forward, despite our exhaustion.

Silently, throwing a cheeky look at me, Raylan turns the treadmill up to 11.0. I try to do the same, barely able to keep pace enough to reach up and hit the button.

"I'm a lot of things," Raylan says to me, "but never a quitter."

My lungs are burning, and so are my legs. I've never sprinted for so long. I can feel my knees getting wobbly beneath me.

All of a sudden, the roof and the floor swap positions. My legs give out from under me.

"Riona, what the hell!" Raylan shouts.

He jumps off the belt and grabs me right before I hit the floor.

I can hear the treadmills still whirring away at top speed, but white sparks are flashing in front of my eyes. Raylan grabs his water bottle and splashes cold water in my face.

"Are you insane?" he cries.

"Get off." I push him away. "I'm fine."

I don't know why I'm angry at him. Maybe because I lost. Maybe because I'm embarrassed at almost passing out like that.

"What the hell is wrong with you?"

"You were racing *me*," I snap back at him.

My head is pounding, and I feel simultaneously too hot and too cold. I can feel sweat running down my chest, even though I'm not running anymore.

"You'd rather kill yourself than let me win?" Raylan's smile is gone. He looks properly pissed.

"Just leave me alone," I say, getting to my feet. I'm planning to stalk away from him, but my legs are too wobbly, and I almost fall over again.

Raylan grabs my arm. "Calm down, and get your breath back."

I know it's good advice, but I hate the way he thinks he knows what's best for me.

"Don't tell me what to do!" I yank my arm away from him.

Thank god we're the only people in the gym. I'd hate to have anyone else witness what an asshole I'm being right now.

"What's your problem?" Raylan demands. "I'm only here to help you."

"I don't need your help!"

"The fuck you don't."

He's not letting go of my arm, and that really pisses me off. I shove him hard in the chest, feeling how hot he is from running.

Raylan yanks me back again. When I try to shove him once more, he grabs me by the face and kisses me. It's a rough kiss, his black stubble scratching my face. It's hard and violent, and I can taste the salt of his sweat.

I wrench away from him and slap him across the face. "Don't you fucking kiss me!"

Raylan's blue eyes are blazing, and he looks completely different from his usual cheerful self. He's all wolf now, teeth bared and jaw rigid. He grabs me by my ponytail and kisses me again, even harder.

He lets go of me, and we pull apart, staring at each other and panting audibly. My heart is hammering against my ribs like I'm still on the treadmill. I can practically hear his doing the same. We both know we crossed a line. Actually, we jumped over the line with both feet.

I can't look him in the eye.

I grab my water bottle and towel and walk back toward the elevators.

Raylan follows me, five feet behind.

No matter what insanity just passed between us, he's not going to stop guarding me. Not for a second.

We get into the elevator together, silent and awkward.

I think of a dozen things I should say. But I can't seem to make up my mind whether to apologize or shout at him some more.

So I just stay quiet.

We ride back down to the twenty-eighth floor and go into my apartment. Then I head straight to my room, while Raylan stays in the living room to sleep alone on the couch.

CHAPTER 10
RAYLAN

I DON'T KNOW WHAT THE FUCK HAPPENED YESTERDAY.

I've never acted like that in my life. I was raised to be a gentleman—not to grab a girl and kiss her like a wild bandit.

Maybe it was the adrenaline from racing Riona. Or the fact we've been in constant proximity for the past eight days. Or the fact she manages to get under my skin in a way I don't quite understand.

I don't know what it is about her. I've always had this compulsion to overcome challenges. And Riona is a constant challenge. She's strong-willed and stubborn as fuck. Determined not to be impressed by me. Intent on always doing things her own way, damn the consequences.

Maybe I shouldn't have raced her at all. I know how competitive she is. But for fuck's sake, so am I! I thought it would be fun. Then I saw how seriously she was taking it. And I guess I realized I was taking it pretty damned seriously, too.

Well, now I feel like a horse's ass.

She was right to slap me—I deserved that.

I know damn well she's got a boyfriend.

I don't like that guy, though. I get that he's good-looking and a fancy surgeon and all that shit. On paper he's a good match for Riona. But she doesn't need somebody stiff and proper like that.

She needs somebody who can make her laugh. Who can help

her relax a little. Not someone who's going to amp her up even more.

I guess that sounds like I'm describing myself—I'm not. I know I'm not the right guy for her either. We'd probably murder each other. Plus, my lifestyle doesn't exactly leave a lot of room for romance.

No romance—just a whole lot of experience.

I've seen a whole lot of ugliness and greed and violence.

But I've seen gorgeous things, too. I've seen the sun setting over Victoria Falls. I've ridden camels over sand dunes bigger than any ocean wave. I've taken a chopper over a volcano half a day before it erupted and walked on black sand beaches that look like an alien planet.

I keep a list of the best places. Maybe so I can show them to somebody else someday. Maybe just so I don't forget them.

I can hear Riona showering and getting ready for the day. I go and do the same so she won't have to wait on me.

It takes me a lot less time to shower. Probably 'cause I don't have two feet of flame-red hair to deal with. I get ready, then poach some eggs and put some toast on. And I make the coffee extra strong 'cause I know Riona likes it that way. It's a peace offering. I can guess it's gonna take a lot more than coffee and a good night's rest to cool her off, though.

Sure enough, she comes sweeping out of her room without even a glance at me. She pours herself a mug of coffee and ignores the poached egg I set all nicely on a piece of buttered toast for her.

"Morning," I say to her.

"Good morning," she replies coolly.

"About yesterday—"

"We don't have to talk about that," she interrupts.

"I'm not tryna go on about it," I persist. "I just wanted to say…I'm sorry."

Her green eyes flit up at me for just a second, then look away again. I can't tell if she's still mad or embarrassed or what. Maybe she's just surprised I apologized.

"Just—let's leave it alone," she says. "The whole thing was embarrassing."

"Okay."

Riona grabs her coat, and we head down to the underground parking garage. I check the vehicle over carefully before we enter, including looking under the carriage for any unwanted additions. As we drive up to street level, I can tell it's an ugly day. Freezing cold, windy, and gray as slate. Little bits of sleet whip against the windshield, fine and hard as sand.

I've been in too many hot places for too long. I'm fucking cold, even with the heat turned up in the car.

"I can't believe this," I say to Riona. "After all the nice things I've heard about Chicago winters…"

Riona gives a little snort. "It's only November. It'll get a lot worse."

"How could it possibly be worse?"

"Just wait."

We drive the four blocks to Riona's office. I bet she's glad now that we borrowed Dante's SUV. That wouldn't be a pleasant walk.

Usually, I'd be a gentleman and drop her off right in front of the building while I find parking, but we need to stick together at all times. Especially now that I know Djinn is apparently such a relentless motherfucker.

Riona and I park half a block away, then run for the double glass doors.

Compared to outside, the inside of the office building feels warm and pleasant. I can smell coffee and fresh muffins from the café on the ground floor.

I escort Riona all the way up to her office. Most of the people on her floor have gotten used to seeing me by now, especially the paralegal Lucy—she gives me a little smile and wave.

I settle down in my favorite chair in the corner of Riona's office while Riona dives right into her work. I see her plowing through folder after folder every day, but the pile of stuff she needs to get done never seems to shrink. She must be adding to it constantly.

After about an hour, we're surprised by a knock at the door.

It's Dante and Nero. Dante's wearing a proper peacoat, but Nero only has on a black T-shirt and jeans. I'm guessing he's too hotheaded to ever feel the cold.

Dante says to me, "I thought you might want to go talk to that ex-employee with me. Nero can stay here with Riona."

"I don't need a babysitter," Riona says without looking up from her papers. "I can be here alone for an hour. There's a hundred people on the floor with me."

"Well, I'm already here," Nero says. "So you may as well enjoy my company."

He slouches over to my chair, flopping down on it as soon as I've vacated the spot. He goes to put his feet up on Riona's glass coffee table. Still without looking up, she says, "Don't even think about it."

Nero grins and swings his legs over the arm of the chair instead, sitting sideways.

It's strange. I never had a problem with Nero—I like all Dante's siblings. But I find myself not wanting to leave him here with Riona. I tell myself it's because I'm supposed to be watching her, keeping her safe. But if I'm totally honest, I look at Nero with his outrageous good looks and that air of menace that appeals to women in a very specific way, and I feel something just a little too close to jealousy.

Which is idiotic. Dante already told me that Nero is head over heels for some girl named Camille, and Riona's already taken. So there's nothing to be jealous about here. Not even a little bit.

Still, I leave the office in a strange kind of mood.

Back in the elevator, Dante says, "How's it going with Riona?"

"Good." I nod.

"Actually good?"

"Yeah. I mean, we've got our differences…"

Dante chuckles. "I bet. She's great, though. Once you get below the prickly surface."

"That's what I'm finding,"

I'm not planning to tell Dante about my fight with Riona. I'm definitely not going to tell him about the kiss. That was pure stupidity. I won't do it again.

Instead, I say, "You want me to drive? I got a pretty sick ride."

Dante chuckles. "You better. Nero brought me over in some hunk of junk that felt like it was gonna fall apart trying to carry me around. I don't think they built cars for people my size back in the fifties."

"I don't think they *had* people your size."

"Exactly. You ever seen a bodybuilder from the fifties? They were like a hundred and seventy-eight pounds soaking wet."

"You could have a real career in the circus if we could get you a time machine, take you back to the old-timey days."

"Thanks." Dante snorts. "Nobody delivers a compliment like you, Long Shot."

Dante has the address for Luke Barker, the guy Oran fired after he apparently tried to get touchy with Riona at the company Christmas party.

It's been almost a year since then, so it seems unlikely to me that the guy's still holding a grudge. Worth running down every lead, though.

Dante and I drive out to his house in the Loop. It's a pretty, Tudor-style place on a tree-lined street. Looks nice enough from the exterior.

"You sure he's home?" I ask Dante. "In the middle of the day?"

"Yeah," Dante says. "I called him earlier."

Despite that, it takes quite a while for Barker to answer the door after we knock. I hear something being knocked over in the hallway and an irritated curse. Then he pulls the door open, still dressed in a bathrobe and looking bleary-eyed and unshaven.

"What?" he says. Then, on spotting Dante: "Oh, right. Come in."

The inside of the house is a lot less well maintained than the outside. It smells musty and stale, and half eaten take-out boxes litter the counters in the kitchen. A yappy little Yorkie runs around barking at our ankles. Barker says, "Shut up, ya little fucker!" which the dog completely ignores.

The Yorkie is wearing a sparkling pink rhinestone collar. That and the throw pillows on the couch that say *Live, Laugh, Wine* and *Cuddle Time* lead me to believe that a woman used to live here not too long ago. Probably not now, however—when Barker opens his fridge, the only thing inside is a pizza box, a dozen bottles of Budweiser, and a bunch of condiment bottles.

"You want a drink?" Barker says, taking a beer out for himself.

I'm guessing it's not his first of the day.

"Sure," Dante says. He's probably trying to seem friendly.

Barker pops the caps off the beers and slides one over to Dante.

"I'm good," I say.

Barker takes a long pull off his beer. He eyes us with narrowed bloodshot eyes.

"What's this all about? You know I don't work for Griffin, Briar, Weiss anymore."

"Yeah," Dante says. "I know that. I was wondering if you could tell me why they let you go."

"You know why," Barker says.

"No," Dante replies calmly. "I don't."

"Because of that bitch," Barker says, taking a swig of his beer.

The venom in his tone makes my heart rate spike.

"Are you talking about Riona Griffin?" I say, trying to keep my tone neutral.

"Yeah. She was flirting with me all the time…couldn't keep her eyes off me. Then, at the party, we both have a couple of drinks. One thing leads to another…and then she goes crying to her uncle."

I can't imagine Riona "going crying" to anybody. And I also can't imagine her flirting with this sloppy sack of shit. He's got at least ten years on her, and even if he were shaved and showered and dressed in a nice suit, he'd still have that smug look on his face I can't imagine Riona appreciating.

"What do you mean by 'one thing leads to another'?" I say through gritted teeth.

Dante glances over at me. He can tell I'm getting pissed.

Barker doesn't seem to notice. He takes another swig of his beer.

"You know. We're talking, having drinks...she's wearing this low-cut dress. Every time she moves, I can see the top of her tits, and she knows I can see it. She acts all uptight, but you know what redheads are like...they're all fuckin' animals in the sack. So she's all like, 'Excuse me,' and walks over to the bathrooms, and I can see the way she's walking, shakin' her ass—she definitely wants me to follow her. So I do, and I shove her in the bathroom and pull up her skirt and—"

I don't know at what point in the story I snap, but the next thing I know, my hands are around Barker's throat and I've flung him against the refrigerator. I'm choking the fucking life out of him while he gags and sputters, trying to pry my fingers off his neck.

The fact this arrogant piece of shit thought Riona was interested in him, the fact he followed her into the bathroom and put his hands on her...it all makes me want to murder him. Just snuff him out of this world.

Dante's pulling me off Barker, shouting, "Long Shot, take it easy!"

I release my grip on Barker's throat just a little—enough that he can talk.

"Did you hire somebody to come after her?" I snarl. "Were you trying to get even because she got you fired?"

"She didn't just get me fired!" Barker spits, still trying to pry my hands off his neck. "My wife left me, too! She's divorcing me! She cleared out the bank account and took my car and left me with this fuckin' dog!"

"Did you hire someone to kill Riona?" I roar in his face.

"What? No!" Barker sputters. "Are you insane?"

I squeeze his throat a little harder, lifting his feet off the kitchen tile.

"Why not?" I snarl. "She ruined your life, right?"

"Even if I wanted to, I don't have any fuckin' money!" Barker chokes, his face turning puce. "Plus the Griffins..."

His voice trails off 'cause he's not getting enough air. I have to relax my grip again so he can speak.

"What?" I say. "What about the Griffins?"

"They're fuckin'...Mafia," he says hoarsely. "I was pissed. But I'm not suicidal."

I let go of Barker. He rubs his throat dramatically, coughing and wheezing. I can see the imprints of my fingers on his neck. I don't feel bad about it. I'd like to do a whole lot worse to him.

Dante looks at Barker gasping dramatically against the fridge. The guy looks pathetic as hell. It's pretty clear that he can't even clear out his pizza boxes, let alone plot revenge against Riona.

"Let's go," Dante says to me.

"Yeah, get the fuck out," Barker cries petulantly. "You fuckin' psychopaths. Drinking my beer, then trying to kill me."

I turn, ready to leave Barker's musty house.

As I take three steps away from him, I hear Barker mutter, "I hope somebody *does* off that uppity bitch."

I turn around and clock him—a right cross straight to the jaw. It slams him into the fridge, and he slumps down on the tiles, knocked out cold.

When I face Dante again, he's watching me, his eyebrows raised. "You okay?"

"Of course." I shake out my right hand. "Why wouldn't I be?"

"I don't think he had anything to do with hiring the Djinn."

"Neither do I. But he's still an asshole."

The Yorkie is running around our feet again, barking, but not at us—just yapping in general. It doesn't seem too concerned about its owner slumped down on the floor over by the fridge. In fact, it runs into the living room and pees against the leg of the coffee table, without a care in the world.

Once we're outside in the chilly air again, Dante takes a deep breath. "That's better."

"He's a mess." I grunt. "I doubt a shit stain like Barker has the gumption to hire the Djinn or the money to pay him, if what he said about his wife cleaning out the bank accounts was true. If it wasn't Barker, and it wasn't the Russians, that only leaves the Hartford family."

"Yeah." Dante nods slowly. "Only problem is I don't exactly want to threaten them. They've been through enough already."

"We don't have to go in guns blazing."

Dante cocks an eyebrow at me. "You gonna be chill this time?"

"Of course." I shrug off his look. "I'm fine."

I'm not fine, though. I don't know what the fuck that was in there—I completely lost my temper. That's twice in two days.

Maybe I'm not cut out for this bodyguard life. I'm getting overly invested. All wrapped up in this thing with a level of emotion that isn't usual for me.

As we get back into the car, my phone buzzes with a text from my brother:

You missed mom's birthday. And the anniversary.

He means the anniversary of our dad's death. It happened only two days apart from Mom's birthday, so it's always a hard time of year for her.

I text him back:

I called her.

A pause. Then he replies:

Calling isn't the same as visiting.

I haven't been home in a while. Almost three years. But who's counting?

I can picture the ranch as clearly as the busy Chicago streets right in front of me. I can see the stands of birch trees and almost smell the scent of clean hay and warm horseflesh.

I feel a pull to be in a warmer, greener place than here.

But I also feel a deep sorrow and shame at the thought of visiting home.

So I text back:

I'm on a job right now.

Grady fires back:

You're always on a job.

There's a pause where he waits for me to respond. When I don't, he texts again:

Mom hurt her foot. She's getting too old to do this full time.
We need to talk about what we're gonna do with the ranch...

I turn my phone off and stuff it in my pocket, annoyed.

"Problem?" Dante says.

"No." I shake my head. "No problem at all."

CHAPTER 11
RIONA

WHILE I'M WORKING, NERO IS FUCKING AROUND WITH HIS switchblade.

I used to think he played with it to try to look tough, but watching him now, I realize it's almost like meditation for him. The blade moves through his fingers with incredible speed and fluidity. He zones out, his eyes becoming calm and focused, and his breathing slows down until his chest is barely rising and falling.

It's funny to think he and Dante are brothers when Dante is so rough and brutal looking and Nero is, for lack of a better word, simply beautiful. In temperament they're opposites, too—Dante deliberate and disciplined, Nero impulsive and ferocious.

Or at least that's how he used to be. Today he seems relaxed and in a surprisingly good mood.

Dante told me Nero's head over heels for a girl he knew in high school—Camille. I thought Nero would be the last person in the world to fall in love, but I guess that's me instead.

Seeing Nero transformed into an almost-reasonable human makes me believe miracles can happen after all.

Maybe that's what it takes: an unexpected pairing. Cal fell in love with the daughter of our worst enemy. Nessa is married to her own goddamned kidnapper. Nero got his heart stolen by a girl he barely noticed in high school. And Dante is back together with the woman who ripped out his heart.

In that case, maybe Nick and I are doomed. He's exactly my usual type. Exactly what I always pick for myself.

And we're barely getting along at all now.

We had one rather awkward coffee date earlier in the week. This time Raylan kept a respectful distance at a different table— pretending he had some emails to answer, but I suspect he was just trying to give Nick and me some space for ourselves.

It didn't really help. Nick was sulky. He kept asking me how long this whole ridiculous bodyguard thing was going to go on.

"I don't know," I said testily. "If we can't find the person who tried to murder me, I guess the alternative is that he succeeds in offing me. Either way, you won't have to worry about it anymore."

"Oh, come on Riona." Nick rolled his eyes at my melodrama. "You know I don't want you to get hurt." He reached across the table and grabbed my hand. "I just miss you. And I'm tired of these Victorian-era chaperoned dates."

I pulled my hand back. "I know. But there's not a whole lot else I can do about it."

The truth is, I could tell Raylan to drive me over to Nick's house for a proper date. Raylan could monitor the house while Nick and I ate dinner on our own, then went upstairs for a little private time. That's how you'd treat a normal security guard.

But Raylan isn't a normal security guard. And not just because he's friends with Dante.

There's something about Raylan that doesn't let you keep him at arm's length. He's too perceptive and too goddamned *personal*. Too honest and too…himself. There's no layer of professional distance between him and me. There never has been.

Even Nero sees it.

He looks up from his switchblade, fixing me with his cool-gray eyes. "So, are you and the cowboy fucking yet?"

That's a classic cross-examination tactic—ask a question bluntly and abruptly to shock the defendant into answering honestly.

"No," I say, without giving Nero the pleasure of an emotional response. "I have a boyfriend."

"But you would otherwise."

"No. I wouldn't."

Nero snorts, obviously thinking I'm full of shit.

I inform him, "I know this will come as a shock to you, but most people don't fuck every single person they meet."

"They do if they're hot."

"Oh, so you think Raylan's hot?" I say innocently.

To my surprise, Nero grins. "Yeah. Real dreamy."

Wonders never cease. Nero Gallo showing an ounce of self-deprecation—he really must be in love.

To test that theory, and to shift the focus off myself, I say, "Dante told me you're dating someone."

"I am," Nero says, unembarrassed.

"Is it serious?"

"Yes," he says with simple finality.

This is so bizarre to me. Nero was the epitome of a Lothario. He didn't seem to give a fuck about anyone or anything. "What's different about her?"

"It's got nothing to do with being different," Nero says in his cryptic way.

Nero reminds me of the Cheshire Cat—he'll respond to questions, but he doesn't give a damn if you understand his answers.

Usually, I'd just ignore him. But I'm genuinely curious about this. I want to know how he could change so drastically; I used to think people didn't change at all.

"Explain it to me," I say, putting down my pen and giving him my full attention. "I really want to know."

Nero closes his knife and slips it back in his pocket. He sits forward, his elbows on his knees.

"Camille and I are the same," he says simply. "Not in circumstances or experiences. Not on the outside. But in the things that matter, we're aligned. What we care about. What we want. What we feel."

I really don't understand love. I was just thinking that opposites attract. Now Nero's saying it's all about finding someone the most like yourself internally.

"So...you're just really similar."

"It's more than that," Nero says. "There are the parts that are the same and the parts that fill the holes in each other. You don't know what's missing inside you until you find it in someone else."

I never thought I'd be discussing love with Nero. This month has been utterly bizarre. I have more questions I want to ask, but Raylan and Dante interrupt.

"Any luck?"

"No." Dante shakes his head. "Barker's an asshole, but a broke and unmotivated asshole, as far as we could tell."

I glance over at Raylan, who looks strangely guilty. Nero, ever eagle-eyed, notices the same thing.

"What happened to your hand?" he demands.

"Nothing." Raylan stuffs his hands in his jeans' pockets, but not before I see what Nero was referring to—the knuckles of his right hand are definitely swollen.

"Did he attack you?" I ask. Barker's an asshole all right, but I can't imagine him having the balls to take a swing at Raylan—especially not with Dante right there backing him up.

"No," Raylan says. He's not looking at me, and he seems irritated by the questions.

"We talked to John Hartford as well," Dante says quickly, changing the subject. "Virginia's older brother. He's pretty pissed at my family—he knows we helped Bosco Bianchi, which I fucking wish we hadn't, but I don't think he knows you were involved at all. So, if he wants revenge, I don't think it would be pointed in your direction."

"So we learned...nothing whatsoever," I say.

"Yeah, pretty much." Raylan nods.

"Great." Nero pushes himself up from the chair. "Sounds like an afternoon well spent."

"I'm sure you had way more important things to do." Dante snorts, shaking his head at his little brother.

"Oh, I'm not complaining." Nero shoots a glance in my direction. "Riona and I were having a real nice chat."

Dante raises his eyebrows at me, clearly having as much trouble imagining what that would look like as I would have trying to explain it to him.

Dante and Nero head out, and Raylan takes his customary chair in the corner. But he's not in his usual good mood. Actually, he looks pretty wound up about something.

"What?" I say. "Are you mad because you didn't find what you were looking for?"

"No," Raylan says shortly.

"What, then?"

"Nothing."

I roll my eyes. I don't want to have to guess what he's annoyed about.

After a few minutes of silence, Raylan says, "What did Nero mean?"

"About what?"

"About having a nice chat."

"Oh. We were just talking about him and Camille."

"Is that all?" Raylan says suspiciously.

"Yes..."

If I didn't know better, I'd think Raylan is jealous of Nero. He's acting very odd.

I ask, "Are you going to tell me what happened to your hand?"

"No."

I make an irritated sound and go back to my work.

When it's finally time to leave, Raylan seems to have relaxed a little. He grabs my coat and holds it so I can slip my arms into the sleeves. Then he opens the door for me.

Usually, I don't like when men go over the top with chivalrous gestures, but Raylan does it naturally, not making a fuss about it. Everything he does with his hands is smooth and easy: cooking, driving, getting the door. He probably is great at chopping wood, just like he said.

I can see Oran's light still burning in his office, so I make a detour down the hall to say good night to him.

He's bent over a stack of papers, looking intent and exhausted.

"'Night, Uncle Oran," I say. "I'm headed out."

"Good night," he replies distractedly.

Uncle Oran is as well-dressed as ever, but there's more gray than black in his hair now, and he's got bags under his eyes. I sometimes forget he's almost ten years older than my father.

"Your uncle never got married or had kids?" Raylan asks as we get into the elevator.

"He's had girlfriends—one for six or seven years. She was nice. Her name was Lorelei. She worked at a gallery in River West—it was for self-taught artists. 'Outsider Art,' they called it. But they split up. I don't know why."

"You're close to him," Raylan says. It's not a question.

I nod. "He got me interested in law. Cal was always the heir to the empire, and Nessa was the baby. You know she's such a sweetheart, everybody loves her. So I guess…there wasn't anything special about me. Uncle Oran made me feel special."

"Classic middle child," Raylan says with a little smile.

"You're probably the oldest." He reminds me of Callum and Dante—competent and responsible.

"Yup," Raylan admits. "But I'm not the biggest. My little brother Grady's got me beat. He was six foot in seventh grade, and he hasn't stopped growing since."

I've heard Raylan mention his siblings before. Always with a tone of affection.

"What's he like?"

"A lot like me, but with worse judgment. He was always getting into trouble growing up, and not much has changed. His wife settled him down a bit—they've got a couple of kids now. He's the hardest worker I know. Does the job of four men on the ranch."

"What about your sister?"

"She's smart as hell and good with the horses. But she gets bored easy. And she's got a temper. Not with animals, just people."

I like listening to Raylan's description. His voice is so warm and animated, anything he says comes alive.

"And your mom?"

"She's kind," Raylan says simply. "She always made us feel like we were the most important thing in the world. But she made us work our asses off, too, so that was good for us. If we ever quit a job before the last little bit of it was done…that was the one way to really piss her off."

I want to ask about Raylan's father, too, but I know from comments he made in passing that his dad is dead. It doesn't seem right to bring him up, especially since Raylan hasn't mentioned any specifics. I don't know if they were close or estranged or what killed him.

"What's the ranch like?" I ask instead.

"Depends. You like horses?"

"I've never touched a horse in my life," I admit. "Never even seen one up close. I guess that makes me a city slicker or whatever."

"A greenhorn," Raylan says, grinning. "Or a tenderfoot."

"I don't know if I like any of those."

"Maybe just a girl who loves Chicago, then," Raylan says.

We've gotten in the car and we're back at my place before I realize it. Raylan is telling me stories about the ranch. He's easy to talk to and even easier to listen to.

Raylan starts cooking while we're still chatting. Despite the fact I loathe cooking, he ropes me into chopping carrots for him.

"I'm shit at this," I warn him.

"That's because you're holding the knife wrong."

He comes around behind me and puts his hands over mine. His hand is slightly rough and very warm.

"You gotta rock the blade like this," he says, showing me how to rock the chef's knife so it slices through the carrot in uniform discs, without sending the pieces rolling wildly in every direction.

Raylan smells nice—not like expensive cologne like Josh, just like soap and laundry detergent and clean cotton. There's something natural about him that I like. He doesn't put product in his hair—it's soft and messy. He rarely shaves, and he's got calluses on his hands. But all that seems exotic to me, compared to the tanned and coiffed men I usually date. Raylan is masculine in a different way—by not giving a damn about his clothes or his car or his social status.

As usual, when I notice something appealing about him, I feel an equal compulsion to pull away.

"I've got it," I say, taking control of the knife myself.

"All right." Raylan goes back to browning meat, well seasoned with salt, pepper, onion, and garlic.

He cooks us pasta with tomato sauce made from scratch. It doesn't look that hard when he does it, though I doubt I could replicate any of it. It's delicious as hell, though. The right blend of rich, spicy, tart, and fragrant.

"Who taught you to cook?" I ask him.

"Everybody. My grandpa, my grandma, my mom, my dad, people I've met on my travels…it's the universal language. Everyone likes food that tastes good. You can bond with anybody over a good meal."

I guess that's true. Even Raylan and I seem to get along when we're eating together.

Raylan probably gets along with everyone, though.

I thought he was just a typical cocky-soldier type when I first met him. But he actually has a very calming presence. He knows when to talk and when not to, when to just have a companionable silence. He's not always trying to fill the air with nonsense.

After dinner, we go sit out on the balcony attached to my living room. We look out over the city lights—the other high-rises, each with their individual boxes of light representing offices and apartments, each containing some other person living their life. The streams of cars on the roads below are the same—each one carrying a person to their own individual destination. To them, what they're doing is the most important thing in the world. To us, it's just another light bobbing down the road, the same as all the others.

Usually, that thought would make me feel isolated and insignificant. But tonight, I think most of those people are probably going home to somebody—maybe to make pasta or watch a movie. And even if those activities are mundane, they're peaceful and happy.

"Do you see your little sister much?" Raylan asks me out of nowhere.

"Nessa?"

"Yeah."

"I do, actually. I meet her for lunch. Sometimes I go see what she's working on at her dance studio—she's a choreographer."

"Dante told me what happened with her husband—with the Polish Mafia."

Nessa met Mikolaj when he kidnapped her. We were in conflict with the Polish Mafia at the time. In what I first thought was Stockholm Syndrome, Nessa and Miko developed feelings for each other. He let her go, which almost cost him control of his men and his own life. Nessa went back to him, and they married.

"Do you know what's funny?" I say to Raylan.

"What?"

"I actually like Miko."

Raylan laughs. "You do?"

"Yes. I mean, don't get me wrong—he's intense. But he's smart and ruthless and devoted to Nessa. He's so cold, but she blooms with him."

"What's Nessa like?"

"Everybody who meets her loves her. She's kind—like your mom, I guess. She's always been that way. Even when she was little, she couldn't stand to see anybody sad. She'd share anything with you."

I pause, thinking.

"Sometimes she used to annoy me because she could be childish, too. Too passive, too gentle, too eager to please my parents. Maybe I was jealous. She's so likable, and I know I'm…"

"What?" Raylan says.

"A lot."

Raylan laughs.

"But anyway, she grew up, moving out of my parents' house, getting married. She's always been creative, and she's been making these ballets that are just wild and gorgeous. I don't know shit about dance, but they really are beautiful. And I respect that. I don't know—maybe it was just both of us getting older. But we seem to have more to talk about now."

"I feel that way, too," Raylan says. "With my siblings."

"You do?"

"Yeah. You get older, and when you get together, instead of talking about the people you know and the things you used to do, you can just talk about life, about books and movies and the world, and you've grown up, and they've grown up, and all the little petty shit you used to fight about as kids doesn't matter anymore."

"Right," I say. "Exactly."

We've been sitting out on the balcony for a long time now. I have a blanket wrapped around my shoulders to keep me from freezing, but Raylan is just wearing his normal button-up shirt.

"Aren't you cold?"

"Nah," he says. Then, after a minute, he grins and admits, "Actually, yeah, I'm pretty fuckin' cold."

We go back inside the warmth of the apartment, closing the sliding glass door behind us.

Raylan and I linger in the living room, a strange kind of tension between us now.

I say, "I guess I'll go to bed."

"Good night." Raylan nods.

I go into my room, brush my teeth, and slip under the covers.

But it's a long time before I actually fall asleep. I lie there restless and confused, wondering why I felt so relaxed on the balcony but so troubled now.

I wake to someone jerking me out of bed.

The air is thick with black smoke so thick that I'm hacking and coughing and my eyes are streaming with tears. I can't pull in a breath.

"Get down!" Raylan barks, pulling me low to the carpet.

It's a little easier to breathe down here but not much.

Raylan is tying one of his T-shirts around my face, making a makeshift bandanna. I hear sharp cracking and popping sounds, and it's so hot that sweat is pouring down my skin.

"What's happening?" I rasp. My throat feels raw and choked, even with the T-shirt over my face.

I can't see anything. The smoke and heat are getting worse by the second.

"We've got to get out of here." Raylan yanks the blankets off my bed, and the sheets, too.

He throws a blanket over both of us and pulls me along, staying low to the floor.

As we leave my bedroom, we're met with a solid wall of fire. The front door, the entryway, and the kitchen are engulfed in flames. Floor to ceiling, it rages, spreading into the living room.

The heat is immense, indescribable. I can't even look at it or it burns my eyes. My body is screaming at me to get away, but there's nowhere to go.

"We're trapped!" I gasp.

Grimly, doggedly, Raylan pulls me toward the balcony. "Hold on," he says, unlatching the sliding glass door.

I don't know what he's trying to prepare me for, but as he yanks open the door and shoves me out, the cool night air rushes into the apartment. The influx of oxygen gives the fire a new breath. The flames roar across the ceiling and throughout the room, igniting the rest of my apartment in an instant. Fire billows out, hitting us like a wave.

The comforter Raylan threw over our heads catches fire. Raylan throws it off, and I watch it tumble end over end, burning like a torch as it falls the twenty-eight floors to the street below.

Using the sheet to protect his hand, Raylan forces the glass door shut again, but I can see the heat has singed the hairs all along his arm. The glass and metal are already hot to the touch, like a fireplace grate. The door won't hold for long. And we're trapped way up here on this tiny balcony, with no fire escape.

I'm trying not to panic. I'm still hacking and coughing, and so is Raylan. His whole face is dark with smoke, cut by the tracks of sweat running down his skin.

We're going to burn to death. We're trapped. The fire is going to burst through the glass any second. No fire truck can reach up here. I don't understand how the fire spread so fast through the apartment. I don't understand what's happening.

I can hear distant sirens but not the fire alarm itself. The roar and crackling of the flames are too loud. I never knew how loud fire could be.

Raylan is tying my bedsheet around the balcony railing. I don't understand why.

"Get on my back!" he shouts at me. His voice is hoarse and

choked with smoke. His eyes are bloodshot, but the irises still gleam bright blue against his sooty face. It's the only part of him that still looks familiar. Still, I don't understand his plan.

"What?"

"GET ON MY BACK!" He grabs my hand and wraps my arms around his neck. I'm only wearing a silk camisole and shorts, with bare feet. He's shirtless in boxer shorts, but his feet are stuffed into his boots at least.

We're both so sweaty and filthy that it's hard to hold on to his neck. And I just realized he's climbing over the railing.

"ARE YOU INSANE?" I shriek.

We're twenty-eight fucking floors up in the air. So high up that you can barely see the streets way down below us. So high that the frigid November wind is blowing hard against us.

If we slip and fall, we'll fall for five or six seconds before we hit the pavement. And when we land, our bodies won't just break—they'll explode.

"If we don't get off this balcony, we're dead!" Raylan shouts back.

I look at the glass doors, barely holding back the raging flames. Even as I watch, the glass begins to crack and warp.

"Oh my god..." I whisper.

I cling to Raylan's neck, my legs wrapped around his waist from behind.

"Don't choke me," he says.

I try to relax my grip just a little while still holding on tight.

He swings his leg over the railing, gripping the bedsheet with both hands.

I'm dangling over bare, empty space, holding on to his back.

Raylan starts to lower us, going hand over hand on the sheet.

The fabric is taut and straining under our combined weight. I can see his arms rigid with strain and his hands gripping the slippery material. His fingers leave sooty prints on the white sheet. His knuckles are pale and tight.

I can't watch. I squeeze my eyes shut, holding on to him with all my might. I can feel his shoulders and back trembling with the strain of carrying our weight.

Raylan's hands slip, and we drop two feet before he catches his grip again. I bite back my scream, my eyes still tightly shut. I can hear the fabric starting to tear.

"Almost there..." Raylan grunts.

I hazard a look.

We're down at the level of the balcony below us, but we're still hanging over open air. The balcony is recessed. We can't quite reach the railing.

"I'm going to swing us. You have to grab it," Raylan mutters, his jaw clenched tight with strain.

"I don't...I don't know if I can." It's taking all my strength just to hold on to his back. We're both slippery with sweat and smoke.

"You can do it," Raylan says in his deep calm voice. "I know you can."

He kicks his legs to swing us out and in. The movement is horrible. It makes my stomach clench. Holding on tight to his neck with my right arm, I reach with my left. My fingers slip helplessly across the slick metal railing. I miss.

"I can't get it!" I cry.

"Yes, you can," Raylan says. "One more time—grab it tight."

He swings us again, harder this time. I hear the awful purring sound of the sheet ripping apart. I grab the railing with all my strength and pull us toward it. Raylan throws his arm over, too. The railing hits me in the ribs, and it fucking hurts, but I get my arm around it and hold on tight. Raylan shoves me over it, and we tumble onto the cement. My heart is thundering in my chest. I'm panting and coughing harder than ever.

The apartment itself is dark—nobody inside. Either they already evacuated the building, or they were never home to start with. I pound on the glass door, but it's pointless. The door is locked, and nobody's coming to open it.

"Stand back." Raylan grunts.

He kicks through the glass with the toe of his boot, then reaches through the hole to unlock the door.

Smoke billows out in our faces. Even a floor down, the heat and smoke and noise are intense. It radiates down from my apartment above. I can see the ceiling sagging.

"Hurry," Raylan says. "That could collapse any second."

We run through the apartment, which is the exact same layout as mine. We shove through the door into the hallway, where I can finally hear the steady blare of the fire alarm. Several other residents are stumbling down the halls, trying to carry out reluctant pets or belongings they don't want to risk losing.

"Don't take the elevator," Raylan tells me unnecessarily. There's no way I was going to risk trapping myself anywhere else.

We run to the stairs instead, my bare feet soon filthy from the endless descent down twenty-seven flights of concrete steps.

The stairs are choked with other tenants. The descent is tediously slow. Some of the people from lower floors are complaining, thinking the whole thing is only a drill. That is until they see Raylan and me, black with smoke and Raylan burned down his right arm from forcing my balcony doors closed.

Everything I own is burning over my head. Should I have tried to grab something before we ran out to the balcony? Stupidly, I think of my brand-new electric toothbrush that I only used twice. Now it's melted plastic. Or maybe just ash.

I think I'm in shock.

I feel numb. My head is a balloon, floating above my shoulders, barely tethered.

If it weren't for Raylan's arm around my shoulders, leading me on, I think I might pass out.

Raylan takes me all the way down to the parking garage. He pulls the car keys out of his boot. That impresses me. I don't know how he had the presence of mind to grab them. I don't know how he kept his calm through any of it.

I feel like I'm barely clinging to my last shred of self-control.

"How did that happen?" I croak, my throat still raw with smoke. "How did the fire spread so fast?"

"I think he must have poured an accelerant under your door," Raylan says grimly. "I woke up to this whooshing sound, and in two seconds, that whole half of your apartment was on fire."

I can hear more and more sirens wailing on street level—fire trucks and police cars coming to the building from all sides.

"We need to get out of here," Raylan says. "We're exposed. That might not be all he had planned."

I nod numbly and climb into the passenger seat.

Raylan does a sweep of the vehicle to make sure there's nothing planted inside or underneath. Then he gets in the driver's side and starts the engine.

My head is still throbbing from the smoke. I lean my head against the window and close my eyes.

CHAPTER 12
RAYLAN

Riona sleeps for several hours.

I drive through the dark night, the city lights receding.

I look over at her from time to time, reassuring myself that she's just dirty from the smoke, that her delicate pale skin wasn't burned by the flames.

I've never seen a fire spread so fast.

I ran into her room, afraid that by the time I pulled her out of there, we'd be completely engulfed.

I don't know how the fuck to protect her. When you're constantly in a defensive position, you're at a disadvantage. It's too easy for your opponent to choose the time and place of his attack. You can't prepare for the unknown.

So it's up to me to shift the battleground.

I'm taking Riona out of Chicago. Taking her away, somewhere this so-called Djinn can't find her.

Tracking down this motherfucker and protecting Riona can't happen in the same place at the same time. Let Dante and Cal do the searching—I'm going to take Riona somewhere far away.

By the time Riona wakes up, we're already halfway to Louisville. She sits up, rubbing her sore eyes and blinking in confusion at the long empty stretch of highway in the early-morning light.

"Where…where are we?"

"I-65," I tell her. "We passed through Indianapolis, but you were sleeping."

"WHAT?" she shouts. "Where the hell are you taking me?"

"I'm taking you to Tennessee," I tell her calmly.

"To Ten—I'm not going to Tennessee!" Riona shouts.

"You definitely are."

"Raylan," Riona says, trying to maintain a semblance of calm. "Turn the car around right this second."

I keep on driving. "I'm not going to do that."

"Stop the fucking car!" she shouts.

I can tell she's pretty pissed, so I keep my eyes on the road as I try to explain my thought process to her.

"If we stay in Chicago, it's only a matter of time until this guy hits us again. I'm going to take you somewhere he can't find you. Your brother and Dante will track down the Djinn. And in the meantime, you'll be safe."

I can feel Riona's furious gaze fixed on me. She's radiating almost as much heat as that apartment fire. If looks could combust, I'd be a charcoal briquette.

Still, she tries to keep her voice calm.

"I can't go to Tennessee, Raylan. I have work. I have meetings. I have responsibilities."

"You can't do any of that if you're dead," I tell her bluntly. "We've got Internet at Silver Run. I'll get you a laptop, and you work from the ranch."

"The RANCH?" Riona cries. "I don't want to be at a ranch! I don't have any clothes. Or a toothbrush. Or my files…"

Her voice trails off as she realizes she wouldn't have those things at home either. Because they all just went up in flames.

"Fuck," she says. "My briefcase…"

"Yeah," I say. "I'm really sorry. I couldn't get anything out."

Riona sits silent for a minute. I know she's mentally tallying up everything that was in that apartment. Every fancy pair of shoes or favorite book or keepsake she loved. All gone.

Finally, she says, "You got *me* out."

"It was pretty fucking close. But we got out of there together."

Now I do hazard a look in her direction. Her pale green eyes are large and sad in her filthy face. The sooty streaks make her look young, like a kid who was playing in the dirt. Her hair is so tangled and smoky that it looks closer to brown than red. There's no telling what color her silk camisole set used to be.

The effect is pathetic. It gives me a pang of guilt. I should have protected her better. It was my job to be her bodyguard, and I let her whole apartment burn down around her.

"I'm sorry," I say again.

Riona sighs, covering her face with her hands. "You don't have to apologize," she says quietly through her fingers. "You saved my life."

"Well," I say, "keep that spirit of gratitude. 'Cause I am taking you to Silver Run. Even if I have to throw you over my shoulder and carry you there."

She raises her head, green fire flaring in her eyes again. "You think you always know best, don't you?"

I shrug. "Any idea's better than no idea."

Riona frowns, crossing her slim arms over her chest. "We're going to have to stop somewhere. I need clothing. Also, I'm starving."

"Me, too," I say, smiling a little. "At least we can agree on that."

We stop in Seymour and pay for a room at the Motel 6 so we can both shower and clean up. While Riona is in the shower, I go to the outlet store next door to buy clothes for both of us. The clerk gives me a bland stare as I walk through the door, filthy, in my boxer shorts, boots, and an oversize hoodie I found in the trunk of Dante's car.

"I need a shirt," I tell him.

"You want pants, too?" he says.

The women's section doesn't have a whole lot of selection, but I pick out a few things for Riona that I think will fit her. I don't bother with coats because even after a few hours driving south, I can already feel the temperature warming. November in Tennessee is nothing like November in Chicago. It'll probably be seventy degrees.

The clerk bags up my purchases, and I carry them back to the motel, not wanting to be gone too long.

I lay out Riona's stuff on the cheap scratchy bedspread. Then I trade places with her once she comes out of the shower. I try to give her room in the confined space and not look at her with just a white towel wrapped around her body, her wet hair dark around her shoulders. It's hard to keep my eyes on the floor. This is the only time Riona looks vulnerable—without the armor of her professional clothing, her sleek hair, and her classy makeup.

This is her stripped down, at her most natural and lovely. But I know she doesn't want anyone to see her like that, least of all me. So I don't let my eyes roam over her like they want to.

Instead, I strip off my own dirty clothing, relieved to have the pungent smell of smoke away from me.

It's a shitty little bathroom, the shower cubicle barely large enough that I can close the glass door while standing inside. But the hot water feels incredibly relaxing after the insane night we had. It beats down on my shoulders, making me realize how sore I am from the climb to the lower balcony with Riona on my back.

I don't know if I've ever experienced a more desperate moment. I could hear the glass of the balcony doors cracking above us. I could feel the fragile sheet tearing in my hands under our combined weight. I could feel Riona's arms slipping from around my neck.

I thought I was going to drop her.

I thought we might both burn in the inferno.

I'm fucking furious at this Djinn, this boogeyman stalking us.

Part of me wants to stay in Chicago and track him down, even if it means setting a trap and staking it out for days. But I can't do that with Riona—my number one priority has to be keeping her safe. And that's what I'm going to do.

I finish cleaning up, and I brush my teeth with one of the cheap little disposable toothbrushes provided by the motel.

When I go back out into the room, Riona is wearing the clothes from the outlet store—jeans, a pair of cowboy boots, and a Western-style button-up shirt. Her hair is damp around her shoulders—bright red and wavy. I didn't realize it was wavy. She always styles it so straight and smooth. I've never seen her in jeans before either. The denim clings to her long legs. She looks pretty fucking hot, actually.

I try to keep my thoughts professional, but I'd have to be blind not to notice.

Riona gestures at the entirety of her person. "Seriously?" she says.

"What?"

"They didn't have any normal shoes?"

I laugh. "Those are normal shoes. Normal enough. What's the problem? You look good."

"I look like my new country album is dropping any day now."

"Well...we're not far from Nashville. So if that's a dream of yours..."

"It's not."

I grin, imagining Riona onstage with a guitar slung around her neck. I really can't picture her singing for other people's enjoyment. Or doing anything for other people's enjoyment.

"Trust me," I tell her. "You'll blend in better wearing that than one of your Ally McBeal suits."

Once we're both dressed, we go across the street to the run-down '50s style diner that promises BREAKFAST ALL DAY! on its faded sign. Since it's currently 7:20 in the morning, I assume we're getting breakfast either way.

Riona and I slide into one of the vinyl booths. She wrinkles her nose at the laminated menu and the wobbly Formica table.

"Coffee with cream, please," she tells the waitress.

"Same. Also pancakes, bacon, ham, scrambled eggs, and hash browns, please," I say.

Riona shakes her head at me. "Nothing can dampen your appetite, huh?"

"I think that whole experience made me hungrier. I probably burned a lot of calories, running and climbing. Plus driving all night. Probably should have ordered an omelet, too."

Riona snorts.

Despite all that, when the food comes out—greasy and crispy and smelling delicious—I can see her eyeing my bacon. I shove the plate toward her.

"Go ahead. There's plenty."

Riona picks up a fork tentatively and takes a bite of the hash browns. The potatoes are nicely browned, covered in salt and pepper.

"See? Pretty good, huh?" I say.

I know she's hungry. I know she wants more.

"Not terrible," she admits.

"Have as much as you want."

She eats half the plate in the next two minutes. Much as she doesn't like to admit it, the craziness of the night had its effect on us both. She's starving, too.

"So where is Silver Run, anyway?" Riona asks me.

"Right on the foothills of the Smoky Mountains. Close to Great Smoky Mountain National Park. Not far from Gatlinburg or Knoxville."

Riona stares at me like I'm speaking Mandarin.

"Never heard of any of that?" I tease her.

"I know the Smoky Mountains, obviously," Riona says defensively. "And Knoxville."

"Oh, yeah? What do you know about Knoxville?"

"Well..." She blushes. "That it's in Tennessee."

I laugh. "Don't get out of Chicago much, huh?"

"I've been places," Riona says stiffly. "New York. Paris. London. I've traveled."

"Not down to the heartland, though."

"No. I never had a reason to."

I grin. "You're gonna love it."

CHAPTER 13
RIONA

I COULD NOT FEEL MORE OUT OF PLACE IF RAYLAN WERE TAKING me to Morocco.

I've never had a pair of cowboy boots in my life. I've never eaten at a diner. And I've sure as hell never ridden a horse, let alone visited a ranch.

I almost think he's taking me here just to torture me. There are a lot of other places we could go that are less...foreign.

On the other hand, I definitely feel a million miles away from Chicago. And that does make me feel safe, in a strange way.

Before we leave the motel, Raylan calls Dante and lets him know where we're going. My phone and laptop burned up with everything else in my apartment, so I don't have any way of contacting anybody.

"It's better that way," Raylan tells me seriously. "Dante will tell Cal. But I don't think anybody else should know. The whole point of taking you here is to keep you completely off-grid. Hopefully your brother and Dante can figure out what the fuck is going on, sooner than later. But in the meantime, I don't want to risk this guy being able to track you."

I don't really like the idea of running and hiding, disconnected from my family and especially my work. But that fire scared me. More than the near drowning. It felt like an escalation—like a mark of this guy's desperation to get at me, no matter how safe and protected I might think I've made myself.

"I do need to call Nick," I tell Raylan. "If I just disappear and I'm not answering any calls or texts, he might call the cops. Bare minimum, he'll come to my apartment and probably notice the hole in the side of the building."

Raylan considers this.

"Fine," he says at last. "Call him, too, from the motel phone. You have the number memorized?"

I nod. "Yeah, I know it."

I always remember numbers—addresses, phone numbers, birthdays, and the numbers in legal files. I don't know why they stick in my brain. I could tell you case file numbers from years back. It's useless information most of the time—I'd rather keep the brain space for something else. But that's the way my mind works.

Raylan frowns, like he's annoyed that I know Nick's number. Like he thinks it means something.

I say, "Can I get a little privacy?"

"Don't tell Nick where you are. Don't tell him where you're going."

"*I know.* I won't," I promise.

Raylan goes out to wait for me in the car. He doesn't have to carry any bags out because, of course, we don't have any bags. We threw the remains of our old smoke-stained clothing in the trash.

I pick up the phone sitting on the nightstand and hit the button for an outside line. I can't remember the last time I made a phone call on a landline. It feels weird holding a receiver instead of a cellphone. Weird to stay connected to the base of the phone by a long spiraling cord instead of being free to wander around during the call.

It's so funny how things change so fast. One minute a piece of technology is a novelty, and before you've even noticed, it's the most normal and natural thing in the world. And the old way seems like a distant dream.

I hear the phone ringing. I'm planning to leave a message if Nick doesn't pick up.

Instead, I hear his grumpy and sleepy "yeah?" on the other end of the line.

"Nick, it's me."

"Riona?" His voice is husky and confused. "What number are you calling from?"

"I'm at a hotel," I say, remembering Raylan's injunction against specifying our location.

"Why are you at a hotel?" Nick's voice contains equal parts bewilderment and annoyance.

"My apartment, uh, burned down last night."

"WHAT?"

"Yeah. I'm gonna be staying somewhere else for…a while."

"Where are you?" After a second's hesitation, he adds, "You can stay at my place, you know."

"Thanks, but I'm still with…I still have Raylan watching me."

"He's with you now?" There's an edge to his tone.

"Not right next to me. But yes, he's at the hotel." I say *hotel* instead of *motel* to make it sound less sordid.

"Are you staying in the same room?"

"We're not…we didn't sleep here last night. We just used the shower. Not at the same time," I hasten to clarify.

"So you're sharing showers and hotel rooms with him now." Nick's jealousy is obvious. And it's obvious he's trying to pick a fight.

"He's a bodyguard," I say, not even trying to hide my annoyance. "Quit trying to make it sound like something it's not."

But even as I'm saying the words, I'm remembering that kiss in the gym. I tried to shove it down to the very bottom of my brain. Tried not to think about it again. It was just a moment of insanity on Raylan's part—we were both hopped up from the race, annoyed at each other for our own stupid reasons. It was impulsive and irrational. It didn't mean anything.

Still, the memory steals the ring of truth from my statement. It makes me sound petulant instead of certain. It leaves a hint of doubt for Nick to hear.

"I'm not okay with this," he says. "I'm not okay with any of this. Somebody's stalking you and trying to kill you, and I'm just supposed to act like that's normal? You've got some bodyguard with you twenty-four seven, like you're the president? This is fucking weird, Riona."

"I'm so sorry that someone trying to *kill me* is an inconvenience for you," I say acidly.

"This is fucking crazy! You're with this guy and—"

All of a sudden, I'm exhausted. It's been a long night and a strange morning, after one of the most traumatic experiences of my life. Nick's not going to understand that. He was never going to understand any of this.

I cut him off mid-rant. "You're right, Nick."

"I...what?" That's the last thing he expected me to say in the middle of an argument.

"You're right," I repeat. "You shouldn't have to deal with any of this. Let's take a break, and maybe when I'm not in the middle of running for my life, we can pick things back up again."

There's silence on the other end of the line. Then Nick says, "You're *breaking up with me?*"

"Yes," I say flatly. "I think so."

"Un-fucking-believable."

I hear a click and then dead air.

He hung up the phone.

I set down the receiver, my heart thudding.

I kind of said it on impulse. But I don't think I regret it. When I examine what I feel, it's a lot closer to relief, actually. I've got too much to deal with without having to baby Nick's feelings, too. This is for the best.

I leave the motel room, joining Raylan in the car.

"So?" he says, putting the Escalade into drive.

"So, what?"

Raylan hesitates, like he's wondering if he should push for details. "Everything okay?" he says at last.

"Yeah," I say, looking out the window. "Everything's great."

I don't know why I don't just tell Raylan that Nick and I broke up. I guess it's because it seems embarrassing in some way. Also maybe because I'd prefer to keep that barrier between us for now.

I know Raylan is as aware as I am that there's no relationship between the two of us. He's been hired to do a job, which is to protect me. We're not friends. And we're definitely not lovers. We can barely stand each other half the time.

Still, there is that weird energy that arises every now and then.

Like that moment in the gym. Or even our conversation last night.

I don't want to have to deal with any more of that. So I think it's better if Raylan believes I'm in a relationship with somebody else. It's safer that way. For both of us.

We drive the rest of the morning and into the afternoon. Mostly in silence. Raylan puts the radio on, and we go in and out of local stations. I hear an endless stream of country songs, punctuated by the occasional rock or pop song and some oldies.

I can't deny that Tennessee is surprisingly beautiful. I didn't realize it was so green. The fields are green, and the smaller mountains that are really more like hills. Beyond that, I spy the deep-blue peaks of the Smokies.

There's so much open space between towns. Raylan is right—I really don't get out of the city much. I can't believe we could drive to a place that looks so different within a day.

As we drive down into a valley between two tall green hills, the radio crackles, and a new song comes on, bright and clear. It's "Please Mr. Postman" by the Marvelettes.

♫ *"Please Mr. Postman"—The Marvelettes*

My mom used to play that song. She loves it—I have no idea why. She loves a lot of Motown and early rock and blues.

"Mr. Postman" is so cute and catchy that it was a favorite of Nessa's, and mine, too. Mom would play it, and we'd jump up on the couches and dance and sing along to it, pretending we were holding microphones, pretending we had beehives and sparkly dresses, and we were an old-school trio. Nessa, ever concerned with choreography even at a young age, would try to make us coordinate and shimmy in a period-appropriate manner.

I can't help tapping my fingers against the car door, nodding along to the song.

Raylan looks over at me, his thick black eyebrow cocked. He reaches over and twists the knob to turn up the volume.

That's another thing nobody does anymore—no one waits for a love letter from the postman. But the cheerful, wistful tone of the song is as relatable as ever. And the upbeat piano riff. It makes me want to shimmy my shoulders like Nessa and I used to do. Especially as Raylan turns the music up even louder and drums along to the beat on the steering wheel.

I can't help smiling. I sing along for a couple of bars, not caring that I'm shit at carrying a tune. Raylan laughs and turns the music up more. He doesn't know the lyrics, but he does the "*wa-ooo*" accompaniment like he's my backup singer.

It only lasts for two minutes. Those old Motown songs are short. The song switches over to something else I don't recognize, and Raylan turns the volume down again.

We're driving in silence once more.

But we're both smiling.

We get to Silver Run just before dinnertime, having driven almost the whole day long with only a brief stop in Lexington to pee and

buy some snacks. Neither one of us needed a real lunch, not after the massive breakfast we ate at the diner.

I can tell when we get close because there's a new tension in Raylan's shoulders. He sits up a little straighter, looking around at fields and forest that he obviously recognizes in a very intimate way. I know without asking that this is where he grew up. This is his home.

"How close are we?" I ask anyway, just to be sure.

"This is it," Raylan says. "Two hundred and twenty-eight acres all around us. This road only goes one place."

We pass through an open gate with an iron arch at the top. Recessed letters spell the name BOONE RANCH. It's the first time I've seen Raylan's name spelled out. I like the look of it in a funny kind of way—though it reminds me that I'm about to meet a bunch more Boones.

We're driving steadily upward on the winding road. The slope is small and gradual, but soon a view unspools below us. The ranch house was built at the highest point for miles around.

I see several large barns and stables on either side, but the winding road takes us directly up to the ranch house itself. The house is three stories tall, with a high peaked roof and large plate-glass windows across the front to take advantage of its aerie-like positioning. It's built of deep reddish-brown boards that aren't much different from the ones on the side of the barn. Yet the house is much grander in shape and scale, with tall doorways, those expansive windows giving views on all sides, and generous verandas encircling the house on all three levels.

Large leafy trees shade the windows and the decks. A pretty, old-fashioned swing hangs from the ancient oak closest to the front door.

I didn't hear Raylan's conversation with his family—I assume he called them while I was in the shower. But he promised that he warned them we were coming.

In a way, that's worse. As we pull up to the house, I can see several other cars parked in the drive, like they've all gathered for dinner. I know they must be excited to have Raylan home. He told me he hasn't been back to visit in over three years.

I feel like I shouldn't be here for this reunion. This is too personal, too intimate.

Too late now, though. The door flies open, and a short deeply tanned woman in jeans and a button-up shirt very like the one I'm wearing—though much more faded—comes hurrying out of the house. She's limping, one foot in a walking boot, but that's not really slowing her down that much.

She throws her arms around Raylan and squeezes him tight. She only comes up to his chest in height, but she looks strong and fit, her graying hair pulled back in a sensible low ponytail. Her nails are cut short and unpolished, and her small hands look highly capable as she grabs Raylan's arms and pulls back to look up into his face. I can see that her eyes are just as bright a blue as her son's.

"You look skinny," she says, and she laughs.

Raylan isn't skinny in the slightest. He's broad and muscular. But as his brother comes out of the house, I can see how Raylan would be considered skinny by comparison. His brother looks like a bear that learned to walk on its hind legs. He has a massive black beard and shoulder-length hair, and he's three inches taller than Raylan and much broader. I can see the muscles in his arms and shoulders beneath his flannel shirt, but his bulk also includes a generous belly.

"RAYLAN!" he roars.

He throws his arms around both Raylan and his mom, squeezing them tight until his mother shouts, "All right, don't break my back. Let me out of this hug!"

He grins, letting her go. "I didn't even see you there, Ma."

It is unbelievable that Raylan and his brother came out of this much smaller lady. Hard to imagine either of these men being little enough that she could hold them in her arms.

"You must be Riona," Celia says, coming over to shake my hand.

Just as I expected, her grip is firm and competent. I can feel the calluses on her palm.

"Thank you for letting us come stay with you," I say politely.

"This is Raylan's home," she says. "He's never a visitor here."

There's no rebuke in her tone. Just a simple statement of fact.

"And you're equally welcome," she says to me kindly.

Grady isn't content with a handshake. He pulls me against his broad chest for a hug. I usually would hate this—but despite his wild appearance, Grady smells nice, like soap and woodsmoke. And his grin shows slightly pointed incisors very like Raylan's. I find myself liking him immediately, despite the fact he's loud and overly familiar, things I usually hate.

Raylan's sister is the only one who hangs back in the entryway, watching us all silently.

She has long thick black hair like her brothers. But her complexion is darker—even deeper than her mother's. Her eyes are brown, not Raylan's blue. And she has none of her brothers' laid-back charm. If anything, she looks fierce and a little bit wild. Like she doesn't really want to be inside a house at all.

Raylan introduces us. "Riona, this is my little sister, Bo."

She watches me, unsmiling. Not holding out her hand to shake, her arms crossed firmly in front of her.

"Nice to meet you," I say anyway, giving her a respectful nod.

I'm not offended when people aren't friendly. Actually, it just mirrors how I feel inside. So I'm quite comfortable with it. Neither of us has to pretend.

"Come on in," Celia tells us. "Dinner's all ready."

The interior of the ranch house is open and airy, not crowded and cozy as I expected. All the furniture is arranged to focus on those massive windows and the sprawling view of the Boones' land.

Everything is made of natural materials, the bare wooden boards of the walls and ceiling and the worn floorboards. It all looks weathered and natural, though perfectly clean. The furniture likewise looks like someone made it by hand, including the huge farmhouse table on which Raylan's mother has spread out enough food to feed an army.

Grady's wife, Shelby, is already seated at the table with their two sons, who look to be about five and seven years of age.

"Hi!" she cries as we come in. She's pretty and petite, with her blond hair in a plait and freckles across her cheeks. Her boys are likewise freckled, though they both have the same black hair as the Boone siblings. They're staring hungrily at the food, impatient for the adults to sit down so they can eat.

"Sorry I didn't get up," Shelby says, pointing to her heavily pregnant belly. "It's a lot of effort to stand these days."

"Stay right where you are, and stay comfy," Raylan says, bending down to kiss her on the cheek.

She throws an arm around his neck and kisses him back with friendly affection.

"You almost missed your first niece!" she accuses him.

"I might still," Raylan says. "I don't know how long we're staying…"

Everyone at the table turns their eyes on me, like it's my decision. I should inform them that Raylan practically kidnapped me, driving me halfway here while I was sleeping. But I don't want to tell anyone my personal business, least of all why we came in the first place.

"I don't know either," I say.

"Don't worry." Celia shakes her head. "We know nobody can tell Raylan what to do. Least of all us."

There *is* a note of reproach now. I glance over at Raylan. It's clear that everybody at this table adores him. Yet he spends most of his time on the other side of the world. Why is that, exactly?

I'm not usually interested in people's family drama. But I'm curious in this particular instance. There's a lot more to Raylan than meets the eye. I want to know more about him, while simultaneously feeling that I really shouldn't get close to him in any way, shape, or form. It can only lead to trouble for both of us.

CHAPTER 14
RAYLAN

I DIDN'T EXPECT TO FEEL SO MUCH EMOTION BEING HOME AGAIN.

I thought I was over everything that happened in this house. Every convoluted tie I have to it.

But it's all rushing back much harder than I expected.

In a way, I'm glad Riona is here with me. It gives me something to focus on, and it keeps the conversation with my family from getting too personal. I know they want to demand I explain why I haven't come back to visit more often. But they can't attack me with that in front of Riona.

I am glad to see them.

My brother, Grady, never hides anything he's thinking or feeling. And my sister, Bo, thinks she keeps it all bottled in, but I can always read her face. And Mom…I know she missed me most of all.

Lawson and Tucker look like two completely different kids from the ones I met last time. Lawson was only a toddler, barely speaking, and Tucker was shy and sweet. Now they're both talking away a mile a minute to each other and fiercely fighting over the last roll, until Shelby separates them and makes them sit on either side of her.

Riona is sitting stiffly upright in her chair next to mine, obviously feeling like a fish out of water. Southern hospitality can be a lot. It's warm and welcoming but also overwhelming and smothering when you're not used to it.

She's a city girl through and through. I'm sure the endless green hills and the wooden furniture and the smell of horses and the massive platters of ribs, biscuits, and corn on the cob are all as bizarre and exotic to her as if I'd taken her to Shanghai and fed her fermented fish.

I like that, though. I like seeing Riona out of her element, not in control of the situation. I like seeing her sharp green eyes examining everyone at the table so she can adapt and overcome. Riona has a certain relentless drive to excel in any circumstance that I relate to. I'm the same.

At first she's trying to eat her ribs tidily, using her knife and fork, but soon she realizes that's impossible. She sees the rest of us—especially my brother—attacking the ribs like wild animals, and she eventually picks one up with both hands and takes a big bite.

"This is *really* good," she tells my mom. "I can see where Raylan learned to cook."

"He always picked it up the best." My mom nods. "He makes apple pie better than I do. While poor Grady could burn water."

"Bo's the worst cook," Grady says. He's just stating a fact, not deliberately trying to piss her off, but my sister shoots him a venomous look all the same.

"I don't like cooking," she says.

"Neither do I," Riona says.

Bo looks slightly mollified to have someone agree with her for once.

"What do you like doing?" she asks Riona.

"Working," Riona says promptly. Then she seems to realize that you're supposed to have hobbies as well, so she adds, "Running and swimming, too. And traveling."

I think she tacked that last one on because it's a good, safe answer.

"I was on the swim team at school," Bo says.

"I find it calming," Riona says. "Same with running."

"You ever ride a horse?" Bo asks.

"I've never sat on a horse," Riona admits. "Never even touched one."

We all can't help smiling at that because, around here, that would be like saying you've never ridden in a car in your life.

"Well," Bo says, "it's a lot like swimming in the way it clears your head and washes your stress away. So you might like it."

"That does sound nice," Riona says as if she's actually considering it.

That would be brave of her. Most adults who have never ridden a horse aren't keen to try it out all of a sudden.

Maybe she's just being polite.

To test her, I say, "Let's go for a ride in the morning."

Riona fixes me with her stubborn stare. She knows I'm challenging her. And I know she hates to back down from a challenge.

"I'd love that," she says without a flicker of anxiety.

It's hard not to grin. I fucking love provoking Riona, and I love making her do things just to spite me.

"Put her on Penny or Clover," my mom says in a warning tone. She's naming two of our sweetest and gentlest horses.

"Of course."

"So tell us about your job!" Shelby cheerfully says to Riona. "Raylan says you're a lawyer?"

"Yes." Riona nods.

"That must be so interesting! Making dramatic speeches and arguing in court…"

I chuckle a little at the idea of Riona making a dramatic speech.

Riona lifts her chin haughtily and says, without looking at me, "It's *very* interesting."

"What was your best case ever?" Shelby asks, in much the same way you'd ask about someone's favorite movie or TV show.

"Well…" Riona really considers the question. "This isn't the sort of work I usually do. But my paralegal was having trouble with an ex-boyfriend. He was stalking her. It was difficult to get the police to do anything about it because what he was doing wasn't explicitly threatening. He was leaving flowers for her everywhere she went. A rose on her car, another on the bench at her yoga studio, roses outside the door of her apartment, even sometimes at her mom's house. She'd be shopping at the grocery store and turn down the aisle to see a rose lying there. It scared her, obviously, because it showed he was following her everywhere she went. But when she called the cops, the responding officer told her she should be glad her boyfriend wanted to give her flowers.

"He'd do other things, too—call her phone and our office dozens of times a day from different numbers. But he wasn't leaving messages, so, again, hard to prove.

"Eventually, we got security footage from the grocery store and yoga studio to show he was following her around. And Lucy knew his Reddit username, so we took screenshots of some very... graphic...posts he had made about her. The posts were violent and threatening. That was enough to get a restraining order.

"He violated it twice. Spent sixty days in jail. And finally, he moved to Florida. So Lucy's been a lot more relaxed since then. And I've been happy about that."

Riona's cheeks flush pink. She's pleased by the memory of the win and the weight lifted off Lucy.

I would have expected her favorite case to be one where she accomplished something important for her family or earned a promotion.

Riona surprises me often. Like when she was singing in the car. I don't think I've ever seen her look so uninhibited and simply... happy. She has such a tough personality that it's easy to believe the impression she gives off deliberately: That she isn't vulnerable or emotional. That she can't be hurt. That she isn't human enough to take joy in simple, silly pleasures like singing along to an old song on the radio.

I like both sides of her. I like her grit and her drive. And I like that she does feel things, underneath. I think she feels them intensely, actually.

———————

Riona and I are both exhausted, so I get her set up in one of the guest rooms right after dinner.

I can see my sister glancing curiously down the hall from her room—checking to see if Riona and I are staying in the same guest room together. We're not—I'll be sleeping in my old room on the other end of the house like I always do.

My room is tiny and almost exactly the same as I left it when I joined the army at eighteen. Movie posters all over the walls and a tiny bed that I know my mother makes up fresh every couple of months, even though nobody's sleeping in it.

Riona gets the nicest guest room. It has a pretty view down to the paddocks behind the house and to the garden. It's got a queen-size bed and an en suite bathroom.

I'll be sharing the bathroom in the hall with Bo. It's packed with her stuff scattered all over the countertops and overflowing the drawers. That's fine with me—means I can steal her shampoo.

Bo just had her birthday, too. She's eighteen now. Same age I left. I wonder if she'll run off for a while like I did. She's always been the wildest one of all of us.

Grady never left, and he never would. He met Shelby in his tenth-grade English class. She's the only girl he was ever interested in. She wouldn't marry him until she came home from college, but he waited here patiently, driving up to visit her at the University of Tennessee every weekend. Now they live in the little house Grady built a mile south on the property. You could see it from the front porch, if not for all the trees in the way. It's close enough that they can drive over for dinner in two minutes but far enough to give them a little privacy.

Shelby's an equine veterinarian, so she works with our stock and the animals on neighboring farms. She's incredible at helping with difficult births—almost never loses a foal.

Grady handles most of the care of the animals and the land itself. He has ranch hands he brings on a few months at a time, but he's so industrious that he doesn't need them often. He told me he's been making handmade saddles in his spare time, though I don't know when that spare time might possibly take place.

Bo is good at training. Even though she's impatient with people, she never loses her temper with the horses.

My mother is the same way. She may be small, but there isn't a job she can't do on the ranch. We were all taught to do every part of the work. She taught us, and so did my father.

Looking out my bedroom window, I'm thinking of him most of all. I can see the cherry trees he planted all along the side of the house because he knew how much Mom loved the blossoms. The cherries were sour. He made them into tarts.

I can almost see him sitting on the wooden fence around the paddock: Long black hair. Sun-faded shirt. Jeans loose on his hips.

But I can only picture him from behind. I can't see his face.

CHAPTER 15
RIONA

I WAKE UP EARLY IN THE MORNING. EVEN EARLIER THAN I DO WHEN I have to get to the office.

It might be because I fell asleep at eight thirty the night before. Or it might be the birdsong right outside my window. It's not louder than city noise—I can usually hear traffic sounds or muffled thumps from the neighboring apartments in my building. But I'm used to that.

The birds are shrill and insistent. Not an unpleasant sound, but one that cuts right through my sleep because I haven't heard anything like that before. Not right outside my window, first thing in the morning.

The sunlight seems different, too. Brighter and more direct. Not filtered through buildings. Pale yellow.

There's a certain energy that comes from waking up in an unfamiliar place. I feel alert and curious, wanting to see more of everything in full daylight.

I slip out of bed and put on some of the clothes Bo lent me the night before. She's almost as tall as I am and close to the same build. There's definitely more muscle on her frame. The ranch is more strenuous than the gym, I guess.

I pull on Bo's jeans, comfortably worn. Her shirt is likewise soft and clean with that fresh laundry smell. I pull my hair into a ponytail.

I don't have any of my usual supplies—my four-hundred-dollar hair straightener is probably a lump of melted metal now, so I can't make my hair sleek and smooth like I usually do. In fact, in the humidity, it's heading past wavy into almost curly.

I hate when my hair gets unruly. It makes me feel powerless. If I can't control my own hair, then how can I control anything in my life?

It's frustrating not to have any of my things here—clothes, underwear, eyeliner. I keep thinking that if I go back to Chicago, it will all be there waiting for me, but I know that's not true. It all burned up. The only thing waiting is the enormously daunting task of filing an insurance claim for everything I lost. Some of which can never be replaced.

At least I didn't have anything truly priceless at my place— another reason to be glad grandma's ring is safe on Nessa's finger.

I don't regret telling Mom to give it to her.

At the time I was certain I'd never get married. I mean, I am still certain. And it always suited Nessa better. She loves things that are beautiful, vintage, and sentimental. Things that have history. That's why she loves living in Mikolaj's ancient mansion. I think the place is creepy as fuck, but she adores every inch of it.

What would my perfect house look like?

I thought it was my condo. Because it was a space that belonged only to me.

Now the idea of buying another place like the one I just lost…it doesn't excite me. In fact, it makes me feel a kind of empty dread that I don't quite understand. I loved that apartment—why don't I want another one? Am I afraid of being there alone? Afraid of someone pouring gasoline under my door again?

I don't think that's it. But I feel confused when I try to think about what I want in the next month or the next six months. Usually, my path forward is so clear. I know exactly what I want to accomplish.

All of a sudden, I'm strangely lost…

Finishing the messy ponytail, I brush my teeth and wash my face and then head downstairs.

Raylan's already sitting in the kitchen with a mug of coffee in front of him and another steaming mug in front of the empty chair next to him.

"Is that for me?" I ask him.

"Of course."

I sit down and take a sip. The coffee is rich and dark.

Raylan looks more himself than ever. His scruff is almost becoming a beard. There's something wild and animalistic about his hair, the way it springs up thick and black from his head, the way his dark brows look devilishly pointed above his bright blue eyes, and the way his facial hair outlines his lips and jaw like bold strokes of ink.

I can't imagine him without that hair. It's as much a part of him as the blue of his eyes, or his wolfish white teeth, or the shape of his hands resting on his blue-jeaned thighs. His hands are large, rough, calloused, and scarred in spots. A shiver runs up my spine, looking at them. One of his hands tenses slightly against his thigh, as if it can feel me looking.

I pull my eyes away, taking a sip of hot coffee so hastily that it burns my mouth.

"You want some breakfast, too?" Raylan asks.

I can hear that he's smiling even before I look at his face. "Did you already eat?"

"Yup," he says. "I've been up a while. There's oatmeal on the stove, though."

"I'm fine," I tell him.

"Well," he says, pushing back his chair from the table. "You want to come out for a ride still?"

"Of course."

I'm trying to sound confident, but I'm regretting what I committed to last night. I am curious what it's like to ride a horse, but I'm also realizing how totally out of control I'm going to be sitting on the back of an animal five times my size. Or more—fuck, I have no idea what a horse weighs.

I could ask Raylan; I'm sure he knows. But that will make me look even more ignorant.

All I can do is follow him out the back door, into the sprawling grounds behind the house.

I see a large vegetable garden and another garden full of fruit and flowers: raspberry canes, rosebushes, lilacs, and apple trees.

Then, beyond that, I see the stables, two barns, and several large paddocks.

Everything looks clean and well maintained. The barns look freshly painted, and the fields are nicely mowed. No trash or tools lie out of place anywhere in sight.

I can see two horses standing next to the stable, already saddled and bridled. One is huge and dark gray—so dark, he almost looks black. The other is a pretty, caramel-colored horse with a black mane and tail. Her coat is so smooth and shiny that she almost looks metallic.

"The big one is Bruce," Raylan says. "The other is Penny. She's a sweetheart—the nicest horse we've got. So you'll ride her, while I take Bruce. He's not as nice, but he gets mad if Penny goes anywhere without him."

I give Bruce a wide berth. He looks over at me with his large black eye, on which I can't see any white. He doesn't seem friendly, but he's not aggressive.

Penny, by contrast, eagerly puts her velvety nose into Raylan's palm, then rubs the side of her head against his shoulder, making a gentle snuffing sound.

"You miss me, Penny?" Raylan says in his low, husky voice.

I don't know why, but hearing the tone he uses with the horses has an effect on me, too. It sends little prickles down my arms.

"All right," Raylan says to me, calm and confident as ever. "Here's what we're gonna do. I'm gonna get you set up on Penny first... you're gonna put your left foot here in the stirrup, and you're gonna grab this little knob here on the saddle. It's called the pommel. And I'm gonna help you swing your right leg over the horse. I'll kinda help boost you."

Trying not to show how nervous I feel, I slip my left foot into the closest stirrup. Raylan is holding Penny steady, though I suspect she would have stood there patiently either way. Even though she radiates gentleness and she isn't nearly as massive as Bruce, she's still much taller than I expected. I don't quite see how I'm going to get my other leg over her back when that back is higher than my shoulder.

However, as I step up into the stirrup, Raylan puts his large hands around my waist and helps lift me. With his boost, my right leg swings easily over the saddle.

Now I'm sitting on Penny's back, and it's damned high up. She's wider than I expected—I'm lucky that I'm relatively tall and long-legged, otherwise I'd have a hard time getting my thighs around her. But the saddle is comfortable. It smells nicely of leather, and Penny smells nice, too—like clean hay and sunshine. Beneath that, a not-unpleasant scent of animal sweat.

Raylan passes me the reins and shows me how to grip them.

"Just sit tight for one second while I get up, too."

He hops on Bruce's massive back in one smooth motion that looks as easy as stepping up on a curb. I can see this is second nature to Raylan. He sits comfortably on the large dark horse, directing Bruce with the smallest motion of his hand on the reins or his heel against the horse's side.

"Give her a little tap with your heels like this," Raylan directs me. "Don't worry, you won't hurt her."

I give Penny a gentle tap, and obediently she starts walking forward. She's probably following Raylan and Bruce more than listening to me. Still, I'm glad to see that she doesn't take off galloping.

Even walking jolts me around more than I expected. Her shoulders and haunches roll beneath me in a way that isn't quite regular. It's hard to catch the rhythm so I don't bounce around in the saddle.

"You're doing great!" Raylan says.

I have to laugh at that. We've only taken a couple of steps. I'm not doing great at all.

Raylan stays close to me, Bruce just a little ahead of Penny so that it's clear who's leading. He keeps the pace slow to start. We amble across the meadow. The grass is a little higher here and full of tiny white butterflies that flutter upward in papery clouds as the horses swish through. The early-morning sunshine makes the dew sparkle. The grass smells sweet, and the air is fresher than any I've tasted before, with no tang of exhaust like in the city.

It's cool—maybe sixty degrees. But I don't feel chilly with the sun shining on my head and warm horseflesh beneath me.

After I've gotten used to walking, Raylan shows me how to trot. This is less comfortable—I have to stand more in the stirrups, and I feel ridiculous bouncing on the horse.

"It's actually more comfortable to gallop," Raylan tells me.

"I don't know about that..." I say hesitantly.

"Just grab the reins like this"—he shows me—"and lean forward more so you're closer down to her neck..."

He helps me get in a better position. Then he shouts, "HA!" and the horses take off.

We're out in an open field, bright green and velvety. The ground is soft underneath us, so I'd probably be all right if I fell. But I don't want to test that theory. I cling to Penny with my knees, leaning low over her neck, gripping tightly on the reins until they almost cut into my hands.

Her hooves thunder beneath me. Raylan is right—it is actually easier to follow the rhythm of her movement at a gallop. The wind streaming into my face is cool and clean and invigorating.

Bruce seems thrilled to be running. He's stretching his neck out low, his powerful legs churning, not even seeming to feel the weight of Raylan on his back. The two horses run in tandem, only a couple of feet between them.

It's beautiful, utterly beautiful. The vast stretches of the ranch seem endless all around us. The sky is like a huge inverted bowl, brilliantly blue like Raylan's eyes, almost cloudless. My heart is racing—partly from fear but also from exhilaration. My hair comes loose from the ponytail, and it streams out behind me like Penny's tail. I'm not gripping the reins so tightly anymore. I'm squeezing Penny with my legs, wanting her to run faster and faster. Wanting to feel exactly this, more and more.

Raylan's right beside me. He lets out a whoop, partly to urge on the horses and partly out of pure happiness. It's the most gorgeous day I've ever seen. These animals are powerful and brilliant. They love to run. They seem to know how pleasurable it is for us, too.

Raylan keeps looking over at me, making sure I'm comfortable and safe. Making sure I'm enjoying this as much as he is.

I've never felt anything like this. A lot of the things I do for pleasure—swimming, running—are meant to calm me down. Put me in a zen state.

This is the opposite. I feel enlightened. I feel alive. I feel terrified and exhilarated and thrilled, all at once. I can see every golden hair on Penny's smooth coat, every blade of bright green grass, every bird soaring overhead. I can smell the trees and the grass and even Raylan's skin more acutely than ever.

My muscles are aching from the strain of doing something so foreign to my usual activities. But it feels good. I feel powerful like the horse. Limitless like the open space. Wild like…like Raylan, I guess. He always seems like a force of nature. Like he could never belong to a city or a place. He's just himself at all times. Wherever he might be.

At last Raylan makes a clicking sound and pulls back on the reins. Bruce reluctantly obeys, coming to a trot and then a gentle walk. Penny matches his pace exactly. I can feel her rapid breathing and the heat of her body. I'm the same—panting and sweating. But exhilarated. Not wanting to slow down.

"Why are you stopping?"

"There's a stream up here," he says. "The horses can have a drink."

He leads us over to a thicket of trees. Sure enough, I can hear water running through. The trees grow in a double line on either side of a small river. It's like an oasis in the grass.

The day is heating up, the sun coming more directly overhead. I'm hot from the ride, as are the horses.

Raylan gets down from Bruce's back and helps me dismount. He takes off the horses' saddles and rubs them down. They roll around briefly on the grass, which alarms me for a moment as Bruce flops over abruptly, then rolls with his legs in the air like a dog would do. I laugh, amused to see such a massive animal behaving that way.

Penny does the same as soon as the saddle is off. It makes me happy to see them enjoying themselves after they carried us all this way and gave me an experience like I've never had before.

Once they've rolled around, they drink from the stream and then start cropping the soft grass, pulling up mouthfuls.

"Can they eat that?" I ask Raylan.

"Of course."

"I don't know anything about horses," I admit. "Or any animals, really."

"You rode so well," Raylan says. "I can't believe you've never done it before."

"I think it's easier on Penny."

"It is," Raylan acknowledges. "We've had a lot of good horses. But none as intuitive as she is."

Raylan is sweating, too. I can see the clear sweat running down his neck into the open collar of his shirt. I can smell his scent, warm like the grass, strong like the horses.

"Are you hot?" he asks me.

"Yes," I admit.

"The water's clean," he says, unbuttoning his shirt. He pulls it open and strips it off, so he's standing there bare chested in just his jeans.

I can't help staring. I've seen Raylan shirtless several times now, but this is the best he's ever looked—his muscles swollen from riding, his skin bright with sunshine and sweat, his waist looking impossibly tight compared to his broad shoulders and his worn blue jeans.

Raylan isn't as massive as Dante, but he's aesthetic in a completely different way. If Dante is a bull, then Raylan is a stallion. He looks fast as well as strong. Lean and capable.

He's exotic to me like no man I've met before. I've known gangsters and businessmen and high rollers of all kinds. But I've never known a man with Raylan's charm and authenticity. I've never known a man who's good at so many things. Nick was the best thoracic surgeon in the city, but he couldn't fix his kitchen sink to save his life. I think you could put any tool in the world into Raylan's hands, and he'd figure it out.

Maybe I'm losing it, after all the things I've been through the past few weeks. But I find myself staring at him in awe. Thinking I've never seen a more attractive man.

That's when he starts unbuttoning his jeans.

"W—what are you doing?" I stammer.

I never fucking stammer. I'm a lawyer. I'm endlessly articulate. But as Raylan unzips his jeans, I couldn't form a sentence to save my life.

"I'm gonna cool off in the water." His mouth quirks up in a half smile. "Care to join me?"

He drops his jeans. Then, keeping his brilliant blue eyes fixed on mine, he hooks his thumbs in his boxer shorts and pulls those down, too.

His cock hangs between his legs, thick and heavy and uncut. It's even darker than his tanned body, with trimmed black hair around it as thick as the hair on his head.

My heart is hammering against my ribs so fast that it feels like one continual beat. My mouth is salivating, and I can't stop staring at his cock. I'm flushed with heat, and I feel an aching, clenching sensation between my thighs.

I have never felt this response to a man's cock. I don't know what the fuck is happening to me.

Maybe it's because I've never seen one that big. Or that animalistic. It's making me respond like I'm in heat.

This is so unlike me. I'm never rabid. I'm never out of control.

I rip my eyes away from his body. I've seen Raylan nearly naked several times. But completely naked…that's a whole different thing. There's something about seeing him stripped down outdoors, in his natural element. It's vastly more powerful.

I'm in his space now. On his land. In his control.

As if sensing the same thing, Raylan says, in his deep commanding voice, "Take off your clothes."

He's never ordered me around before. Nobody orders me around.

My natural inclination is to toss my head and tell him to fuck off. That's what I'd usually do.

But then Raylan takes a step toward me, and more gently—in the same tone he used with Penny—he says, "Come on. Strip down. Get in the water. You'll like it."

And like he's fucking hypnotized me, I find my fingers unbuttoning my shirt. Baring my skin to the sunshine and the breeze. I take off my shirt and the bra underneath.

I can feel Raylan's eyes roving hungrily over my bare breasts. My breasts are small and extremely pale. The nipples are light pink, barely darker than my flesh.

I unzip my jeans and pull them down—my underwear, too.

I have a tuft of trimmed hair as vibrantly red as the hair on my head. Men go insane for it. They obsess over it.

I look at Raylan's face to see what he thinks of my body.

His eyes are so bright that they look as if they're on fire, like the blue flame under a gas burner. His lips are parted hungrily, and I see a glint of those sharp white teeth.

"Come on," he says huskily.

He steps into the stream to a place where the river widens and flattens, creating a small pool. The water is perfectly clear, so you can see the smooth stones beneath.

Raylan gives me his hand to help me down.

His touch is like an electric jolt. The energy runs up my arm, and I feel my nipples stiffening. Every step I take seems to make my pussy lips rub together. I've never been naked outside before. I've never been nude in front of a man like this—a man I'm not supposed to be dating or fucking.

The water is cold, but it doesn't jolt me nearly as much as Raylan's skin. I can barely feel the water on my flesh compared to how intensely I feel his eyes roaming over me.

I've never seen him look so ferocious. His warmth and humor have all burned away, replaced by an intensity I never would have guessed he possessed.

I sink into the stream, hoping the cold water will help cool my lust.

Raylan does the same. He splashes the clear water on his face and chest, washing himself clean of sweat. He dunks his head under and shakes the sparkling droplets out of his thick black hair.

I try not to stare at him. But every movement flexes the muscles on his broad frame. When he turns, I can't help but stare at his wide back and his tight round ass cheeks. When he rinses his hair, his biceps bulge like softballs, and I can see the narrow bands of muscle running across his ribs and down his torso.

And then there's that heavy cock that swings and hits his thigh with an audible *thwap*. It doesn't shrink in the cold water. In fact, when Raylan runs his eyes down my body again, I think it's swelling with arousal.

I can feel the cool water between my thighs. The flowing stream runs between my pussy lips. No matter how I try to shift to stop the stimulation, it only becomes more intense. I can feel the flush on my pale skin. I know Raylan can see it, too. He can see my rock-hard nipples and my flaming-red face.

I tell myself we're just skinny-dipping.

I tell myself that nothing is going to happen.

Raylan is a professional. He's my bodyguard. That's all. That's it. He knows I don't want anything else…

But, of course, that's a fucking lie.

I want *him*. I want him right now. It's all over my face. I can't hide it.

"Are you still dating Nick?" Raylan asks me bluntly. His voice is low and intent. His eyes burn into mine.

"I…I…"

That fucking stammering again. I should lie and tell him we're still together.

Raylan is tempting in a way that terrifies me. I've never been so aroused by a man. I've never felt this desperate.

I'm used to being pursued. I'm used to having the upper hand.

I have no advantage with Raylan. If I let go right now, if I give in to this desire, I'll be completely out of control. I'll be in totally uncharted territory. I don't understand my desire for him or how I feel about him as a man. Sometimes he drives me insane. And sometimes I admire him, against my will. None of that is normal for me. None of it is comfortable.

He scares me. My only protection is pretending I don't want this. Pretending I'm committed to another man.

But I can't lie to Raylan. He's too honest, too open. And too damned perceptive. He'll know if I lie. It's pointless.

"I broke up with him."

"Why didn't you tell me?" Raylan growls.

"I wanted you to think I was taken," I confess.

What the fuck am I doing? Why am I admitting that?

"Why?" Raylan says.

I lick my lips, tasting the cool, clear river. "You scare me."

I've never admitted to being intimidated. I've never admitted to being afraid, period.

"This…scares me," I say, gesturing between the two of us.

Raylan steps closer to me, closing the gap between us. I can almost hear his heart pounding as fast as mine is. I'm sure I would hear it, if not for the noise of the running water.

He says, "I told myself I wouldn't kiss you again without your permission."

I swallow hard.

"But that was a stupid fucking promise." He grabs my face between his hands, and he kisses me hard, harder even than he did in the gym. His bare burning-hot chest presses against mine. His tongue thrusts into my mouth. His beard scratches my face.

I kiss him back, my hands thrust into his thick black hair. His hair feels hot from the sun, thick and coarse and alive like animal fur. The scent of his skin is sharp and wild.

He lifts me and throws me on the riverbank, in the sun-warmed grass. Then he climbs on top of me and kisses me even harder, grinding his naked body against mine. I feel his cock standing straight up now, harder than a poker.

His lips devour mine, and then they run hungrily down my neck, down to my breasts. He sucks and nibbles on my nipples, making me moan and arch my back. Meanwhile he's touching between my thighs, stroking my pussy lightly at first, then a little harder as his fingers become slick and wet.

I'm soaking wet. Wetter than I've ever been before. It started the moment I saw him naked, and it only got worse. The river couldn't wash it away. My pussy is swollen and aching, throbbing at his touch.

I grind against his hand. I'm rabid for him. Ravenous.

He reaches up with his other hand to caress my face, and I seize his fingers between my teeth and bite them, then suck on his index and middle finger, taking them all the way into my mouth.

I've never behaved like this in my life.

Quite honestly, I'm a selfish lover, doing only what I personally like. I don't get down on my knees and suck men's cocks—that would be degrading. I let them worship me, but I don't respond in kind.

With Raylan, I have no pride. He's unleashed a hunger in me that I never knew before. I'm fucking wild for him. I would do anything for him right now. I want to taste him, touch him, lick him absolutely everywhere. I want him like I've never wanted anything before.

I want that cock. I want it inside me right now—anywhere, anyway.

I grab Raylan's cock in my hand. It's so thick that my fingers don't close all the way around the shaft. It feels like it's two hundred degrees of burning heat. I feel it throbbing like a live thing.

I shimmy down in the grass so I can close my mouth over the head.

I'm literally salivating. I want to taste Raylan. I need it.

I close my mouth around his cock, and I start sucking. Immediately, my mouth is flooded with thin warm precome. It tastes fucking delicious. I'm ravenously hungry from skipping breakfast and riding around all morning. That precome tastes like the most satisfying thing I've ever had in my mouth. It's salty and rich, and it tastes like Raylan's skin and sweat. It's like a drug—the more I get, the more I want.

I attack his cock with my mouth, sliding my tongue up and down the shaft, sucking hard on the head. I use both my hands, alternating between sucking him off and taking his balls in my mouth while I slide my hands up and down his slippery shaft.

This is the most enthusiastic blow job I've ever given. It's the most I've ever enjoyed oral sex. Raylan is groaning, his hands thrust in my hair. His powerful hips are pumping toward my face, and that

huge, thick head of his cock is banging against the back of my throat. It's sloppy and wet and primal, and the fact it's happening outdoors in a field makes it all the more animalistic.

Raylan grabs my hips and twists me around so we're facing opposite directions. Now I'm on top of him, with my pussy over his face. He pushes my thighs apart and buries his face in my cunt.

I always thought sixty-nines were stupid. Now, for the first time, I understand the point. When you're completely lost in oral sex, you just want more, more, more. I want more of his taste and scent. And more of our bodies grinding and touching.

Raylan is eating my pussy like a ten-course dinner. He's licking and fingering and shoving his tongue inside me. It feels fucking fantastic. And at the same time, my mouth is full of his cock and the taste of his precome that comes in spurt after spurt, like a reward for sucking him off just the way he likes.

Sucking his cock upside down is more difficult, but the angle helps his cock slide even farther down my throat. I relax my jaw and try to take as much of it as I can. I can't bob my head up and down as much, but it doesn't matter because he's thrusting his hips and doing a lot of the work himself.

Which is good because I can barely concentrate. I'm lost in the insanely pleasurable sensation of his tongue lapping at my clit and his fingers thrusting in and out of me. His fingers penetrate my pussy at the same time as his cock thrusts in my throat. He's stimulating me orally as well as vaginally. The dual sensation is wildly intense. I never knew a blow job could feel good for me, too. I never knew my lips and tongue could be so sensitive.

Our bodies are pressed tightly together, my thighs wrapped around his face and his cock skewering my throat. I can feel Raylan pumping even harder, getting closer to the edge.

I'm close, too. The orgasm building inside me is totally out of my control. I'm grinding on his face, squeezing my thighs, but Raylan is the one teasing the climax out of my body. It's his fingers rubbing on the perfect spot inside me and his tongue pressing against just the right place on my clit.

The pleasure is thrumming through my whole body. I feel it pulsing down my legs and arms, all the way to my fingers and toes. My whole frame is vibrating with one long, endless sensation.

I moan around Raylan's cock. I cry out, my mouth still stuffed full.

I'm coming harder than I've ever come in my life, with an orgasm that twists my body in knots.

And while I'm coming, Raylan is, too, deep down my throat. His cock is twitching and pulsing, unleashing thick white come, a torrent of it. I usually never swallow, but right now I have no choice. His cock is shoved too deep in my throat to pull back.

And I love it. I want him to come as hard as I'm coming. I want it to feel as good for him as it does for me.

I feel his thick load pulsing into my throat. I'm choking and gagging on it, and I don't give a fuck. Because I'm still coming, too, all over his tongue.

It goes on and on and on. Time stretches out. The pleasure stretches and increases and stretches again.

Then, finally, it's over.

Raylan takes his cock out of my mouth, and I roll limply onto my back, bright flashes popping behind my closed eyelids.

Raylan rolls on top of me, kissing me. I can taste my pussy on his lips, and I'm sure he can taste his come in my mouth. This is totally unsanitary—something that would disgust me usually. But I do not give one single fuck. I'm still in a state of blissful eroticism, where everything is sexy to me and nothing seems wrong.

"Oh. My. Fucking. God," I moan.

Raylan says, "I've been wanting to do that for a long time."

CHAPTER 16
RAYLAN

My head is buzzing on the ride back to the house.

That was…so much more than I expected.

I knew that Riona had a whole lot of something bottled up inside her. Anger, or determination, or something…

But I had no idea she'd be so fucking wild.

She was raw and primal. Ten times sexier than I expected.

And that body…fucking hell.

I've never seen skin so creamy and flawless or a pussy that fucking perfect. Standing in the water with her red hair all wild and wavy around her shoulders, she looked like Aphrodite. Like a goddess made flesh for the very first time.

And like a goddess, she had a kind of terrifying intensity. Her skin was paler than normal from the cold water. Next to that, her red hair and green eyes looked as vivid as a venomous snake. Maybe more Medusa than Aphrodite.

I would have been intimidated if I weren't so fucking aroused.

I had to splash myself with the cold water to keep my cock only semihard. Because Riona naked was the most gorgeous thing I'd ever laid eyes on.

I got my erection tamped down. Then I looked over at her and saw those green eyes fixed on my cock, and I knew she was almost as aroused as I was. I knew I had to have her.

I clarified the little matter of the ex-boyfriend—for Riona's benefit, not because I give a fuck about the surgeon. I knew from the second I met him that he isn't the right man for her. He doesn't have a fraction of the strength it takes to tame a woman like Riona. To grab hold of her and force her to respect you.

Riona's a fighter. She's driven to lock horns with any man who tries to assert his power over her. She won't be taken gently.

I suspected that she was tired of Nick for a while and only dragging things out because he was a useful shield between her and me. A way to make me keep my distance.

Hearing that she had already broken up with him told me everything I needed to know. I knew Riona wanted me, whether she'd admitted it to herself or not.

So I grabbed her and kissed her and buried my face in that sweet shell-pink pussy with its tuft of wild red hair. It was intoxicating. She tasted sweet and spicy, like cinnamon. I could feel her responding to me immediately, her body betraying any restraint she tried to maintain.

And the way she sucked my cock...good god, it was like she was starving. Like she needed my come to live. I never would have thought she'd let go like that. I thought it might take months to dig down to that kind of ferocity. But it was waiting right below the surface. Dying to be released.

Now I want to be close to Riona. I want to grab Penny's reins and pull her over so I can rest my hand on Riona's thigh and tell her she's fucking gorgeous, and sexy, and brilliant, and stubborn. That she drives me insane, and I can't get enough of her.

But I know I can't do that. Riona will spook.

Already she's silent and pale, deliberately not looking over at me. Mulling over what just happened between us.

I've spent every minute of the past two weeks with her. I've gotten to know this woman better than she'd like to admit. I know that it terrifies her to lose control. It terrifies her that I've seen through her armor, seen the actual person beneath.

Now that she's been exposed to me, she wants to clam up again. She wants to rebuild those walls.

That's fine…I'll let her think that it's working. That she's still in control of this thing between us.

And then, when the moment is right…I'm going to capture her again. I'm going to find her most vulnerable places, the cracks in her armor, and I'm going to split it wide open. I'm going to grab hold of her—stripped down, raw, and genuine. And I'm going to force her to admit what she actually likes.

But not just yet. Right now, I need to pull back and give her space. Let her get comfortable again. Let her think she has control.

Meanwhile, I'm just biding my time.

We ride back the way we came, slower on the way back because I'm sure Riona is sore from riding. This is an unfamiliar exercise to her, unfamiliar motion.

I was surprised by how well she did.

I guess I shouldn't have been—she's smart and competitive. Quick to catch on to something new. Wise enough to respect the horses.

When we get back to the house, I see Grady in the round training ring, chasing a brand-new horse. It's an Appaloosa, probably two years old. Its front half is a smooth glossy black, while its back is white with dappled black spots, like a rug thrown over its hindquarters. It's a beautiful animal, with long legs and a well-shaped head. But I can tell immediately that it's wild and bad-tempered and totally unbroken. It bites and snaps at Grady when he tries to get near it. He hasn't gotten the bridle over its head.

I halt the horses a good way back—I don't want Bruce getting riled up by the sight of the other horse and its fury. Grady tries again, unsuccessfully, to fit the halter over its head.

I lead Bruce and Penny the long way around to the stable, where I show Riona how to remove their saddles again, then how to feed and water and rub them down. She seems genuinely interested in that, not jumping off and wandering away the moment the ride is done like so many tourists do after their first ride.

Riona is highly attentive to Penny, brushing her coat and patting her affectionately. "She's such a good horse…"

"She is." I nod. "So's Bruce, but you have to remind him of that."

I give Bruce a good scratch on the shoulders like he likes and feed him a couple of carrots. Penny gets apples since they're her favorite.

"What are they doing to that horse in the pen?" Riona asks.

"Looks like Grady's trying to break it."

"What does that mean?"

"You gotta teach a horse how to accept a rider. That one looks like it's never had a person on its back."

Riona goes to the doorway of the stable so she can watch.

She stands motionless, her head slightly tilted, watching Grady try again and again to slip the bridle over the horse's head. It snaps and bites at him or slips its head away at the last minute, forcing Grady to swing the horse around again, holding tight to its mane.

"How long does it take?" Riona asks.

"Could be a couple of hours. Could be all day." I chuckle. "Could be forever if Grady doesn't calm that horse down a little."

Grady is dogged and tenacious, but he doesn't always know how to connect with a horse. He treats each one the same. And no horse is the same.

Once Penny and Bruce are comfortably eating, I walk over to the ring with Riona.

The Appaloosa is highly agitated, trying to rear up but prevented from doing so by Grady's grasp on its mane. The whites of its eyes show as it tries to jerk its head away from Grady's grip.

"Where'd you get that one?" I ask him.

"From the Fosters. Name's Star. She's been running wild with her mother and brother on their land 'cause Allan Foster broke his leg and hasn't had a chance to do shit all with her. Jemma Foster sold her to me cheap 'cause she says she's too vicious to train."

As he's talking, the horse rips its mane free with one sharp toss and starts galloping around the pen. Grady has to jump up on the rail to keep from being trampled as Star circles 'round again.

"Fucking hell," Grady shouts, barely pulling his legs up in time.

"You want some help?"

"You think you're still the horse whisperer when you barely seen one in three years?" Grady laughs.

"I think I remember 'em all right." I glance over at Riona. "You okay if I take over here for a bit?"

I know I don't have to follow her around every minute while we're on the ranch. We're in the middle of nowhere, fenced off from the world. She's safe here.

But it feels strange to leave her alone for any amount of time after we've been attached at the hip for so long.

"Go ahead," she says. "Your sister told me I can borrow her laptop. If your Internet is decent, I can probably log in to my Google Docs and get some work done from here."

Riona heads back toward the house. I feel a strange pull to follow her.

But Star is still galloping around the pen, snorting furiously, and Grady already looks hot and flustered with the job barely begun.

I slap him on the shoulder. "Go ahead and grab some water. I got this."

I drop into the pen, standing in the center so the horse can get used to me. I stay still and relaxed, holding up my hands and saying, "Whoa. Calm down now," in a low comforting tone.

Eventually Star drops to a trot, though she's still skittering around me, eyeing me warily.

"Relax. Relax," I say.

As she starts walking, I take hold of her mane, but gently. I let her keep moving, walking around me, giving her the freedom to lift and shake her head as she likes.

When she's calmed a little, I touch her face and ears and run my hand down her neck so she gets used to being touched around the head.

"That's not so bad," I say, patting her cheek.

She's still not exactly comfortable with me. But she's calmed down a bit.

I hold the bridle close to her face so she can see and smell the rope. She shies away again, and I wait patiently until she's accustomed to the pale blue rope and the texture against her cheek.

After a long while, I slip it over her head.

She doesn't like that one bit. She tries to rear up, whinnying, but I gently hold her down, patting her head, rubbing her neck, and speaking softly to her.

Grady comes back out of the house, having gotten a drink and probably some food, too. "How's it goin'?"

Just from the sound of his voice, Star rears up again and yanks at the bridle, trying to pull away from me.

"Stay back over there," I say to Grady, though using my softest tone so it doesn't startle Star. "You're ugly, and you're scaring her."

"I've heard that too many times." Grady grins. He stays back out of sight of Star.

I start resting my hand on the horse's back. Just getting her used to weight and pressure.

She's never had a rider on her back, not for a second. She's never carried anything, not even a saddle.

Eventually I press a little harder on her back. Letting her feel a small amount of weight.

She keeps circling around me, held in place by my hand on her bridle. I start to lean on her back and even pull myself up for a second or two. She startles and skitters away the first couple of times I do it, but eventually the pauses between feeling my weight against her back and her jerking away become longer and more spread out.

I like to break horses bareback, without a saddle. They hate the feeling of the saddle when they're not used to it. It's more tolerable to them to feel a person alone, at least to start with.

It's better for me, too. I can feel the horse's heartbeat thundering, feel how overheated it's getting.

So when I finally pull myself all the way up onto Star's back, I do it with just the bridle and rope, nothing else. No bit in her mouth. Trying to make it as pleasant as possible.

Still, she bolts and starts running. She's trying to throw me off, though she's not quite enraged enough to buck or roll. She thinks she can sprint away from me if she runs fast enough.

I'm not trying to hold her back. Actually, it's the opposite—I lean low across her neck, and I whisper in her ear, urging her on faster and faster.

We gallop around and around the pen. When she starts to slacken her pace, I squeeze my knees against her sides and urge her to run harder. She's galloping full out, running faster than she probably ever has before. She was loose on the Fosters' land, galloping around wherever she pleased. But she had no predators, nothing chasing her. She's never run flat out with all her might.

Soon I can feel her heart thundering and her pace slacking again.

Horses can only gallop full out for a couple of miles. They can go a long way in a day. But they're not tireless.

In fact, the animal with the greatest endurance is a human. You could run a horse into the ground if you had unlimited time and distance to chase it. We're not as fast as them or as strong. But there's no creature more tenacious than we are.

Star will tire before I do. I knew that before we started. And that's why I already knew the outcome of this struggle.

There was no battle between Star and me. I already knew who would win.

That's why I approached her with gentleness and patience. I wasn't afraid of her or afraid she might beat me.

I only had to show her I'm not her enemy, not her adversary.

I ride Star at top speed until she tires. Then I let her canter around and around the pen. Finally, she drops to a trot and then a walk. She's tired—not beaten and broken down. Just exhausted enough to be at peace with me on her back.

CHAPTER 17
RIONA

RAYLAN IS OUT IN THAT PEN FOR HOURS.

I find myself drawn back to the window again and again to watch him.

I have Bo's laptop, and I was able to access my personal files. Not the ones for all of Griffin, Briar, Weiss because they don't allow remote access from unknown IP addresses. But anything I scanned in myself, I can still open, read, and edit.

So there should be plenty for me to do. Plenty to hold my attention.

Instead, I'm back at the kitchen window, watching Raylan gallop around and around that pen with infinite patience.

He doesn't seem to be trying to calm the horse. Actually, it looks like he's urging it to run faster. I guess that tires it out sooner.

I don't know why I feel so agitated watching him.

I'm impressed by his patience and by his skill in riding the horse bareback, balancing flawlessly, barely even shifting when the horse abruptly startles or turns, trying to throw him off.

And yet…I feel a sort of anxiousness, too. Almost an antipathy toward Raylan. I look at that beautiful wild horse, and I almost want it to fling him off so it can kick its way out of the pen and go thundering across the field again.

That's an immature impulse, I know.

It's just a horse. It was bred and raised for work.

But there's a stubbornness in me, a contentiousness, that wants to see that horse rebel. I hate to see it broken.

I force myself to sit at the kitchen table again, to return to the endless rows of data in my purchase-agreement spreadsheet. There are a couple of numbers that aren't adding up in the deposit column, and I'm trying to figure out which figures are causing the discrepancy.

I've always been good at spotting patterns, especially in numbers. I wouldn't like to admit this out loud, but I have a burning passion for Excel spreadsheets. I love the formulas, the neat tables of data, the way the cells can be manipulated to provide answers to all sorts of questions.

Finally, I spot the issue disrupting my perfect structure.

There are two properties with almost the same name—one is listed as Benloch Commercial Lot 29 and the other as Benloch Commercial Lt 29. At first I think it's just a typo, but then I see there really is a purchase agreement for both and two separate wire transfers for the payments.

It's odd. We had to purchase almost a hundred properties for the South Shore development. Still, I'm surprised two had such similar names. Especially with a numerical signifier at the end. I'll have to get the original documents from the office to see if this is accurate.

I send a quick email to Lucy asking her to scan the documents and send them to me.

With that done, I find myself wandering back to the window again to check on Raylan's progress.

The horse has finally slowed its gallop. It's trotting around the pen now, clearly exhausted. It still holds its head high, though. And I see Raylan is only gripping the rope loosely, letting the horse think it has control of its own motion.

It doesn't, though. It's trapped in that pen. And it couldn't throw Raylan off no matter how hard it tried. It's broken, whether it knows it or not.

I shift, pressing my hand into the small of my back. I'm going to be sore tomorrow when I wake up. All that riding around today will catch up with me.

Bo comes into the kitchen. She's wearing an oversize man's shirt—probably a hand-me-down from Raylan or Grady. Her black hair is in a loose plait. I can't help noticing how beautiful she is. She has Raylan's striking wolfish features, but in feminine form. Her eyes are narrow and slightly tilted up at the outer corners, her lips fuller.

"That laptop work for you?" she asks.

"It did. Thank you."

She acknowledges the thanks with a nod. "You going to the dance tonight?"

She has an abrupt way of speaking, without any of Raylan's laid-back charm. She seems impatient, like the rest of the world is moving too slowly for her.

I understand that. I often feel like people are thinking and speaking at half speed. It's a constant struggle to maintain the appearance of patience.

"I don't know," I say. "This is the first I'm hearing about it."

"You can borrow clothes," Bo tells me. "I know you don't have any. Raylan said your whole apartment burned up."

There's a hint of sympathy in her tone. Not much, but enough to prove Bo isn't totally unfeeling. She's certainly been generous with her clothes and toiletries. I get the impression she doesn't give a shit about "stuff," but I still appreciate it. It's hard for me to accept kindness. I wouldn't be able to stand it if she made a big deal out of the favor.

"Thank you," I say again. "I know this whole thing is weird. Us showing up here."

Bo shrugs. "Raylan likes trouble. He always has."

"Is that why he didn't stay here? It wasn't enough adventure for him?"

Bo narrows her eyes at me, looking me up and down like she's analyzing the motive behind my question. "He had his reasons for leaving," she says at last. Then she turns on her heel and leaves the kitchen.

I feel like I offended her, but I have no idea how. Or maybe she wasn't offended—she just didn't want to leave space for any more questions.

I look out the window again, my eyes irresistibly drawn back to Raylan.

I feel a pull toward him unlike anything I've experienced before.

I don't know what the fuck happened between us down by the river. I've never felt anything like that. I was completely out of control. And usually I hate that sensation. Hate it more than anything.

But in this particular instance…

It was almost worth the trade. Giving up my sense of security and dignity in return for the most transcendent sexual experience of my life.

I've never felt pleasure like that.

I can feel my face flaming just remembering it.

I don't understand how it happened. I've never been so wildly attracted to someone. Never felt my body respond like that…

And now I want to shut it off again. I want to turn it off like a faucet because I don't know where this will take me. I don't know what will happen if I give in to that impulse again.

I want to leave and go back to Chicago.

I'm overwhelmed by Raylan's ranch, his family, his personal life. Overwhelmed by seeing him here in his element where he's most comfortable, most himself.

He's at his most powerful here, and I'm at my most confused and off-kilter. I don't have any of the trappings of my normal life—my clothes, my routine, my career, my own family. Those are the core elements of my identity. Who am I, stripped down to nothing and brought to this strange place?

Raylan and I missed lunch when we were riding around all

morning. I made myself a sandwich while I was working, but he stayed out in the pen, probably getting hungrier by the minute.

He spends so long with the horse that he almost misses dinner, too.

I'm alone in the kitchen with Celia when she starts the evening meal. I'm working away on Bo's laptop, but I feel guilty watching her peel potatoes and chop carrots, knowing I'll be eating the food when it's finished. Especially considering she's doing all this work with a clunky boot on her right foot.

"Can I help?"

"No need," she says. "You're already working."

Her tone is genuine—she's not trying to nudge me into offering again. But I close the laptop and stand anyway, feeling like I should contribute since I'm staying in her house, wearing her daughter's clothes, and eating her food.

"I don't know what the hell I'm doing," I tell her honestly. "But I'd like to help."

"Do onions make you cry?"

"I don't know."

"Try cutting these up."

She hands me a couple of yellow onions, plus a worn cutting board and a large chef's knife that has been sharpened so many times, the blade is honed to fragile thinness.

I take the counter space next to her and try cutting and peeling the onions.

I can tell I'm wasting too much—it's hard to get the skin off without taking a ring or two off the onion as well. Then my pieces are all different shapes and sizes, not uniform like when I've seen Raylan do this. I try to use the grip on the knife that he showed me, and the rocking motion. That helps a little.

The onions are stinging the hell out of my eyes. I blink hard, sending tears running down my cheeks. I swipe my eyes with the back of my hand, but that only makes it worse.

"Some people seem immune to onions," Celia says. "Not me, that's for sure."

"My pieces are wonky," I point out.

"Doesn't matter. They'll taste the same regardless."

Celia uses the knife to scrape the onions into a cast-iron fry pan already sizzling with butter. She sautés carrot, onion, and celery pieces all together, filling the kitchen with their savory scent.

"How did you like riding this morning?" Celia asks.

For a second, I can feel myself blushing as if Celia might guess what happened at the river. Then I remember nobody knows that— all they saw was me trying out a horse for the very first time. So I say truthfully, "It was much better than I expected. Really incredible, actually."

"Most people are scared of horses if they haven't ridden before."

"I was scared at first," I admit. "I would have been more afraid if I were on Bruce instead of Penny."

Celia looks over at me, her blue eyes searching my face.

"I can see why Raylan likes you," she says. "You're honest. That's important to him. He can't stand being lied to."

"We don't… We're not…" I want to tell Celia that we're not dating, but I can't exactly say there's nothing between us.

"I know, I know," she says, stirring the contents of the fry pan. "He told me you weren't together. But he's never brought a girl home before."

Despite the fact I don't want Celia getting the wrong idea, her statement gives me a warm flush of pleasure. I would have been jealous at the thought of Raylan bringing another woman here, introducing her to his family, taking her on horseback for the first time. Even though I don't particularly want the distinction, I'm enjoying it anyway. Knowing this is all as new to him as it is to me.

"Here, cut this up in bite-size pieces," Celia instructs, handing over some cold chicken out of the fridge.

While I'm working on that, she flours the countertop and rolls out a large lump of pastry. She lines two pie pans with the dough while also making some kind of white sauce on the stove that smells buttery and delicious.

"What will this be?" I ask.

"Chicken pot pie."

I've never tried that before. My expression betrays me. Celia laughs, saying, "Don't worry, it's good."

"I'm sure it is," I say hastily. "I'm not picky."

As I watch her assemble the pies with the chopped chicken, the sautéed vegetables, and the gravy-like sauce, it reminds me of an Irish dish.

"My family makes something like this," I tell her. "Chicken and dumplings."

"Sure," Celia says. "That's similar."

She shows me how to top the pie pans with another circle of pastry, then crimp the edges to seal the top and bottom of the pie. Then she makes little slashes across the top of each pie.

"What does that do?"

"Lets the steam out." She slides the pies into the oven. "There. Those'll be done in an hour."

I know I should probably use that time to shower and change my clothes, but I find myself lingering in the kitchen, which is warm and cozy and smells like sage and browned butter. I want to talk to Celia for longer.

So I say, "Raylan's so good with horses."

"One of the best I've seen," Celia agrees. She wipes a strand of hair away from her forehead with the back of her flour-dusted hand, giving me a little smile. "And I'm not just saying that because he's my son."

I hesitate, hoping I'm not about to offend her.

"Why did he enlist? He seems to love it here…"

Celia sighs. "I think…I think he felt he had to leave. For a while, at least."

I frown, not understanding.

"Has Raylan told you anything about his father?" Celia asks me.

"No." I shake my head. "Nothing at all." An omission I noticed immediately since he talked openly about all the rest of his family.

Celia hesitates for a moment, as if she's deciding how much to tell me. I've seen this before in depositions—the human desire to share information, battling the endless unknowable consequences of our own words. I can see she wants to explain but doesn't want to anger Raylan.

At last, she says, "I didn't grow up in a house like this—big and beautiful with every amenity. I was the kind of dirt poor you only see in the South. I had one pair of shoes, and when they got too small for me, I slit the front of them so my toes could poke out. I had seven brothers and sisters. I was the oldest, so most of the care for them fell on my shoulders. Getting food for them was a constant battle. I'd get a loaf of Wonder Bread and make margarine and brown sugar sandwiches, if we had margarine or brown sugar. And then the whole loaf was gone, and I had to find something else."

She presses her lips together as if wincing from the memory of hunger pains. And I realize the massive meals she cooks that fill the table might stem from a long-ago desperate desire to feed the people she loved with as much delicious food as they could stomach.

"I left school in the tenth grade, and I got a job. I was working as a waitress at a roadside bar. I wasn't supposed to be serving drinks—I wasn't anything close to twenty-one. But the owners knew my situation, and they needed the help.

"It was rough. I know things look rugged around here now, but it's nothing to how it was thirty years ago. Silver Run was the kind of place where people didn't stick their noses in other people's business. Which is why nobody did anything about the fact my parents were too high to feed or clothe their kids or make sure any of us attended school. And if something did happen that crossed a line—people were more likely to take the law into their own hands than to call the sheriff."

I nod slowly. I know exactly how that works. In the Irish Mafia, it's the same—each family runs their own affairs. And when there's a conflict, you take it to one of the head bosses. Never to the police or to any other outsider.

"So," Celia continues, "I served drinks and food to all types. Ranchers and truck drivers, farmers and line workers. Most of the men were local and reasonably respectful to me. They'd flirt or tease or maybe give me a little slap on the ass now and then. But I was relatively safe and making enough money that my next two siblings down the line could stay in school and, hopefully, graduate. Then, one night, somebody I'd never seen before came in to eat."

A shiver runs down her frame, like a cold breeze just blew on the back of her neck.

"He was about forty years old, tall and handsome. He wasn't dressed like the men I usually saw. He had on a proper suit, and his hair was freshly cut. What I noticed most of all was how clean he was. Not a speck of dirt on his shoes or trousers. And his fingernails were spotless. I'd hardly ever seen a grown man look like that. He wasn't tanned either. His face and neck and hands were pale like they'd never seen the sun. So he caught my eye at once.

"I went over to his table. He was sitting with two other men I didn't recognize, though they had on the usual Wranglers and button-ups. And they were normal-looking men. They didn't draw the eye the way Ellis did.

"That was his name—he introduced himself as soon as I came to take his order. He had a soft, cultured voice. A Northern accent that made him sound exotic to me then. He said, 'I'm Ellis Burr. What's your name?' so politely and with such genuine interest.

"I think I was blushing redder than a stop sign. I don't even know if I managed to say my name properly. He ordered a Grey Goose martini, which I also thought was unutterably fancy. His friends got whiskey. And he asked me what I wanted to drink.

"I said, 'I can't drink. I'm only sixteen.' And he smiled, showing the most white and perfect teeth I'd ever seen. I should have realized then what a warning that smile was, but when you're a teenager, you don't realize you're just a child. You don't realize how different adults are from you. You think you're one of them—or close to it. You don't know that in innocence and vulnerability, you're like a kitten padding around next to a tiger."

I feel a sick sense of dread at where this story is going, but I don't want to interrupt Celia, not even to encourage her. I've learned that when someone is in the flow of a narrative, the worst thing you can do is derail them. Not if you want to learn something.

"He asked me a few more questions about myself as I brought their drinks and then their food. I didn't dare ask anything about him. I found out later, from the regulars, that he was a big shot at a building-materials company in Knoxville. He'd just built some big estate thirty miles outside Silver Run.

"Ellis paid the bill for the table, which came to maybe sixty dollars. And he laid three crisp, new hundred-dollar bills on the table.

"If he would have been there when I picked them up, I would have said, 'That's too much,' and refused to take it. But the men had already left. So I just picked the money up, staring at it like it was a gold nugget. Like it was something magic left by a genie in a fairy tale.

"Then, a couple of hours later, when I had wiped down all the tables and we'd closed for the night, I went out behind the restaurant to get my bicycle. And there was a sleek black car parked ten feet away from my bike. Ellis got out of that car and said, 'Let me give you a ride home.'

"I never took rides from men at work. Not even if it was raining. But I felt like I couldn't refuse him because he'd given me all that money. So I got in his car.

"I'd never been in a truly luxurious space before. The gleam of the dashboard and the scent of the leather...it was like I was sitting in a mobile palace. And Ellis himself seemed ten times as powerful and intimidating now that I was in his space, sitting right next to him.

"But his voice was as soft and gentle as ever as he asked me all about my parents and my siblings and why I wasn't in school.

"He drove me straight home, respectful as can be, and dropped me off in front of the house.

"When you're poor...you can be incredibly practical. By the time I was eight years old, I was paying our electrical bill. I understood a lot of awful things that no child should understand. And yet...I lived in a fantasy world, too. I had to create these dreams for myself. Possible futures I might have someday. If I won the lottery. If I became a famous actress—never mind that I was horribly shy. If I won a trip to Paris somehow...

"So, when I left work the next night and Ellis was waiting for me...I finally felt special. And chosen. As if fate had noticed me at last.

"He was so kind to me at first. He bought me gifts, and my siblings, too. Never asking anything in return. He never laid a hand on me. I almost imagined at first that he might want to adopt me, like Daddy Warbucks in Annie...

"Of course, that was innocent in a way I should not have been innocent since I knew better by then what men want from girls. I was a virgin, but only thanks to several narrow escapes.

"Eventually, Ellis did expect favors back from me. But by that point, I was so deeply in debt to him...thousands of dollars in gifts and dinners and even cash...I felt like I had to give him whatever he wanted.

"Looking back on it now, he probably spent less than three thousand on me. Which seemed like all the money in the world. Now I think how cheap I sold myself to him."

I can't keep quiet at that. I say, "You were a child. And you were desperate. You didn't sell yourself—that implies you made a choice."

Celia sighs. "I saw the path I was on. And I never tried to leave it. I knew about birth control... He refused to use it. I continued anyway. And, of course, I was soon pregnant. Pregnant with Raylan.

"Ellis proposed. I accepted. Though even as he slipped the shiny ring on my finger, I didn't feel excitement. I knew I was trapped. No going back.

"The cracks in his kindness had already started to show. I knew I was never allowed to say no to him—not about anything. If he ordered dinner for me and I wanted pasta instead of steak, I never spoke up. If I did, he'd punish me later. Not in an obvious way. But with something subtle—like closing the car door on my hand 'accidentally' or forcing me to miss my sister's school play.

"The first time he slapped me was over something so small...I was carrying a pitcher of lemonade out to his deck. He had a massive house out in the middle of nowhere. I had only visited it a few times then. I tripped over the ledge leading down from the kitchen to the deck. I dropped the pitcher, and it shattered, spilling lemonade everywhere.

"He slapped me across the face, hard. It hurt. But it shocked me more. My parents were addicts, but they didn't beat us. I remember his pale blue eyes watching my face. Watching to see how I'd react.

"I stood there stunned for a second. Trying to decide whether to cry or run away. And then, instead, I said, 'I'm sorry.' And he smiled. That's what he wanted to hear. He wanted me to accept fault, even for an innocent mistake. And he wanted me to accept my punishment."

Celia pauses to dampen a rag so she can wipe down the countertops while we talk.

"Anyway," she says, "I don't have to tell you every detail of what happened next. I'm sure you can guess. Men like Ellis like to think they're original, but they couldn't be more predictable if they were operating out of a literal playbook. As soon as we were married, as soon as he had me alone in his house, as soon as I was pregnant and unable to leave...he escalated. Day by day his restrictions tightened, and his violence increased.

"He never left marks that someone else could see. But the rest of my body…I was covered in burns. Cuts. Bruises. And sometimes worse. I begged him to be careful, not to hurt the baby… Thank god he didn't. For his own reasons, not because he gave a damn what I wanted. He was excited about the baby. Another human completely under his control.

"Of course, for me, the pregnancy was a time bomb. A countdown to my greatest fear of all—that what was being done to me might eventually spill over onto an innocent child.

"Ellis was so excited when he found out we were having a son. I told myself that meant he would never hurt the baby. No matter how angry or violent he got, he never actually lost control. He never broke anything that mattered to him or left a mark on me that might be visible in public. It was all so calculated.

"But then one day he truly lost his temper. One of my brothers came to the house to check on me. It was the next oldest of my siblings, Abott. He was only fifteen, but tall. Like Grady is tall." Celia smiles, faintly.

"Ellis had cameras set up all around inside the house and on the property so he could watch me constantly, even while he was at work. He saw Abott come to the door, and he saw me open the door. Even though I didn't let him inside and I made him leave immediately, Ellis was already on his way home.

"I saw a rage in him that night that I'd never seen before. He hit me again and again in the face. Then he poured a glass full of bleach. He held it out to me, and he said, 'Drink.' I begged and pleaded, but it was like talking to a mannequin. His face was so still and blank. Only his eyes were glittering.

"He grabbed my face and brought the glass to my lips. He was going to force it down my throat.

"I said, 'Please don't make me. It will kill the baby.' That was the only thing that shook him out of it. But it was close—too damned close. I didn't know if he would listen next time.

"I ran away the next day. I was terrified, of course. I knew he'd kill me if he found out. I never would have had the courage to go if the baby weren't due a month later. I was out of time. And I never would have made it out if I didn't have help. As I mentioned, people here will handle things themselves if it gets bad enough. Despite all Ellis had done to isolate me, I had one friend left…"

She trails off. I'm wildly curious about this part of the story, but after all she's told me, I know I don't have the right to push for more.

"Sorry." She shakes her head. "I didn't mean for this story to be so long. You're probably wondering why I even brought it up. But I'm about to get to the point."

"I want to hear it all," I assure her.

"I got away," she repeats. "I had the baby. Not here—over the border in North Carolina on Cherokee land. It was the only place that felt safe. The only place Ellis couldn't go.

"My friend who helped me…his family took me in. His sisters helped me with the birth and with the baby. I was afraid that I might not feel everything I should for the baby after it was born. Because I thought it might remind me too much of Ellis. But from the moment I saw Raylan, I loved him like I'd never loved anything. More than my parents or siblings or my own self.

"I stayed there for six years. My friend…became more than a friend to me. We were married. He had always treated Raylan like his own son. After we had two more children…it seemed wrong to make unnatural divisions between them. I always meant to tell Raylan the truth. But the truth was so ugly.

"And they adored each other. Even though Raylan wasn't technically his son, they were more alike than Waya and his own blood children.

"We were so happy; no day seemed like the right day to tear that happiness apart, to put such an ugly burden on Raylan. Especially because Ellis died. So there was no chance of him ever finding us."

I can see tears in the corners of Celia's eyes. Not tears of sorrow—tears of happiness, remembering that time when she was free again and married to a man who actually loved her, with three beautiful small children running around.

"I waited too long," she says. "We got this ranch. We moved here, all together. The children grew up so fast. Time flew away from me.

"Raylan found my old wedding certificate in a box in the attic a week before his eighteenth birthday. He did the math and realized the truth. He was so angry at us. He felt betrayed. I think, though he's never said this, he felt like he no longer belonged to this ranch or to our family in the same way. We promised him it didn't matter—that all three of the children would inherit the ranch as we'd always said.

"I don't think he believed us. He enlisted right after.

"Waya said it was all right. Raylan would go and see more of the world, his anger would fade, and eventually he'd come back to us.

"But then..." Now her tears are certainly tears of sorrow. "Waya was killed in a car crash. He was driving Bo home from a party. Another car ran them off the road—we never knew who. If it was intentional, or drunk driving, or a stupid accident.

"Raylan came home for the funeral. We hoped he would stay. But..."

She breaks off, pressing her fingers into her eyes and taking a moment to compose herself.

"I think the guilt was too much for him. He never had a chance to reconnect with Waya. To tell him...that he knew Waya was his father. Regardless of blood. And that he loved him. Waya knew all that, of course. And Raylan knows it, too. But when you don't get to say the words..."

I understand that.

I often find it hard to say out loud what I actually feel. To tell people what they mean to me.

If Cal or Nessa or my mother or father died, or Uncle Oran, I would have many regrets. Things left unsaid that would eat at me.

Knowing that, you'd think I'd call them right now and let it all be said.

But that's not so easy either.

My sympathy for Raylan is intense. For Celia as well.

That's another thing that's hard to express. How can I tell her how much I appreciate her sharing this with me? How can I tell her that my heart hurts for her younger self? That I admire that she did manage to leave and that she kept Raylan safe?

All the words that come to mind seem pithy and weak.

I swallow hard and say, "Thank you for telling me that, Celia. I…care about Raylan. And you know when you care about someone, you want to understand them."

That doesn't seem like quite enough, so I add, "You were so brave to leave. You're strong."

Celia squeezes my shoulder gently. "I haven't talked about that in a long time. But I wanted you to understand why Raylan coming home again means so much to us. And to him, too, I think. He brought you here for a reason."

I don't know exactly how to respond to that, so I just say again, "Thank you."

Celia smiles. "Go on upstairs. You've got just enough time to wash up before this pie is done."

I scale the creaking staircase back up to my room.

The guest room is a beautiful space, like all the rooms in the ranch house: light, airy, and open. The walls and ceiling are white-washed wood, and the floor is dark oak, partly covered by a hand-woven rug. The pretty blue quilt on the bed against the white walls makes me feel like I'm inside a cloud, way up in the sky.

I can see an article of clothing laid out on the bed—a dress. It's light and summery, pale green with a prairie floral print. It looks too feminine to be something out of Bo's closet. Surely she's the one who put it here for me, though.

I take a shower, then try to battle with my hair, which is becoming less cooperative by the day. I usually straighten it with all kinds of expensive salon shampoos and serums and an arsenal of tools. Here I don't even have a proper blow dryer. I have to let it air dry while I borrow some of Bo's makeup.

We don't share the same coloring, and Bo clearly leans toward the minimalist look with a swipe of heavy black eyeliner. Still, she's got enough selection that I can add a little color to my pale face. I use her blush and her lip gloss.

Then I slip into the dress, which fits quite nicely.

It's nothing I would wear usually—too girly and too country. But I'll admit, it's pretty, with a ruffled skirt and a row of tiny buttons down the front.

Right as I finish dressing, I hear Celia calling, "Dinner's ready!" from the kitchen.

I can hear footsteps hurrying from all corners of the house. Sounds like everyone else is as hungry as I am.

We all crowd in around the table, which is set with the mismatched crockery of several different generations. Grady has brought Shelby and the boys over for dinner again, and Bo is already seated, dressed up a little more than usual in torn black jeans and a sleeveless top, with beaded earrings dangling from her ears.

"How come you look so fancy?" Grady says.

"I don't." Bo scowls.

"Leave her be," Shelby says. "You're the last person in the world to give fashion advice."

I go to the window to check if Raylan is still out in the pen.

"Don't worry, he came in a while ago," Grady says.

"Where is he now?"

"Probably cleaning up. He was a mess."

Nobody else seems inclined to wait for Raylan—Bo starts dishing up a hearty helping of the chicken pot pie, and Celia passes around a basket of warm rolls.

"Do you always eat together?" I ask Shelby.

"Most nights," she says cheerily. "But sometimes Celia and Bo come over to our place instead."

Raylan pointed out their house to me—it sits about a mile away, not visible from the front yard because of the birch trees all around. From what I could see, it's a little smaller than the ranch house but newer.

I understand that kind of family structure—mine is similar. You grow up and start your own family, but you all stay intertwined. This ranch is too large to be run by one person or two—it's an empire of its own type. Like my family's web of influence in Chicago.

"Hey, save some for me," Raylan says, coming into the kitchen. His hair looks blacker than ever, still damp from the shower. I can smell the clean scent of his soap and see the flush on his skin from the hot water. He's actually shaved for once. It makes him look younger and reminds me that he's quite startlingly handsome beneath the beard. I've gotten comfortable with him over the past couple of weeks. Now I feel thrown off- kilter, like he's a stranger all over again.

He sits down right next to me. The sleeve of his flannel shirt brushes against my bare arm. It feels warm and soft and familiar. I relax just a little.

"You want pot pie?" he asks me. "I'll get it for you."

His voice is as low and drawling as ever—as familiar as his shirt. It's funny to hear him talking the same, out of this face that looks leaner and sharper now that it's shaved clean.

He dishes me up a huge serving of pie.

"Riona helped make that," Celia says.

"Don't give me any credit." I shake my head. "I only chopped onions."

"That's the hardest part," Celia says, smiling at me.

The pot pie is delicious. It is similar to chicken and dumplings, but honestly Celia's cooking is better than my mother's. Celia is a master at seasoning the food so it's rich and flavorful but not over-the-top. Just like how Raylan cooks.

She urges me to have a second helping and makes sure everyone has whatever they want to drink.

She's been tirelessly kind to me the whole time I've been here, making sure I've got fresh towels and any toiletries I need. Bo is the same. I guess that's Southern hospitality. Specifically, the way they offer things with such warmth and genuine concern so you'd feel worse declining the favor than accepting it.

"You look stunning," Raylan says, eyeing the borrowed dress. "That one of yours, Bo?"

She nods. "Auntie Kel gave it to me for my birthday. I've never worn it."

"Kelly's still trying to turn you into a little lady, huh?" Raylan laughs. "I admire her persistence, if not her grip on reality."

"Well, all things work out in the end," Celia says. "Because it looks beautiful on Riona."

I have a hard time accepting compliments or warmth of any kind from people I don't know well. I'm always looking for the ulterior motive, the hidden agenda. But for some reason, maybe because I know Raylan pretty well by now or maybe just because his family all has that same attitude of honesty and practicality, I feel relaxed around them. I can enjoy their friendliness and their interest without feeling like they're prying at me, searching me for flaws.

"You coming to the dance, too?" Raylan asks Bo.

"I guess," she says without much enthusiasm.

"Wish I could go," Shelby says wistfully, resting her hand on her swollen belly.

"You could still come," Bo says.

"Yeah, but I can't dance, so what's the point?" Shelby pouts.

"I'll swing you around." Grady grins, slinging a heavy arm around her shoulders. "Might make the baby come faster."

"That's true," Shelby says, perking up a little.

"Go on," Celia urges. "I'll put the boys to bed."

We all coordinate clearing the table, rinsing the dishes, and loading them into the dishwasher. I participate in this as if I've done it a hundred times before. Nobody leaves the kitchen until the last crumb is wiped off the table. It's clear that in the Boone family, everyone works together until the job is done. No matter how small that job might be.

Then Raylan, Grady, Shelby, Bo, and I all load into a beat-up Ford truck so we can drive to the dance.

It takes us longer than I expected to get there. I forget that everything is spread so far apart in the country. The Wagon Wheel is almost forty miles away, and that's forty miles over winding bumpy roads where you can't travel at nearly the same speed you would on a freeway.

I'm not sure what I thought the Wagon Wheel would look like—I guess I was picturing some pokey little rec center with a handful of hicks in attendance.

Instead, I see a large historic building, strung with lights and already bumping from the music inside. The lot is packed with trucks of all types, from gleaming Platinum models all the way down to rusted-up Chevys that look held together with twine.

"I didn't think that many people lived around here," I say in surprise.

"The dances are popular," Raylan says. "People come from all over."

He leads me inside the building.

The dance floor is packed with people, as is the entirety of the room. It's a good twenty degrees hotter in here than it is outside. It smells like leather, sweat, liquor, and cigar smoke. Up on stage, a five-piece band plays at full volume. I have no idea what song they're performing, but it's loud, upbeat, and raucous. There's a fiddle and a banjo mixed in with the usual bass, guitar, and drums.

I hadn't planned to dance. For one thing, I don't really know how. Not to country music, at least. And I'm not sure if I can look Raylan in the face after what we did this morning.

Still, I find my foot tapping to the swinging beat.

♫ *"Dirt on My Boots"—Jon Pardi*

"You want a drink?" Raylan asks me.

"Sure."

I watch Raylan head over to one of the beer stands. It's hard for him to push his way through the crowd—partly because it's so packed in here and partly because he keeps bumping into people he recognizes who want to slap him on the shoulder and ask what the hell he's been doing the past few years. I see more than a few women greet him with particular friendliness. I feel a hot flush on my cheeks as a pretty brunette gives his arm a squeeze and tries to keep him talking for as long as possible. Raylan is cordial, but he keeps moving.

He waits in line and returns a couple of minutes later carrying two plastic cups of foamy beer.

"That's all they had," he says apologetically.

I take a sip. I don't usually like beer, but there's something about the sharp effervescent taste that seems to pair well with the smell of leather and hay. The beer is nice and cold, refreshing in the hot humid space.

Raylan drinks his down in a matter of seconds. Then he crumples the cup and grins at me.

He always attacks his food and drink like that, as if it might disappear if he doesn't swallow it fast. As if it's the most delicious thing he's ever tasted.

He pulls me out on the dance floor the same way, like there isn't a moment to lose.

Raylan has so much restless energy, so much active drive.

"I don't really know how to—" I start, but he's already pulling me into his arms, one hand on my waist and the other clasping my right palm.

I know some basic ballroom dancing—you pick it up going to fancy parties and events. As far as I can tell, country dancing doesn't seem to have structured footwork in the same way as a waltz or salsa. Instead, there's a basic rock-step and then a whole lot of twirling and spinning.

Raylan directs me with his big strong hands, sometimes resting them both on my waist to spin me one way or another, sometimes switching his grip between my hands or holding both my hands over my head as I twirl.

I'm clumsy at first, stumbling a couple of times. But it's a whole hell of a lot easier to dance in cowboy boots compared to the stilettos I'd usually wear. And Raylan's lead is truly flawless—he directs me effortlessly, shifting my momentum one way and another, dipping me over his blue-jean-clad thigh and then pulling me back up again.

He makes it all look so easy. He moves with a kind of casual grace that belies the fact he's really fucking good at this.

I'm not a great dancer. But I am a quick learner. Once he puts me through a particular move once or twice, I can anticipate it the next time around. Soon I'm doing a kind of three-part spin, where I duck my head under his hand on the third rotation, and a move where Raylan wraps my arms around my body, walks me around, and then flings me out to the end of his reach like a yo-yo before pulling me back and wrapping me in his arms again.

At first, I'm focused on learning the moves. But the more I can follow his lead without thought, the more I notice the heat coming off his body and the tension of his arms when I press against his chest. I can smell the spicy scent of his aftershave.

I find myself relaxing, melting against him like butter in a hot pan.

The dance floor is packed with people. All kinds of country boys—tanned, muscular, and charming. But none of them is as handsome as Raylan, not even close. And none can move like him. I'm not the only woman who can't take my eyes off him. I'm sure

plenty of these girls would love to cut in for a dance, but Raylan doesn't pause for an instant between songs. He's grinning and brimming with energy, dancing faster and harder by the minute.

I can't believe he's got this kind of stamina when I know he spent all afternoon breaking that horse.

Actually…the way he leads me through the dances reminds me of the way he rode that horse. Directing it so subtly and gently that the horse thought it had the freedom to run, while all the time it was doing exactly what he wanted.

He's doing the same thing now: directing and training me without me even noticing. He's got the lead, and I'm totally under his control.

I stiffen, resisting his motion.

Raylan puts his hand on the small of my back and pulls me closer, trying to swing me around in his orbit. But now I'm pulling away from him, my pleasure in dancing evaporating.

I don't want to be trained. I don't want to be broken.

"What's wrong?" Raylan says, standing still but holding my hands.

"I don't want to dance anymore."

"All right," Raylan says easily. "Let's get another drink."

"Just water," I say. I blame the beer for the warm flush that made me think I could dance. It made me think it was a good idea to let Raylan spin me and dip me any way he wanted.

Raylan goes to get us a couple of bottles of water. I lean against the wooden railing that borders the dance floor, looking around the room. I see Grady and Shelby dancing the best they can with Shelby's belly in the way. They're mostly just swaying, Grady's hands on his wife's hips, and Shelby stretching up as high as she can reach to link her hands behind his neck.

I hate the idea of being pregnant—of being essentially debilitated, unable to walk or run like normal, my body stretched out and taken over by another living thing. I never get that vicarious excitement other people seem to experience. Quite the opposite—when I see a pregnant lady, I want to wince and look away.

Even when Cal and Aida had their baby, I felt discomfited. I was happy for them, but at the same time, I felt like some kind of strange spell took hold of them both, changing them forever. It wasn't a bad thing. But my brother is a father now. He's irrevocably a different person than he was before.

I can see Bo standing just outside the doorway on the wraparound porch that encircles the building. I walk over to speak to her, drawn by the pensive set of her shoulders and by my own desire to breathe fresh air for a moment.

Bo is looking out over the dark fields. Washed in moonlight, the fierceness has vanished from her face. Her dark eyes look wistful.

"It's nice out here," I say to her.

The cool breeze feels lovely after the heat of the dance floor.

"I saw you dancing," Bo says.

"Do you like to dance?" I ask her.

She shakes her head. "I don't like crowds." Then, with a half smile, she admits, "But I don't really like being alone either. So I guess that's why I'm standing out on the porch like an idiot."

I laugh softly. I understand that feeling—sometimes I go to a club or a party, and the minute I get there, I'm annoyed by the noise and smoke. But then as soon as I get home again, I feel a kind of blank emptiness.

I say, "I wish I could enjoy things as easily as everyone else seems to."

Bo glances over at me, her dark eyes glinting beneath her thick lashes. "Sometimes I think they're just pretending to have fun. And other times I think it really is that simple for the rest of the world. They're a bunch of clocks that run right, and I'm just missing a gear somewhere..."

The end of her sentence is drowned out by a retro-style motorcycle roaring into the lot. It's one of those old-school bikes that looks like it should be ridden by a mail carrier in World War II. Maybe it was—this particular bike is missing so much paint that it's impossible to tell the original color, and the noisy engine spits out a plume of black smoke.

The rider is slim, dressed in torn jeans and a battered jacket that looks as old as the bike. When he pulls off his helmet, he shakes out a mane of black hair that falls below his shoulders. He's got high cheekbones, an aquiline nose, and dark eyes even fiercer than Bo's.

Bo tenses at the sight of him. She looks like she might run inside the Wagon Wheel but then changes her mind and stays put.

"I thought you said you weren't coming," the rider says, setting his helmet down on the bike seat and striding toward Bo.

"I changed my mind." Bo tosses her head.

"I could have picked you up."

"I don't need a ride from you."

The boy walks right up to Bo so they're almost nose to nose. She stands her ground, refusing to step back, her arms folded in front of her chest.

The air between them crackles with tension. Even though their sentences are innocuous enough, each word carries an undercurrent of challenge and resentment.

"Who's this?" the boy says without actually looking at me. His eyes are fixed on Bo's, furious and unblinking.

"Riona, this is Duke." Bo introduces us in a monotone.

"Nice to meet you," I say. Duke totally ignores me, but I don't care because I'm fascinated by the tension between these two. I don't want politeness—I want to know what the hell is going on.

"You promised to dance with me," Duke says, grabbing Bo's wrist.

She wrenches it out of his grip and shoves him hard in the chest for good measure. "The hell I did!"

Duke makes a sharp hissing sound, like the noise you might make to correct an unruly animal. He shoves between Bo and me, stomping into the Wagon Wheel.

The silence he leaves behind is thick and poignant.

I'm torn between my desire to ask Bo for details and the knowledge that she probably wants me to mind my own damned business.

"There you are!" Raylan says, handing me a bottle of water. "I was looking all over for you."

"Where's my drink?" Bo says.

"I didn't know you were out here—you can have my water."

"Water isn't a drink," Bo says sullenly. She ignores the proffered water bottle and heads inside to get something more satisfactory.

I twist off the lid and gulp down the water, dehydrated from my long session of dancing.

Raylan cocks his head, watching me. "Why'd you come out here?"

I slip the question, saying instead, "What's the deal with Bo and Duke?"

Raylan chuckles. "They were best friends growing up. A couple of hellions, getting into trouble constantly. I don't know exactly what they're beefing about since I haven't been around lately, and I only got a few things secondhand. But I gather that Duke wants to be more than friends, and Bo is pissed about it."

"She doesn't like him that way?"

Raylan looks over at me, his dark eyebrow cocked. "Women don't always know what they like."

I feel the color rising in my face. "That's pretty sexist."

Raylan shrugs. "Okay. *People* don't know what they like." He grins. "Especially women."

I frown at him, my temper rising. "I know what I like and don't like."

He keeps smiling at me in that infuriating way. "I don't think you do."

I want to slap his smug face again, but I wouldn't give him the satisfaction.

This is exactly what I suspected. He thinks he can manipulate me. He thinks he can break me.

"Let's go back," I say coldly. "I'm tired."

Raylan's expression clearly shows that he thinks I'm pouting, not tired. But all he says out loud is, "I'll go get the others."

As we step back inside the Wagon Wheel, the heat and humidity are higher than ever. The band is stomping the stage while they play, and the boots of the dancers likewise thunder against the wooden floor. It seems to shake the whole hall.

Raylan heads over toward Grady and Shelby, who are still dancing together in the corner, away from the wildness of the other dancers.

I look around for Bo. I spot Duke instead, dancing with a pretty redhead. He's got his hands on her hips, and she's looking up at him with a flirtatious expression, obviously pleased to be this close to him.

Bo is standing at the edge of the dance floor, likewise watching them while she gulps down half her beer. Her eyes are narrowed, and two bright spots of color flame in her cheeks.

Duke is not paying much attention to the redhead. He keeps glancing back at Bo. He looks defiant but also slightly uncomfortable, like he's regretting his strategy.

As the song winds down, the redhead reaches up to tuck a lock of hair behind his ear.

Seeing that, Bo whirls around and starts to push her way through the crowd, heading toward the exit. Duke abandons the redhead on the dance floor so he can chase her. He catches up to Bo about five feet away from where I'm standing, so I have a full view of what happens next, though I can't hear what they're saying over the noise of the music and the crowd.

Duke grabs Bo's arm. She shakes him off angrily. He shouts something at her, waving his hands in frustration. She rolls her eyes and tries to turn away from him again. He grabs her shoulder and spins her around. Then she flings the remains of her beer in his face.

This has an effect similar to throwing a match in the middle of a pool of gasoline. Duke looks ready to strangle her, his face so full of fury that even Bo looks slightly abashed.

But the beer didn't confine itself to drenching Duke. It splashed the backs of the necks of the two men standing behind him. The two cowboys whirl around, their fists already raised.

The cowboys don't seem to care that Duke got hit with more beer than they did. They're looking for somebody to blame, and he's the obvious culprit. After a brief exchange of insults, the bigger of the two cowboys throws a haymaker right at Duke's face. He ducks under the punch with a speed and fluidity that shocks me, and shocks the cowboy, too. The cowboy looks baffled, like he just witnessed a magic trick. His buddy reacts a little quicker, hitting Duke from the side with a sucker punch.

Even though she was fighting with Duke five seconds earlier, Bo shrieks with rage and runs at the two cowboys. She kicks cowboy number two right in the gut with the heel of her boot, then cracks him across the jaw with a right cross. The bigger cowboy seizes her from behind, pinning her arms to her sides, and she kicks both legs out in front of her, hitting his friend again.

Now Duke is properly pissed, and he throws his arm around the big cowboy's neck, choking him until he releases Bo. But the cowboys apparently didn't come alone—at least six other guys are joining the fight from all sides.

I'm frozen in place, not knowing what the fuck to do. It's a melee of people, and I'm not entirely sure who's on which side. Especially once Raylan and Grady jump into the fray. Raylan rips one of the cowboys off Bo and flings him over the wooden railing into the dance floor. Grady is throwing punches left and right, taking a hit to the face that would knock out a grizzly bear but simply shaking his head and coming back for more.

The brawl spreads outward like a virus. Within seconds, it seems like everyone is fighting, and I can't tell if there are teams or sides or just a whole lot of people taking the opportunity to release their aggression on whoever's standing next to them.

Somebody grabs my arm, but it's only Shelby pulling me toward the door, her arm cradled protectively around her belly.

"Come on!" she shouts.

"What about Bo?"

"Raylan'll bring her." Shelby pants.

She pulls me outside to the porch, which is already crowded with the dancers who likewise wanted to flee the brawl. Some people are laughing and peeking in the windows, commenting on the riot within. Others are heading to their cars, obviously feeling like they had enough fun for one night.

I hear the wail of a single siren, distant but distinct. Somebody called the cops, though I don't know how a single sheriff is going to break up this mess.

Raylan comes barreling through the doorway, half carrying and half dragging Bo along. Grady is right behind him. Together they frog-march their sister back to the truck. Raylan's lip is swollen, and Grady has the beginning of an impressive black eye. But both are grinning.

"You said you weren't going to fight tonight!" Shelby says, slapping her husband's arm furiously. He seems to feel it about as much as a moose feels a mosquito. Still, he pretends to be cowed.

"I didn't start that!" he says. "Duke did."

Bo looks mildly guilty. She knows that if anybody started the fight, it was her. But she doesn't pipe up, and I'm not going to rat her out.

Once Raylan has stuffed Bo in the back seat, he grabs my shoulders and looks me over.

"Are you okay?"

"Yeah, of course. I'm fine," I assure him.

"Just making sure you didn't get hit by any stray shrapnel," he says. "You know…Solo cups. Tobacco juice. Cowboy sweat."

I smile. "No. Nothing like that."

"Thank god," Raylan says. "You get a drop of cowboy sweat on you, and you're never getting that smell out."

"You're a cowboy," I say, low enough that nobody else will hear. "And I'm pretty sure I've gotten your sweat on me…"

Raylan grins. "That's different…"

"So, how'd you like your first country dance?" Shelby calls up to me from the back seat.

"It was…pretty fun," I admit.

"You got the full experience," Grady says. "No good dance ends without a brawl."

"There are plenty of good dances without any fighting!" Shelby cries.

"Name one," Grady says.

Shelby bites her lip, obviously at a loss for an immediate answer.

"Carrie's wedding!" she blurts.

"Uh-uh. Jonny White beat the shit out of Carl Oakton halfway through the reception. Right before they cut the cake."

I can see Shelby scowling in the rearview mirror, but she can't seem to think of any other examples to prove her point.

Grady grins smugly, throwing his arm around his wife's shoulders and squeezing her tight.

Bo sits next to the pair, silent and frowning.

Raylan glances back at her. "You okay, sis?"

"Yeah, of course." Bo grunts. "I'm fine."

Raylan nods and turns back to the road, but I can see him thinking, probably piecing together what happened.

CHAPTER 18
RAYLAN

A KIND OF PEACEABLE SILENCE SPREADS IN THE CAR. I CAN TELL Shelby is getting sleepy, her head leaned against Grady's chest and her eyelids drooping like a child's. Bo is looking out the window, even though the night is black as pitch and she can't see anything in the fields and forest we pass.

I don't know what the fuck is going on with her and Duke, but I don't exactly feel like I'm in a position to give advice. I'm chasing after a girl who barely tolerates me, who seems determined to slam the drawbridge down on my head every time I try to wriggle my way through her castle wall.

Goddamn, Riona looks so gorgeous tonight. I love her in her lawyer clothes, but I've never seen anything prettier than her creamy skin against that pale green dress with her red hair all loose and wavy around her shoulders.

She looked relaxed and free in a way I've never seen before. Strangely, she looked more herself than she did in Chicago. She was smiling and laughing, dancing with me like she'd been doing it all her life. She tries to be so rigid and stern, but that's not her, not really. The real Riona is adventurous, climbing on a horse when she's never been within ten feet of one before. She's graceful, spinning around in my arms like she was born to dance. She's perceptive, getting to know Bo when Bo's as prickly as a cactus and can't get along with anybody, including her own damned best friend.

That's what I see when I look at Riona. A woman who can be anything and do anything she wants.

But she seems determined to deny it.

I felt her pulling away from me as we danced. I saw that resentment flare in her eyes again, that refusal to let herself enjoy something she was obviously loving just a few minutes before.

I don't understand her.

But goddamn, do I want to.

I want it more than anything. I want to crack the code of her psyche. I want to win her over. I want to make her mine.

And it's not just 'cause it's a challenge. Maybe it started out that way—Dante calls me *Long Shot* for a reason. If you tell me I can't have something, I want it ten times more.

But it's gone way past that with Riona. The more time I spend with her, the more I realize she has a force of will inside of her stronger than a hurricane. I admire it.

I never wanted some sweet-tempered country girl. I adore Shelby—she's just the right kind of angel to put up with my brother. But I don't want that for myself.

I want an equal. Someone who pushes me and challenges me.

I want a partner.

The only problem is you can't make somebody your partner against their will. And I don't think Riona wants to tie herself to me for one goddamned second. I think even the idea of that would terrify her.

I don't know how to convince her to give me a real shot.

But I've got a couple of ideas.

"You can just drop us at the house," Grady tells me.

"Sure," I say, turning right at the fork in the road that leads to their place. I drop them off in front of their pretty white house, waiting just a minute to see if my mom will be coming out. The door remains shut—I'm guessing she probably fell asleep right next to the boys when she was putting them to bed. That's what usually happens.

So I drive Bo and Riona back to the ranch house instead. Bo hops out as soon as I shut off the engine. She goes stomping into the house, still steamed about whatever happened at the dance and not wanting to talk to Riona or me about it.

Riona starts walking in the same direction, but I grab her arm and gently pull her back, saying, "Hold up a second, I want to talk to you."

"It's cold," Riona says.

It's not really cold—mildly chilly at most. But I say, "Come in here, then. It'll be warmer."

I pull her over to the smallest of the barns, the one closest to the house. It's empty of animals at the moment—actually, it has been for years. My father used it as a workspace for a while, and now Grady uses it to make saddles. It smells like clean hay, apples, and a faint whiff of Mary Jane, because Grady smokes in here when it's rainy.

There's a wooden pommel bench in the center of the room where Grady places the saddles that are works in progress. His tools are laid out on a table nearby, along with a lantern, scraps of leather, and spare bits of thong.

I light the lantern, throwing a faint golden glow around the space and creating a forest of long, distended shadows. Riona's pale skin looks luminescent, and her green eyes gleam like the eyes of a fox prowling around the edge of a campfire. She looks wary of me, wrapping her arms around herself and keeping distance between us.

I ask her, "What happened tonight?"

"The fight?" she says. "I couldn't really hear what Bo and Duke were saying…"

"No, not that. Before—when we were dancing."

Riona's eyes meet mine for a second, then determinedly look away. "I don't know what you mean."

"Yes, you do. We were dancing together. You were enjoying yourself. And then you pulled away from me. You were upset, and you wanted to leave."

Riona's lips are pale, and her jaw looks stiff. "I was tired of dancing."

"You're lying."

Her eyes flash up at me, bright and furious. "I don't lie!"

"Yes, you do. Tell me the truth. Tell me why you wanted to stop."

"None of your damned business!" she shouts.

Her arms have uncrossed, and now her fists are balled at her sides instead. From defense to offense mode. That's fine—I'd rather fight than beat my head against a brick wall.

"Tell me why you were angry at me all of a sudden."

"I didn't like the way you were leading me!" Riona cries.

That's not at all what I expected her to say. "What are you talking about?"

"When we were dancing—you were acting like we were dancing together. But you were the one in control."

"That's what dancing is. The man leads, and the woman follows."

"I don't want that!" Riona snaps. "I don't want to follow someone else. I don't want to be controlled by someone else."

"It was just a dance!" I say, with an incredulous laugh. "I know how to two-step. You don't."

I shouldn't have laughed because that just makes her angrier.

"It's not just the dancing!" Riona hisses. "It's everything. You're trying to trick me by being calm and charming and funny…"

I can't help smiling just a little. "You think I'm funny?"

"No!" Riona shouts.

"But you just said—"

"You're trying to put a bridle on me without me noticing!"

"I…what?"

"I saw you out there with that horse. You were acting all calm and patient with it. Lulling it into a false sense of security. Then you put the bridle on it, and then you got on its back. And soon you were riding it around. And the horse was galloping as fast as it could, thinking it could get away from you. But it didn't realize it was already trapped. And then you just wore it down until you broke it. I'm not going to be that fucking horse!"

I stand there silently for a second, taking in what she said. Then I shake my head at her. "You don't know a damn thing about horses."

Riona scowls. One of the things that's so damned infuriating about this woman is that she looks even more beautiful when she's mad. Her cheeks get as red as her hair, and she looks fierce and imperious, like an empress. It's very distracting. But right now, on this one thing, I'm right and she's wrong. And I'm determined to prove it.

"What do you mean?" she says.

"You don't *break* a horse. Not in the way you're saying. You could beat a horse, and whip it, and yell at it, and eventually you could break its spirit, but what the hell good would it be then? It'd be scared of you, skittish and jumpy. It'd probably startle when you least expected it and throw you off so you break your neck."

Riona tilts her head, still frowning but also considering what I'm saying. She likes to argue, but she will listen, too.

"That horse had never been ridden in its life. So, yeah, I had to calm it down, ease it into accepting me. You're right about that. But once I got on its back, we both wanted to run. She started galloping, and I urged her on to go faster and faster. She'd been galloping around out in the fields, but she'd never been chased. She'd never raced before. She'd never *really* run. I didn't break that horse. I set it free. I showed her what she could do. And she fucking loved it."

I take a step closer to Riona, closing the space between us. She stays exactly where she is, only tilting her chin up a little to look me in the face. Her eyes are wide and unblinking.

I trail my thumb gently down the delicate curve of her jaw toward her full lower lip. "I don't want to trap you. I want to unleash you. I want to set you free. I want to show you what you really are…"

I run my thumb across her mouth.

Riona's lips part.

I move my thumb and replace it with my tongue. I slide my tongue across her bottom lip and her top and then the space in between. When she opens her mouth a little more, I thrust my tongue inside, tasting her. I grab her thick red hair, wrapping it around my hand like a rope, and I pull her face into mine, penetrating her mouth with my tongue. This is no chaste kiss—this is me taking her mouth. Violating it. Filling her up.

I want her to be dizzy and overwhelmed. I want to remind her of how good it feels when she lets me have my way with her.

Sure enough, she melts into me, her whole body sinking against mine. She moans around my tongue. I can feel her lips swelling from the rough kiss, increasing in sensitivity. I can feel her jaw relaxing, letting me in deeper and deeper.

I pull her hair to tilt her head back all the more, exposing her creamy-white throat. Then I lick from her sternum all the way up her neck to her right ear, making her shiver with pleasure. Her nipples stand out in hard points against the cotton dress.

I growl into her ear, "I want you to give yourself to me. I want you to do exactly what I say. And if you don't love every fucking minute of it...I'll leave you alone for good. I'll never bother you again. Do you agree?"

Riona hesitates, and I pull her hair a little harder.

"Yes or no?" I hiss.

"Y-yes," she stammers.

"Good." I let go of her hair. Instead, I grab the front of her dress and tear it open, the buttons popping off and flying in all directions. Her bare breasts spill out, bouncing once, the nipples harder than glass.

"Don't—" Riona protests, too late. She's worried about ruining the borrowed dress.

I grab her by the throat and growl in her ear, "Shut the fuck up. You promised to do what I say."

I see that fire of rebellion in her green eyes, but it's swallowed by lust. She wants this as much as I do, though she hates to admit it. I feel her pulse fluttering against my palm. I can see those gorgeous bare breasts heaving from her rapid breaths.

I grope her breast roughly with my free hand. I squeeze its exquisite softness, pulling on the nipple, rolling it between my finger and thumb. Riona gasps.

Keeping hold of her throat, I fondle her other breast. I go back and forth between them, pinching and squeezing, until her pale pink nipples are swollen and darker by two shades.

I duck my head and take her nipple in my mouth. I flick it gently with my tongue until I feel her squirm. Then I suck hard. Riona lets out a long moan of relief.

I squeeze her breast with my hand while I suck the nipple, as if I were milking her. I can feel her knees going weak, her arms circling my neck for support.

I work one breast and then the other. Riona grabs the back of my head and presses my mouth harder against her breast, wanting more and more.

Instead, I straighten and drag her over to the pommel bench. It's about waist height, just wide enough for a saddle.

I bend her over the bench and push her legs apart with my feet. Grabbing a coil of rope off the wall, I tie her hands in front of her and secure them to the bench. Then I tie her ankles, one at a time, so they stay spread apart.

I can practically hear her heart rate increasing. She squirms against the ropes, scared of being restrained, wanting to resist me. But I know she's curious, too—curious about what will happen if, for once in her life, she relinquishes control.

Once I have her firmly tied, I step back to admire the view. She's bent over the bench, utterly helpless. Her bright red hair hangs around her face, half blinding her. Her bare breasts are pressed against the wood, her ankles tied about two feet apart.

I walk behind her and pull up her skirt so the remains of the dress are bunched around her waist, revealing her creamy-white ass cheeks, round and full and luscious in the pale golden light.

She's wearing a lace thong. The only thing covering her now.

I pick up a pair of shears off the workbench, their blades gleaming in the light. I open and close them once so Riona can hear the vicious snapping sound. She shivers, trying to look behind her.

I place the blade against the tender skin of her hip, slipping it under the waistband of the thong, cutting her panties off in one sharp snap. I do the same on the other side, pulling away the shreds of fabric to bare her smooth pink pussy lips and the little puckered opening of her ass.

Now she's completely vulnerable. Her legs tremble. Wetness gleams between her pussy lips. My mouth waters.

But it's not time for that yet.

Instead, I go back to the wall and take down a freshly made riding crop. It's a little longer than my forearm, made of fragrant black leather. The handle is stiffly braided, with a little loop of leather at the head. I smack that loop against my palm, making a sharp cracking sound. Riona flinches, trying to look around at me but pinned in place.

I trail the crop down the side of her bare breast. She shivers at the touch, and her nipples harden again.

I run the riding crop down her spine, admiring the tightness of her waist, flaring out to her beautiful heart-shaped ass. I trail the crop down her left ass cheek, down her thigh, then gently tease the little loop of leather across her bare pussy, and all the way up her ass crack, making her moan aloud.

I rest my free hand on the small of her back.

"If you do what I say, I'll reward you. If you disobey…I'll punish you."

Her back tightens under my palm as she rebels against the idea of reward and punishment. But curiosity and arousal keep her silent.

I say, "Just so we're clear, this is what punishment feels like."

I swing the crop through the air, whipping her smartly on the ass.

Riona yelps, trying to pull away, but she's tied tightly down over the bench.

The crop leaves a long pink welt on that snow-white ass. Her skin is extraordinarily delicate. The sight of that mark makes my cock throb with lust.

I whip her again on the other side. She flinches but manages to bite back the cry this time.

I give her one more smack, and this time she hardly jumps at all. She can't stop herself from trying to maintain control over her reactions.

That's fine—we'll see how long it lasts.

"That was punishment," I say. "This is reward…"

I massage her reddened ass cheek with my hand, gently soothing the sting. Riona relaxes and exhales softly, unable to resist my touch.

I reach between her thighs and touch her pussy, running my fingers over the soft lips. I can feel her swollen clit protruding. I let the ball of my thumb dance across it, making her draw in a shuddering breath.

My fingers are slick with her wetness. I massage her pussy, slipping my fingers between her folds but not penetrating her yet. Just teasing her clit, letting my thumb slide over it again and again until I feel her trying to grind against my hand as much as she can while tied down by the ropes. Her breath quickens. She's already on the edge of climax from pure arousal.

I pull my hand away.

Riona groans in frustration.

"Not yet," I say. "You haven't earned it."

I walk around to the front of the bench. I stand directly in front of Riona and unbutton my jeans, pulling out my cock, heavy and throbbing and already dripping precome.

I grip my cock by the base and hold it out to her.

"Suck," I order.

For a moment Riona presses her lips together, contemplating disobedience. But she's craving reward. So she opens her mouth and lets me feed her my cock.

Her hands are tied; she's immobilized over the bench. All she can do is relax her jaw and let me thrust in and out of her mouth. I feel her tongue sliding on the underside of my cock from the base all the way up to the head.

I thrust shallowly at first, then deeper as my cock is lubricated by her saliva. Soon I'm bottoming out in her throat, making her gag.

It's incredibly dominating using her mouth like this. It wouldn't mean fuck all if it were some random girl, but Riona is a queen. It's like I've captured Cleopatra as my spoils of war. I feel like a fucking emperor.

I pump in and out of her mouth, my cock so swollen and hot that I feel like I might split my own skin. Come boils in my balls, begging to be released.

Not yet, though. I've barely gotten started.

Instead, I pull out of her mouth saying, "Good job, baby girl."

"I'm not your baby!" Riona says furiously.

"Oh, you're not?"

I stride around her, picking up the crop again and bringing it down hard on her ass. Riona can't help crying out.

"Ow!" she yelps.

I whip her again, in the same spot.

"Fuck!" she shouts, squirming and twisting.

CRACK!

CRACK!

CRACK!

I whip her ruthlessly until her entire buttocks are bright pink.

Then I drop the crop, and I thrust my fingers inside her. She gasps, her warm wet pussy twitching. Now she's squirming for an entirely different reason.

"Oh god," she moans.

I'm rubbing her clit and fingering her in a steady rhythm. She rocks against my hand, her thighs trembling and her pussy clenching around my fingers.

"Only good girls get to come," I tell her in a low voice.

She groans and presses harder against my hand, desperate for release.

"Say you're my girl," I demand.

Silence for a moment. Then she gasps, "I'm yours!"

"Mine to protect?"

"Yes," she pants.

"Mine to ride?"

"YES!" she cries, right on the edge.

I stop fingering her. She cries out in frustration.

But she doesn't have long to wait. I grip her by the hips and thrust my cock into that tight wet pussy. She screams with pleasure as I fuck her from behind. Holding tight to her hips, I slam into her again and again, my hips smacking against her ass even louder than the riding crop.

I reach down to rub that swollen little clit in time with my thrusts.

It only takes three seconds to tip her over the edge. Her pussy clenches around my cock, and she lets out a long strangled cry as I finally allow her to orgasm.

The climax goes on and on and on. Each thrust seems to wring another wave of pleasure out of her.

I'm dying to explode inside her at the same time. My balls are throbbing. The rhythmic squeezing of her pussy is almost irresistible. I hold back, just barely, by pulling my cock out of her and squeezing hard under the head. My cock is soaked and slick, her cream streaked down the shaft.

I drop behind her and bury my face in her pussy. I lick her clit, feeling how hot and swollen and tender it is against my tongue.

Riona cries out, too sensitive from her orgasm. I keep going, gently at first and then with a little more pressure as I feel her relax and start rocking against my tongue. I lick her steadily and deeply, building a second climax.

"Oh my god…oh… I can't…" She pants.

"Come for me again," I demand, my face buried in her cunt.

Her pussy feels like it's on fire. She tastes sweeter than ever. Her clit is velvet against my tongue. I lap steadily harder, pushing my fingers inside her.

"Ohhhh, YES!" she screams as she starts to come again.

This orgasm hits her like a hammer. Her whole body tenses. She grimaces as if she's in pain, but really, it's pleasure, pleasure so intense, it's almost unbearable.

She gives a soft little sob as her body finally releases. She's draped over the wooden bench, weak and spent.

I untie the ropes around her wrists and ankles, and I lift her off the bench.

She's as limp as laundry fresh out of the wringer. She can't even hold up her head, which lolls against my arm. I pull off the remains of the dress so her slim body is completely nude.

I'm not done with her yet. I'm going to fuck her senseless.

Like the horse that galloped to pure exhaustion, I'm going to show Riona the peak of pleasure I can give her if she'll give herself to me.

I lift her, her arms around my neck and her legs around my waist. Then I find a bare spot on the barn wall, and I press her against it, sliding my cock inside her once more. I fuck her against that wall with the speed and ferocity of a stallion mounting a filly. I drive into her again and again, her legs locked around my waist and her clit rubbing against the flat patch of stomach right above my cock.

I lock my hands under her ass, pulling her tight against me. Making sure my cock fills her all the way up so every inch of her is stimulated.

Her bare breasts rub against my chest, the friction on her hard little nipples making her gasp.

I seize a handful of her hair and kiss her again, tasting those orgasms on her breath, tasting sweat and blood from my own split lip.

I'm about to come. I can't hold back much longer.

But I'm determined to force one more orgasm out of Riona first.

She's exhausted, but I can feel her clit grinding against me, and her pussy beginning to tense and tighten again.

"Come for me," I growl in her ear. "Come for me right now."

Riona bites down hard on my shoulder, strangling her yell. She's coming for a third time, her thighs clenched tight around me and her arms clinging to my neck.

This time I couldn't stop if I wanted to. I erupt inside her, an orgasm that feels like an aneurysm. My head explodes at the same time as my cock in a brilliant, blinding rush that almost knocks me out. I'm coming harder than I ever have in my life. Violently hard, with shocking intensity.

I have to drop Riona on a pile of clean hay. I fall on top of her, still blinded by flashing lights, with my cock still pulsing and dripping come even though I've pulled out of her.

I wrap her in my arms and squeeze her tightly, unable to speak.

Riona looks delirious, her eyelids fluttering.

We're both drenched in sweat, though I didn't realize it until now. I think the temperature in the barn has gone up by thirty degrees.

"That was insane..." Riona groans when she can finally speak again.

I kiss her once more, still hungry.

Both of us are too weak and exhausted to move.

Insane is an ambiguous word. It could be good or bad.

But I don't have to ask if she enjoyed it. I know what Riona needs.

CHAPTER 19
RIONA

RAYLAN HANDS ME HIS SHIRT. I TRY NOT TO LET HIM SEE ME shiver when I slip into the scent of his sweat and soap. He walks me back to the house and all the way up to the guest room. I think he's planning to tuck me into bed, but I say to him, unexpectedly and surprising him as much as me, "Will you stay with me?"

Raylan looks surprised but pleased. "I'd love to."

Even though it's a queen-size bed, Raylan is big enough that we're still close together on the mattress, his weight causing us to roll together in the middle of the bed. With my head resting on his chest, I can feel his heart thudding against my ear, steady and strong. It's an incredibly peaceful sound. As regular as ocean waves.

I feel my heart rate slowing to match his. My breathing getting deep and heavy like the air slowly rushing in and out of Raylan's lungs.

I feel exhausted like I've never been before. Every muscle of my body is loose, warm, and still steeped in pleasure chemicals.

I've never been so satisfied. Not just sexually—mentally and emotionally, too. That sex stimulated my brain and my desire unlike anything I've experienced.

It's paradoxical because I would have thought I'd *hate* to be treated like that. I fucking hate being restrained, controlled, or bossed around. But not by Raylan…

I don't understand it.

How could everything I hate be twisted and turned to such a degree that I found it wildly arousing?

Even as I'm drifting off to sleep, I'm pondering that question. Trying to understand what I just experienced.

Right before I fall asleep, I see a glimmering answer, like a nugget of gold in the silt of a riverbed.

It's because I admire him.

I've never fucked a man I actually respected before. I'm so fucking arrogant that I looked down on every man I dated. They didn't impress me. Outside my own family, one of the only men I truly respect is Dante. But I was telling the truth to everyone who asked—our feelings for each other have never passed platonic.

I've never experienced what it's like to fully esteem a man. To want to impress him. To want to please him.

There was a particular pleasure in being conquered. Raylan is so handsome and rugged and capable that I felt like he deserved to have me. He deserved to have me any way he wanted.

On top of that, there was a deep and potent relief in letting go...in letting him take charge of the sexual experience. I didn't have to think or plan or maintain my rigid hold on the situation like I usually would. Instead, I could set my brain free. There was no governor on my thoughts or on my physical response. I was free to simply experience what was happening with no distractions.

Then, of course, there was a third element—how deeply filthy and taboo it all felt. He tied me down! He whipped me! He fucked me like an animal!

I should be furious and disgusted.

Instead...I fucking loved it.

The perverse and rebellious part of me takes a deep pleasure in enjoying what I'm not supposed to like. In embracing what I'm supposed to reject.

It would only work with Raylan, though, I know that. I would never respect another man enough to allow him to do that. Enough to *want* him to do it. And I would never trust anyone else like that.

That's the core of why I was able to let go…because I do trust Raylan. However dominant and aggressive he might have seemed in the moment, deep down I knew he would never actually hurt me. I allowed him to tie my hands because I knew that what followed would be pleasurable for both of us. I knew that even though he was pretending to use me for his own enjoyment, all the while he was watching my responses, gauging my arousal and my desire so he could pull back from the edge of pain at just the right time and soothe me with exactly the right kind of touch.

I trust him.

Just that thought alone hits me like a hammer.

I've never trusted anybody outside my own family (I include Dante in that because he is my brother-in-law, after all).

But I trust Raylan. I really do.

If his heavy warm arms weren't currently wrapped around me, I think that realization might terrify me. But I'm too calm, too drained, and too comfortable to feel any negative feelings right now.

Instead, I slip off to sleep simply marveling that something so unexpected has happened to me.

The next morning, I wake up to Raylan's tongue between my thighs.

He's down under the blankets, gently licking and lapping at my clit.

I'm so flushed and warm with sleep that my pussy is incredibly sensitive. Each stroke of his tongue is utterly intoxicating.

My brain is still in that floating half asleep state. My memories of the night before are both vivid and fantastical—real and dreamlike. With every touch of Raylan's tongue, I feel like I'm experiencing the best parts of our sexual encounter all over again.

I remember the look of his body in the lantern light: Every muscle bulging with exertion. His skin glowing. His bright blue eyes intense and animalistic. The glint of his teeth when he growled at me or when he threw his head back in pleasure.

I remember how he seemed to transform into the most commanding, most powerful version of himself. The more dominant he became, the more my arousal grew. I wanted to please him. And the more I pleased him, the more pleasure I felt myself, in an endless feedback loop.

He knew exactly what I needed. His attention was fixed on me 1,000 percent. Those bright blue eyes were focused and intent, and his hands seemed to have a supernatural ability to wrench a reaction out of my body.

I've never known anyone as perceptive as Raylan. I know I can be difficult—stubborn, cold, contentious. Most people don't understand me at all.

But Raylan sees through all that. Those blue eyes cut through the barriers I've built. They cut through all my contradictory impulses. And he finds my real, true desires. The things I want that I would have sworn I didn't want at all.

Like right now—he's eating my pussy gently and carefully so there's no jolting awake. Instead, I'm recovering consciousness gradually, extending that state of dreamlike bliss for as long as possible.

By the time I'm fully awake, my pussy is throbbing with pleasure, the waves of elation radiating outward through my sleep-warmed body.

Right as I come fully awake, Raylan climbs on top of me, his cock raging hard. He slides into me easily since I'm soaking wet. But it's still a tight fit with a delicious level of friction that I've only ever experienced with him. As if his cock and my pussy were made for each other. As if every other partner we'd been with was the wrong-sized shoe on the wrong foot—uncomfortable and always rubbing raw.

He fills me perfectly, his cock stimulating every single pleasure zone. The head of his cock rubs against that sensitive place deep inside me; his girth stimulates all around my opening. And my clit grinds against his hard flat belly with exactly the right amount of pressure.

He braces himself with bent arms on either side of my head, and he looks directly down into my face.

I look up at him, thinking about how unusual it is for a man to be so handsome up close. Most people are better viewed from a distance. That's why we close our eyes when we kiss.

Not Raylan. With his face only a few inches from mine, I see the clarity and brilliance of his eyes. They're a vivid and electric blue, crackling with energy. His irises are encircled by a ring of deep black, the same color as his hair. That ink-black hair looks enticingly thick and soft, so much so that I have to reach up and run my fingers through it, marveling at how it feels like ermine, vibrant and alive like every other part of Raylan.

I can't stop touching him. I trail my fingers down the side of his face where his thick prickly stubble is already growing back. I like the way it outlines his lips and jaw, giving him a roguish, wicked look.

Then I touch his shoulders and chest, straining with the effort of holding himself up on the soft bed and the exertion of slowly thrusting in and out of me.

He has a large tattoo on his right shoulder, shaped like a shield. Inside the shield is a kneeling knight holding a sword. The background of the shield is a night sky speckled with stars and a crescent moon. I know it must be from his mercenary company, the Black Knights. I bet all his brothers-in-arms have the same mark.

I've seen mercenary tattoos before—skulls, daggers, snakes, and guns, usually.

It strikes me that the Black Knights chose something quite different as their sigil—a kneeling man in a penitent pose. It's not aggressive or violent. Instead, it seems to indicate chivalry and honor.

Raylan is a good man.

He's been good to me.

He's protected me. He brought me to his own home to keep me safe.

I look up into his face, and I *do* feel safe. I feel cared for.

These are not sensations that come easily to me. Sometimes I struggle to feel that way even with my own family.

But Raylan isn't obligated to care about me like my family is. If he likes me, if he protects me…it's simply because he wants to. It's real and genuine.

I can feel my climax building—it's been building steadily since he was eating me out, but now it's at the top of a very high peak. And I'm about to go plummeting down.

And for the first time in my life, I look right in a man's eyes while I come. It's not awkward or distracting. Instead, the eye contact amplifies the sensation a hundredfold. It takes sexual pleasure and pairs it with gratitude, admiration, and adoration. It stitches together sensation and emotion into one explosive climax. Instead of crying out, I make a sound almost like a sob.

"Are you all right?" Raylan asks, his blue eyes full of tenderness.

"Yes!" I cry.

He nuzzles his face against the side of my neck, inhaling my scent. He lets go, too, coming inside me with a long groan that thrills me from my head down to my toes.

When we're finished, we lie there for a long time, with Raylan still inside me and my arms still wrapped tightly around his neck. I'm smelling the warm clean scent of his skin, which is endlessly enticing to me. I can't seem to stop pressing my face against his chest, inhaling slowly and deeply.

At last, we hear the noise of breakfast below.

Raylan says, "I guess we better get up before they start shouting for us. That's the downside of ranch life—nobody can stand to see anybody sleep in."

"That's all right," I say. "I hate sleeping. It's a waste of time."

But for the first time, that's not actually true. I had the best sleep of my life last night. Not a waste of time at all.

Raylan and I pad over to the shower.

This is something else I'd usually avoid—cramming two full-size adults into one tiny shower. I've always viewed that as a ridiculous inconvenience.

Today, I want to be close to Raylan. I want to be right next to him for as long as I can. I don't care that it takes longer to shower or that sometimes we have to trade spots under the warm spray, and for a moment, I'm shivering until he pulls me back under again and helps me rinse out my hair.

It feels lovely having his strong thick fingers massaging my scalp, feeling our bodies pressed together all slippery and wet and clean.

When we get out to towel off, the foot or two of space between us seems like too much. Having fallen into this unprecedented intimacy, I'm afraid to let us drift apart again in case it never rematerializes.

"Are you hungry?" Raylan asks, toweling off his thick dark hair.

"Starving," I admit.

I feel like I could eat an entire outrageously sized Raylan breakfast, down to the last bite of toast.

As we thump down the creaking stairs, a cornucopia of delectable scents hits my nostrils. The Boones never disappoint when it comes to food. The table is piled high with plate-sized pancakes, bacon, sausage, scrambled eggs, poached eggs, biscuits and gravy, and, bizarrely, what looks like freshly sliced papaya.

Tucker and Lawson are each attacking a stack of syrup-drenched pancakes that would stymie grown men—or at least grown men who aren't Boones.

Grady and Shelby are sitting next to their sons. Grady has a black eye as dark as a ring of boot polish. He looks like he's wearing a giant monocle.

Celia is digging into a poached egg on toast. She looks up as her eldest son comes into the room. "You were fighting, too!" she says accusingly, spotting Raylan's split lip.

"Ah, it was nothing," Raylan says dismissively. "Just a little dustup. Nobody got stabbed or shot. Sheriff Dawes was pulling in as we left— I'm sure he cleared out anybody who hadn't had enough already."

Celia looks over at Bo. "Tammy Whitmore said Duke started it."

Bo flushes guiltily. "Not really," she says, without confessing exactly what happened.

"I saw him dancing with Lindsey," Shelby says, knowing she's skirting the edges of the truth.

"Was he?" Bo pretends indifference.

She doesn't seem to have much appetite this morning, sticking only to a mug of coffee and a couple of slices of papaya.

I'm piling my plate high with bacon and scrambled eggs, torn between my curiosity about whether Bo is going to admit what actually happened and my desperate need to eat a ton of food as quickly as possible.

But Bo simply pushes her chair back from the table, saying, "That's enough for me."

"You barely ate!" Celia protests.

She turns to me, probably expecting me to make a similar comment. I've got both cheeks as full as a chipmunk, and I'm still shoveling in more.

Celia can't help laughing. "At least we're having a good influence on you."

"Yesh," I mumble, my mouth full and my belly happy.

Raylan laughs, too, loving that he's managed to sway me over to the joys of breakfast if nothing else. His laugh is loud and mischievous, the kind that pulls everyone else into mirth. The boys start giggling, and soon Shelby and Grady are, too.

I like this family so much.

They're warm and welcoming, unpretentious and hardworking. They love animals and the outdoors.

I like them and respect them, as much for our differences as our similarities.

I don't know why they seem to like me, too—maybe they're just kind to everyone. I'm grateful all the same.

"What's your plan today?" Celia says to Raylan and me.

"I've gotta run into Knoxville this morning to get some new horse-stall mats." Raylan asks me, "You wanna come with me before you start working?"

"Temping…I do love shopping for horse-stall mats."

Raylan chuckles. "I thought we could get you some toiletries and clothes. I'm aware that horse-stall mats aren't a big draw."

"You don't know what you're missing," Grady says. "A nice thick flexible mat with that fresh rubber smell…they oughta make that into a candle scent."

"Are you going to the crêperie after?" Bo asks.

"Sure," Raylan says easily.

"Then I'm coming."

"Me, too," Grady says.

We all pile into Raylan's truck. I'm starting to like the comfy wide bench seats and the view of the dusty roads from way up in the cab. Unlike with bucket seats, there's nothing separating Raylan and me. It makes the drive strangely intimate, our free hands just inches apart on the seat.

Grady insists on picking the music, which is all country and mostly all awful. That doesn't stop him from singing along to every song and drumming on the back of the seats. I'd usually find this annoying, but today it just makes me laugh. Maybe it's all the pleasure chemicals still zipping around in my blood. Or maybe it's the huge breakfast I just ate. Whatever the cause, I'm in a bizarrely good mood.

As we drive into Knoxville, the city strikes me as surprisingly pretty. The streets are tree-lined and shady, and the high-rises are built along the banks of a river, similar to Chicago.

It's busier than I expected. The shops and cafés are crowded with people, and the downtown streets look prosperous. There are no empty or boarded-up shops, and only one small brick building is for sale.

There's a pleasant air of friendliness—people smiling or nodding as they pass us on the sidewalk. I don't know if it's a Southern thing or if Raylan's grin just makes people want to smile back at us.

Raylan waits while I step inside a CVS to buy what I need. Then we go next door to something called the C-A-L Ranch Store. Bo wanders off to the firearms section while Grady and Raylan get the mats. I'm distracted by several incubators full of eggs in which dozens of chicks are currently hatching. The chicks look wet and bedraggled and not nearly as cute as the fluffy yellow ones in the next box over, who have apparently been hopping around for at least a day or two. Still, I'm fascinated by the slow, painstaking process by which they break out of their shell prison.

I'm still there when Raylan returns from hauling mats out to the truck.

"You want some chickens?" he asks me with a grin.

"No." I laugh. "I'm just amazed they can do this when they look so weak and floppy."

"They're tougher than they look."

He scoops one of the clean fluffy chicks out of its glass box and places it in my hands. I'm amazed at how light it is and how soft. I can feel its heartbeat against my thumb, ten times faster than my own. The chick nuzzles down in my palm, enjoying the warmth.

All our purchases complete, we head over to the French Market Crêperie as Raylan promised. Raylan and I split a banana, Nutella, and walnut crêpe, and I have to admit, it's pretty damned good. Not far off the crêpes I ate in France.

We head back to the ranch, the heavy rubber horse-stall mats weighing down the bed of the truck.

While Raylan and Grady are unloading, I head back into the

house. I want to go back over those purchase agreements again so I can puzzle out the discrepancy one more time.

Opening Bo's laptop, I notice the deep quiet of the kitchen, punctuated only by a few creaks from the older parts of the house and the odd distant animal sound from outdoors.

It feels strange to be alone.

I'm surprised at how quickly I'm getting used to the noise and bustle of the ranch and the near-constant companionship of Raylan himself. Twice I find myself looking up from the work, about to make a comment to him, only to realize he's out in the stables, not in the kitchen with me.

I shake my head at my idiocy and try to lose myself in the numbers like I usually do.

I asked Lucy to send me those documents. I'm pleased to see she managed to find everything I needed and sent it in several emails so none of the attachments would be too large.

I download them all and start sorting the data, comparing it to my previous spreadsheet.

After a couple of hours of intense comparison, I'm finally able to slip into that state of almost hypnotic focus where the numbers seem to flow and float through my brain, rearranging themselves into patterns that seem to occur almost outside my control, as if I'm watching what's happening instead of actively organizing it.

Numbers have always had a particular personality to me. Six is lucky, seven is quixotic but powerful. Nine can be tricky. Two is useful. Five can always be depended on. I know this is irrational, but it's a device that allows me to rearrange and memorize sequences of numbers as if they were people or objects, not just symbols.

I'm looking at the computer screen, but I'm seeing the flow of numerals in my brain. I'm watching them twist and reform in kaleidoscopic patterns. Until at last...at last...*I see it.*

I see the irregularity.

I see it, and I understand it.

I let out a long slow breath.

"Motherfucker," I whisper.

Josh Hale has been stealing from us. And not a little bit...a whole fucking lot.

When we had to purchase all that land for the South Shore development, he duplicated some of the properties. He copied the purchase agreements almost exactly—omitting only a single number or letter per page. That way, the documents would look identical to the naked eye but could be sorted into separate folders in the computer system.

But where did the money go? That's the question.

The numbers all add up in the spreadsheet, with the duplicate properties removed.

Which means the money we paid for the properties is gone. Siphoned off to some other account that I can't see here.

I know it's Josh because the only properties with double documents are the ones signed by him and him alone.

But I don't know where the fuck he sent the money.

We're talking almost fifty million dollars...

I guess Josh figured out he wasn't getting the partnership. And he thought he deserved to be paid.

I sit back in my chair, my mind whirling.

I have to tell my family, obviously. Especially Cal. I'm pretty sure I just discovered why Josh wants me dead. He poked his head in my office and saw me working on the purchase agreements. He must have thought I already knew about the duplicates—or was about to find them.

But strangely, I don't rush to call Cal.

I want to talk to Raylan. I want to explain what I think I've found and see if he thinks my conclusions are sound or if I've missed something.

It's not that I doubt myself—I just want his opinion. I've come to trust him over these weeks. Sometimes he sees things that I don't.

So I wait for Raylan to come back from fixing the mats.

He strolls into the kitchen, sweaty and a little sunburned, but looking cheerful.

"You want some lemonade?" he says, taking the jug out of the fridge.

"No. Well…maybe a little." The lemonade looks pretty damned good.

Raylan pours us each a glass. We drink it standing up, next to the sink.

"What are you about to tell me?" he says, smiling. "You look excited."

I explain what I found and what I think it means.

Raylan listens, his face still except for a line of tension between his eyebrows.

"So?" I say when I'm finished. "What do you think?"

"That's pretty quick for that Josh guy to hire a hitman," he says. "Just a couple of hours at most from seeing the documents on your desk to the time the Djinn got in the pool…"

"He knows where I live. He probably even knows I like to swim, the nosy fucker."

Raylan is quiet, twisting his empty glass between his thick fingers.

"What?" I say.

"I dunno. It makes sense…if this guy's been stealing money from your family, he'd do anything to cover it up. But something's off…"

I feel flustered that Raylan isn't entirely agreeing with me. I know I asked for his opinion, but it's unsatisfying to hear that I might not have solved it.

"Where did you get the extra files from?" Raylan says.

"I asked Lucy to send them to me."

He frowns. "Did you tell her where you're staying?"

"No, of course not."

"But you emailed her from this laptop?"

"Yes…Does it matter?"

"Probably not," he says, but he looks troubled. "Have you called your brother yet?"

"No. I wanted to talk to you first."

"Well, call him now if you like."

He hands me his phone. It's an old one of Bo's that Raylan's been using, since his cell phone got burned up in my apartment along with everything else.

I dial Cal's number, putting it on speaker so Raylan can hear the tinny ringing at the same time as me.

Cal picks up after only a couple of rings, sounding slightly out of breath.

"Hello?" he says with that slightly suspicious tone he always has when he doesn't recognize a number.

"It's me."

"Oh, right," he says. "Sorry, I keep forgetting to make a contact for this phone—"

"It doesn't matter," I interrupt. "I think I know who hired the Djinn."

"You do?" His tone is eager and tense. "Hold on, I'm putting you on speaker. Dante's with me right now."

I hear Dante's rumbling voice: "What happened? What did you find out?"

I quickly summarize again.

There's silence when I finish, Cal and Dante digesting what I've said.

Then Cal says, "That slimy little shit."

Cal's only met Josh once or twice, but I don't think he liked him any more than I do. Cal's always had a particular hatred of suck-ups and brownnosers. I think it comes from his days at that fancy private school where other kids would try to leech onto him because of our family name.

"If we leave now, we can probably get him at the office," Dante growls.

"Better call Uncle Oran and warn him," I say. "If you just show up there and grab his employee, he's going to be startled."

"Yeah, I will," Cal says.

"We'll get the contract details out of Josh so we can call off the hit," Dante assures me. "I don't care if I have to pull out every fucking fingernail and tooth in his body."

"I doubt it will come to that," I say. "He's kind of a little bitch."

"It won't take long," Cal says. "You can start packing your bag to come home again."

My heart gives a little lurch in my chest.

I glance quickly over at Raylan to see his expression. His face is still, but a muscle jumps at the corner of his jaw.

I had almost forgotten I'd be going back to Chicago once we figured out who the fuck was trying to kill me. As soon as Cal and Dante get Josh, they'll be able to wring the details of the hit out of him. Then they can call back the marker. The Djinn is just a hitman for hire—he doesn't have any grudge against me.

The idea of being free of that shroud is certainly appealing. I want to be able to go where I like and do what I like again, without worrying about some boogeyman popping out at me.

But on the other hand...I'm not entirely excited to leave the ranch. I was actually enjoying myself here.

Still, Cal's waiting to hear my response. So I lick my dry lips and say, "Yeah. I'm excited to come home. I miss you guys."

"I'll let you know as soon as it's done," Cal says.

He hangs up without actually saying goodbye, like he's in a movie. Aida always teases him about that. *Too busy and important to waste half a second, Mr. Alderman?*

I don't mind. I'm impatient, too. And I don't care about little formalities.

I'm much more concerned with the strange tension between Raylan and me. It started with our disagreement over Josh. And now it seems to have expanded to fill the whole space of the kitchen.

"I'm sure Dante and Callum will handle it," Raylan says as if he's reassuring me.

"I know," I reply.

I don't think that's what either of us is actually worried about, but it's the easiest thing to address.

Raylan hesitates. His blue eyes search my face as if he's trying to read me like he usually does, but for once he's coming up blank.

"Do you want to go back?" he asks.

"Well…I have to. I've already missed so much work. And with Josh gone…I know it sounds stupid because, apparently, he's a treacherous asshole, but he did handle a huge workload. Somebody's got to pick up the slack. Not to mention it's pretty clear who's getting the partnership now."

"Congratulations," Raylan says dully.

My chest feels tight. I know I should be happy. I'm finally getting what I worked toward for years. I'll have my name on the door and on the letterhead. I'll be a partner, not just an employee. I'll be equal to my uncle in my father's eyes. And I can just imagine how Uncle Oran will sweep me into one of his stiff, tight hugs that smells of cigar smoke, saying in his raspy voice, *Well done, girl.*

I want those things, as badly as I've ever wanted them. But I also want the look of hurt to disappear from Raylan's eyes.

"You'll come back with me, won't you?" I ask.

He lets out a little exhale of air. "Well…you won't exactly need a bodyguard anymore, will you? And that's a good thing," he hastens to add.

"Right," I say.

It's true. Still, I feel a little dull at that realization.

Which is ridiculous. Did I think Raylan was going to follow me around everywhere for the rest of my life?

The whole point was to figure out who hired the hitman and get back to normal existence. That's done. Or almost done.

"Besides," Raylan says quietly. "I don't plan to go out on any more jobs. At least not in the foreseeable future. You probably saw my mom broke her foot—it'll heal up fine, but she's gonna break it again if she keeps working as hard as she has been. I've let her and Grady and Bo run this place for too long. It's time for me to make a choice if I want a stake in it or not. It's not fair for me to let them do all the work, acting like I can come back anytime I want."

"So...you want to be a rancher?"

"I am a rancher," he says. "I just did other things for a while. I don't ever want this place chopped up and sold. This is home."

If Raylan would have told me that before I ever saw this place, I would have thought he was crazy. Who would want to live in Tennessee after having traveled the world?

But I've seen with my own eyes how beautiful the Boones' ranch is. How endless in scope. I've seen how connected Raylan is to his family and the animals and the people around here. He was gone for years, and when he came home again, it was like barely any time had passed. That's how strong his bond is with this place—it can't be eroded by time or distance.

I feel the same way about Chicago, in some ways. I've lived there all my life. I know its sights, its sounds, its smells. But I'm just one person out of millions in Chicago. Whereas Raylan is needed here. His family and the ranch depend on him for survival, in the long term.

"I understand," I tell him.

"You do?"

"Yes. This is a corner of the earth you own. That's different than just living somewhere."

He nods slowly.

Of course, there's the other part of it. I know from what Celia told me that Raylan left here in anger, thinking he didn't actually belong to this place. But that was never really true. It was always his home. And he was always meant to come back here, to heal that wound.

I think he's finally ready to do that.

I shouldn't say anything to prevent that from happening. I think he needs it. Badly.

I don't know how to bring up what I know, but I don't want to keep it secret from him either.

I say, "Your mom told me what happened right before you enlisted. She told me about your father."

"Waya was my father," Raylan says at once.

"I know!" I say quickly. "That's what I meant."

Raylan looks at me with a strange expression. "I'm surprised she told you. She doesn't like to talk about that. Obviously." He gives a mirthless short laugh, totally unlike his usual laugh. "Since I never heard about it for eighteen years."

"You belong here," I say. "I just wanted you to know…that I understand that."

Raylan looks pained. His voice is tight. "Does every family have an ugly history?"

"Mine certainly does."

You could write a thousand-page saga of the pain and bloodshed in the Griffins' history. Another for the Gallos, too.

I want to ask Raylan what I couldn't ask Celia because I didn't want to seem intrusive after all she'd told me. But the lawyer in me knows there's more to the story. From what she told me about Ellis, he never would have let her get away easily…

"Your mom told me what happened. But not how she got away from Ellis Burr."

I don't say *your father* or even *your biological father* because I know Raylan doesn't view him that way.

Raylan lets out a long breath. "I'll tell you," he says. "But not in here. Come for a walk with me."

CHAPTER 20
RAYLAN

I walk with Riona down along an avenue of birch trees. Their leaves have fully changed from green to gold, later in the year than usual as it's been a warm autumn after a lengthy Indian summer.

I'm surprised Mom told Riona about Ellis but also glad in a way I can't quite express to her. It's a story I wouldn't have told without my mother's permission. And I want Riona to know it. I want her to know everything about me.

As well, it shows that my mother thinks highly of Riona. She trusted her with our family secrets. She obviously intuited how I feel about Riona, though I haven't explicitly told her.

The other part of the story is something our family has never shared with anyone. I never expected to tell it myself, even to a future partner. But Riona is different. As she said, her family has its own dark secrets, its own history of violence. I know she won't be shocked by anything I tell her. I can trust her to take the story to her grave. Only a Mafia daughter understands true discretion.

So I'm not nervous as we walk along.

I'm just rolling the story over in my head, trying to think how best to explain.

"My mother had a friend," I say. "A boy she knew from the time she was little. Similar to Bo and Duke. They went to elementary school together. Eventually, his family moved back to North

Carolina, to Cherokee land. But my mother and Waya still kept in touch—he would visit her when his family came back to Silver Run for any reason. Though at the time she got married, she hadn't seen Waya in almost three years. She also had two younger brothers— maybe she told you?"

Riona says, "One of them was named Abott, and he was big like Grady, right?"

"That's exactly right. Uncle Abott. The other was Uncle Earl. At the time she got married, they were only thirteen and fifteen years old. But they were both tall, and hardened, if you know what I mean."

Riona nods. I'm sure she's seen plenty of boys become men at a young age.

I continue: "Before Mom got married, she was still seeing her siblings regularly. Still taking care of them. As soon as she moved into Ellis's house, he cut her off from them entirely. They weren't allowed to call or visit. And my mother was barely allowed out of the house at all. Never without Ellis right beside her.

"Of course, they were worried about her. And not just because there was nobody to take care of them anymore. They tried to slip notes to her when Ellis would bring her into town. And two or three times, they tried to visit.

"There were gates all around the property, and cameras. Uncle Abott climbed the wall and managed to speak to her when she was pregnant with me. Right before she was about to give birth, actually.

"She tried to tell him that she was all right and he needed to leave her alone. But she was wearing a white shirt, and he could see bruises all over her arms, even through the shirt.

"So he left. But he called Waya. He said, 'Celia needs help. Will you help her?' And Waya drove in that night with two of his sisters.

"They waited outside the property all night till the early morning, with Abott and Earl in the car, too. They were scared, arguing over whether they should go in right away. They were worried that Ellis might be hurting her if he'd seen Abott on the camera. Which, of course, was exactly what was happening. But they also worried he might do something worse to her if he caught them trying to break in. My mother had told them he had dozens of guns in the house— one in every room.

"So they waited, staying up all night. Then, in the morning, Ellis didn't leave for work at the usual time. They debated again what to do. Finally, Ellis's black BMW pulled away with him sitting in the driver's seat.

"They waited for him to get all the way away from the property. Then one of Waya's sisters went to the door. They knew Ellis wouldn't recognize her on the camera.

"She had to climb the fence. Then she sprinted up to the door. She rang the bell, terrified in case nobody answered. In case my mother *couldn't* answer.

"But she did. My mother peeked through the window, then opened the door. Her face was so battered and swollen that she couldn't even really see Ama, only out of one eye.

"Ama said, 'We're leaving right now. What do you want to take?' And my mother said, 'Nothing. I don't want a single thing from this house.' She stripped off her wedding ring and left it on the floor in the front hall.

"They had to run across the property, knowing Ellis was probably already speeding home as fast as he could. They got to the wall, and my mother couldn't climb it because of how pregnant she was. Ama got down on her hands and knees so my mother could get on her back, and then she boosted her up. Waya was on the other side to catch her.

"They drove off as fast as they could. They'd left the car down the road, out of sight of the cameras, so Ellis wouldn't know who had taken her."

I pause. The next bit is the part nobody outside my family knows. Or at least nobody still alive. I look over at Riona. We've been walking side by side all this time, not touching each other but the closest thing to touching. Our hands only an inch apart.

Riona looks tense and expectant. Her face is paler than usual, I think out of sympathy. I know she likes my mother and doesn't enjoy thinking about her beaten, battered, and heavily pregnant.

It's strange to think that I was technically present for all these events. Just a nearly grown fetus, carried along for the ride. I don't remember any of it, obviously. I'm only going off what my mother told me after I found her wedding certificate in the attic.

She was willing to tell me everything once I knew the truth. She described it all in perfect detail, and Waya added anything she didn't know or couldn't remember.

It's all burned into my brain. It was the most unexpected thing that's ever happened to me. I was so safe and secure in my life. I had never suspected for a second that Waya wasn't my "real" father.

God, I was so angry at them. I'm ashamed of it now. I can picture them standing there, my mother sick with guilt and regret, Waya looking at me with his gentle dark eyes. Both of them trying to say anything they could to comfort me. And me shouting at them, wrapped up in my own emotions without a thought for what they'd been through or what they were feeling.

It was dumb luck I found the wedding certificate. It was all folded up, stuffed into a folder with a bunch of documents. I wasn't looking for it. If you can believe it, I was looking for an old set of Ninja Turtle action figures I'd stashed up there, thinking maybe I could sell them on eBay for a couple of bucks.

Instead, I found the old certificate, which was actually a copy ordered later so my mother could finish the paperwork to get remarried.

She looked horrified at the sight of it. Like it was a snake that might bite her. I'm sure she wished she'd thrown it away. At the time, I wished she had, too.

Now I don't regret that I found it. I only regret how I reacted.

Some things can't be taken back.

I've taken too long to continue, lost in thought. Riona reaches out and touches my arm, saying, "Are you all right?"

I clear my throat. "Yes. Of course. Where was I? Oh, right... My mother wanted Waya to stay with her. She was so scared. But he passed her over to his sisters, and they drove back over the border to Cherokee land, not stopping once. Waya stayed with my uncles.

"The next bit was the tricky part. They had to make sure everyone in Silver Run knew that my mother had run off and that Ellis was looking for her. But they couldn't let him actually get close to finding her.

"So, Waya, Uncle Abott, Uncle Earl, and some of my mother's younger siblings kept watch everywhere they could. It was easier than they hoped because Ellis was in a fucking rage. He went to the sheriff and reported my mother as kidnapped. He went to the bar where she used to work. He went to her old high school and her friends' houses. My grandparents' house, too.

"He screamed at them and threatened them. Even smashed a couple of windows in their house. Beat my grandfather within an inch of his life, though he was probably too high to notice. Then Ellis grabbed one of the youngest siblings—my aunt Kelly. She was only four at the time. He grabbed her and acted like he was going to drag her out of the house. Maybe he thought he'd keep her hostage or something to force my mother to come back."

"Jesus," Riona whispers.

"Well, Uncle Abott came running into the house with his junior league baseball bat, and he said, 'Let go of her, or I'll crack your fuckin' skull.' Ellis let go of Aunt Kelly and left.

"They followed him around for three days. At one point he came face-to-face with my auntie Lane as she was tailing him outside a gas station, but he just looked right through her and kept going. It was ironic because Ellis had given her a skateboard as a gift when he'd been pursuing my mother. But he didn't even recognize her face. Maybe he was just too enraged to notice.

"Anyway, on the fourth day, some people in town were spreading the rumor that my mother had been seen on Cherokee land. Ellis hadn't heard it yet as far as my uncles knew, but they also knew it was only a matter of time until he did.

"So they put a slow leak in the tires of his car while he was eating at the bar where my mother used to work. He kept going back there to threaten the owners and harass the other customers. He bribed a few, too. It didn't work—if anybody knew where my mother was, they didn't tell him.

"Ellis got back in his car, more than a little tipsy. He started speeding down the road back to his property. At first he didn't notice the tires were getting flat. Waya and my two uncles were following along behind him in a borrowed car. Ellis kept speeding, even when the back right tire was wobbling and flopping.

"Finally, the car started to fishtail, and he swerved and went off the road. He rammed the BMW into the space between two trees. It was jammed in there tight. So tight that he had to climb over the seat and go out the back door.

"He had a big cut on his forehead, but otherwise he was fine. Just swearing and complaining. Still dressed in one of his fancy suits.

"Waya pulled up and said, 'You need a lift?'

"Ellis might have been suspicious if he hadn't been drinking. But he just said, 'Yeah,' not even saying thanks. And he started walking over to the car. He got about five feet away, and he stopped and squinted at the car windows. I think he saw there was somebody in the back seat.

"Waya opened the driver's side door, and Ellis reached into his jacket like he was gonna grab a gun. He had one, but he'd lost it in the crash. By the time he realized, my two uncles and Waya had all jumped out of the car and surrounded him."

I pause, glancing over at Riona to see if she knows what's coming next. I can tell by her solemn expression that she does.

"They dragged him off into the woods. Uncle Abott wanted to

kill him slowly. He wanted to cut and burn and beat Ellis, like Ellis had done to my mother. But Waya said no. It would be messy and noisy and leave too much evidence. And he said, 'We're not like him.'

"So they marched Ellis a full ten miles out into the woods and shot him in the back of the head. They dug a hole and buried the body under enough dirt and rock that no animal would dig it up. Waya and Abott did it. Uncle Earl stayed behind to move their car in case someone came along and saw the crash.

"Then Waya drove my uncles home, and he went back to his own house, where my mother was staying with his sisters. She went into labor a week later.

"After I was born, he told her what they had done. He didn't want to upset her, but he didn't want her worrying about Ellis finding her either.

"She wanted to go back home to her siblings. Waya convinced her to stay. He said they had to wait—to make sure there wasn't going to be any trouble for her. He thought it would look suspicious if she came back home like she knew Ellis was dead.

"Ellis was reported missing at first. His work called it in. The sheriff found Ellis's car shortly after. There was a hunt through the woods—they thought maybe he hit his head in the accident and wandered off, confused. But they didn't think an injured man could wander far, so they only went a few miles in. They found some blood on the ground. So some people thought an animal had got him.

"Everybody knew he'd been drinking at the bar. He wasn't a local, and he wasn't liked. So nobody looked too hard for him.

"Meanwhile my mother stayed where she was. She fell in love with Waya—or fell in love with him all over again. They'd always cared about each other, growing up.

"Uncle Earl came to live with her. So did a couple of her youngest siblings. She got pregnant with Grady. Married Waya. Then a couple of years later, she had Bo.

"Ellis stayed a missing person for several years. Then eventually his work wanted to claim their insurance policy on him, so they did the necessary footwork to get him declared dead.

"When they did, my mother found out she was the beneficiary of a pretty hefty insurance policy herself. Plus Ellis's estate. He had no will, so it all went to her.

"She sold the house they'd lived in together without ever stepping foot inside it again. She used the money to buy the ranch. We all moved here.

"Of course, none of us kids knew anything about what had happened or where the money had come from. Kids don't think about things like that. We were all just excited to have such a big house. Except for Bo—she was pissed we were leaving. She loved living on Cherokee land with all our dad's family around us.

"He used to take us back all the time. That's how Bo and Duke stayed so close. They were cradle mates—born the same week in August. My mother and Duke's mother became close friends during their pregnancies, and they'd put the babies in the same hammock together to nap.

"Bo and Duke used to fight like wild animals as they got older. But they were best friends, too."

"They got in a fight at the dance," Riona tells me. "Duke was dancing with another girl."

"I guess he's desperate. Trying to make Bo realize she's jealous."

"You think they have romantic feelings for each other?"

"I know they do. You can't have a best friend you're attracted to. That's what being in love is. It's wanting to fuck your best friend."

Riona laughs. "That's all love is?"

"That's what it should be."

She looks up at me with those sea-glass eyes, then drops them again just as quickly.

I say, "What is it?"

"I was just thinking…there's a third part."

"What?"

"You can fuck a lot of people. And anyone can be a friend. But there's a third part to love…admiring the person."

"Admiring them?"

"Yes. That's a lot rarer. There are only a few people I really respect."

In this moment, I want more than anything to be one of those people. To be respected and admired by a woman like Riona is a real accomplishment. I know she doesn't give her approval easily.

"Do you count me in that favored few?" I say, trying to keep my tone casual.

"Yes," Riona says evenly. "I do."

The way my chest swells up, you'd think I just won the Kentucky Derby.

"Thank you," I say. For some reason, my throat feels tight. "You know I think the world of you, Riona."

"I do know that," Riona says, her green eyes looking up at me, clear and wide. "You're better than I am at showing what you feel."

"I think I've got a pretty good guess with you," I say. "Most of the time, at least."

"What am I thinking right now?" Riona asks quietly.

I know what I wish she were thinking. But I don't know if I have the courage to ask her.

I gently touch her cheek, our faces only inches apart. Her expression is more vulnerable than I've ever seen before. I don't know how I ever called this woman an ice queen. Riona isn't only one thing. Once you chip past the frost, she has a whole universe inside her.

I open my mouth to speak, but before I can say a word, Bo comes jogging up to us, red-faced and irritated.

"Shelby's having the baby! Mom's going over to their house to watch the boys, and I'm gonna drive them to the hospital. I'll probably stay there in case they need anything—so Grady doesn't have to leave."

"What do you need me to do?"

"Handle the horses. Get 'em all fed and put away for the night."

"Sure thing." I nod.

"Why'd you two walk so damn far?" Bo complains, turning around to jog back to the house.

I look back at Riona, wanting to pursue our conversation. But the moment has passed.

She says, "We'd better hurry back, sounds like."

"Yup," I say. "But I want to continue this later."

CHAPTER 21
RIONA

RAYLAN AND I HEAD BACK TO THE RANCH HOUSE.

We linger outside the kitchen door, both of us feeling there was more to say to each another. When Bo interrupted us, I think Raylan was about to tell me something else. After he'd already told me his family's story.

I don't take that lightly. That's a secret they've kept for thirty years.

He told me because he trusts me. I wish there were a way to show him that I trust him, too.

But all I can say is, "Good luck with the horses."

Raylan grins. "Thank you. When I get back, let's have a drink together. It's a full moon tonight. We can sit out on the deck."

"That sounds beautiful."

I intended to go inside and do a little more work. But I feel strangely flat after what I discovered about Josh. It makes me feel as if the project is tainted in some way. I know that's stupid, but it bothers me how the truth was hiding right under the data without me seeing it. It's like realizing there's a crocodile floating right under the water. Even if you manage to pull it out, you don't look at the lake in quite the same way.

I guess I'm embarrassed I didn't see it sooner. I didn't think much of Josh. I'm surprised he was able to fool us for so long.

I expect Cal and Dante have found him by now. They'll probably call me any minute.

Idly, I turn Raylan's phone over in my hands, waiting for the screen to light up with the call. When it doesn't, I set the phone down on the kitchen table and open the laptop instead.

I'm still distracted. My brain keeps floating back to my walk with Raylan down the birch avenue.

I miss him.

That sounds so ridiculous, but it's true. I've gotten so used to him being by my side almost constantly. When he goes anywhere else, I feel his absence.

Raylan has become like sunshine on my skin. Warm, comforting, enlivening. When he goes someplace else, I feel chilled and dull. Like a flower just waiting for the sun to return.

That's ludicrous, I know. I tell myself to shake it off and get back to work. To lose myself in charts and documents and purchase agreements, to find my pleasure in labor like I always used to.

I can hear the house creaking and groaning as the sun sinks lower and the warmth of the day fades away. The temperature change makes the old wood contract. It almost sounds like someone walking around upstairs, though I know Raylan and I are the only ones on the property at the moment.

I hadn't bothered to switch on the lights. Now that the sun is going down, the kitchen is becoming dim and shadowy. The laptop screen is illuminated, so I don't really need the light to work. But I still feel an impulse to get up and flip the switch. I feel uneasy, the tiny hairs rising on my bare arms.

Raylan's phone buzzes on the table, startling me. I pick it up, seeing Cal's number.

"Hey," I say.

"Hey. I wanted to update you—we don't have Josh."

My stomach sinks like an elevator. "What happened?"

"We called Uncle Oran, and he said Josh hadn't come into work today—he called in sick. So we went to Josh's house instead. But there was nobody there. The place was a fucking mess. It was hard to tell if he'd packed up and cleared out or if he's just a slob."

"His office is like that, too," I tell Cal.

"We searched the streets to see if his car was anywhere around. Bribed his neighbor, but he said Josh left that morning at the normal time and he hadn't seen him come back. We've got eyes out anywhere we can think of..."

"Did you check his girlfriend's apartment?"

"Yeah, Uncle Oran told us about her. She was at work—said she hadn't talked to him that day. We took her phone, tried texting and calling him. No answer. We made her give us her key and searched her flat. Fucking nothing."

I don't like the sound of that at all.

We end the call.

My stomach is clenching and twisting. I feel prickled with anxiety.

Why did Josh take off all of a sudden?

He must know we found out what he'd done. But how could he know that?

Is it a coincidence? Was he always planning to take the money and run once he'd amassed enough?

I don't believe in coincidences that big. He disappears the very day we come looking for him? That seems off.

Maybe he found out Lucy sent me those files. I never told her to keep it a secret.

I remember how Raylan reacted when I told him about the emails back and forth. He seemed uncomfortable with it, like I'd made a mistake. Is it possible to trace an IP address? If I emailed Lucy from this laptop, could someone locate where my email came from? Could they have found out where I'm hiding?

I tell myself I'm just being paranoid. I'm safe here—that's why Raylan brought me all the way to the ranch.

It was just an email.

Still, I wish Raylan were here beside me and not all the way out in the fields, rounding up the horses.

Quietly, I slip out of my chair and walk over to the counter where Celia's knives are all fitted neatly into their slots in a carved wooden block. I pull out one of the knives—not the cleaver, which is too large and unwieldy. I take a fish knife instead—long and slim and deadly sharp. Then I go back to the table again.

The kitchen is getting quite dark. I could turn on the light, but something tells me not to. Instead, very quietly, I close the laptop screen, snuffing out the last bit of illumination.

Then I sit in the dark, listening.

I hear a tiny creak from overhead. I know the ranch house pretty well by now. I think that noise came from the guest bedroom. *My* bedroom.

I remember how the Djinn lay in wait for me in the swimming pool. How he waited for almost an hour, quiet and still, at the bottom of the pool. He must have seen me slip into the water. He watched me stroke back and forth across the pool, over his head. Watching me from below like a shark. No…like an eel in a cave.

The Djinn is an ambush predator.

He likes to hide himself, waiting and watching. Taking pleasure in his victim's obliviousness. Letting them wander closer and closer.

Then, when the moment is right…he pounces.

My heart is thudding against my ribs. This could all be complete fantasy. There's no reason to think the Djinn found me here. No reason to think he's hiding upstairs in my room just because I heard a couple of creaks.

But I can't get that picture out of my mind—a dark figure lying in wait under my bed. Waiting for me to lie down and sleep so he can rise from below and wrap his arm around my throat again.

I'm frozen in place, wanting to go out to Raylan but afraid to cross the dark fields alone. I'm gripping the handle of the fish knife in my fist, rigid and motionless in the kitchen chair. My ears strain for any other sounds that might tell me if what I'm imagining is real or only a paranoid fantasy, like a child who runs up from the basement thinking there's a monster at their heels.

Silence. Total silence.

I'm an idiot. I'm just making myself scared, sitting alone in a dark kitchen.

Still, I want Raylan more than I've ever yearned to see anybody. If he were sitting next to me on the deck, each of us with a drink in our hands, I wouldn't be scared of anything.

He's got to be almost finished with the horses by now. I'm going to go out to meet him.

Still holding the knife, almost forgetting I have it, I walk swiftly toward the kitchen door. It's so dim that I reach out half blindly, fumbling for the knob.

Right as my fingers close around it, an arm locks around my neck.

I hadn't heard anything. Not a creak. Not a breath.

The Djinn grabs me from behind and jerks me back off my feet.

His arm is a steel bar around my throat, closing off my air in an instant. He lifts me off my feet, inhumanly strong. And he squeezes harder.

It's all too familiar—we're in air instead of water, but I'm plunged back to exactly where we were. I'm drowning again, choking to death in the arms of the Djinn.

His other hand is clamped over my mouth. It doesn't matter—without air, I can't scream. And even if I could, Raylan is too far away to hear me.

The Djinn watched and waited. He knew I was alone in the house.

The loss of air is so sudden that my limbs go weak. My fingers loosen. I almost drop the knife.

Almost…but not quite.

With every last shred of control, I grip it tightly. I blindly swing backward, aiming for his body.

The fish knife plunges into his side. I hear a grunt of pain and fury in my ear. The first sound I've heard him make. But he doesn't let go.

I keep hold of the handle and wrench the knife out again, then swing it back toward him. He jerks away with his body, avoiding the blade. But he has to loosen his hold on my throat.

As soon as I feel his forearm loosen, I turn my chin to the side and drop with all my weight, slipping out of his grasp. I swing the knife wildly, and this time it sticks into his thigh. I lose my grip on the handle. The Djinn gives a strangled yell and backhands me.

I slide across the kitchen tiles. For the first time, I get a good look at the Djinn in the flesh. Or at least as good a look as I can get in the dark. He's dressed in a skintight black suit, not so different from the one he wore into the swimming pool. His head is covered by a tight hood, and his eyes look monstrously enlarged, like a house fly's, because he's wearing night-vision goggles. The fish knife protrudes from his thigh.

That's all I see before I scramble to my feet again and run for the door. I wrench it open and sprint out of the house into the backyard. I'm running barefoot across the path between the vegetable and flower gardens. I scream as loudly as I can, "RAYLAN!" I have no idea how far away he is or if there's any chance he can hear me.

We're so far away from anything. If I try to run to the main road, I'll have to go over a mile down the driveway. It's pitch-black out, the only lights located directly around the barns and stables. I can't stomach the idea of running alone through the dark. Especially when I know the Djinn can see much better than I can.

So I run toward the stables instead. I slip inside, smelling the warm scent of the horses, clean hay, and scattered oats. I can hear the horses shifting around in their stalls, their feet thudding gently on the wood floor.

I find Penny's stall, and I go inside with her. She recognizes me, giving a soft little whicker. She rubs the side of her head against my body.

I say, "*Shh*," very quietly.

Then I stand next to her, my heart racing.

I'm regretting not looking around for some kind of weapon—even a shovel or crop. I wanted to get in here as quickly as possible, afraid the Djinn would pull the knife out of his thigh and come out of the house so he could see where I'd run.

I listen closely without hearing anything. That doesn't mean much—I've already learned how quietly he can move.

Where did he go?

I can't hear anything but horses.

Now I'm afraid for a completely different reason. What if Raylan comes back? The Djinn will ambush him. Raylan has no idea what's going on—as far as he knows, Cal and Dante grabbed Josh and canceled the hit. He has no idea that anyone could come here looking for us.

I shift on my feet, wondering if I should try to cross the fields to find him. I can't just stay here hiding while Raylan's in danger, too.

Right as I'm about to move, I see Penny's ears stand up stiffly, and she takes a quick step to the side. I hear Bruce's angry snort in the next stall over. The horses smell somebody else. Someone they don't recognize.

The Djinn is inside the stable.

I stay perfectly still. Barely breathing. Time seems atrociously slow.

I don't know if he saw me come in here or if he's just searching the most obvious places. I don't know how carefully he'll look or if he's just glancing around before leaving. I don't know if he has a gun or the fish knife.

I wait, my pupils so dilated that I can see every hair on Penny's bright coppery coat. She seems as tense as I am. She can probably smell my fear.

I don't hear footsteps. I'm hoping, praying the Djinn has left.

Then Penny's stall door creaks open.

I see the Djinn's booted feet standing just past her back hooves.

Without thinking, I slap Penny hard on the flank. She kicks backward with both feet, hitting the Djinn square in the chest. He goes flying backward, crashing through the door of the stall opposite Penny's.

I'm running again, out of the stable, across the open yard.

I don't scream for Raylan this time. The Djinn is too close. I don't want him to hear me.

No…he's not close…

He's right behind me.

I hear his boots on the gravel—it's impossible to be quiet here. I hear his ragged breathing. He's gasping for air, groaning with each breath. He's obviously injured—Penny possibly broke a few of his ribs. But that motherfucker is still gaining on me. He's fast and relentless. He's never going to stop. I have no more weapons. If he gets his arm around my throat again, I'm dead.

He's closing in. So close that I feel his hot breath on my neck.

Out of nowhere, Raylan hits him from the side. He barrels toward us from the direction of the house, tackling the Djinn sideways, taking him out at the knees so they roll over and over on the crushed stone.

"*Run, Riona!*" Raylan shouts.

He's wrestling with the Djinn. He's got no weapon either. Silver flashes as the Djinn swings the fish knife toward Raylan's eye. Raylan grabs his wrist, barely twisting the blade in time so it cuts his cheek instead.

Raylan is actually the bigger of the two men, but I've never seen someone as fast as the Djinn. He sends slash after slash at Raylan, some blocked and some cutting Raylan on the forearm and the shoulder. Raylan has one hand on the Djinn's throat, and he's squeezing while trying to block the knife with the other hand. All this happens in the span of two seconds while I'm rooted in place, staring at them in horror.

I don't know what to do.

We're right next to the barn where Grady makes the saddles. Where Raylan and I had our encounter.

I run into it and grab two items off the bench: the lantern and an awl. I sprint back to Raylan, who's locked in a trembling, static position with the Djinn: the blade of the fish knife pointed at Raylan's throat, the Djinn bearing down on the handle with both hands while Raylan tries to push his arms back.

The Djinn looks inhuman, those bug-eyed lenses fixed on Raylan and his face a rictus of fury. I turn the lantern directly at his face and switch it on.

The light flashes right into the night-vision goggles. The Djinn howls and staggers back, tearing the goggles off his face. He's stumbling and blinded.

"Raylan!" I cry.

I toss him the awl.

He catches it in his right hand and plunges it into the Djinn's chest. The Djinn shrieks, unable to even see what's hit him. He feels for it blindly. But unlike the fish knife, he can't pull the awl out. It's too deeply embedded in too vital a place.

Instead, he sinks to his knees with a long gurgling moan. He falls over on his side, the gravel biting into his face.

Raylan kicks the Djinn over with the toe of his boot. The Djinn rolls onto his back, his mouth still working soundlessly.

I step closer, looking down at him. I hold up the lantern so I can see his face.

Without his goggles, he looks...utterly average. He has a soft, plain, almost gentle-looking face. Brown eyes, wide and bloodshot now, but almost pretty with their dark lashes under his straight brows. Thin lips and a weak chin. A man you would never look at twice, passing on the street.

I suppose that was helpful in his profession.

I look up at Raylan instead.

He's panting heavily, his shirt slashed open on his shoulder, his right cheek bleeding.

His blue eyes find mine, and I see infinite relief in them as he looks me over, as he sees I'm safe.

He pulls me into his arms, holding me tightly against his warm chest.

"You're okay. You're okay," he says.

I think he's reassuring himself.

CHAPTER 22
RAYLAN

I can't let go of Riona. I'm holding her, probably too tightly, but I can't relax my grip.

I should never have left her alone at the house.

How the *fuck* did the Djinn find her?

It could have been the emails—he might have tracked the IP address. Or maybe it was the phone calls.

Either way, I wasn't careful enough. That won't happen again.

I kiss Riona, tasting the remnants of adrenaline on her lips. I can feel her shaking from her sprint across the yard.

"What are we going to do with him?" she asks, looking down at the body of the assassin.

"I'll bury him somewhere out on our land."

"Don't go right now," Riona says.

"I won't," I promise.

I'm not letting go of her, even for a second. Instead, I scoop her up in my arms, and I carry her into the house. I carry her all the way up the stairs to her room, and I lay her down on the bed, on top of the covers.

Then I kiss her, pinning her against the pillows. Running my hands over every inch of her body, making sure no part of her is injured.

We're both still keyed up at full throttle. We're full of nervous energy that has to go somewhere.

Riona strips off her clothes and climbs on top of me. Her pale skin gleams in the moonlight streaming through the window. Her hair looks dark auburn, and her eyes are green as moss. She looks like a creature you might find deep in the woods. Something that would lure you off the path, that you would gladly follow to your doom.

I shuck off my jeans.

She straddles my hips, stroking my cock with her pussy lips. It feels so good that I think I'm already inside her, even though I can see I haven't even penetrated her yet. She's just slowly grinding her clit against the shaft of my cock.

I could watch her slim body writhe on top of me for hours. She looks inhumanly beautiful. Almost too beautiful for me to reach up and touch.

But, of course, I can't resist doing exactly that. I caress her breasts. She leans forward to let them fall into my hands. She rolls her hips, letting her nipples brush against my palms in time with her grinding. Her breasts are soft, and her nipples are stiff.

I slide my hands down her sides to the curve of her waist.

Her body reminds me of a violin—perfectly shaped, perfectly balanced. I want to play her like an instrument. I want to tease the most outrageous sounds out of her.

Riona reaches down and grips my cock, finally sliding it inside her.

Oh, my fucking god, that sensation…warm and painfully tight. But so smooth and slippery. She rolls her hips harder, riding me steadily.

Now I slide my hands down to her ass. Riona is slim, but she has a full round ass. Firm from running and swimming. It fills my hands. I can feel the muscle squeezing with each roll of her hips.

She leans forward so her breasts hang right in my face. I take one in my mouth, sucking her tits while she rides me. I'm half propped up on the pillows, and I press my hand against the small of her back to pull her closer so I can take more of her breast in my mouth.

Riona moans. She hooks her arm around my neck, keeping my face pressed against her breast. She's riding harder and faster, her hips moving in frantic short arcs as she increases the pressure against her clit.

I grab her waist again, helping to press her down hard on my body. Thrusting my cock deeper inside her.

Her warm wavy hair has fallen all around my face. I love the scent of it and the way it tickles my skin.

I can't get enough of her. Every time we get close like this, I want more of it. I never want it to end.

I grab her face, and I kiss her as she starts to come. She moans directly into my mouth as the climax washes over her, as her pussy clenches rhythmically around my cock and her whole body becomes as tense as a bowstring.

Then she collapses on top of me, and I have to roll her over so I can climb on her and finish myself.

When I roll her onto her stomach, I mount her from behind, pinning her down flat on the bed and sliding my cock inside her again. I fuck her hard, each thrust of my cock shaking the entire bed on its frame.

All I can think of while I do this is, *You're mine. I kept you safe… and now you belong to me.*

That thought makes me explode inside her. I feel like I produce ten times the come as normal when I'm with Riona. I can feel it pulsing out of me, spurt after spurt. The volume of it gives me an intense sense of relief. The wet warmth is erotic and primal. I feel like I'm marking her. Claiming her as mine.

We fall asleep like that, facedown on the bed, me still inside her. It seems impossible to sleep after the night we had.

But that's how powerful our release is together…it washes away even the most intense stress. Leaving nothing but peaceful warmth in its place.

———

As soon as the first gray light of dawn comes through the window, I get up again.

I can't leave the body of the Djinn lying in the yard.

"Where are you going?" Riona says sleepily.

"I've got to move…you know."

Riona sits up. She looks outrageously sexy in the morning light—her hair wild and tangled, her skin flushed pink with sleep. Her eyes are surprisingly alert. "I'll come with you."

"You don't have to do that."

"I want to."

We dress quickly, going downstairs and out through the back door.

For a minute I have the sick sensation that the Djinn might have vanished. That he might be unkillable. But his body is lying right where we left it—dusty, bloody, and strangely pathetic.

Riona looks at it, then turns away, her face pale and nauseated.

"Don't bother with him," I say. "Just get a couple of shovels out of the shed."

I point to the outbuilding where we keep most of the tools.

While Riona's getting the shovels, I take Bruce, Penny, and Horatio out of the stables. I saddle the first two horses, then heft the Djinn's body onto Horatio's back. Horatio snorts, taking a few nervous sideways steps. He seems to know there's something wrong with his rider.

I help Riona climb on Penny's back, while I carry the shovels with me on Bruce. We head out across the fields. The sun is just coming up, bright and cold and sparkling on the frost-dusted grass.

We ride out to the most distant and least-used corner of the ranch. I deliberately pick an unattractive spot. I don't want to mar any scenic place with the memory of the Djinn.

We start digging.

I'm surprised how doggedly Riona applies herself to the task. I shouldn't be—I know her work ethic. But it's another thing to see her lifting shovelful after shovelful of heavy, rocky earth until the sweat drips down her face and her palms are blistered.

"Let me finish," I say, trying to get her to stop.

Riona shakes her head stubbornly. "I can help."

At last we have a hole deep enough. I kick the Djinn's body into it. Then, unceremoniously, we begin the task of covering him again.

When I told Riona what happened to Ellis, little did I know she and I would likewise bury a body twelve hours later. One of those little jokes the universe plays on us.

Riona seems to be thinking the same thing. She looks at me with solemn eyes and says, "Now we have our own little secret."

When we're almost finished filling in the grave, my phone vibrates in my pocket. I pull it out, seeing Callum's number. I pass the phone over to Riona.

"Hello?" she says.

I can hear the buzz of Callum's voice but not actually make out the words. I watch Riona's face as she listens, her dark brows drawing together in a frown.

"All right," she says. "Thanks for telling me." She ends the call and hands the phone back to me.

"What did he say?"

"They found Josh."

I help Riona mount Penny once more. I climb on Bruce, leading Horatio behind me. He trots along cheerfully now that he has no load to carry.

"They found his car in airport long-term parking," Riona says. "He was in the front seat, dead. It looks like he shot himself in the head."

"It *looks* like it?"

Riona shrugs. "So they say."

I frown. "They think he was trying to get a flight out of town… and what? He lost his nerve? Figured your family would catch up with him one way or another, so he might as well just end it?"

"I guess."

I let out a long breath, thinking.

"So, what now?" I say at last.

"I guess...I go home," Riona replies.

It's what I was expecting. But her words hit me hard anyway.

I don't want Riona to leave. And I don't think that's what *she* wants either. Not really.

I say, "You could stay."

Riona makes an impatient, dismissive sound. "And do what? Become a rancher? I love my job."

"Do you?"

She looks defensive. "Of course I do."

"I don't know if that's true."

She tosses her hair back, narrowing her eyes at me. "What are you talking about?"

"I think you're good at your job. And I think it keeps you busy. But I don't think you're actually that attached to building up the Griffin empire."

That green fire flares in her eyes again. I know I'm pissing her off, but I don't care.

"You spend a few weeks with me, and you think you know what's best for my life?" Riona snaps. "You think you know better than I do?"

"I do know you, Riona," I say calmly. "You think you're independent and invulnerable. You think you want power in your family. But I know you need so much more than that."

"What?" she demands.

"You need to be loved," I tell her. "You're not above it any more than I am. You've been happy here with me. Happier than you are at home. This is where you belong—here with me."

Riona stares at me, her lips pressed together. I can tell she's angry, but she doesn't throw back an answer as quickly as I expected.

She swallows hard. "I do like it here. But I'm not going to

abandon everything I've worked for in Chicago. I want that partnership. I earned it. I'm grateful for everything you did for me…everything your family did. But I don't belong here. This is your home, not mine."

Disappointment washes over me, heavy and dark.

I hadn't realized how much I'd been hoping Riona would stay. After everything we've been through together. Everything we've learned about each other…I thought she had bonded to me like I bonded to her.

But I was wrong.

She's anxious to get back home. The Djinn is gone, and Josh Hale is as well. Nobody is out to get her anymore. She doesn't need me. I did my job a little too well.

"I'm sorry," Riona says softly.

She doesn't ask me to come back to Chicago with her again. She understands what I owe my family after leaving all that time.

Still, neither of us is happy in this moment. We're determined but not content in our choice.

We ride back the rest of the way to the house in silence.

CHAPTER 23
RIONA

Bo comes back to the house at about ten in the morning, looking exhausted but happy.

"Shelby and the baby are fine. They're naming her Frances."

"Frances?" Raylan says, like it's a foreign word.

"I know." Bo shrugs. "But they seem really excited about it, so don't say anything."

All of a sudden, I feel like an intruder here. I'm sure Raylan wants to go to the hospital to see his new niece. I don't think I should be a part of that. The Boones should be able to enjoy all this together, without me in the mix.

Speaking quietly to Raylan, I say, "I'm gonna drive back home today."

"By yourself?" he says. "I'll drive you."

"No." I shake my head, "It's too far. And you'll have to fly back again. Stay here with your family. Go see your niece."

Raylan doesn't look happy, but he doesn't argue with me.

I don't have much to pack. I brought nothing with me, and I've mostly been wearing Bo's clothes.

I do plan to take back the cowboy boots Raylan bought me at the outlet store. I know I won't have anywhere to wear them in Chicago, but I feel irrationally attached to them. They're damned comfortable, if nothing else.

I offer to reimburse Bo for the dress Raylan and I ruined. She snorts and shakes her head. "You were doing me a favor ripping that up. Aunt Kel is always trying to get me to dress more feminine. I wish she'd save her money or get me something I actually like."

"Like a grenade launcher?" Raylan interjects.

"Yeah." Bo grins. "That would be much better."

Bo heads over to Grady and Shelby's house so she can help Celia get the boys dressed to go visit their baby sister.

Raylan feeds and waters the horses while I get ready to leave.

We meet in the yard—Raylan looking tired and dusty, me gripping the keys to the Escalade in my hand.

"You sure you want to drive back alone?" he asks.

"I think that's for the best."

I look up at his handsome scruffy face. I wish he'd give me his charming smile one more time—the one that drove me crazy at first. Now I think it would just make me feel warm and happy.

Instead, Raylan pulls me close in a hug.

As he lets go, he brushes my cheek with a rough kiss.

I grab his face and kiss him softly on the mouth instead.

"Thank you," I say again.

I turn away from him and hurry over to the car. I don't look back at him, but my ears are straining. Listening in case he calls out to me.

Raylan doesn't shout for me to stop. He just watches as I get into the SUV and start the engine.

I wave to him in the rearview mirror. He holds up his hand in return as I drive away.

It takes me all day long to drive back to Chicago. It's the longest and most depressing drive of my life. Every moment of it feels wrong. My stomach is tight, and my temples throb with a headache.

I tell myself I'm doing the right thing.

Raylan and I are too different to be together. We want completely different things out of life. He told me he wants to get married and have kids someday. I've sworn a hundred times that I'll never get married, and I'm not too keen on children either.

He wants to stay on that ranch, and I want to run a law firm.

We're just not compatible.

It's like Nero said—he and Camille have the same plans, the same goals. Internally they're the same.

Raylan and I are different inside and out. Yes, we learned not to drive each other crazy. And we learned how to work together pretty well. And sexually speaking, we were pretty fucking compatible...

But you can't build a whole relationship around sex. I'd like to... but I can't.

Still, I feel utterly dull as I drive back into the heart of Chicago. It's nighttime. A chilly wind blows bits of trash across the road. Not many people want to brave the cold, so the sidewalks are emptier than usual.

Raylan gave me his phone. I use it to call Dante.

The phone rings and rings without answer. I was going to ask him if I could swing by to drop off the SUV, but I don't want to drive over there if he's not actually home.

Without thinking, I head in the direction of the office instead. It's more home than my actual home. And unlike my condo, it wasn't burned to a crisp.

The office tower looks as grand and imposing as ever. It used to give me such a thrill walking through the double glass doors every day. Thinking this would be a piece of the city I'd own someday.

Looking up, I can see two or three windows on our floor still illuminated. My own office is dark. But Uncle Oran seems to be working away.

I want to go up and sit in my chair behind my desk. I want to remind myself of who I am and what I'm working for. I haven't felt like myself in weeks. Slipping into that cushy leather chair again will be like slipping back inside my own skin.

I park Dante's car and head inside, waving to the security guard at the front desk. Carl gives me a little salute, hitting the button under his desk that activates the elevators. He's used to me coming and going at all hours.

I push my way through the expensive glass doors bearing the names Griffin, Briar, and Weiss. As soon as Weiss retires, I intend for that door to say Griffin, Griffin, and Briar. There's no way I won't be getting the partnership now, with Josh out of the way and me being the one who uncovered his theft.

The familiar scent of the office hits me immediately—paper, printer ink, the freesia perfume Lucy wears, and lemon-basil furniture polish from the cleaning crew.

I feel a flush of nostalgia even though I've only been gone less than a week.

I flip on the light in my own office. I expect to feel the same comforting rush, but instead I notice how stark and cold the space feels. The bookshelf looks staged, like a furniture catalogue, and the polished desktop is so empty that you'd think nobody worked here at all. Everything looks gleaming and expensive but lacking in personality and warmth.

It makes me think of the ranch house, where every piece of furniture and every bit of decor seems to tell a story of the person who made it and the people who used it over the years. The Boones' house is a home. This is just an office where I spent countless hours working alone.

I sit behind the desk anyway, trying to recover my sense of purpose and drive. This is where I always felt most powerful and most myself.

I need to feel that again.

I switch on my computer, thinking it's the work that's missing. I should immerse myself in my old projects.

But when I start sorting through files, I realize half my projects are missing. Deleted off my computer without a trace.

Before I can search to find what's missing, Angela Pierce pokes her head into my office. "Hey, there you are!" she says. "We missed you!"

Angela is one of the senior attorneys who works directly under Uncle Oran. She's clever, argumentative, and stubborn, so we get along great. But I don't know what Uncle Oran told everyone about why I disappeared, so I try to be vague.

"I missed you guys. You know I hate taking time off."

Angela grins. "I was counting down the days on my last vacation. There's only so much relaxation I can handle before I'm itching to fight with somebody again."

"You done for the night?"

"Yup. I was going over some tax filings with Oran. He's still back there if you want to say hi."

"Perfect. I'll do that."

She wrinkles her nose, looking me up and down. "What are you wearing?"

I forgot I'm still wearing jeans and cowboy boots.

Angela looks like me from three weeks ago—flawless cream blazer, cigarette pants, and Gianvito Rossi heels. Beautiful but severe.

"Just…trying a new look," I say.

Angela smiles. "Not bad—we should see if we can get Oran to agree to casual Friday once Weiss retires."

"Good luck with that." I laugh. "You know Oran loves a three-piece suit more than anyone."

"True." Angela lowers her tone, leaning into my office a little farther. "Hey, did you hear about Josh?"

"What?" I ask, playing dumb.

Angela grimaces. "He killed himself."

"He did?"

I'm a terrible actor, but Angela doesn't seem to notice. She's too wrapped up in the drama of this particular piece of gossip.

"Yeah. Just yesterday. It's so weird—I never thought he was

the type. You know, he always seemed so full of himself. I guess I shouldn't say that now that he's dead."

"Why did he do it?"

I want to know if anybody's heard about the embezzlement. Angela always knows what's going on in the office—if there's a rumor circulating, she'll be the first to hear it.

She just shakes her head. "Who knows! He was fighting with his girlfriend. But I bet it wasn't that."

"Huh," I say. "I guess you never know…"

Angela steps all the way inside, speaking even more quietly. "I bet it was a work thing."

"What makes you say that?"

"Well…" She casts a quick glance back over her shoulder in the direction of Uncle Oran's office. "I saw Oran giving him shit a couple of times. Pulling him into his office for private chats, and then Josh came out looking stressed as fuck, like he got dressed down. And he was bragging to Lucy that the partnership was in the bag…but the rest of us thought you were going to get it. So if he found out it was yours…I could see him losing it."

She catches the look on my face, quickly adding, "Not like I'm blaming you for what he did! It's not your fault—you deserve to make partner. You've worked your fucking ass off. So you shouldn't feel bad about it. I'm just saying…he seemed kinda delusional about it. So I could see him freaking out if it came as a surprise."

"Yeah," I say slowly. "You might be right."

"It's just so weird," Angela says, wide-eyed. "He acted totally normal all day long! And then he leaves and shoots himself…"

I'm about to nod, but something catches in my brain—like a nail snagging on fabric.

"Wait," I say. "Josh came to work yesterday?"

"Yeah." Angela nods. "He was here all day."

"I thought he called in? Said he had the flu or something?"

She frowns. "He definitely didn't have the flu. He was strutting around like usual, giving Lucy shit over some letter she forgot to type up for him and complaining about the espresso machine."

"What time did he leave?"

"I don't know—about four or five o'clock? Early enough that I thought he probably had a date with his girlfriend. Why?"

I look at her blankly, my mouth open. "I...no reason."

"It's weird as fuck for sure," Angela says, tossing back her long dark hair. "Anyway, glad to see you back."

"Thanks," I say. "See you tomorrow."

Angela strides off toward the elevators in her sky-high heels, her briefcase in hand.

I watch her go, my thoughts chaotic and troubled.

I need to talk to Uncle Oran.

CHAPTER 24
RAYLAN

I DRIVE MY MOM, BO, AND THE BOYS UP TO THE HOSPITAL TO SEE the baby. Even though this is his third time around, Grady looks like he's over the moon at becoming a father again. He keeps saying, "She's the prettiest little thing you've ever seen. You've never seen a prettier baby. Call up those people who make the Baby Gap ads—I bet they'd pay a million dollars for a picture of her."

Shelby looks a lot more exhausted than Grady but equally pleased. She's sitting up in the hospital bed in her blue gown, her blond hair in a messy bun on top of her head. The baby is all wrapped up like a little hot dog in a bun, lying parallel across her lap.

The boys stare at the baby like she's an alien.

"I thought it was gonna be a girl?" Tucker says.

"She is a girl," Shelby tells him.

"Then how come her hair's so short?"

"That's just how babies come out," Grady says. "You were bald as an egg till you were two. Look, she's got a little hair at least." He points to the pale blond fluff on top of her head, which makes her look like a fuzzy yellow chick.

"She's *gorgeous*," my mom says. "Let me hold her!"

Shelby passes the baby over obligingly. To me she says, "Where's Riona?"

"She went home."

"Oh." Shelby looks disappointed. "How come?"

"She doesn't need me anymore," I say. "As a bodyguard."

"When's she coming back?" Lawson asks.

"I don't know." In my head I think, *Probably never.* But there's no point telling Lawson that.

My mom looks over at me, her first little granddaughter cradled in her arms. "You're going to stay, though, aren't you?"

"Yes," I promise her. "I'm staying."

"Good," Mom says. "Hold your niece."

She passes the warm bundle of the baby into my arms before I can answer. Frances is lighter than I expected—too light to be a whole entire person, and yet that's exactly what she is.

I've carried guns and grenades, newborn colts and lambs. But never a human only a few hours old. I feel unexpectedly nervous, and I sit down in the chair next to Shelby so I can be sure I don't drop the little bundle.

The baby's skin smells sweet and milky. Her tiny hand looks like a curled-up rosebud. Her fingernails are so minuscule that you can barely see them, but all five are present and perfectly formed, even the pinky nail.

I stroke the back of her hand. It feels too soft to be real. Softer than satin or silk.

Her face is red, with a little bruise on the bridge of her nose. She must have gotten stuck during the delivery. But her tiny features really are quite lovely.

I wonder what it would feel like to hold my own child. To see a mix of my own features and the features of the person I loved best in the world. I can imagine the gratitude I'd feel to my wife for carrying my child and going through the pain and labor to bring the baby into the world. I can imagine the overwhelming impulse to take care of them both. To provide for them and keep them safe.

I felt that impulse toward Riona. When I heard her scream my name, I ran back toward the house at a speed I've never even touched before. And when I saw the empty kitchen with its overturned chair and the spatter of blood on the tiles, I was afraid like I've never been afraid before.

I ran back out into the yard, and I saw her sprint out of the stable with the Djinn right behind her. I charged at him without a weapon, without any plan. Just knowing I had to save her at all costs.

I still feel that impulse. I know it's all over now and she should be safe in Chicago. Josh is dead, the Djinn is dead, and she has her family to protect her.

But still…I feel like she needs me.

Or maybe it's me who needs her.

I pass baby Frances over to Bo.

"You want a drink or anything?" I ask Shelby.

"I'd love a snack," she says. "Those damned nurses wouldn't let me have anything but ice chips while I was in labor."

"They gave you breakfast after," Grady says.

"I know, but I'm still hungry."

"I'll get you something," I say. I saw a café on the way up, and there are vending machines on every floor.

I walk down to the café first, thinking Shelby might like a pastry or a cup of soup. While I'm scanning the menu, Bo joins me.

"You hungry, too?" I ask her.

"Nah," she says. "I just want coffee."

We place our orders—coffee for Bo and me, soup and a sandwich for Shelby. I get her the full-size order because I'm sure Grady will eat half of it.

"Better get some cookies for the boys," Bo says. "And coffee for mom."

While we're waiting for the food, she says, "What are you gonna do about Riona?"

"What do you mean?"

She fixes me with a look like I'm being deliberately stupid.

"You're obviously crazy for her. You're gonna act like you're just gonna let her go back to Chicago and never see her again?"

"You're one to talk."

"What's that supposed to mean?"

"You and Duke."

She flushes, scowling at me. "He's my best friend."

"He's been in love with you since you guys were twelve years old. Maybe even before that. And you lose your fucking mind if another girl so much as looks at him."

"No, I don't," Bo snarls.

"You're gonna lose him as a friend, one way or another. Either you let the relationship develop…or you'll lose him to somebody else."

Bo doesn't like that at all. She flings back her sheet of black hair, her eyes blazing at me. "What do you know about it? You're never here. You don't know what our lives are like."

"I'm here now," I tell her. "So you better get used to it. I'm your big brother—that means I give you big-brother advice. Whether you like it or not."

Bo grinds her teeth, considering the many retorts she could give me. Finally, she settles on this: "Well, let me give you a piece of little-sister advice. If you found a girl who can stand you, you shouldn't let her go so easily. 'Cause it might not ever happen again."

With that, she snatches up her coffee and flounces away from me, leaving me to carry the rest of the food.

I bring it all into Shelby's room, juggling the various Styrofoam cups and paper bags.

"Thank you!" Shelby says gratefully, ripping open the sandwich wrapper. As I suspected, Grady hovers around like a mournful Saint Bernard until Shelby passes him half her BLT.

My mother lays the baby in the bassinet so she can drink her coffee. Her eyes are drawn back to the infant again and again.

"I wish Waya could have seen her," she says. "He loved babies."

Sometimes after a person dies, everyone else feels obligated to speak highly of them. To exaggerate their merits and forget all their flaws.

With my father, it's the opposite. You could never do justice to how good a man he really was.

He didn't just love babies—he was incredibly kind to all children. He laughed and joked with us. Taught us with infinite patience how to tie a shoelace, or skip a rock, or milk a cow. Never shouted, even when we did things that were stupid and aggravating. He'd answer any question—if you asked him why clouds float or where bears sleep, he'd give you an explanation you'd actually understand.

The only time he was stern was if he saw us acting cruel. That he never allowed.

I miss him. God, I miss him.

I wish he could have seen this baby. And I wish he could have met Riona. He would have admired her fire and her determination.

All my memories of my father are good.

The only regrets I have are things left unspoken. The things I should have told him when I found out we weren't related by blood—but I never got the chance.

Sometimes opportunities come once and never again.

I think of Riona driving back to Chicago alone.

I think of our walk through the birch trees. Before Bo interrupted us, I wanted to tell Riona that I've never felt about anyone the way I feel about her. That I think I'm falling in love with her.

I almost said it.

I wish I had.

The moment passed. And it won't come again.

"What's wrong?" my mother asks me quietly.

"I think...I might have made a mistake with Riona."

She looks at me with her clear blue eyes. Ellis had blue eyes, too. But I choose to think my eyes came from my mother. My sense of humor and my cooking skills, too. From Waya, the desire to care for and protect the people I love. And the means to do it. He taught me to hunt, to shoot, and even to fight. He always said, *Be slow with your fists. But fight for things that matter.*

"Most mistakes can be fixed," my mother says.

"I promised you I was home for good this time."

She gives me a smile that crinkles up the corners of her pretty blue eyes. "I'm not worried. You'll come back when the time is right."

I can tell she actually means that. My mother never says anything she doesn't mean.

I give Bo the keys to the truck. She doesn't ask me where I'm going because she already knows.

I run out of the hospital and jog over to the taxi stand.

"I need to go to the airport," I tell the driver.

CHAPTER 25
RIONA

THE SILENCE IN THE OFFICE BUILDING IS ALMOST TOTAL.

With Angela gone home for the night, only Uncle Oran and I remain.

The walk down to his office seems long. I can hear every soft thud of my boots on the carpet as well as the gentle hum of the overhead lights.

Uncle Oran has the biggest office in the firm. Bigger even than Jason Briar's or Victor Weiss's. It's a beautiful room, with floor-to-ceiling shelves stuffed with expensive leather-covered books. The walls are covered with vintage maps and framed botanical samples. A massive painted globe sits on a golden stand next to Uncle Oran's desk, which was built from old ship timbers like the Resolute desk in the Oval Office. The desktop is clean other than his twelve-hundred-dollar Caran d'Ache pen and his letter opener that looks like a medieval broadsword.

His office smells pleasantly of beeswax, cigar smoke, and brandy—the scent of Uncle Oran himself, which has always been one of my favorites. If Uncle Oran was coming over, it meant I could eavesdrop on good conversation and off-color jokes. And secrets, too. Because Oran always had secrets to tell.

His door is cracked only an inch. I pull it a little wider so I can step inside.

Oran looks up at once, his dark eyes deeply shadowed. The only light in his office comes from the lamp on his desk.

I can't tell if he's surprised to see me or not. All he says is, "You're back."

"Yes."

"Where's your handsome bodyguard?"

"At home in Tennessee."

"Ah," he says, nodding and setting down his pen. "So you gave him his walking papers."

"I didn't think I needed constant surveillance anymore. Since the Djinn is dead."

I watch his face closely. This time I do see a flicker of something in his eyes...not surprise. I almost think it's anger.

"The hitman is dead?" he says.

"That's right."

"Are you sure?"

"I watched him die. Then I buried him in a field. So, yeah, I'd say he's pretty fucking dead."

Uncle Oran leans back in his chair, his fingers steepled in front of him. "Always so blunt, Riona. So frank."

"You used to compliment me on my honesty when I was a child."

"That I did. Come...have a seat."

He gestures to the chair across the desk from his. It's a large chair, comfortably upholstered. I've sat in it dozens of times. Tonight it looks different. The straight back and stiff arms look stern and unyielding. They remind me of the wooden chairs used to electrocute prisoners.

I sit down across from him.

"I don't like this outfit," Uncle Oran says with a tsk. "Or the hair. I'm sorry to say, my dear, you're not looking your best."

I could say the same thing to Uncle Oran. The lines on his forehead are the deepest I've ever seen them, and the bags under his eyes look like bruises. I think he's even lost weight. His suit, usually so impeccably fitted, seems to hang off his shoulders.

Instead, I say, "It's been a strange couple of weeks for me. Very strange."

"Nothing soothes a troubling week like a drink."

Uncle Oran stands and walks over to the globe. I know from past visits that bottles of liquor are concealed within, as well as cut-glass tumblers. He pours himself a glass of brandy and scotch for me. Those are our usual drinks. When he passes me the glass, I set it down on his desk without drinking.

Uncle Oran takes a long sip, leaning against the edge of his desk and looking down at me.

"I always thought if I had a daughter, she'd be like you. There's a ruthlessness, an arrogance in you that I recognize from myself. But the honesty...I don't know where that comes from." He chuckles. "Certainly not from any Griffin."

"I think it comes from my father," I tell him coldly. "He'll at least stab you in the front instead of the back."

"Fergus?" Oran says, with a little curl in his upper lip. "He's as conniving as they come."

"Maybe you and I don't have the same definition of 'conniving.'"

Uncle Oran drains his glass and sets it gently down on the desk. "Perhaps not."

I'm studying his face, wondering how I could have misread it for so long. I don't always express myself as I'd like, but usually I'm good at reading everyone else.

I always saw so much affection there. Now I think it was calculation instead.

"Shame about Josh," I say.

"How so?" Uncle Oran raises an eyebrow. "I thought you despised each other."

"We did. But it was very inconvenient of him to blow his head off before Dante and Callum could talk to him."

"Or before we could recover the money he took," Uncle Oran says smoothly. "How much did you say it was? Twenty million?"

"Why don't you tell me?"

Uncle Oran smiles thinly. "You're the forensic accountant. I'm just the man humiliated by the fact all that money disappeared on my watch."

"My father will be very angry about that," I say. "But not as angry as he'll be when he finds out his own brother's been stealing from him."

Oran's face darkens. It's like watching clear water grow cloudy—his real emotions muddying his smooth facade. "That's a very serious accusation, Riona. Especially from my own niece. What evidence do you have?"

That's the point of this game—to discover what I know.

I say, "It never made sense that Josh hired the Djinn. He only found out that I was working on the purchase agreements that afternoon. But you knew long before—with more than enough time to put out a hit. And you knew better than Josh what time I swim laps every night. You even saw how late I worked that particular evening. You told me I should go home…but I stayed. Did you have to wait down on the street, watching for my light to go out? I'm sure that was annoying."

My uncle's eyelid twitches, and I'm sure I guessed right. He really must have stood down there on the cold street, cursing my attention span.

I say, "You took the purchase agreements off my desk. You put them in Josh's office. But I went in and grabbed them again, then took them home with me. Of course, that wouldn't have mattered if I'd drowned. That's why it had to look like an accident—so no one would come looking for the killer or even wonder *why* I'd been killed.

"I'm assuming the Djinn took my phone so you could check my emails and calls. See if I'd tipped anyone off about the properties. You thought I already knew…but that's the irony, Uncle Oran. I had no fucking clue. I hadn't figured it out. You thought I kept taking those purchase agreements because I was already on to you...but that wasn't it at all. I just wanted to impress you! I wanted the partnership."

His lips tighten in irritation. He's not answering me, but I already know that everything I'm saying is true. As much as it contradicts what I thought I knew about my relationship with my uncle, it's the only explanation that makes sense. This man who was my friend and mentor, this man whom I thought loved me like a daughter...he's the one who tried to kill me. To save his own skin.

"You still needed those files gone, so you had the Djinn incinerate my apartment. You hoped that would get rid of me, too. Unfortunately for you, I had digital copies on my computer. Lucy sent them to me. I'm guessing you figured that out later because they're gone now. All deleted.

"You knew there was another layer of protection, though—you had Josh sign all the documents. That's why you were always passing all that work to him. Because you knew he wouldn't notice the discrepancies. He was a decent lawyer but a much better ass kisser. He wouldn't question anything you told him to do.

"He was the perfect patsy. Everybody saw he and I were enemies. We were rivals for the job, and we hated each other's guts. It seemed believable that he'd hire someone to kill me.

"But you knew if Dante and Cal got their hands on him, Josh would sing like a bird. Did he know about the embezzlement? Was he in on it?"

Uncle Oran's impassive face gives away nothing. Only the glitter of his dark eyes shows he's still listening intently.

"It doesn't matter," I say. "You had to get rid of him. So you sent him home early before Dante and Cal could show up here. Told them he'd been off sick all day. Then you drove out to the airport with him and forced the gun up under his chin. Or did you hire someone for that messy little job? I can't imagine you getting blood and brain matter all over one of your suits."

Oran's lips twitch with distaste, which makes me certain he did it himself. He's older than Josh, but he had surprise on his side. Josh didn't expect to be betrayed by Oran any more than I did.

"No," I say. "You did it. You couldn't risk some so-called hitman fucking up the job again. Once Josh was out of the way…I assume you wired some of the money into his accounts to make him look guilty. Not enough to put a serious dent in what you stole, but enough that we'd know Josh hadn't saved it from his salary.

"And I suppose you thought the Djinn would get rid of your last loose end in Tennessee. It would look like Josh never got a chance to call off the hit. All the evidence would be gone. I'd be gone. Josh would take the fall. And you'd…what exactly? What in the fuck did you even want that money for?"

This is the one part where Oran can't keep silent. His eyes narrow to slits, his yellowed teeth bared as he hisses, "I want it because it's *mine*. It's owed to me."

"How do you figure that?" Uncle Oran gets a 50 percent share of the profits of the law firm, a hefty amount of money. Double what the other partners get. "You get paid plenty for running this place."

"I shouldn't be *paid* at all!" he cries. "A share in the law firm…I should get half the empire! Or more! I'm the eldest son, not Fergus."

"You're the bastard son," I say coldly. I never cared about that, but I'm bitterly angry at Oran, and I want to hurt him like he hurt me. "This empire is ten times the size it was under grandfather because of my dad. He's the one who built it up to where it is today. You didn't do that. You couldn't."

"You have no idea what I can do, girl," Oran hisses.

Maybe he's right. Because faster than I can blink, there's a gun pointed at my face.

I scoff. "You're going to shoot me? Right here in the office? You don't have anybody else to blame it on this time. You kill me, and my father will hunt you down like a dog and cut the flesh off your bones an ounce at a time."

"I'm not going to kill you," Oran sneers. "You're going to kill yourself."

He reaches into his desk and pulls out a bottle of pills. My stomach squirms as I read the label. It says, *Riona Griffin.* He got a prescription in my name.

I tell him, "You're not going to get away with the same trick twice."

"I don't know about that..." Oran says. "I don't think anybody believes you're happy, Riona. Not really. What do you have in your life besides work? Nothing."

When he asks that question, for one wild moment, my brain responds, *Raylan.* Until I remember I don't have him anymore. I only had him for a brief moment. Then I shoved him away.

Oran pops the lid off the pill bottle and shoves it toward me. He brandishes the gun in my face. The muzzle looks as dark and empty as Uncle Oran's eyes.

I don't know what the pills are, but it doesn't matter. I can puke them up after. For now, I have to pretend to cooperate. Or else he'll just shoot me.

Oran is hanging by a thread. I seriously underestimated my uncle's desperation.

I came in here to confront him, thinking he was still the man I knew. I thought I could reason with him. At the very least, I thought he would recognize that it was over—he lost.

I didn't realize how much hatred was simmering below his skin. Hatred against my father...and against me. He never loved me. He never respected me. He used me when it was convenient. And when I got in his way, he tried to drown me like a rat.

I trusted him. But he never deserved that trust.

Raylan did. I wish I could scream for him like I did outside the barn. I wish he could swoop in and save me. But he's five hundred miles from here. I spent all damned day driving away from him.

I'll have to save myself if I want to survive.

"Pick it up," Oran barks at me.

I pick up the pill bottle. It's small and light. The white pills rattle around inside.

"Swallow them," Oran hisses.

I shake a few pills into my palm. Then I swallow them with a gulp of scotch.

The clock is ticking. I probably only have thirty minutes or so before these start to kick in.

"Take them *all*," Oran orders.

It probably doesn't matter how many I take. I'll have to puke them all up anyway. Or Oran will shoot me—and the pills won't matter for a completely different reason.

I swallow the rest of the pills with the remainder of the scotch.

Tick tock, tick, tock.

"What now?" I say.

"Now you write your suicide note."

"I need paper."

Oran rummages in his desk. He pulls out a sheet of thick creamy parchment paper. Only the best for Uncle Oran.

"What do you want me to write?"

Oran tilts his head back, his eyes closed, as he thinks about what it should say. I lift his gold-plated pen off its stand.

"*Dear family,*" he begins. "*I'm so sorry to do this to you. But I think it's for the best. I'm in so much pain. I just can't take it anymore…*"

He continues to dictate. I scribble nonsense on the paper, pretending to write it down word for word. His suggestions are dramatic and ridiculous—not at all what I would write. Not that I would write anything at all because I'd never fucking kill myself. Cal will know that, and Nessa will, too. No matter what happens, they're not going to believe this bullshit.

"Sign it, 'Love, Riona,'" Oran orders.

I scribble a signature that looks nothing like my own.

"Is that what you wanted?" I say, sitting back so he can examine the paper.

Oran leans on the desk, bending over the page so he can read what I wrote. His eyes scan the page, angry color suffusing his face.

"No!" he cries. "That's not—"

I grab the letter opener and stab it onto the back of his hand. The tiny medieval sword goes all the way through his hand, pinning it to the desk.

Oran howls and swings the gun toward my face, but I grab his wrist with both hands and shove it upward. He jerks the trigger, firing into the ceiling three times. Plaster dust rains down on our heads.

I stomp on his foot hard with my cowboy boot, then bring my knee up into his groin. Oran doubles over, groaning and swearing.

I wrench the gun out of his hand.

Oran may not have actually been in the IRA, but he does know how to fight. As soon as I yank the gun away from him, he punches me right in the face. The blow knocks me backward, and the gun goes skittering out of my grip, disappearing under my chair.

Oran tries to rip his hand free from the desk, but it's stuck. He howls with pain then grabs the hilt of the letter opener to pull it free.

Meanwhile, I'm down on my knees, groping under the chair, trying to feel for the gun. I don't know if it's because of the haymaker from Oran or because the pills are starting to kick in, but my head is swimming. The floor seems to rock back and forth underneath me, and I can't find the gun.

Uncle Oran jumps on top of me, slamming me into the carpet with his full weight. He knocks the air out of my lungs, so I'm gasping for breath, my head spinning worse than ever. Then he tries to drag me up again, pulling me away from the gun.

Right at that moment, my hands close around something cold and hard. I grip the handle and curl my finger around the trigger.

As Oran yanks me up, I swing the gun around and point it right at his face.

He freezes, his hands locked on my shoulders.

"You wouldn't shoot your uncle..." he says, his yellowed teeth bared in a stiff rictus of a smile.

"I absolutely would."

I pull the trigger, shooting him right between the eyes.

Oran's limp hands release me, and he falls backward. I tumble back as well, unsteady on my feet. When I fall, the back of my head hits the carpet with a thud.

I roll over, and the whole room rolls around me. I jam my fingers down my throat, trying to make myself vomit. I gag, but nothing comes up.

Shit.

I try again, but my hand feels numb and floppy on the end of my wrist. My throat is swollen. Maybe that's why I can't throw up.

I try to get to the phone instead, but it seems a million miles away on Uncle Oran's desk. I'm crawling and crawling but not actually moving anywhere. My knees slide on the oriental rug.

Oh my god, I think my idiot uncle is finally going to succeed in killing me when it won't even help him anymore.

I think I'm still crawling toward the phone, but my cheek is pressed against the carpet, so I can't actually be moving.

I feel cold. Very cold.

I wish Raylan were holding me. There's nothing warmer than his arms.

God damn it. What a sad way to go. With so many regrets in my heart...

Suddenly, I feel myself float upward. I'm still freezing cold, but I'm pressed against something warm. I hear a steady thud against my ear.

I open my eyes and see Raylan's face. That's impossible, so I know I must be dreaming.

If this is my last dream, I'm going to enjoy it.

Raylan's strong arms lock around me, carrying me out of the office...

CHAPTER 26
RAYLAN

When I land in Chicago, I take a cab right to Riona's office building. I feel certain that's where she'll be, and sure enough, I see a light burning in her corner office.

Carl is manning the front desk. He recognizes me from all the days I tailed Riona, and he waves me in saying, "She's already upstairs."

I take the elevator up, my heart beating hard. I already went over all the things I want to say to her on the flight over. All I'm doing now is hoping against hope that when she sees me, her face lights up with happiness, not annoyance.

But when I get to her floor, her office is empty. Her light is on, and her chair is swiveled around as if she was sitting in it not long before. But there's no one around. The floor is silent.

I stand there waiting, wondering if she went to the bathroom. Carl said she was up here—he would have noticed if she'd left.

I peek my head out the doorway and see a faint glow of light down the hall.

I head in that direction, recognizing the route to Oran's office. I'm walking slowly at first, thinking Riona must be talking to her uncle. But it's too quiet, too still. There's a metallic scent in the air and something else—a faint whiff of smoke. I start to jog, and then I run. I shove my way through Oran's door.

Oran is spread-eagle on the carpet, his blank eyes staring up at the ceiling. A round black hole marks the middle of his forehead, and a stain spreads from under his head like a dark halo. Riona lies ten feet away, facedown.

An inhuman sound comes out of me—halfway between a roar and a sob. I run over to her and roll her over, terrified at what I'm about to find.

Her face is bruised and pale—paler than I've ever seen it. Her lips are turning blue. But she isn't dead. Putting my fingers to her throat, I feel a pulse. Weak and erratic, but there.

I scoop her up in my arms, and I run for the elevators. She feels too light and too cold—her skin is clammy, as if she just came in from the rain. As we're riding down, I'm already calling an ambulance.

The paramedics take her to Northwestern Memorial and pump her stomach on the way. They ask me what she took, but I have no idea. Whatever it was, I'm pretty sure she didn't take it willingly.

The nurses put an IV in her arm and fill her with fluids. Within minutes of the saline drip running into her arm, the color comes back into her cheeks. Just a light tinge of pink, but it fills me with hope.

I've already called Dante. He calls Callum and Fergus. Fergus is the first to arrive at the hospital. He comes into Riona's room, his face chalk white with fury. "*Where is he?*"

"Oran?" I say. I'm mindful of the fact that whatever he may have done, Oran is still Fergus's brother. "He's back at the law office. But I'm sorry to tell you, sir—he's dead."

I see a twitch at the corner of Fergus's mouth. A grimace of pain, immediately swallowed by his cold fury. "He's damned lucky, then," Fergus says.

He sits down next to Riona's bed, stroking her hair back from her forehead. That red hair is the only color on her person at the moment. It looks more brilliant than ever against her pallor.

I'm torn because I think Fergus might want to be alone with his daughter. But I don't want to leave Riona's side—not for an instant.

Fergus can feel me standing behind him, my eyes fixed on Riona's face.

"You don't have to leave," he tells me. "It's because of you she's alive."

"I shouldn't have let her drive back alone."

Fergus lets out a small chuckle. "I doubt you had much choice about that. I know my daughter. She makes her own decisions."

He turns around to look at me fully. His face gives me a bit of a shock because it's so similar to Oran's. Other than some small differences in coloring, Fergus could have been the man I saw lying dead on the carpet an hour ago. But there's a fierceness in his face that Oran didn't have. Men have the ability to recognize leaders— it's clear at a glance that Fergus is a boss.

"Parents love all their children," he tells me. "But not all children are equally able to accept love. I've tried to show Riona how much I value her. But I don't think she's ever understood how much she means to me." He touches her hair again, gently, just like Imogen did in the kitchen. "I'm not blaming her," he says. "I only wish I spoke her language better."

I look at Fergus, and I think about my own father. I think about the day I discovered Waya wasn't related to me by blood. He was only my father by caring for me, teaching me, protecting me, and loving me. He was only my father in all the ways that mattered.

I wasn't able to accept his love in that moment.

But I've felt it every day since.

"She knows," I say to Fergus. "Trust me, she knows."

Fergus nods slowly. "I hope you're right." After a moment, he adds, "I owe you a debt. Whatever we were paying you—"

I interrupt him. "There's no debt."

Fergus persists. "Yes, there is. Forgetting a debt doesn't mean it's paid."

He can see that I'm uncomfortable. That I don't want to be rewarded for taking care of Riona.

Not by him, anyway. Only Riona can give me what I actually want.

"You think on it," he says. "Then come find me."

Most of Riona's family comes to the hospital that night. Imogen arrives shortly after her husband. They stay for several hours in the hopes that Riona might wake up. Dante and Callum come at three o'clock in the morning, delayed by the necessity of disposing of Oran's body first.

"Can't have the other lawyers finding him in morning," Dante mutters to me.

"Did you take the carpet out, too?" I say, remembering the bloodstain.

"Of course. That's how we carried the body out. Cal shut off the cameras and told Carl to take a smoke break."

"Where's the body now?"

"Buried on the South Shore property," Cal says. "He can rot on the land he used to defraud us."

Cal seems to have no compunction about burying his uncle's body. None of the Griffins have shed a tear for Oran. Riona would have. But the fool tried to kill the only person who actually loved him.

Early in the morning, right as the sun is coming up, a slim, pretty girl with light-brown hair and a smattering of freckles comes into Riona's room. I've never met her before, but I know immediately this is Riona's little sister, Nessa. The way she moves and stands gives her away as a dancer. Plus, she's carrying a huge bouquet of peonies, which I know are Riona's favorite.

"Oh!" Nessa cries, her green eyes filling with tears at the sight of the bruise on Riona's cheek. "Dad said she wasn't hurt…"

"She's okay," I tell her. "Just sleeping."

Nessa grabs Riona's hand and squeezes it. She's dropped the

peonies on the nightstand, totally forgotten in her anxiousness over her sister.

She's truly crying now, tears running down both her cheeks.

"I'm sorry," she says. "I just...Riona seems so invincible. It's hard to see her like this."

"I know. She'll be all right, though. I promise."

Nessa looks over at me, really seeing me for the first time. "You're her bodyguard," she says. "Raylan?"

"That's right."

"I'm Nessa."

"I know," I say. "Riona talks about you a lot."

"She does?" Nessa's eyes are bright with pleasure.

"Yeah," I say. "A lot more than Callum. She barely likes him at all."

Nessa laughs. Her laugh is higher than Riona's, but the cadence is the same. "You're funny," she says. "That makes sense."

"What does?"

"Riona pretends to be so serious. But she likes to laugh...you just kinda have to make her."

"I figured that out over time. She doesn't like to do anything the easy way."

"Better not say that too loudly." Nessa smiles. "In case she can hear us."

"I wouldn't dare say anything behind her back that I wouldn't say right to her face."

Nessa looks at her sleeping sister, her face full of affection. Then she bites her lip, her expression troubled again. "Poor Riona," she says. "She was so close to Uncle Oran...I can't believe he would do that to her."

I think about what Fergus said. And I think of what I'd like to do to Oran if he were still alive. Fergus is right. Oran got off easy with a clean shot between the eyes.

Nessa sees the murderous expression on my face. Far from frightening her, it seems to please her.

"I'm glad she has you here," Nessa says. "You're going to stay with her?"

Firmly, I say, "I'm not going anywhere."

"Good." Nessa leans over and kisses Riona softly on the cheek. "Tell her I came to see her. I'll come back again in the afternoon."

"I'll tell her," I promise.

I'm glad I'm the only one in the room when Riona finally wakes. I'd hate to sit back and let the others crowd around her. I'd hate to try to hide what I feel.

When her eyelids flutter open, the first thing she sees is my face. I watch her expression. I see the relief and happiness in her eyes.

"Raylan," she whispers.

Her voice is hoarse because of the tube they put down her throat.

"You don't have to talk," I tell her.

"Yes, I do."

I grab the tumbler of ice water the nurses left, and I hold the straw to her lips so she can take a sip. Once she's swallowed it, she can speak a little easier.

"You saved me," she says. "Again."

"You saved yourself. You shot Oran."

She scowls. "That asshole. He stole the money, not Josh."

"I figured as much. I didn't think you shot him just for having bad taste in pocket squares."

Riona gives a raspy little chuckle. "Don't joke—I can't laugh right now."

"I can't help it," I say. "I'd do anything to make you smile."

She's smiling now. She reaches up and touches my face gently. "I can't believe you came back here."

"I'd go anywhere for you, Riona. I'd do anything. I know I probably shouldn't tell you that. You don't like anything if it's too easy. But it's true—you've got me wrapped around your little finger."

"I could say the same to you," she says, arching one perfectly shaped eyebrow. "I know what *Long Shot* means."

"Yeah? Well, you were the longest shot I ever took. What do you think? Did I make it?"

She tries to hold back her smile but can't. "I don't know how you did it, but you hit the bull's-eye."

I can't stop grinning. I have to lean over her hospital bed to kiss her. And what was supposed to be a gentle, careful kiss turns into something much harder and deeper. Because I'm flooded with too much emotion: Relief that this woman I adore is safe and sound in my arms. Happiness that she wants me here. And that intense desire sparked by the softness of her lips and the scent of her skin. A desire that doesn't give a damn that she's stuck in this bed with an IV in her arm. I still want her. I want her more than I've ever wanted anything.

I don't know what I'd do if the nurse didn't interrupt us.

"Don't crush the patient! You know I wasn't even supposed to let you stay the night."

I say, "You'd need a whole lot more nurses to drag me out of here."

"We've got a nurse named Barney. He was a lineman for Penn State."

"All right." I grin, stepping back so the nurse can take Riona's vitals. "Don't sic Barney on me."

CHAPTER 27
RIONA

THE NURSES MAKE ME STAY IN THE HOSPITAL FOR THREE WHOLE days.

This is almost intolerable—to the point that, despite my gratitude for their excellent care and all the cups of ice water they bring me, I might have gotten in a serious fight with them. Except that Raylan is right beside me, laughing and joking, smoothing over my grumpiness at having my blood pressure taken for the eight hundredth time.

He's my rock. The only person who can soothe the pain I feel knowing Uncle Oran tried to kill me. It's a betrayal that cuts deep. Not only because I truly respected my uncle, but because I misjudged his character so badly. It puts a crack in my perception of my own good judgment.

But I was right about one person at least: the man sitting next to me. Raylan flew to Chicago to make sure I was safe. He saved me when nobody else was there to do it. He hasn't left my side since except to brush his teeth or use the shower in my hospital room.

We're so happy to be together again that it's all we talk about.

We don't discuss the looming question of how we'll stay together in the long term. I know Raylan's family wants him back home. But my family needs me here, more than ever. With Uncle Oran gone, they need me to take over the law firm. Not just as a partner but as the managing partner. It can't go to anyone else—only a family member can be trusted with our most vulnerable secrets.

There's a more urgent reason I need to get out of the hospital: I don't want to miss Dante and Simone's wedding.

It's going to be small and intimate—fewer than twenty people in attendance. Including me and Raylan.

Dr. Weber insists on running a hundred tests on me before I'm allowed to leave. At the end of it all, he concludes that I might have some mild liver damage, but I'm otherwise unscathed by Uncle Oran's attempted poisoning.

"Watch your alcohol intake over the next few months, and hopefully any damage will heal," Dr. Weber says.

"I assume that doesn't include wine."

"It definitely includes wine."

"What about scotch?"

He shakes his head at me, unamused.

Raylan says, "I'll make sure she behaves herself."

"You're going to bodyguard me against liquor now?" I give him an incredulous look.

"If that's what I gotta do."

I fling my hair back over my shoulder. "I'd like to see you try."

Raylan grabs my arm and pulls me close so my body is pressed right up against his broad chest. His stubble scratches my cheek as he leans over to whisper in my ear:

"Don't you think you're safe just 'cause we're in Chicago, darlin.' I can find a riding crop if I need to."

The wave of lust that hits me almost knocks my knees out from under me. If he weren't holding me up with that iron grip on my arm, I'd definitely stumble.

Still, I look up into those bright blue eyes with my haughtiest expression. "I'm not going to make it so easy for you next time."

"Easy or rough…I'll take what I want," Raylan growls.

I have to turn away from him before he sees my cheeks flaming as red as my hair.

Once we exit the hospital room, Raylan and I part ways briefly to change clothes before the ceremony. I can tell he doesn't want to let me out of his sight, even for an instant.

"It's okay," I tell him. "There's nobody left to try to kill me."

"I'm not so sure about that," he says, his eyebrow cocked. "You had a pretty hefty list of enemies here, if you remember."

"I'm not worried. I'm getting pretty handy in a fight."

"Can't argue with that," Raylan says, giving me one last quick kiss.

Nessa's waiting for me out front of the hospital in her army-green Jeep. She witnesses the kiss and the prolonged conversation before Raylan and I part ways.

I can feel her excitement as I slide into the passenger seat.

"Was that just top-quality customer service?" she says. "Or does the bodyguard have serious feels?"

"Please don't call it 'feels,'" I groan.

"Riona Griffin, you better tell me *everything* right now!" Nessa cries.

"All right," I say. "But you have to promise not to freak out. It's been a pretty…intense couple of weeks."

"I will not freak out," Nessa promises, but she's already bouncing in her seat, barely able to pay attention to the road as she pulls away from the curb.

"Don't crash the car either."

"I would never!" Nessa sniffs. "My driving has vastly improved— I've only gotten two tickets so far this year."

"I'm going to pretend you didn't say that."

I tell Nessa the CliffsNotes version of what I've been doing since my apartment caught fire. I can tell she's dying to interrupt a hundred times, but she keeps a lid on it so she can hear the rest of the story. When I finally get to the end, she squeals, "*I can't believe it! Is my big sister maybe, possibly, actually…in love?*"

I frown. "Did you miss the part where our future goals have us living five hundred miles apart?"

"No," Nessa says serenely. "I just don't think that matters."

"How does it not matter?"

"Because love finds a way!" she says. "Look at me and Miko. He *hated* our family. And you all hated him."

"Well, he did abduct you and try to extort us..."

Nessa rolls her eyes.

"And he framed Dante for murder..."

"Exactly!" she says cheerfully. "And look how well it all turned out! If Miko and I can get through that, I'm sure you and Raylan can figure out a way to make things work."

Usually, Nessa's relentless optimism would annoy me. I guess it's a sign of how desperate I am that today I find it comforting. I do want to find a way to be with Raylan, without either of us losing the other things in our lives that matter to us.

Nessa and I go shopping on the Mag Mile, popping in and out of fancy boutique shops until we've found the perfect dresses for the wedding.

It's easy to find something for Nessa because everything looks perfect on her slim dancer's figure, against her creamy skin and her chestnut hair. She ends up buying a lavender gown with a slit up the thigh and long puffed sleeves. It reminds me of something a 1940s film star might wear. Nessa always chooses things that look vintage in some way, and they always suit her because she has that delicate, timeless beauty that would fit any era.

It's harder for me because a lot of colors clash with red. Plus, I've always avoided showing too much skin because I want to be taken seriously. But today, still flushed from my last conversation with Raylan, I choose a backless dress in a rich, dark teal. The cool silk flows around my body, caressing my skin.

"Oh my god!" Nessa says when she sees it. "I've never seen you look so...dangerous."

"Is it too much for a wedding?"

"No! You have to buy it. It's the best you've ever looked."

I buy the dress, not worried that I'm going to outshine Simone. She's literally the most gorgeous woman in the world, with the modeling paychecks to prove it. There's no way she could ever be upstaged at her own wedding.

By the time Nessa and I have our hair and makeup done at the Asha Salon, we have to head straight to the venue. Luckily, I bought my gift for Dante and Simone weeks ago, and even luckier that I stored it at my parents' house. Nessa brought it with her in the Jeep.

"What did you get them?" she asks me.

"It's a sound wave of the first song they ever danced to. It's printed in gold leaf, and I had it framed."

"I wish it wasn't wrapped so I could see it."

"What did you get them?"

"Salted bread and a bottle of Château Mouton Rothschild. Also, gold ingots for Henry and the baby. Mikolaj picked them—they're traditional Polish wedding gifts," Nessa explains. "I thought Simone would enjoy that since she's been everywhere."

"I'm sure she will," I agree. I've never met anyone more cultured than Simone—she's a diplomat's daughter, and she lived all over the world even before she started modeling.

Nessa and I drive over to Le Jardin, the massive greenhouse where Simone and Dante will be wed. I'm guessing they picked this place because they wanted greenery and flowers all around them even though they're getting married mid-November. No one suggested they should simply wait for summer—after being separated for nine years, I doubt Dante would wait a single day longer to make Simone his wife. Besides that, Simone is pregnant with their second child. She probably wants to tie the knot while it's still easy to fit in a standard wedding dress.

Even though it's getting colder by the minute, Raylan is waiting outside for me. He grins as we pull up, excited to show me what he looks like in an actual tux.

He should be pleased with himself—he looks damned good. Even better than I expected. The smoke-gray jacket is perfectly fitted, and his beard and hair look blacker than ever by contrast. His blue eyes have taken on a steel-colored cast under the gray autumn sky.

He takes my arm, looking me up and down with obvious appreciation. "Goddamn, woman…just when I think you couldn't impress me any more than you already have, you step out of that car and blow my fucking mind."

"You clean up pretty nicely yourself." I smile. "Where's your boots?"

Raylan grins. "In the car. Don't tempt me, or I'll go and grab 'em."

The interior of the greenhouse is lush and humid, though not uncomfortably so. Flowers and vines run across the trellis overhead, entwined with fairy lights. A bearded cellist plays a cover of "All of Me."

♫ *"All of Me"—Brooklyn Duo*

An iron archway marks the place where Dante and Simone will be wed. The arch is woven with greenery and cream-colored flowers: orchids, peonies, and roses.

Raylan and I take a seat on the groom's side of the aisle. We're sitting behind Enzo Gallo, the patriarch of the Gallo family, and Aida and Callum. I can see little Miles peeking over Callum's shoulder. He's been pacified with a soother stuffed in his mouth, but his gray eyes still look furious, and his dark hair sticks up in all directions.

Aida turns around to whisper, "Hi!" She squeezes my knee as we sit down. I can see her looking Raylan over with great curiosity.

Two rows back, Nero's sitting with his arm around the shoulders of a pretty girl with dark curly hair. That must be Camille. I check her hands—sure enough, I spot the faint remnants of oil at the edges of her fingernails. Just the same as Nero's hands—proof of their mutual love of combustion engines. They're talking intently, their heads close together as if they're the only two humans in the world.

Nessa has dropped our gifts off at the reception table, and now she's sliding into her seat next to Mikolaj, directly behind me. Miko was silent and scowling up until that moment, his pale face and white-blond hair in stark contrast to his all-black suit. When Nessa sits beside him, his expression changes entirely. His sharp features soften into a smile, and a light comes into his ice-blue eyes, until he hardly looks like the same person. Now he seems almost approachable and not like he might murder all of us. He lifts one heavily tattooed hand to tuck a lock of hair behind Nessa's ear. In his accented voice, he says, "You look stunning, *moja mała baletnica*."

Across the aisle, I see a tall trim Black man in a navy tuxedo. He's sitting with a slim blond woman, with Henry sandwiched between them. Clearly that's Yafeu Solomon, Simone's diplomat father, and his wife, Éloise, Simone's mother. Henry is Simone and Dante's nine-year-old son. He looks much taller than nine, with a head of soft dark curls and a gentle expression on his face. He's quietly solving a Rubik's Cube while he waits for the ceremony to begin. Behind Henry is a pretty young woman whom I believe is Henry's tutor and nanny. She's obviously been invited because she's close to Simone, not because Henry needs to be supervised.

My parents come in next, taking a seat behind the Solomons because there's no more room on Dante's side. My mother squeezes my shoulder on her way to her seat. She came to visit me in the hospital every day even though I told her it wasn't necessary. She brought me clothes, toiletries, books and magazines, Brazil nuts, dried fruit, and chocolate. She brought treats for Raylan, too, until there was barely room for anyone to sit down anymore.

I think my parents feel guilty about Uncle Oran, though none of that was their fault. The funny thing is, whatever grudge I might have held against them when I felt like Callum was their heir and Nessa was their favorite...it all drifted away in those moments when

I lay dying on the carpet. In those last few seconds of life, I didn't feel anger or resentment. I thought to myself, *I've been loved.* My only regret was that I hadn't shown that same love strongly enough in return.

The last person to arrive is the youngest Gallo brother, Sebastian. He's here alone, without any plus-one. He's the tallest of the Gallo boys, taller even than Dante. He walks with a lanky kind of grace, having finally shaken off the persistent limp that plagued him after my brother smashed his knee. His face is somber, though, with dark shadows under his eyes.

I don't know Sebastian well. I know he used to be a basketball star with dreams of playing professionally. It was my family that ended those dreams. The Griffins and the Gallos called a truce, and Sebastian's never shown any resentment toward us since. But I can't imagine it doesn't burn somewhere deep inside him.

He had no interest in the Mafia life. He's been slowly drawn into it by the violence and conflict of the last few years. I know he shot one of Mikolaj's men—probably the first person he'd ever killed. I wonder if it eats at him. Or if it felt like an inevitable step. A fate always destined to find him, one way or another.

All I know is that he doesn't look happy today. He sits behind my parents, apart from his own family members.

The cellist pauses, and a different song begins to play, light and hopeful:

♫ *"First Day of My Life"*—*Bright Eyes*

I look down the aisle to where Simone and Dante are standing hand in hand. Simone is tall, slim, as bronze as a goddess against her stark-white gown. I'm sure any designer in the country would have gladly given her their most ostentatious or outrageous gown. Instead, Simone's dress is simple in the extreme—unadorned, off the shoulder, clinging to the figure lauded as the most perfect in the world. Her flat stomach shows no hint of the baby she's carrying, though I'm sure its existence is one of the factors making Dante look happier than I've ever seen him.

Dante can't take his eyes off Simone. He's so massive and brutish that he usually looks terrifying in any type of clothes, even a tuxedo. But today Simone's loveliness radiates with such power that even Dante looks genteel. He looks like the only man in the world who could deserve such a beauty.

They walk down the aisle together, then face each other under the arch. Henry comes to stand between them, looking shy but happy. He's got the rings in his pocket, and he takes them out even before Enzo Gallo can stand to perform the ceremony.

"Welcome, friends and family," he says. "I don't think any union has been more fervently anticipated. And I know no couple has loved each other with greater intensity. Dante, would you like to say your vows?"

Dante takes both of Simone's hands in his own. His massive fingers swallow her slim hands so they can't be seen at all from the outside.

"Simone," he says. "I've loved you from the moment I saw your face. I know that will sound shallow since I'm talking to the most gorgeous woman in the world. But I promise you, in your face I saw your bravery, your intelligence, and your kindness. As soon as you spoke to me, it was like a door opened into your mind. I saw this whole other universe of creativity and cleverness. A way of looking at things that I'd never imagined. And I wanted to walk through that door. I wanted to live in your world. You made such an impact on me that I never forgot you. Through all the time we were apart, I thought of you constantly. I dreamed of you. I longed for you. To have you back in my arms brings me a joy that I can't express. The reality of you is a hundred times better than my imagining."

He pauses for a moment, and he looks down at his son. He lays his heavy hand on Henry's shoulder.

"Thank you, Simone, for coming back to me. Thank you for bringing our son. Thank you for raising him. Henry, you're a good man already. I'm so proud of you."

I've never heard Dante talk like this, with raw openness and honesty. He always keeps his feelings stuffed down tight. Or at least he did before Simone came back into his life.

It's having an effect on me I never would have expected.

I'm starting to feel emotional.

I have never cried in public, not once in my life. I certainly haven't cried at a wedding. But all of a sudden, my eyes feel hot, and my face is stiff.

"I will love you every moment of my life," Dante says. "I will cherish and protect you. Anything you want, I'll get it for you. I'll be your best friend and your ally. I'll make your life better, always, and never worse."

Simone is freely crying, her tears silver on her flushed cheeks. She is so beautiful that it's hard to even look at her. She's glowing with happiness, illuminated by it.

"Dante, you are everything to me," she says. "My heart and my soul. My happiness and my safe haven. Life without you was lonely and bitter. The only thing that brought me joy was Henry, our son. He's a piece of you and me, the best thing we ever did. I love him for himself, and I love him for how he reminds me of you.

"I promise to choose you for the rest of our lives. To choose you over fear or selfishness. Over ambition or other cares. I promise to never let you down again. To always be there for you. I promise to give you every bit of joy this life has to offer. You are the most incredible man I've ever known, and I promise to be the wife you deserve.

"I'm so lucky today. I'm the luckiest person in the world."

She, too, puts her hand on Henry's shoulder, still looking up into Dante's face.

I want to look at Raylan, but I can't. I know I'm about to cry, and I don't want him to see it.

The tears are partly for Dante and Simone—I'm so, so happy for them.

But they're also tears of anguish because I'm realizing I love Raylan. I truly, truly love him. And that terrifies me.

Simone's words are like an arrow in my heart.

I promise to choose you over fear or selfishness. Over ambition and other cares.

Is that what love is? Is it putting the other person above your own fears and desires?

I thought that might be the case. And that's why I thought I'd never fall in love.

But now I have, by accident.

And I want that love. I want Raylan.

I think I might want him more than all the things I wanted before. More than my fears and, yes, even more than my ambitions.

Does that make me weak and pathetic?

Do I have to give up myself to have love?

I feel wetness on my cheeks, and all of a sudden, Raylan puts his arm around my shoulder and pulls me close to him so my face is hidden against his chest. He's doing that for me—because he knows I'd hate to have anyone see me cry. Even my own closest friends and family.

He knows me so well. He knows exactly what I need.

I remember what he said in Silver Run. I was so angry with him at the time. Now I wonder if he was right all along:

You're happier here. This is where you belong: here, with me.

I'm afraid. But I want to choose Raylan over that fear.

CHAPTER 28
RAYLAN

THE WEDDING IS THE LOVELIEST I'VE EVER SEEN. I HOPE IF I GET married, it's in a place like this with only the people I love the most around me.

After the ceremony, we drink and dance and eat until everyone is pleasantly exhausted, including Henry and the cantankerous baby Miles, who spits out his pacifier and begins to howl. Callum and Aida hustle him away at top speed after blowing one last kiss to Dante and Simone.

Riona is quieter than usual. I don't mind 'cause she still asks me to dance. We waltz around under the glass and the stars, the air full of oxygen from all the greenery. This time she doesn't pull away from me—we dance in perfect tandem, our bodies pressed close together and her head against my chest.

After the ceremony we go back to the Intercontinental Hotel, where I've rented a suite for the night. I only hoped to sleep next to Riona—she just got out of the hospital, after all. But as soon as the door closes behind us, she jumps on me, kissing me with all her might.

I have to force myself to kiss her back with a reasonable degree of gentleness. I want to tear that dress right off her. She's been driving me insane all night, her skin looking as pale and bright as the moon next to the rich darkness of the dress. Her hair is like a lava flow down her back, warm and smoky.

She's never been more beautiful. It's funny—we were in a room full of gorgeous women, but I only had eyes for her. Riona has a fierceness that grabs me and holds me fast. I want to know what she's thinking and feeling, always. She's both blunt and a mystery. Strong and powerful, but also fragile.

And above all, she's so goddamned sexy. She's all over me with an intensity I've never seen before: ripping my shirt open so the buttons pop off, tearing off my pants.

I lift her and throw her down on the bed, equally desperate to have her.

When I kiss her mouth, she tastes of champagne.

"You weren't supposed to drink!" I accuse her. "When did you get champagne?"

"I only had a sip," she says. "While you were congratulating Dante and Simone."

"You naughty little thing," I growl, seizing her by the throat—not too hard. "How should I punish you?"

I pull down the front of her dress and take her breast in my mouth. I suck her nipple hard until she squeals.

"Stop that!" she cries, slapping me away.

I grab both her hands and pin them over her head. Then I return to her breasts, noting that both her nipples are standing up straight, tightening her tits.

Lightly, I trail my tongue around her nipples without taking them in my mouth. I tease them with my tongue until her arms are shaking in my grip.

"Stop?" I say. "Or keep going?"

"Keep going," she gasps.

"Say, 'Please, Daddy.'"

She scowls at me, and I could laugh out loud at the pleasure of teasing her. I knew she'd hate that. I flick her nipple with my tongue, making her moan in frustration.

"Please, Daddy!" she says petulantly.

I close my mouth around her nipple again, and I suck gently. I caress her breast with my tongue until she gives a long groaning sigh of satisfaction.

Then I slide down her body and go to work between her legs instead. I put her legs up on my shoulders, and I eat her pussy until I feel her thighs clenching around my head, her hands thrust in my hair and her clit grinding against my tongue. My mouth is full of the sweet and fiery taste of her, like cinnamon and sugar, like pure, raw arousal.

I've never tasted anything so good. I could spend hours down here.

I let her control the pace for a while, rolling her hips against my tongue. Then, when I can feel she's close to the edge, I grab her hips in my hands and I increase the pressure of my tongue. I lick faster and harder until she's gasping, until she digs her fingernails into my scalp, screaming, "Oh my god! Oh my gooooood!"

She's still half wearing her dress, and my shirt is still on, though torn open. I don't care. I like us half dressed. I like the look of her: clothes pulled up, hair wild and messy, makeup smeared. I love the immediacy, the impatient lust that won't let us take even another second to properly undress.

I flip her over, and I enter her from behind, with me sitting back on my heels and her on my lap, sliding up and down on my cock. Sinking myself inside Riona is pure fucking heaven. The feel of her is addictive. The taste and scent, too.

She's sitting up, and I pull her back tight against my chest, my hands on her bare breasts. I caress her tits as I fuck her from behind, squeezing and pulling on her nipples. I gather the whole of her breasts in my hands, and they fit perfectly, the way every part of her fits me.

I grab her hair and pull her head back so I can kiss the side of her neck. I bite her gently and suck on the tender skin, my other hand still fondling her breasts.

I leave marks everywhere I touch her. Her skin is so delicate that I can see the flushed imprints where I squeeze her breasts, where I bite her neck. It makes me want to whip her again, just for the pleasure of seeing those red welts on her flawless ass. It makes me want to tease and torture every inch of her body.

I love how wild it makes her. The more I push her, the more she wants. She can't get enough of it. She's riding my cock, her head pulled back with my hand wrapped in her hair. She presses my hand tighter against her breast, begging me to squeeze harder, to torment her sensitive little nipples.

I want to know what she was thinking at that wedding. I know she wasn't crying from sentiment. It was a beautiful ceremony, but I know Riona—her mind must have been full to overflowing to make her react like that.

I flip her around on my lap so I can look at her face. I watch her ride me, her bare breasts pressed against my chest. I kiss her deeply, my tongue thrust all the way into her mouth. Tasting the remnants of the champagne.

I can see she's right on the edge.

So am I. I can only hold on for a few more seconds.

I look her in the eyes, and I say, very quietly, "I love you, Riona."

I see her face crumple like it did at the wedding. Like she's about to cry. And then she starts to come, and she buries her face in the side of my neck. She's clinging to me, grinding against me, and I let go inside her. What I feel is so much more than sexual release. It's the relief of saying out loud what I've been feeling for so long.

———

When I wake in the morning, she's gone. The sun is streaming in the windows, illuminating the empty spot on the mattress right next to me.

For a moment, I feel a sick swoop of dread. I think I've scared her off again.

Then I see the note on the pillow.

Before I snatch it up, I tell myself, *Trust her. Trust that she hasn't run away.*

I read the first line in a glance:

> *Don't worry, Raylan, I haven't run away.*

I smile to myself. I know Riona, and she knows me.

> *There's something I have to do this morning. It won't take long. Please come meet me downstairs at 12:00. I promise I'll be there. I want to respond to what you said last night.*

> *XOXO*
> *Riona*

It doesn't say *Love, Riona.* But after all, we're talking about a woman accustomed to legal correspondence. I know the *XOXO* is a big step for her.

I get in the shower and clean myself up. I actually packed a bag this time, so it doesn't matter that Riona destroyed my shirt. I've got a perfectly comfortable flannel button-up to replace it.

Once I'm all spruced up and fit to be seen, I head downstairs to get a coffee and a muffin in the hotel café.

It's eleven o'clock. I'm feeling calm and confident.

The closer it gets to noon, a little bit of nerves sneak in.

I want to believe Riona feels the same as I do. I want to believe she loves me.

But I know as well as she does the barriers that stand in our way. We each have commitments to our families. We each have goals.

I didn't know Riona was still in danger from her uncle—I came to Chicago to chase her. To make this thing work between us.

But I didn't have a real plan. As I mull it over now, I wonder if I can give up on the ranch and my life in Tennessee. If she asks me to stay, will I say yes this time?

I think I have to. I promised my mom I'd come home for good. But I know my mother. I know she wants me to be happy. If I tell her that Riona is the thing that will make me happiest...she'll understand.

With that decided, I finally feel the peaceful spread of warmth in my chest. When Riona comes back, I'll tell her that I'll stay here. I'll learn to love the city life. She'll probably take over the law firm, and I'll...figure something out. I've always been good at making myself useful.

Riona pulls up to the curb in a taxicab. She jumps out, carrying a rolled-up sheet of paper in her hand.

"Hey!" she cries. Her cheeks are pink from cold and happiness. "Are you hungry? There's a restaurant next door..."

"What do you think?" I ask her, grinning.

She grins back. "I think you're always hungry."

"You got that right."

We head next door. As we're walking, Riona slips her free hand in mine. The ease of the gesture makes my heart swell in my chest. I hold the door open for her, and she sweeps through with an unusual lightness in her step.

"Table for two, please!" she says to the hostess.

The hostess sits us in a booth against the window.

Riona is smiling so hard that it makes me laugh. I've never seen her so cheerful.

"You've got to tell me what's going on," I say. "The suspense is killing me."

Her face is glowing. "I bought an office!"

That is not what I expected her to say.

"You…what?"

"Look." She pushes the paper toward me.

I unfurl it, smoothing out the edges so I can see the printed image. I see a brick building with large square windows. It looks familiar, though I'm not sure why.

I read the listing:

> *6800 W Hill Ave*
> *$789,000*
> *2,746 square foot office building on 0.66 acres. Built in 1949, renovated in 2011. Has 12 parking spaces, plus a walkout basement of 838 square feet. Single tenancy. Partial view of the Tennessee River.*

"Riona," I say slowly. "This is in Knoxville."

"I know." She laughs. "I saw it when we went into town to get the horse-stall mats."

"You bought a building…in Tennessee?" I know I sound like an idiot, but I can't quite believe this.

"Yes," Riona says. She's starting to look concerned—either that I'm not as happy as she expected or that I might have brain damage. "It's a bit of a drive from the ranch—but not too bad."

I just can't believe it. I don't want to allow this wild happiness to rise inside me in case it isn't real.

I grab her hands and grip them tightly. "You want to come back home with me?"

She looks at me, her green eyes bright and shining. "Yes," she says simply.

"What about Griffin, Briar, Weiss? Without your uncle…there won't be a Griffin. Unless you stay."

Riona sighs. "I thought about that. For a long time, actually. All the time I was in the hospital, I felt this duty to stay. But then I realized…duty isn't the same thing as desire. What I thought I wanted...I don't want it anymore. Maybe I never really did. And even if I were still hung up on the idea of a big law firm in a big city...I want to choose you, Raylan. I want to choose you over anything else."

I shake my head in amazement. I really thought I was getting the hang of Riona. Then she knocks me over like this.

I say, "I was all set to tell you that I was gonna stay here in Chicago. And darlin', I'm still willing to do it. I want you to be happy, Riona. If that means staying, then I'll stay."

Riona just laughs. "I wasn't kidding—I already bought this place. I sent over the deposit this morning. And even if it weren't a done deal, I don't care. What you said was true, Raylan...the happiest I've ever been was that week on the ranch with you and your family. It's beautiful, it's peaceful, and it feels like home. It's where I want to be, if it means I'll be with you."

I still can't believe it. I lean across the table and kiss Riona to be certain I'm actually awake and not just dreaming.

"I love you," I tell her again. "I really love you."

"I know." She grins. "I love you, too."

I chuckle. "Did that hurt you to say out loud? Was it hard?"

She laughs. "No. I thought it would be hard, but it wasn't. It feels good to tell you finally."

"*Finally?*" I shout. "How long have you known that you love me?"

"I don't know," Riona says seriously. "I didn't even know what it was, at first. But I'm sure now."

I kiss her again. "Let me make you more sure."

EPILOGUE
RIONA

MY PARENTS ARE DISAPPOINTED WHEN I TELL THEM I'LL BE moving for good. There's a mountain of documents and data, all our most sensitive files, that has to be passed along to somebody. And there's no one they can trust quite like family.

"Can you at least stay until the South Shore project is done?" my father asks.

"That could take years," I say gently. "And there's always another project. Another job, another crisis. Our lives have never been calm. I don't think they ever will be. Not here, anyway."

"Is that why you're leaving?"

"No." I shake my head. "I'm leaving for Raylan. But I'll admit, the lack of imminent danger might be a nice side benefit..."

Nessa flings her arms around me and hugs me much longer than I'd normally tolerate.

"I'm going to miss you." She sobs.

"I'm just going to Tennessee, not Indonesia." I laugh. "You can visit me, you know. And I'm sure I'll come back here all the time."

"No, you won't." Nessa shakes her head with surprising seriousness. "When you really fall in love...that person becomes your world. You'll come back sometimes. But mostly you'll want to be with Raylan. And that's okay. I'm happy for you! I'll miss you like crazy, though!"

Dante is infuriatingly smug about the whole thing. He's leaving on his honeymoon to Portugal with Simone and Henry, but he comes all the way over to my parents' house so he can gloat.

"I'm the one who introduced you two." He grins.

"I know."

"I had to do it twice. Because you hated Raylan the first time."

"I *know*." I scowl at him.

"You better name your firstborn after me for all the work I put in."

"I'm not having a firstborn or any born. I still don't want kids. That hasn't changed."

"We'll see," he says with a maddening air of superiority.

"Even if I did, I wouldn't saddle them with the name '*Dante*.'"

His jaw drops. "'Dante' has been popular for eight hundred years. It has history and gravitas."

"It's not even a real name! It's a nickname! You know Dante Alighieri's real name was Durante."

Dante looks both shocked and horrified. I don't think he knew that at all. "You're lying."

"I never lie."

He's crestfallen. "Really? That's really true?"

I start to feel guilty. "Never mind," I say. "It's not so bad. If I were going to have a kid—which I'm not—I guess I could name them Dante."

Dante grins. "I'm holding you to that."

———————

Raylan and I fly back into Knoxville. Our flight is canceled, postponed, then leaves an hour earlier than expected, so we take a cab into town to kill a little time before Bo picks us up.

Raylan says we should walk by my newly purchased office building so he can see it in person. It's not nearly as grand as the massive high-rise in which I dreamed of becoming partner, but I feel a deep flush of pleasure all the same. This building belongs to me and me alone. This law firm will be mine. I'll build it from the ground up.

And it has a view of the river like I always loved in Chicago. A different, gentler river in a warmer town, where even at the end of November, I only need a light sweater.

Even if it were cold, I've got a big, strong man beside me radiating heat from his chest into my back with his arms wrapped tightly around me.

"I'm gonna come visit you here every day," Raylan says. "I'll bring you lunch."

"I'm not going to get any work done if you're around. You're incredibly distracting."

"Me?" he says innocently.

"Yes. When you were supposed to be bodyguarding me, I can't tell you how many times I had to sneak a look at you, all scruffy and handsome in that corner chair."

He grins. "Oh, I know you did. I caught you every time."

"The hell you did!"

"The hell I didn't!"

He kisses me hard.

"I'm proud of you," he says. "I already know you're gonna be a huge success. The best lawyer in Knoxville, guaranteed. Probably all of Tennessee."

"Not the whole country?" I tease him.

"Well…there's that one guy who got OJ off…"

"Johnny Cochrane? He's not even alive anymore!"

"All right." Raylan grins. "You're the best in the whole damned country, then."

With Raylan's arm around my waist, we walk over to World's Fair Park. We take a little stroll around the lake, stopping at the Sunsphere. Its gold-plated glass glitters even though it's not a very sunny day.

On the opposite side of the tower, I see a girl with long black hair standing next to a slim young man in a battered leather jacket. They're standing with their backs to me, but something about the couple looks oddly familiar. They look tense, as if they've been arguing. The girl starts to walk away, and the boy grabs her and pulls her back again. He seizes her face and kisses her ferociously. For a moment she tries to pull away, but then she kisses him back just as hard.

It's only when they break apart that I realize it's Bo and Duke.

"Oh!" I gasp. "Let's go. I don't want them to see us."

"Why not?" Raylan says.

"I don't want your sister to feel embarrassed."

He grins. "She should feel stupid. It's about damned time."

"Come on!" I pull him away, making him walk all the way back to the crêpe shop with me.

"Those silly kids." He shakes his head. "Why don't they know they should fall in love when it's so damned obvious?"

I look up at him, at his wolfish smile and his bright blue eyes. "It's just obvious, huh?"

"Yup," Raylan says. "Sometimes it's clearly meant to be. I knew it from the moment I saw you."

"All you knew was that you were driving me crazy."

He grins. "And I wanted to do it a whole lot more."

WHY WOULD YOU WANT TO RIDE WITH ANYONE ELSE?

A BO AND DUKE NOVELLA

BO BOONE

I'M UP IN MY FAVORITE PLACE, WHICH IS A FORK IN THE GARGAN-tuan white oak that hangs over the river a mile from the house. So when I hear footsteps in the brush, I know it's Raylan way before I see him. Grady wouldn't walk so far, and Duke's too pissed at me to even be in the same damn state.

Raylan got pretty good at walking sneaky in Afghanistan, but I still hear him way before he thinks I will. I slip down from the fork and wait in a clump of ferns.

When he passes, I whap the part of his head that would have a hat on it if Raylan still wore hats. It's purely 'cause of me that he doesn't. Gets a little humiliating chasing your ten-gallon while it rolls away down the street.

"*Goddamnit, Bo!*" He whips around.

I make a *tsking* sound.

"Thought all those gangsters woulda toughened you up."

Raylan's slow grin spreads. You can't rile him up past surprising him, though it's a hell of a lot of fun to try.

"If they were as quiet as you, I wouldn't be standing here right now."

"Don't butter me up."

I can already guess what he came out here to say.

"I even left Bruce all the way back there." Raylan shakes his head, ruefully retrieving his horse.

Bruce looks like he always knew this wasn't gonna work.

"You're embarrassing him," I say to Raylan.

"He deserves it." Raylan has zero sympathy. "The shit he's put me through."

Bruce has never been an easy horse, but of course, that's exactly why Raylan loves him. Took me about a second and a half to know my brother was gonna fall head over heels for Riona, too. A stone-cold bitch like that—he never stood a chance.

"Come on," Raylan says, grabbing hold of the fork in the oak and pulling himself up one-handed. He does that shit to show off, no matter how natural he makes it look.

I shimmy up a few branches higher so my bare feet dangle down in his face. They're hard as a rock and twice as dirty.

"Come sit with me," Raylan says, patiently pulling me down.

I get comfy beside him, because this really is my favorite place. This tree got knocked over in a storm and should've died but didn't—the roots still in the ground spread out wide, and the oak's massive sideways canopy kept sprawling, creating this shady bower over the river.

Below us, Bruce dips his head to drink. Raylan hasn't tied him up, but he doesn't leave.

"I love that horse," Ray says. "I've been through some shit with that horse."

I have a pretty good idea where he's going with this, but I just stare down into the water, watching the bits of grass and chaff on the surface swirl in the mini-currents that inevitably drag them down.

"That horse has run me into trees, into branches, kicked me multiple times..." Raylan smiles. "He's stubborn as fuck, but he's *my* horse, and he's the best goddamn horse in the world."

He looks at me. I can feel it, even though I'm deliberately not looking at *him*.

Raylan gives my elbow a little nudge.

"How many times you think Riona bucked me off when I was trying to lay a little of that cowboy charm on her?"

"Not often enough, 'cause you wore her down in the end."

His smile now is pure satisfaction. "You're damn right I did."

I'm happy for him, but I'm jealous, too. Everything comes right for Raylan in the end. He knows what to do.

Not me.

I hate all my options and there is no winning.

"The lesson, little sis, is that love is hard. Relationships are hard. Nothin' worth doin' comes easy—"

That's about all I can take. "I appreciate the words of wisdom, but me and Duke aren't you and Riona."

Raylan takes the interruption in stride. "How come?"

"'Cause I didn't just meet him five minutes ago."

My brother laughs softly. "Yeah, yeah, I know all about your deeply complicated relationship."

A thousand moments flash through my mind—arguments, escapes, triumphs, betrayals...

"You don't know anything."

"I know he wouldn't be your best friend if he wasn't a good man."

That makes me turn my head. Raylan gazes at me with his clear blue eyes. He's the only one of us who really looks like Mom.

But he looks like Dad, too, impossible as that may seem—when he holds me fixed in his stare and won't let me go.

"Give it a shot," Raylan says. "Of all the things I've called you, I never thought you'd be a coward."

Anger runs like wildfire up my spine, but my brother only smiles and keeps poking at me.

"I went to Chicago and chased down a lawyer. Can't nothing be worse than that." And then, gently, he adds, "You're not a coward, Bo…are ya?"

I take a long, slow breath—and deflect with something that's only a fraction of the problem:

"Mom's trying to make me go to college."

That's not the issue with Duke, but it sure ain't helping. He's been taking digs at me ever since that stupid acceptance letter arrived.

Can't wait to see your letterman jacket.

You think they serve fried pickles in the cafeteria?

You gonna be a lawyer now, too?

That last one had an extra little spin of snark on it 'cause Duke could tell Riona was rich as fuck even when she was dressed in my cast-off clothes. It's the manicure, and also the way she stands, like she's emperor of the room, including all the rooms she's never stepped foot in before.

That's exactly what I like about her, but Duke snubs anybody who drinks bottled water or wears high heels or uses Instagram. He hates anything fake. I say he judges people on petty shit so he can ignore the real ugliness all around.

The truth is, I was never planning to go to Vanderbilt. I only applied to get my mom off my ass, and my swim coach, too.

When the letter arrived, just for a moment, I pictured myself walking across campus, books tucked under my arm. Then I felt that ache that I've felt pretty much every day of my life since I was eight years old, like one of my ribs is missing high up on the left side, and I knew that hole would only get deeper with each step I took away from here.

"Mom tried to make me go to college, too," Raylan says. "Can you picture me as a college boy? Maybe I'd have even got an NBA."

I give him exactly the kind of look he's determined to dredge out of me. "You mean an *MBA*?"

Raylan grins. "Maybe you *should* go to college—you know all about it."

"Don't make that joke around your girlfriend. She'll think you're actually stupid."

Raylan laughs. "Trust me, she knows exactly how dumb I am. But she can't find a better horse, either."

My brother is infuriating. But he's also deeply comforting, like an old favorite shirt. I lean my cheek against his shoulder. He wraps his arm around me and gives me a kind of half-hug.

"All I'm sayin' is, if you and Duke are the friends you claim to be…then why would you want to be riding with anybody else?"

Easy for him to say.

Duke hates me right now.

And in some kind of fucked-up way—that's better than the alternative.

Duke's been pissed at me plenty of times before. We always work it out.

But some lines, once you cross them…you can't ever come back.

Like the day my big brother packed a bag and vanished in the night.

If he thinks he can just stroll back here and start handing out advice, he's got another thing coming.

I scooch away from him, settling my back against the trunk of the oak, pulling my knees up under my chin and wrapping my arms around them. "Why'd you leave?"

I think I know the reason. But I want Raylan to tell me himself.

I was ten years old and he just fucking left. Didn't even say goodbye.

"You remember that?" I say. "It really *fucking* sucked, because I'd moved away from my best friend two years before, and I lost my dad a couple months after. But you didn't come home after that, either."

Raylan looks at me for a long moment. It's hard to guess what my brother is about to say because he'll hold eye contact no matter what he's feeling.

At last he says, "I came home for the funeral."

"But you didn't stay."

"They don't let you come home from Afghanistan. Even if your dad dies."

"That's not what I asked you," I hiss. "I said, *why'd you leave?*"

He runs a hand through his hair and grips it hard at the roots, letting out a sound like a sigh and a groan.

"I was angry."

I've never seen my brother lose his temper. In fact, I've watched him keep his cool in some pretty extreme situations.

"Why were you angry?"

"Well…" His lip twitches, showing a flash of teeth. "I found something out. About our parents."

I wait, suspecting what he's about to say.

"Our dad…wasn't the one who got Mom pregnant. With me." He rushes to add, "It was before they met. Before they dated, I mean. It was fine. It was fine with both of them."

"I know." I let him off the hook. "I read Mom's journal."

"You—*Bo!*"

I shrug. I don't regret that one bit—I knew she was lying to me.

"I was angry," Raylan repeats, his expression miserable. "Angry that they'd never told me. I left and enlisted. Three months later— you know what happened."

Oh yes, I remember. Headlights in the night. Close and then way too close.

Raylan touches my knee so I'll look at him.

"That's my biggest regret, Bo. Our dad said, *I love you,* and I said, *You're not my dad,* and walked out the door. And I never got the chance to tell him what a lie that was because he died right after. So I have to live with the lie I told in anger. Because I can never put it to rest."

He's trying to teach me another lesson.

I need to tell *him* something.

"They ran us off the road on purpose."

Raylan blinks. "Bo—"

"I saw it."

"You were ten and it was two o'clock in the morning, Bo, I'm pretty sure you were aslee—"

"I wasn't asleep! I'm telling you, I saw it!"

Raylan pauses only half a second.

"Okay."

My shoulders relax because I can hear that he believes me. I lick my lips and say, low and quiet, "What if his family did it? Ellis."

Raylan shivers slightly when I say his birth father's name. "No." His lips are pale. "He'd been dead eighteen years. His family never knew anything. It was a drunk driver, Bo, the cops—"

"You never talked to the cops," I remind him. "Mom did."

"No," Raylan says again. But then his jaw moves like he's disagreeing with himself.

"What if they—"

"So what if they did?" he interrupts. "What would you do, Bo? Didn't you hear what I was just telling you? You'll make the worst mistakes of your life when you're angry."

"Speak for yourself."

Raylan sits back like that one hurt him. I flush a guilty red and turn away.

After a while he says, warm and comforting again like the other part of the conversation never happened, "Going to war with my brothers was a choice that I had to make for myself. Going to college is a big decision, too. Mom's giving you good advice. Listen to her. She knows—she's probably right, by the way—we probably both shoulda gone to college. But you gotta make the choice for yourself, not for Mom."

"Yeah, okay," I say. "Thanks."

Raylan drops down from the oak, landing lightly by the river. He slaps my calf lightly as he passes.

"But if I could give you some advice...worry about college tomorrow. Don't let that horse get away."

God, I bet he was saving that the entire time.

In one sense, finding Duke is difficult because he lives way the fuck across the state border on Cherokee land.

In actuality, it's not difficult at all because I know exactly where he'll be when he's in this much of a sulk—tearing around his uncle's ranch with the pack of jackals he calls cousins.

I drive over there in Grady's old blue Ford.

The dogs see the plume of dust from a mile away and all run barking.

When I step out of the truck, one of the cousins buries a crossbolt in the door, right above the handle. I can't tell if he was aiming for my hand. Is it better for him to have homicidal intentions and terrible aim or excellent aim and slightly more restraint?

"Keep practicing!" I call up to the rustling trees.

You can't show fear around the cousins or they'll tear you to shreds.

I find Duke right where I knew I would, by the horses.

He's watching his uncles break a pack of mustangs. The horses are wild in the pen, especially the big male with a lightning-bolt blaze down its face.

When the uncles see me coming, half of them scowl 'cause they hate me and half of them smile 'cause they like to see Duke lose his shit.

Duke pretends like he doesn't see me at all, even when I'm standing right next to him. Even when I can see the pulse jumping in the side of his throat.

I know the exact color of his skin. It's like the color of the earth to me.

I know his smell like I know my own.

Standing next to him is all the good parts of being alone and all the best parts of being around anyone else.

I don't see his uncles or cousins or even the horses anymore—all I see is Duke.

"Did you break your phone again?" I ask.

"Yeah," he grunts.

I knew he must've. He can't go more than a day without texting me, otherwise.

"Were you outside my window last night?"

His jaw goes tight and he digs the heel of his boot into the dirt, hands jammed in his pockets.

"Yeah," he admits at last.

"Why'd you leave when I came out to talk to you?"

"'Cause I'm fucking pissed at you, Bo!"

He turns to face me. My stomach swoops away and doesn't seem to return.

My best friend has gotten a little more beautiful each day until now. I can hardly look at him—even with half-healed bruises scattered across his face. *Especially* with bruises. He has an angular jaw, high cheekbones, narrow eyes, and long black hair, black as a rook. His lower lip is slightly swollen. I bite the same place on my own lip, then catch myself.

A bunch of cowboys jumped Duke after I threw beer on him. Well, threw beer on all of them, I should say.

"I got banned from the Wagon Wheel!" Duke cries.

"They ban everyone, it's not permanent."

He makes a sharp hissing sound through his teeth. "Big surprise, you don't give a shit."

I wish I could care as little what happens between Duke and me as he seems to believe I do.

The smirking half of his uncles scoot a little closer on the fence railing, trying to listen in. The scowling ones are mostly busy in the pen—they do the majority of the work around here.

Duke's cousin Arnie gets bucked off the crazed mustang.

"Did you see that? He tried to kick me in the head!" Arnie crows, the horse's hoof missing his temple by an inch as he leaps backward.

"Look." I grab Duke's forearm. "I'm sorry."

Where our bare skin touches, a calm warmth spreads. Everywhere else, the air is spiky and tense. Especially in the space between our faces.

"What are you sorry for?"

Duke looks right in my eyes. His are so dark you can hardly tell pupil from iris.

I stammer, "I'm…I'm sorry you thought—"

"You're sorry I *thought?*" Duke becomes instantly furious for reasons I don't quite understand.

He drops over the fence into the pen with the horses, grabbing a fistful of the wild mustang's mane and swinging onto its back. The stallion tenses, throwing up its blazing white face, eye rolling madly.

"Show 'em how it's done, Donkey!" Duke's uncle shouts. He wouldn't dare use that old nickname if Duke were on foot.

But Duke doesn't seem to hear. He grips the horse's mane, keeping his seat through the first series of bucks, and rears with the balance of a butterfly. It doesn't even look difficult, because Duke is the only person on this planet I might consider a better rider than me. Not that I'd ever admit it to *him*.

Duke's broken a hundred horses. But as I watch, the mustang gives a spectacular wrench and Duke releases his grip. He goes sailing through the air, tumbling down onto the dirt, rolling over several times, and coming to rest against the fence.

His uncles and cousins descend, scooping him up and pounding him on the back before he can even breathe.

"You're fine, you're lovely!"

They mess up his hair so it hangs loose around his shoulders. He ties it back again, watching me silently across the railing. Blood drips from his nose.

I'm staring right back at him because I have the weirdest feeling he let that horse throw him on purpose.

"What are you sorry for, Bo?" Duke demands.

I lick my lips. "I'm sorry I couldn't—"

"Nope." He grabs the horse where his cousins are trying to restrain it, swinging onto its back again.

"Duke!"

He gallops around the pen, ignoring me, goading the mustang into a fit that ends with Duke chucked right back over the fence.

I run to him, beating his uncles. They shout their jeers, confused why their best trainer is failing so spectacularly.

Duke sits up, blood running down the side of his face and dripping off his fingertips from a gash on his arm.

"What are you sorry for?" he says, doggedly.

"Stop it! Are you trying to kill yourself?"

"Wrong answer."

He lurches up.

I grab his shoulder and he rips free, vaulting the fence, jogging after the mustang in his light, relentless way that never lets the horse escape in the circular pen. He puts his hand on its back and leaps up, though I can tell he's hurt, leaning to the right, favoring that side. Blood runs from his eyebrow to his collar and streams from his nose.

The coppery scent enrages the horse. Its nostrils flare and it whips and spins like a dervish. Duke hangs on with a kind of loopy grace that becomes more exaggerated as he loosens his hold. The look he gives me is plainly a dare.

"Duke!"

He lets go, crashing to the ground once more.

This time he doesn't get up so easy.

"Idiot." His uncle Inota hauls him up. "What do you think you're doing?"

The other uncles stand silent, glowering at me. This is going too far; they're not enjoying it anymore.

I never was.

"Stop," I beg Duke.

He tosses his head. "Tell me, Bo. Why are you sorry?"

Usually Duke makes me so goddamned angry I could combust. But in this moment, covered in dust and blood, he just looks so…defeated.

The fight has gone out of his face, and the fury.

All I see is sadness.

"I'm sorry I hurt you," I whisper.

He nods once, holding my eye. Then he gallops around the pen on the mustang's back, this time holding tightly to its mane, not allowing himself to be thrown.

When he circles around again, he calls, "Go on a date with me. A real date."

That's rank fucking blackmail. Any regret I had a moment before evaporates.

"I'd rather date that horse."

Duke digs his heels in the horses' sides, teeth bared. Five seconds later, the mustang bucks him off so hard that Duke does a half-gainer and lands flat on his back in the dirt.

"You'll never out-stubborn him," Arnie says to me, conversationally.

Arnie's father Gatlin doesn't look nearly as amused. He's never liked me or my mom.

"He's gonna get himself killed," Gatlin says, throwing me a dark look. And then, so low I could have almost imagined it, he mutters, "Just like Waya."

If anybody else talked about my dad like that, I'd break their fucking nose. But Gatlin has already had his nose broken several times, and also he's a rangy old cowboy who would murder me in a fight. Then all the rest of Duke's uncles would bury me somewhere on their ranch, and maybe Duke, too, if he said boo about it. You do *not* fuck around with the Warclouds.

Duke goes crashing to the ground again.

The next time he slams into the dirt, I hear myself shouting, "All right, I'll do it! Get away from that damn horse!"

Duke limps over, covered in dust and blood.

"You couldn't have made your mind up a little quicker?"

———————

I promise to let Duke pick me up for the dance at the cultural center later that night, and then I spend the rest of the afternoon at my grandmother's house, helping her bake bread.

My grandma is the best cook I know. She taught my dad to make incredible beef stew and the best damn pancakes you'll ever eat, but it was my mom who became her real prize student. My dad couldn't believe it when Grandma gave her all her old cookbooks, saying, "I've got the recipes memorized."

"You told me those recipes were secret!" Dad said.

Grandma shrugged. "They needed a worthy successor."

She was probably mad 'cause my dad was always adding things to her recipes—raspberries in her banana pancakes, cinnamon on her fry bread. He couldn't help tinkering.

Dad was tall and skinny and Grandma's short and round, but her hands look just like his when she's cooking or making saddles. She gets more done in a day than most people do in a month.

We knead the dough together. I've got flour up to my elbows. Her apron is still spotless despite the fact that she already canned peaches and mucked out the chicken coop this morning.

I'm trying to distract myself because the dance is only a couple of hours away and the thought of dressing up for an actual date makes me feel like ants are crawling all over my skin.

What I love about being friends with Duke is that it's never supposed to feel like this.

We've fought like cat and dog since we were toddlers. He shot me with a BB gun and I still have the pellet in my ass, too deep to dig out. I once threw a slush-ball at him with a rock in it that knocked out one of his teeth. You can't see the spot anymore, 'cause the rest of them kinda shifted around and filled it in, but now he only has 31 teeth.

We've been in trouble with both the Tribal Police Department and the local sheriff, not to mention Duke's uncles. I've never gone an entire week without seeing him.

He closer to me than my own brothers because he's not just a brother, he's my best friend and my goddamn cradle-mate. We're practically twins.

Except…

Your heart's not supposed to race whenever your twin gets close. You're not supposed to lean over and breathe in their scent when you think they won't notice. Your chest shouldn't hurt when you see them talk to anyone else. And most of all, you're not supposed to stare at their mouth and wonder again and again and again if they taste as good as they smell.

"What did that bread ever do to you?" Grandma says.

"I'm kneading it."

"It looks like you're trying to steal its lunch money."

"Why do they have so many goddamn dances, anyway?" I say, punching the bread again.

Grandma smiles. "Some people like dancing."

"People like a lot of stupid things."

She ignores that like she ignores anything surly that comes out of my mouth.

"What time's Duke coming over?"

"I don't know," I say, irritably. Then, "Seven, I guess."

"Are you going to shower first?"

It's just a question, but the kind of question with a hell of a statement buried inside of it.

"I guess," I say again, even more annoyed.

"Better be sure," Grandma says. "You smell like horses and chicken poop."

"It's your chicken poop!"

"Doesn't make it smell any better."

"All right, all right." I toss my pummeled dough down on the floury countertop. "I'll go shower."

"Borrow something from Koko," Grandma says. "She won't mind."

Koko's my aunt, but Grandma had her so late she's not much older than me. She's also gorgeous and glam and has the wardrobe of a rockstar, so I wouldn't dare raid her closet even if any of it looked good on me. Which it won't.

"Where is Koko, anyway?"

"Work," Grandma says, neatly shaping the dough into little loaves.

Koko reads the morning news at the local station. She wakes up at three-thirty in the morning and goes to bed at dinnertime, which is maybe why she's never had a boyfriend. Or at least, not one she'd introduce to us.

She comes home while I'm still showering. I hear her Trans Am roaring up the road, and then her off-key singing down in the kitchen.

She comes galloping up the steps to bang on the rickety bathroom door. "Ma says you need an outfit!"

The hot water runs out without warning. I yelp and grab a towel, wrapping it around myself right as Koko barges in.

"How about this?" she says, holding up something covered in sequins.

"Hell no. And I've got clothes, thanks."

"Not anymore you don't. Mom's washing them."

"Grandma!" I bellow down the stairs.

"Too late, they're soaked." Koko grins. She knows as well as I do how completely intentional that was on Grandma's part.

This is what it's like to be the youngest sibling and the youngest cousin—everybody bossing you around, trying to fix their own mistakes vicariously through you.

I'm still in the middle of making my mistakes, and I'm nowhere near finished.

"Come on," Koko coaxes. "Let me doll you up."

Koko has been trying to get me to let her make me pretty since I was literally the size of one of her dolls.

I used to run away, trailing ribbons and bobby pins, and deliberately roll around in the mud.

But tonight I keep thinking about the redhead Duke asked to dance at the Wagon Wheel. She was wearing a frilly skirt and cowboy boots with rhinestones all over them.

Beautiful girls throw themselves at Duke all the time—especially the last few years. That redhead looked surprised to even see him talking to me. What kind of looks would I get if we were holding hands? Or dancing together?

Shame heats my face, and that makes me angry. "I'm not wearing a fucking dress!"

"Nobody said you had to," Koko says, placidly.

It takes her an hour of hard work before she pronounces me "not bad!"

She blow-dries my hair so it's soft and shiny, then paints my eyes more than I like but less than she wants.

When it's time to pick out an outfit, I stand in awe inside her closet. "It's like a magazine…"

She laughs. "Now you know where all my paychecks go."

If I had stuff this nice, I wouldn't let anybody touch it. But Koko hauls the hangers down and makes me try on a hundred outfits, each fancier than anything I own, but nothing I could wear without Duke laughing in my face.

"This could be perfect!" Koko says, admiring her own tomato-red jumpsuit.

"Yeah—if I was cosplaying as a tampon."

"That's disgusting." Koko laughs. "And maybe a little bit true."

She hangs up the jumpsuit and takes down a canary-yellow ruffled top instead. "How about this?"

"Sometimes I think you forget where we live."

"I like to dress for where I *want* to live," Koko says, lifting her chin.

That's obvious, because she's currently wearing bell-bottom jeans covered in butterfly patches and a fringed leather vest. I think Koko wants to live at Woodstock in 1969.

In the end, we settle on a pair of leather pants so thin and supple they could be leggings, with a loose, slightly sheer top.

"I was hoping I could convince you to wear something that wasn't black." Koko pouts.

"I want Duke to recognize me." I examine myself in the mirror, still not entirely certain. "Are you sure I don't need to wear something under this top?"

"Nah, it'll be dark in there. And that's kind of the whole point…" Koko winks. "What you can *almost* see…"

Grandma's kind enough not to raise an eyebrow when I descend the stairs. I'm self-conscious enough already.

"You brushed your hair," she says, like I never have before.

"And my teeth."

"Wow, this really is a date."

"Ha, ha," I say, but I actually am smiling.

The minutes tick past on Grandma's old cuckoo clock.

I'm experiencing the weirdest paranoia that Duke isn't gonna show. He went to a hell of a lot of trouble to get me to say yes, but all of a sudden I'm watching the window like it was some kind of trick.

When I hear his ancient motorcycle, my heart leaps and my stomach sinks like a rock.

"Here he comes!" Koko cries. "I'll meet you at the dance!"

Koko is staying up way past her bedtime for her one true love, busting a move. She's wearing sparkly pants and a top that used to be a silk scarf. Koko doesn't give a damn that she's going to look like a disco ball in a sea of jeans and flannels—she lives for the attention.

I wish my superpower was invisibility. Especially right now, as Duke's boots crunch up the walk.

He knocks politely, though usually he'd just come strolling in.

"Why'd you knock, you weirdo?" Koko says, opening the door.

She knows why, but she wants to tease him.

Duke steps inside, looking stiff and completely unlike himself. His hair is loose but neatly brushed back, his face freshly shaven. He's wearing a shirt I've never seen before, soft black cotton with pearl snaps, and dark jeans without any rips. Only his old boots are the same.

He's still covered in faded marks from his fight with the cowboys, plus new cuts on his eyebrow and jaw, but every inch of him is showered and groomed, down to his neatly trimmed fingernails.

We look at each other, my nervousness mirrored in his face.

"You ready?" he says.

There's no way I can answer "yes" to that.

Actually, I can't say anything because my mouth is too dry. So I just nod.

"No drinking on that bike!" Grandma says, sharply.

"I hate drinking," Duke reminds her.

"More for me!" Koko chirps. "Melby will drive me home."

Melby is the local marshal. He's supposed to drive Koko to the drunk tank, but he acts like her Uber instead because of his monster crush on her, shared by every other person who's ever seen her on TV.

I follow Duke back to his bike, wondering how the fuck I'm supposed to talk when we're on a date. Wishing I'd never agreed to this, but also, feeling a kind of sick and heady anticipation...

He pauses at the curb, meeting my eyes for only the second time since he arrived. "You look..."

"What?" I smile, though my stomach is doing backflips.

"Sanitized."

He grins and I grin back at him.

"You, too," I say. "I don't think I've ever seen your hands that clean."

"Scrubbed 'em with a wire brush."

Even though I've ridden on the back of his bike a thousand times, when I climb on the seat and wrap my arms around his waist, it feels different. The engine ignites, the vibration rolling up through my thighs. The same thrumming shakes Duke's frame. I press my cheek against his back until finally we're on the same frequency.

The night is crisp as an apple, the air flowing cool over my face. Duke's hair tickles my forehead, heat and scent radiating from his back.

Light pours from the cultural center, the dance already in full swing. The double doors are flung open, the band on the stage deafening, the pounding of the dancers' boots like another set of drums.

Duke nudges down his kickstand and holds out his hand. "You ready?"

"Yeah. Let's go in."

I put my hand in his.

Walking inside with our fingers linked feels like shouting from the rafters. I swear, a hundred people turn their heads and stare.

Or maybe it's just Duke's uncle Gatlin. He gives me the kind of look a sheriff would give a cattle rustler strolling into his town at high noon. He takes a long, slow pull of his beer, staring me down the whole time.

"Your uncle hates me," I tell Duke.

He shrugs. "He hates me, too. And most of his kids."

We grab a couple of drinks—rum and coke for me, water for Duke 'cause he really does hate alcohol. His older brother and two of his cousins flipped their truck into a ditch on prom night. Only Gatlin's son Arnie survived.

I gulp my rum, hoping it'll do something for my nerves. Really, all that happens is I start noticing how good Duke's body looks in that shirt. The top snap is undone, revealing a triangle of bare brown skin right below his throat that draws my eyes again and again...

"You want to dance?" I say.

"Yeah."

Duke looks angry ninety percent of the time, but when he smiles, the sun bursts through. My legs feel weak and wobbly, and not from a single drink.

The dance floor is packed, the heat immense. Duke presses closer to me than we usually dance. Everything is different tonight, especially the way he touches me. His hand rests on the small of my back, then my hip. He looks into my eyes, our mouths only a few inches apart.

We haven't danced like this before, but we move like we have. Duke is the one in control, the one who pulls me closer and slips his thigh between mine, creating heat and friction every time we sway.

"I had a dream about you last night." His voice is low and husky next to my ear.

I've had more than a few dreams about Duke.

"What were we doing?" I whisper.

"Do you want me to show you?"

My whole body is on fire, every inch of my skin throbbing with the beat of the drums onstage. Duke's scent invades my lungs, cinnamon and diesel, burning in my throat, making my head whirl.

I'm afraid. In fact, I'm fucking terrified. But for once, fear doesn't become anger. Duke calms me. His hands on my hips hold me steady; his eyes search mine. He's my best friend, and also...my whole fucking world.

Instead of running away, I press against him, letting him feel my breasts against his chest through Koko's tissue-thin shirt.

I tilt up my chin until my lips rest right against his ear.

"I want you to show me *exactly* what you dreamed."

Duke's fingers dig into my hips. His eyes are black as gunpowder, glittering in the low light.

He pulls me off the dance floor, but not out through the open double doors—instead, he takes me to the back of the cultural center, then through the rabbit warren of hallways that eventually spit us out by the barns.

The barns don't contain any animals at the moment—they're mostly used for demonstrations of hand-crafts to tourists. But they are full of sweet-smelling hay, which Duke shoves me into with more force than necessary.

He leaps on top of me and we roll around, wrestling like we have a thousand times, but this time with new intensity.

We're fighting like we're both desperate to be on top, but Duke is stronger than me and tonight he's not holding back. He pins me in the hay, his fingers manacles around my wrists. Suddenly, his mouth is on mine. The heat and wetness shocks me. My tongue and lips become fireworks, crackling and bursting as colored lights flood my brain.

He tastes like everything delicious, like every good scent and every good feeling if they were concentrated into Pop Rocks and sprinkled across my tongue.

His hands roam my body wildly, like we only have seconds to spare. But those seconds stretch on and on and no one comes to interrupt us. We're buried deep in the hay, its chaff and prickling points the opposite of Duke's mellow warm skin.

His hands slip under my shirt, finding the softness of my breasts and the electric hardness of my nipples, sparking against his palms. Each touch is a jumper cable right to my heart. I gasp and press against him, his thigh wedged between mine.

He's touching my tits for the very first time—the first time *anyone* has touched them. The sensation is anxious and melting. My heart races and I'm putty in his hands.

I reach my own hands under his shirt, feeling the impossible smoothness of his skin over the hard, flat muscle. His nipples are hard like mine, but so tiny my fingers skate over them. His stomach is ripples of muscle and then a delta that pulls my hand down, down into his jeans…

I slip my fingers beneath his waistband, into the humid warmth of his boxer shorts. I'm nervously groping, guessing at the angle, relieved and terrified when his cock fills my palm.

Duke makes a sound like I'm torturing him, but he presses against me harder, his cock a steel bar wrapped in butter-soft skin. His groan sends a wicked pulse through my brain.

I grip his cock, touching the skin where it's slightly looser around the rim between the head and the shaft, rubbing over that ridge with my thumb.

Duke seizes a handful of my hair and kisses me, wet and messy and ravenous. Every time I squeeze his cock, he thrusts his tongue into my mouth.

Slippery wetness leaks from the head of his cock. My palm becomes slick and I slide my hand further up and down the shaft. Duke presses me down into the hay, his tongue delving deep into my mouth, the breath from his lungs hot and rich and head-spinning.

"I want to taste you," he groans.

"You are tasting me."

"Not there."

Before I fully understand what he means, he slides down my body, unbuttoning the leather pants, peeling them off my thighs.

The underwear beneath sticks to my pussy lips, soaked through from the heat of dancing and the wetness of everything else.

Duke hooks his fingers under the elastic on my hips and looks at me.

I lick my lips. They're throbbing. My entire body is throbbing with each beat of my heart.

Slowly, Duke slides my panties down.

The cool air kisses my wet pussy lips.

I can feel every millimeter of exposed skin. I'm naked like I've never been naked before, exposed in front of the person whose opinion is the one and only thing I give a fuck about.

"You're so fucking beautiful," Duke says.

He's never called me beautiful before.

But when I look in his face, I know he's not lying. I can see exactly how much he means it.

He kneels between my thighs like a worshipper, gazing up and down my body. When he touches me, his hands are gentle and warm, his fingers resting lightly on my hips. He bends and presses his mouth softly against my pussy.

His lips rest against my lower lips, warm and full with the lightest tickle of breath. His tongue sweeps up the cleft between them and I instantly melt. His tongue is velvety wet in a way that feels overwhelming, drenching my brain. I have no control over the sounds I'm making, or the way my back arches and my hips lift to press against his mouth.

My hands scrabble helplessly in the straw. I twist and squirm, locked in his grip as he holds tight to my hips. It's too much and I can't take it, this sensation that's maximum, maximum, more, more, more. There are no breaks, no reductions in pleasure. The feeling only builds, rolling way past what I thought I could take, making me gasp and shriek and groan and beg.

I feel every flick and press of his tongue, but I could never tell you what he's doing down there. Warm waves roll over me, and I heave up on my elbows, crying out, and then I thrust both hands in his hair and pull him tighter against me, flopping backward into the straw, dizzy and helpless.

He holds me locked in place, his hands on my hips, his mouth lapping relentlessly between my thighs. It's nothing like when I've touched myself, nothing like anything I've felt before. Those were little flutters; this is a full-on spin cycle.

My thighs squeeze and tremble around his ears; I'm babbling and begging and telling him again and again how good it feels.

His eyes flash up at me, that look I know too well that means he won't stop for anything.

I might die if he stops.

I might die if he doesn't.

I'm throbbing, pulsing, fucking against his face, his head gripped in both hands. He shoves his tongue inside me like he shoved it in my mouth and I trigger like a gun.

It's not one shot but many, cascading pulses that radiate from my belly all the way down my legs. Wetness floods and every part of me goes loose and floppy like I lost all my bones.

Duke comes up to kiss me, his mouth soaked and messy, musky-sweet.

"Even better than I dreamed," he murmurs against my lips.

His cock rages between us, nudging at my hipbone, rigid and burning hot.

Duke grips it at the base and positions the head against my swollen pussy.

"Wait," I gasp.

He pauses. He's leaning on his elbow, looking down into my face.

My body wants this. I think my brain wants it, too. But I'm still so fucking scared.

This is the line you can't walk back over. Once we fuck, we won't just be friends anymore. We'll be lovers or ex-lovers. And all the pain of whatever is about to happen between Duke and me, come September, will be a hundred times worse.

"I don't want to lose you," I blurt out.

Duke looks down into my face, his expression ferocious. "I'm here right now. And you *are* going to lose me—when you leave for school, you're going to lose me."

"I'm not going to school."

Duke doesn't show his surprise, but the angle of his head changes. "What?"

"I'm not going to school," I repeat. "But I am leaving. When

September comes, I'm taking the money I have saved, I'm gonna figure out who killed my dad, and I'm gonna make them pay for it."

Duke stares at me in a way that's very different from Raylan. With Raylan, I never know what he's going to say. With Duke, I see the intention in his eyes and I watch it harden.

"I want you, Bo," he says. "And I'm not going to settle for part of you. Not anymore."

My family thinks *I'm* stubborn?

They don't know Duke.

If I push him away again, he'll be the one who leaves. And he'll go where I can't find him.

"Take me, then."

My knees fall open. I look up into his eyes, waiting.

Now it's Duke who hesitates. His eyes flick down my body and back to my face. Then hunger sweeps his face. His eyes darken, his lips part, and he swoops down on me, kissing me deeply as he fits his cock against me once more.

His heavy heat presses where it feels like there's no opening— the most sensitive part of me stretches and gives, but only a little at a time, like it's pushing back, resisting. I try to relax, taking deep breaths. The breaths only fill my lungs with Duke's scent, making my heart beat faster.

I'm sweating from the deep, throbbing pleasure that makes me press against him, but the stretching becomes a tearing I can hardly stand. His cock nudges inside me, bit by bit, taking longer than I expected. Is time slowing down or is my brain speeding up?

I'm balanced on the razor's edge, needing more while I can hardly tolerate what I'm getting. I cling to his back, face turned against his neck, thighs wrapped around his hips.

Duke is steady and gentle at first, but each inch of his cock that slips inside me draws a feverish groan from him, and he thrusts with more force, his arms wrapped around me, his hand cradling the back of my head. The sounds he's making directly into my ear drive me wild.

I rock my hips, spreading my legs wider, relaxing as best as I can while my whole body is strung tight as a wire. At last his cock slides home, socketed deep inside me, his body pressed against mine. I look into his eyes, and for a moment the universe pauses.

Then we're moving together, with the same easy grace as when we danced. He's slowly thrusting, I'm rocking at the same pace, we're linked all the way down our bodies, and even our breath is in sync.

I've never felt anything more peaceful or connected—two people sharing the same pleasure at the same time. Two souls laid over each other like panes of colored glass.

It doesn't last long—this is Duke's first time, just like mine. I'm raw inside and he was throbbing fit to burst before he even made it in, but that's what makes it so perfect. No dam could hold the endless weight of anticipation, the thousand stolen glances, the moments our hands brushed, the gifts that were so much more than gifts, the times when I could count on him and no one else…

We've been waiting so long.

"I can't hold it," Duke gasps.

I feel his warm, wet pulses and my body responds in kind—waves of pleasure that join with his until we're surfing the same tide. We come together and we wash up on the straw, panting, sweating, still wrapped in each other's arms.

I'm taking a walk around World's Fair Park, killing time before I'm supposed to fetch my brother and Riona from the airport. Raylan flew to Chicago yesterday just to pick her up and fly back with her today, which tells you exactly how whipped he is.

He texted me that their flight was delayed, but then my phone died right after, so now I'm not sure what to do. I forgot to charge it last night, which I guess was a side effect of being de-virginized.

Or maybe it was a side effect of Duke acting weird as fuck.

He was quiet on the way home, and so was I. We might have talked if we drove all the way back to my place together, but he only took me the short trip to Grady's truck.

He did kiss me once more before I climbed inside, but even that felt brief and strangely distant, like he was thinking about something else.

This is exactly what I was trying to avoid. Now my pussy's aching and I feel like a half-filled garbage bag tossed by the side of the road.

I thought he'd call me this morning. Or at least text me.

I stalk around the Sunsphere, grumpy as fuck, trying not to remember the parts of last night that take my pussy from raw and aching to warm and flushed all over again…

That's never happening again. It was a mistake from the start, I knew it.

I take a kick at a dandelion, exploding its puffy head and sending seeds scattering across the lawn.

"Was that supposed to be me?" a voice says in my ear.

I whip around, shrieking and punching Duke's chest. "Don't *do* that!"

He grabs my hands and holds them still. His are warm and strong. His thumbs press against my palms.

"Where have you been?" I say, peevishly. My chest is tight and I can't quite look him in the eye.

"I've been taking care of a few things," Duke says. "Before we leave."

I stare at him blankly. "Before we…"

Duke shakes his head. His hair is tied back today, and his face looks lean and fierce. But his eyes are the softest I've ever seen as he looks at me.

"Bo, sometimes I think that even though I've spent every damn day of my life with you, you still don't know me at all. I'll follow you anywhere. Just not to Vanderbilt. 'Cause I didn't get in."

The iron bands around my chest fall away and it expands like a hot air balloon. "You applied to Vanderbilt?"

"As soon as you did," Duke admits. "But I guess I shoulda paid better attention in algebra. Or else learned to swim. It made me sick, thinking of you going there without me."

"I was *never* going to go there without you."

"But you think you're going on some revenge mission without me? No fucking way."

Duke grabs me and kisses me hard.

"You're not going *anywhere* without me, Bo. Not now, not ever."

I look at him, wild happiness surging through my veins.

Then I throw my arms around him and kiss him back, twice as hard.

Read on for a sneak peek at the final book in the Brutal Birthright series, *Heavy Crown*

CHAPTER 1
SEBASTIAN

I'M SITTING IN THE CORNER BOOTH OF LA MER WITH MY TWO brothers and my little sister, Aida. It's an hour past closing time, so the servers have already taken the linen and glassware off the tables, and the cooks are just finishing their deep clean of the stove tops and fridges.

The bartender is still doing his nightly inventory check, probably lingering longer than usual in case any of us wants one last drink. That's the perk of owning the restaurant—nobody can kick you out.

La Mer is known for its high-end seafood—halibut and salmon flown in from the East Coast every morning and king crab legs longer than your arm. We all feasted on butter-drenched lobster earlier in the evening. For the past several hours, we've simply been sipping our drinks and talking. This might be our last night all together for a while.

Dante leaves for Paris tomorrow morning. He's taking his wife, his son, and his brand-new baby girl across the Atlantic for what he's calling an extended honeymoon. But I've got a feeling that he's not coming back.

Dante never wanted to become the *capocrimine*. He's been the de facto leader of our family for years only because he's the eldest—not because it was his ambition.

Of course, my father is still the real Don, but his health is getting worse every year. He's been delegating more and more of the running of our family business. It used to be that he personally handled every meeting with the other Mafia families, no matter how small the issue. Now he only puts on his suit and goes out for the direst of situations.

He's become a hermit in our old mansion on Meyer Avenue. If our housekeeper Greta didn't also live there full-time, eating lunch with him and listening to him complain about how Steinbeck should be ranked higher than Hemingway in the pantheon of authors, then I might be seriously worried about him.

I guess I feel guilty because I could be living there with him, too. All the rest of my siblings have moved out—Dante and Aida to get married, Nero to live with his girlfriend, Camille, in the apartment over her brand-new custom car mod shop. Once I finished school, I could have come back home. But I didn't. I've been living with my lieutenant Jace in Hyde Park.

I tell myself that I need a little more privacy for bringing girls home or staying out as late as I want. But the truth is I feel a strange kind of wedge between me and the rest of my family. I feel like I'm drifting—in sight of them, but not on the same boat.

They're all changing so rapidly, and I am, too. But I don't think we're changing in the same way.

It's been three years since we had our last run-in with the Griffin family.

That night changed my life.

It started with a dinner, very much like this one, except it was on the rooftop of our family home while we were all still living there. We saw fireworks breaking over the lake, and we knew the Griffins were holding a birthday party for their youngest daughter.

How different our lives would be if we hadn't seen those fireworks. If Aida hadn't perceived them as a sort of challenge or a call.

I remember the bursts of colored light reflecting in her eyes as she turned to me and whispered, "We should crash the party."

We snuck onto the Griffins' estate. Aida stole their great-grandfather's watch and accidentally lit a fire in their library. Which made Callum Griffin come hunting for us later that night. He trapped Aida and me on the pier. Then his bodyguard smashed my knee.

That was the fracture in time that sent my life shooting off in a completely different direction.

Before that moment, all I cared about was basketball. I played for hours and hours every day. It's hard to even remember how much it consumed me. Everywhere I went, I had a ball with me. I'd practice dribbling and crossovers in every spare moment. I'd watch old games every night before bed. I read that Kobe Bryant never stopped practicing until he'd made at least four hundred baskets a day. I decided I'd sink five hundred daily, and I stayed for hours after our regular practices, until the janitors turned off the lights in the gym.

The rhythm and feel of the ball in my hands was burned into my brain. Its pebbled texture was the most familiar thing in the world, and the most familiar sound was sneakers squeaking on hardwood.

It was the one true love of my life. The way I felt about that game was stronger than my interest in girls, or food, or entertainment, or anything else.

When the bodyguard's boot came down on my knee and I felt that blinding, sickening burst of pain, I knew my dream was over. Pros come back from injuries, but injured players don't make pro.

For over a year, I was in denial. I did rehab every single day. I endured surgery, heat packs, cold packs, ultrasound therapy on the scar tissue, electrostimulation of the surrounding muscles, and countless hours of tedious physiotherapy.

I went to the gym daily, making the rest of my body as strong as possible, packing thirty pounds of muscle onto a formerly lean frame.

But it was all for nothing. I got rid of the limp, but the speed never came back. During the time I should have been getting faster and more accurate, I couldn't even get back to where I used to be. I was swimming against the current while slowly drifting downstream.

And now I live in this strange alternate reality where the Griffins are our closest allies. My sister, Aida, is married to the man who ordered his bodyguard to smash my knee.

The funny thing is I don't hate Callum. He's been good to my sister. They're wildly in love, and they have a little boy together—the heir to both our families—Miles Griffin. The Griffins have upheld their end of the marriage pact. They've been loyal partners.

But I'm still so fucking angry.

It's this churning, boiling fury inside me, every single day.

I've always known what my family did for a living. It's as much a part of the Gallos as our blood and our bones. We're mafiosos.

I never questioned it.

But I thought I had a choice.

I thought I could skirt around the edges of the business while still unfettered, able to pursue anything else I wanted in life.

I didn't realize how much that life had already wrapped its chains around me. There was never any choice. I was bound to be pulled into it one way or another.

Sure enough, after my knee was fucked and I lost my place on the team, my brothers started calling me more and more often for jobs.

When Nessa Griffin was kidnapped, we joined the Griffins in their vendetta against the Polish Mafia. That night, I shot a man for the very first time.

I don't know how to describe that moment. I had a gun in my hand, but I didn't expect to actually use it. I thought I was there for backup. As a lookout at most. Then I saw one of the Polish soldiers pull his gun on my brother, and instinct took over. My hand floated up; the gun pointed right between the man's eyes. I pulled the trigger without a thought.

He went tumbling backward. I expected to feel something: shock, horror, guilt.

Instead I felt…absolutely nothing. It seemed inevitable. Like I'd always been destined to kill someone. Like it had always been in my nature.

That's when I realized that I'm not actually a good person.

I always assumed I was. I think everyone does.

I thought, *I'm warmer than my brother Dante. Less psychopathic than Nero. More responsible than Aida.* I considered myself kind, hardworking—a good man.

In that moment I realized I have violence inside me. And selfishness, too. I wasn't going to sacrifice my brother for somebody else. And I certainly wouldn't sacrifice myself. I was willing to hurt or to kill. Or a whole lot worse.

It's a strange thing to learn about yourself.

I look around the table at my siblings. They all have blood on their hands, one way or another. Looking at them, you'd never guess it. Well, maybe you'd guess it with Dante—his hands look like scarred baseball mitts. They were made for tearing people apart. If he were a gladiator, the Romans would have to pair him up against a lion to make it a fair fight.

But they all look happier than I've seen them in years.

Aida's eyes are bright and cheerful, and she's flushed from the wine. She wasn't able to drink the whole time she was nursing, so she's thrilled to be able to get just a little bit tipsy again.

Dante has this look of contentment like he's already sitting at some outdoor café in Paris. Like he's already starting the rest of his life.

Even Nero has changed. And he's the one I never thought would find happiness.

He's always been so vicious and full of rage. I honestly thought he was sociopathic when we were teenagers—he didn't seem to care about anyone, not even our family. Not really.

Then he met Camille, and all of a sudden, he's completely different. I wouldn't say he's a nice guy—he's still ruthless and rude as hell.

But that sense of nihilism is gone. He's more focused than ever, more deliberate. He has something to lose now.

Aida says to Dante, "Are you gonna learn French?"

"Yes." He grunts.

"I can't picture that," Nero says.

"I can learn French," Dante says defensively. "I'm not an idiot."

"It's not your intelligence," Aida says. "It's your accent."

"What do you mean?"

She and Nero exchange an amused glance.

"Even your accent in Italian…isn't great," Aida says.

"What are you talking about?" Dante demands.

"Say something in Italian," Aida goads him.

"All right," Dante says stubbornly. "*Voi due siete degli stronzi.*" *You two are assholes.*

The sentence is accurate. The problem is that Dante keeps his same flat Chicago accent, so it sounds like, *Voy doo-way see-etay deg-lee strawn-zee.* He sounds like a Midwestern farmer trying to order off a menu in a fancy Italian restaurant.

Aida and Nero burst into laughter, and I can't help letting out a little snort myself. Dante scowls at us all, still not hearing it.

"What?" he demands. "What's so damn funny?"

"You better let Simone do the talking," Aida says between giggles.

"Well, it's not like I actually lived in Italy!" Dante growls. "You know, I speak some Arabic, too, which is more than you two chuckleheads." When they won't stop laughing, he adds, "Fuck you guys! I'm cultured."

"As cultured as yogurt," Nero says, which only makes them laugh harder.

I think Dante would have knocked their heads together in the old days, but he's above their nonsense now that he's a husband and father. He just shakes his head at them and signals the bartender for one more drink.

Becoming a mother hasn't made Aida above anything. Seeing that Dante isn't going to respond to her teasing anymore, she looks across the table and fixes her keen gray eyes on me.

"Seb has a gift for languages," she says. "Do you remember when we were coming back from Sardinia and you thought you were supposed to talk to the customs officers in Italian? And they kept asking you questions to make sure you were actually an American citizen, and you wouldn't say anything except '*il mio nome è Sebastian.*'"

That's true. I was seven years old, and I got flustered with all those adults staring at me, barking at me. I was so deeply tanned from my summer in Italy that I'm sure it looked like my father had snatched some little island boy out of Costa Rei and was trying to bring him back across the Atlantic.

The customs officers kept demanding, "Is this your family? Are you American?" And I, for some reason, had decided that I had to respond in their native language even though they were speaking English. In the moment, all I could think to say was "my name is Sebastian," over and over.

Damn Aida for even remembering that—she was only five herself. But she never forgets something embarrassing she can bring up later at the most inopportune time.

"I wanted to stay on vacation a little longer," I tell Aida coolly.

"Good strategy," she says. "You almost got to stay forever."

I am going to miss Dante. I miss all my siblings, the more they branch out into their own lives.

They can be infuriating and inconvenient, but they love me. They know all my faults and all my mistakes, and they accept me anyway. I know I can count on them if I really need them. And I would show up for them, anytime, anyplace. That's a powerful bond.

"We'll come visit you," I say to Dante.

He smiles just a little. "Not all at the same time, please. I don't want to scare Simone away right after we finally got married."

"Simone loves me," Aida says. "And I'm already bribing my way into your children's hearts. You know that's the path to becoming the favorite aunt—giving them loud and dangerous gifts that their parents wouldn't allow."

"That must be why you liked Uncle Francesco," I say. "He gave you a bow and arrows."

Aida smiles fondly. "And I always adored him."

So did I. But we lost Uncle Francesco two years after that particular gift. The *Bratva* cut his fingers off and set him on fire while he was still alive. That sparked a two-year bloodbath with the Russians. My father was in a rage like I've never seen before. He drove them out of their territory on the west side of the city, killing eight of their men in revenge. I don't know what he did to the *bratok* who threw the match on Uncle Francesco, but I remember him coming home that night with his dress shirt drenched in blood to the point where you couldn't see a single square inch of white cotton anymore.

I still have my favorite gift from my uncle: a small gold medallion of Saint Eustachius. I wear it every day.

Uncle Francesco was a good man: Funny and charming. Passionate about everything. He loved to cook and to play tennis. He'd take Nero and me to the courts and play two against one, smoking us every time. He wasn't tall, but he was compact and wiry, and he could fire a shot into the very back corner of the court so the ball touched the lines while still remaining inside. It was impossible to return. Nero and I would be sweating and panting, swearing this would be the time we finally beat him.

I sometimes wish we could have him back for a day so he could see what we all look like as adults. So we could talk to him as peers.

I wish the same thing about my mother.

She never saw who we turned out to be.

I wonder if she'd be happy.

She never liked the Mafia life. She ignored it, pretended to be ignorant of what her husband was doing. She was a concert pianist when my father first spotted her playing onstage. He pursued her relentlessly. He was much older than she was. I'm sure she was impressed that he spoke three languages, that he was well-read and well-spoken. And I'm sure his aura of authority was impressive to her. My father was already the head don of Chicago, one of the most powerful men in the city. She loved who he was but not what he did.

What would she think of us? Of what we've done?

We just completed a massive real estate development on the South Shore. Would she look at that in awe, or would she think that every one of those buildings was built with blood money? Would she marvel at the structures we brought into being or cringe at the skeletons buried in their foundations?

The bartender brings Dante's drink.

"Can I get another for anyone else?" he asks.

"Yes!" Aida says at once.

"Sure," Nero agrees.

"Not for me," I say. "I'm gonna head out."

"What's your rush?" Nero says.

"Nothing." I shrug.

I don't know how to express that I feel impatient and uneasy. Maybe I'm jealous of Dante leaving for Paris with his wife. Maybe I'm jealous of Aida and Nero, too. They seem sure of their paths, happy in their lives.

I'm not. I don't know what the fuck I'm doing.

Dante stands to let me out of the booth. Before I leave, he hugs me. His heavy arms almost crack my ribs.

"Thanks for coming out tonight," he says.

"Of course. Send us postcards."

"Fuck postcards. Send me chocolate!" Aida pipes up.

I give her a little wave, and Nero, too.

BRUTAL BIRTHRIGHT

Callum & Aida

Miko & Nessa

Nero & Camille

Dante & Simone

Raylan & Riona

Sebastian & Yelena

ABOUT THE AUTHOR

Sophie Lark writes intelligent and powerful characters who are allowed to be flawed. She lives in the mountain west with her husband and three children.

The Love Lark Letter: geni.us/lark-letter
The Love Lark Reader Group: geni.us/love-larks
Website: sophielark.com
Instagram: @Sophie_Lark_Author
TikTok: @sophielarkauthor
Exclusive Content: patreon.com/sophielark
Complete Works: geni.us/lark-amazon
Book Playlists: geni.us/lark-spotify